Not in the Script

A Branded Hearts Romance

K.E. Morrison

Not in the Script

Copyright K.E. Morrison 2021

AJ, Cadence, Edin-ness.
Thank you.

Contents

Chapter One

Charlie

"FINALLY," CHARLIE MUTTERED AS SHE closed the cover on the last exercise book she needed to have marked for the next morning.

Rolling her shoulders backwards and arching her spine forwards, she stretched through her usual post-marking-marathon routine. She clenched and unclenched her right fist, circling her wrist as she did so. Every time she sat down to mark books, Charlie promised herself that she'd build in regular breaks and reward her body with a few yoga poses so that she didn't end up in such discomfort. It never happened. Somewhere between starting the first book and ending the last one, Charlie got sucked into a universe where all that existed were the lined pages in front of her and the words her students had written. All hell could break loose around her, and Charlie wasn't at all convinced she would even notice. It was like time ceased until she crawled out the other side.

Slowly pushing to her feet, Charlie grimaced as something in her lower back crunched back into place. At least she hoped it was crunching into place and not out. She rubbed her eyes before glancing at the clock on her kitchen wall.

"Perfect timing," she congratulated herself, noting that she had just enough time to make a cup of tea before her weekly group chat started. With the kettle switched on, she packed the exercise books back into her bag, proud of the work her students had completed. *Tess of the D'Urbervilles* might be considered a classic, but it was far from an entertaining read for her A-level students and she always found teaching it to be a pretty turgid experience. The essays her girls had produced were far better than she had expected, and she found herself looking forward to their lesson tomorrow.

Tea in hand, she settled into her favourite armchair, the one she sat in every week for their chats. She curled her feet under her, opened the Skype app on her Microsoft Surface, and initiated the call, the familiar ringtone filling the silence around her. As always, Lauren answered first. If there was one thing in life Charlie

3

could rely on, it was that Lauren would be on time. She'd been that way since the group met during their first year at university. Four complete strangers thrust together in the same halls of residence, sharing a kitchen and living space. Never in a million years would Charlie have dreamt that seventeen years later, they would spend every Sunday night filling each other in on their respective weeks.

"Marking all done?" Lauren asked, a slight hint of teasing in her tone.

"Of course," Charlie grinned.

"And how many breaks did you remember to take today?"

"How many do you think she took?" asked Naomi as she joined them.

"Well, I'd put a tenner on it being the same number she takes every week," Lauren replied.

"None!" they both laughed together.

"Yeah, yeah, laugh it up you two. I could just as easily ask you how many times you've made it home from the office before 10pm, Lauren, or how many times you've worked up the courage to speak to that customer of yours you obsess over, Naomi."

"I'm two minutes late joining the party, and you three are already bickering. Nice to see some things never change," Jenna's sarcastic tone jibed. "Honestly, I spend my days surrounded by politicians who play more nicely together."

"Wow," replied Naomi. "You work with politicians? How come you've never mentioned that before?"

"Leave her alone, Nay," chided Lauren. "She didn't mention it until the third sentence today, so that's an improvement on the last few weeks!"

"Har har har," Jenna said, rolling her eyes good-naturedly. "It's not my fault you three rely on me for a little excitement in your lives. I mean, come on. How exciting can your jobs actually be? Charlie spends all day trying to liberate the minds of hormonal teenagers, Nay cuts up carrots and you draw lines on bits of paper, Laur."

"Well, it's a little more complicated than that, actually, Jen. You know they don't give out RIBA National Awards if your lines aren't straight. And I'm pretty sure Nay's Michelin star is for more than just her carrots," Lauren bantered.

"Oh, and thanks for coming to my defence too, Lauren," muttered Charlie. "Seriously, the three of you and your fancy awards. Top architect, top chef, and top journalist. How did I get stuck with you lot?"

"Come on, Charlie, don't sell yourself short," Nay replied. "Didn't you mention that you got a Christmas card from the rock star father of one of your students?" she asked, a huge grin blooming across her face and snorts of laughter coming from the other two.

"Fuck off the lot of you!" Charlie laughed, shaking her head. "Those of us who choose to serve the public don't need the same level of back-patting you private sector wimps seem to need."

"Oh, good god, here she goes again," moaned Lauren. "Have you still got that violin, Jen? Whip it out and play her a few bars, would you?" On the screen, Jen mimed taking a tiny violin out of her back pocket and managed a few imaginary strokes with her bow before joining the other three women in fits of laughter.

It had always been this way with them. Playful prods at each other's achievements in their chosen careers and before that, when they were still students, at each other's chosen degrees. To an outsider, Charlie acknowledged that it probably sounded like the four of them couldn't stand each other, but this was just them. And she wouldn't have it any other way.

"Right, now the niceties are out the way, how did the client meeting go this week, Lauren? The one with the woman you thought might be a bat-shit on the crazy scale?" she asked, steering the conversation back to its purpose. To find out how her best friends' lives were going and fill them in on hers. She smirked to herself, wishing she had something exciting to share with them for once.

"Well," Lauren started, a hint of hesitation in her usually confident voice, before painting a vivid picture of her time with Mrs Neoclassical as she had dubbed her new client.

"So, let me get this straight," Charlie said a couple of minutes later. "She wants you to build a garden studio that looks like the Pantheon?"

"Yup," Lauren replied.

"And by the Pantheon, she does actually mean the famous building in Rome?" Nay asked slowly.

"Yup."

"Complete with columns?" asked Jenna.

"Yup."

"And the hole thingy in the roof?"

"Yup. And it's called an oculus, Charlie," Lauren teased.

"All this in her back garden?" Back to Nay.

"Well, she calls it her back garden, but I think most normal people would refer to it as 'the grounds'. We're talking acres and acres." Lauren replied.

"So, you're going to design it for her?" Charlie asked and Lauren's face fell.

"I don't have any choice, do I?" she sighed.

Over the past few years, Charlie knew that Lauren had become increasingly disenchanted with the projects she had to work on. Being part of a successful firm came with a price, and she struggled with having to create buildings she didn't love.

On more than one occasion, Lauren had talked about striking out on her own, building a firm where she had control over the projects she took and the work that she added to her portfolio. But Charlie understood her reluctance. It was a big deal to go solo, with no guaranteed income at the end of every month, no database of clientele with the money to waste on adding pompous outbuildings to their already lavish dwellings, and no contractors lined up and ready to work with her. Still, Charlie was strongly in favour of Lauren taking the risk, knowing how hard her friend would work to make it a success. She was just about to voice her opinion, when an alert popped up at the bottom of her screen, signaling an email arriving in her work inbox.

"What just happened, Charlie? The scowl on your face can't be about Lauren's project," Nay spoke, bringing Charlie back to the conversation.

"I just got an email from The Velociraptor," she replied to a chorus of groans from her friends.

"What does she want this time?" Jenna asked.

"To see me in her office at 7:30am tomorrow," Charlie said with a shrug. She had absolutely no idea what her headteacher could want.

"Ooh," crowed Nay. "Surely you're not in trouble again, Charlie?" she teased.

Lauren laughed before adding, "A summons to the headteacher's office. Did you forget to dot an 'i' or cross a 't'?"

"Honestly?" Charlie began. "I have absolutely no idea at all and, you know her, it could be anything. Whatever it is, I guess I can guarantee one thing-"

"That it'll mean more work for you!" Naomi interjected. "It always does, Charlie."

"You need to try to stand your ground this time, Charlie," added Jenna. "Don't let her bully you into doing something again. You're an amazing teacher and you work so bloody hard for your students. That woman really doesn't value you the way she should."

"Not that you're at all biased?" Charlie teased, trying to diffuse the conversation. She knew exactly what her friends thought of the way she was treated by her headteacher, a woman that Charlie couldn't seem to please no matter what she did. As much as she loved her friends, there were times when she didn't want to hear what they had to say. The day of her refusing to do something her headteacher requested was simply never going to happen. It just wasn't in Charlie's nature and as hard as it may be for others to understand, Charlie loved her job despite the woman in charge. Her time in the classroom with her students fed Charlie in a way nothing else did. The buzz she got after even a mediocre lesson wasn't something she'd been able to replicate in any other part of her life. Whilst she knew a sleepless night was ahead, as she worried about what The Velociraptor was going to ask of her, she knew in her heart that she would accept.

Charlie tuned back into the conversation in time to realise her friends were winding things up for the night. She made her promises to let them know how she got on in the morning and ended the conversation with her love and wishes for good weeks all round.

With a tentative knock on the door, precisely at 7:30am, Charlie announced her presence to The Velociraptor and was greeted with an instruction to enter.

"Be seated, Ms Evans," The Velociraptor instructed, no other greeting forthcoming.

"Good morning, Mrs Hebdidge," Charlie said as she took her seat. Despite having worked for The Velociraptor for thirteen years, first names were an absolute no-no.

"I won't waste your time, Ms Evans. I'm sure you'll be keen to get yourself set up for the day."

Charlie replied with a tight smile, which The Velociraptor took as a sign to continue.

"I received a call on Saturday evening from Lucinda Armstrong-Miller's mother." Charlie's stomach sank somewhat at the mention of a student from her A-level class. She had met Lucinda's mother on many occasions and had always found the woman a little on the cold side. She had the highest of expectations for Lucinda and that meant she expected all her teachers to bend over backwards to make sure her daughter only achieved the top grades. It didn't matter that Lucy, as she preferred to go by, much to her mother's disgust, was a very long way from being the hardest working student. Mrs Armstrong-Miller would steadfastly refuse to believe that Lucinda's grades were anything but Charlie's responsibility. Since completing her GCSEs and beginning her A-levels, Lucy was taught by Charlie for all three of her chosen subjects: English Literature, English Language and Media Studies. Charlie couldn't begin to guess which one Mrs Armstrong-Miller would be complaining about.

"Yes," Charlie replied tentatively.

"It seems that Lucinda went for an audition recently and heard on Saturday that she had got the part," The Velociraptor continued. "It's being filmed at Pinewood Studios, starting next weekend and lasting for three months, give or take."

"That's fantastic for her," Charlie enthused. "Her family must be delighted. Do they know how long the filming will take? Just so I can work out what Lucy will miss and make sure we can catch her up when she gets back."

"Lucinda won't miss anything," The Velociraptor stated emphatically, drawing a quizzical look from Charlie.

"Surely she's not dropping out?" Charlie replied, that being the only possible way she could see Lucy going off for an extended period and not missing any work.

"Of course she isn't dropping out," The Velociraptor said scornfully, as if Charlie was an absolute numpty for even allowing such a thought to have crossed her mind. "She won't be missing anything," The Velociraptor continued. "Because you will be accompanying her and will teach Miss Armstrong-Miller everything you would have covered here in school."

"I'm sorry, what?" Charlie asked incredulously, aware that her eyebrows had just taken up residence in her hairline. The scathing look on The Velociraptor's face told Charlie that her response wasn't the right one.

"You will be going with her," The Velociraptor said, enunciating each word clearly and slowly to show Charlie exactly how she felt about having to repeat herself. "That is why Mrs Armstrong-Miller telephoned me. To say that she and her husband had only agreed to Lucinda accepting the role if you went along to ensure her studies didn't suffer. I don't need to tell you that the Armstrong-Millers aren't the sort to let their daughter go off on some flight of fancy and have her thinking she's going to be some hot-shot actor who doesn't need an education."

"I'm going with her?" Charlie asked, completely unable to wrap her head around what was unfurling before her. "To Pinewood Studios? Next week?"

"Honestly, Ms Evans, I'm beginning to wonder why on earth the Armstrong-Millers would want you there if you can't wrap your head around a simple conversation."

Charlie's mind raced, flitting from one thought to the next so quickly that she couldn't grasp onto any of them. How on earth was she supposed to head off to Pinewood Studios in the middle of the term? Had The Velociraptor finally lost her marbles completely? Surely this couldn't be happening.

"I don't understand," she said. "What about my classes? All the other students that I teach?"

"Not your concern."

"Not my concern?" Charlie replied, momentarily losing the very tight grip she always kept on her emotions. "Of course they're my concern, they're MY students. I have a responsibility to all of them, not just Lucy Armstrong-Miller. How can I go off on a jaunt with one student when I have a hundred others who are taking their GCSE and A-level exams this year?" Charlie knew her voice was rising, the tone becoming frantic, but this whole thing was just bloody ridiculous.

"Ms Evans," The Velociraptor said sharply. "This is not a discussion. Mrs Armstrong-Miller requested your presence and I agreed; therefore, you will go. Your other classes will be taken care of. The film company had agreed to cover the cost of tuition, so the Armstrong-Millers are going to pass that money to us, and we have arranged for Miss Lambert to come out of retirement while you are away."

For the first time since she had sat down, Charlie felt a moment of something resembling relief. Georgia Lambert had been the Head of the English department back when Charlie had started at Harewood Grammar School as a newly qualified teacher. Georgia had taken her under her wing and the two had grown from mentor and mentee to close friends. Charlie knew without a doubt that Georgia was only coming out of retirement for her, and she wished she could wrap the older woman in a tight hug at that very moment. She took in a breath and slowly let it out, forcing herself to calm before continuing the discussion that wasn't a discussion.

"Okay," she said slowly. "So, what happens now?"

"You teach your classes as normal until Wednesday. Your train to London leaves on Thursday morning. Keep an eye on your email as someone from the film company will be in touch with the actual arrangements. I didn't ask."

Of course you didn't bloody ask, Charlie thought. And you've clearly just agreed to all the Armstrong-Millers' demands without even consulting me.

"Right," was all that Charlie managed to reply, despite the vehement protest inside her head. She knew she was dismissed; the curt nod of The Velociraptor's head, followed by a switching of attention to her computer was an obvious enough signal, even for Charlie. She stood, picked up her bag and turned to leave, her mind racing over everything she needed to put in place before the end of Wednesday.

"Oh, and Ms Evans," The Velociraptor's curt tone cut through Charlie's thoughts, and she turned, wondering if this might be the so far absent thanks. "Don't forget that you are representing Harewood at all times. Do not disappoint us."

Well, that would be a no on the thanks, then.

Charlie opened their WhatsApp group chat and started typing, knowing that no matter what the other three were doing, they'd make time to respond.

Charlie: So, apparently, I'm going to Pinewood Studios for the next three months.

Jen: WTF?

Nay: The actual Pinewood Studios? Where they make Bond films? Are you the new Bond girl?

Laur: Are we okay with this?

Charlie: One of my students got cast in some upcoming film and her parents want me to go along to tutor her. Yes, yes, and no, Nay. We have to be, Laur. Not a lot of choice.

Jen: "Again, WTF?"

Laur: You don't have a choice? How is that even possible?

Nay: A Bond film?

Charlie: No, Nay, not a Bond film! At least, I don't think it is. The Velociraptor didn't have details. Someone from the film company is going to send me something.

Laur: Choice, Charlie. How come you don't have one?

Charlie: Because the parents donate substantial cash every year, so when they ask, The Velociraptor doesn't say no, ergo, I can't say no.

Laur: That's not right, Charlie. Surely The Velociraptor can't make you do something you don't want to do?

Charlie: You mean like designing the Pantheon to go in some old biddy's back garden?

Laur: Touché

Nay: I don't see Charlie saying she doesn't want to go, Laur. Do you want to go, Charlie?

Charlie: I mean, I guess I don't like the way it's happened, but I guess it could be an interesting experience.

Jen: OMG, Charlie. Interesting? Really? It's a film set for god's sake; I think 'interesting' is the least applicable adjective. It's going to be fucking amazing!

Nay: Come on then, Miss Journalist. Which film do you think it's going to be? What rumours have you heard?

Jen: Well... I have heard talk that Robyn White is due to go into the studio soon.

Nay: O.M.G. Robyn White? Seriously?

Laur: Woah! Robyn White! Charlie, you lucky bugger!

Charlie: Ha ha! Firstly, I doubt VERY much it'll be the same film. And even if it is, why on earth would Robyn White want to speak to me?

Nay: Who said anything about speaking, girl?!

Jen: You can just gaze longingly across the set...

Laur: And sneak lots of photos to share with your friends on a certain WhatsApp group chat!

Charlie grinned. No matter how crazy the next few weeks were, she knew her friends would be right there with her. And, if it was the new Robyn White film, well, that would more than make up for the crazy.

Chapter Two

Charlie

AS THE CAR THAT HAD COLLECTED her from the station pulled to a stop, Charlie was absolutely convinced the driver had brought her to the wrong place. When she'd read in her information email from the production company that they would provide accommodation, she'd expected at best a Premier Inn and honestly thought a caravan might be more likely. Not in her wildest dreams had she thought she'd be staying in what could only be described as a stately home. Like, a proper mansion-sized stately home.

The driver, who had introduced himself as Jonny after meeting her at King's Cross, caught her eye in the rearview mirror.

"Don't look so worried," he said gently. "I promise I've brought you to the right place!"

She'd been overwhelmed enough to see him holding her name as she'd headed out of Kings Cross to walk to Paddington to catch a train to Slough before grabbing a taxi to take her to Pinewood. Instead of the slightly frantic cross-London experience she'd been fortifying herself for, she'd ended up nestled in the back of a chauffeur-driven Mercedes, and now, he was trying to convince her that she was staying in what could quite easily have passed for a film set itself. Charlie gave him a pessimistic look.

"You do know that I'm not one of the cast, don't you? I'm not an actor. This can't be right."

"I assure you, Ms Evans, you are exactly where you are supposed to be."

No matter how many times she'd told him to call her Charlie, Jonny just couldn't seem to let the formality slip. He switched off the engine and got out of the car, moving swiftly to the back to retrieve the bag he had insisted on stowing there for her. A fleeting scowl crossed his face when he turned to discover Charlie had opened her own door and managed to exit the car without his assistance. There were some lines Charlie just wasn't prepared to cross. She grinned at him in pleasure, and he shook his head as a small smile tugged at the corners of his mouth.

"This way please, Ms Evans," he said, slightly stressing her name as if knowing it irritated her. She liked this man a lot. "I'll see you to reception and leave you in the capable hands of Ms Ray, our senior production assistant. I imagine she has already been in touch with you via email?" It wasn't really a question and Charlie merely nodded in reply. "Ms Ray explained you'd been a last-minute addition and I know she's keen to sit down with you today and go over everything in detail."

"Thank god for that," Charlie muttered, but apparently not quite quietly enough.

"Indeed, Ms Evans," Jonny added as he led her across the gravel driveway, past the understated fountain, and up the sandstone staircase to the glass-fronted portico.

Charlie couldn't have carried on a conversation with him if she'd wanted to as her senses were in overdrive. The white rendering across the top half of the building stood out in contrast to the sapphire blue sky, its wispy clouds barely marring a perfect vista. Beyond the building were trees, trees, and more trees. How she was less than an hour's drive to the country's capital city was beyond her. The landscaped gardens looked stunning, and she couldn't wait to explore them, if she got the opportunity to. In fact, what she really couldn't wait to do was get on the phone to Lauren and let her know where she was staying.

As she followed Johnny inside, Charlie was mesmerised by the hotel's lobby. The elegance from outside continued inside the building. The marble floor reflected the light coming through the large glass windows that surrounded the front of the portico. Luxurious chairs were grouped around an open fire and Charlie was reminded that this was not the kind of location she was used to visiting. A red-headed woman glanced in her direction, smiled, and closed the laptop she was working on. The smile grew as she pushed to her feet and moved to greet Charlie.

"Charlie Evans?" she asked politely, eliciting a nod in reply. "It's lovely to meet you," she said, extending a hand towards Charlie. "I'm Brittany Ray. Britt," she clarified.

"Great to meet you too," replied Charlie, feeling more relaxed than she had at any point so far that day, the warm caramel eyes across from her somehow instantly putting her at ease.

"I know this has all been so last minute and you must have a million questions, but if you can hang on to them for just a little longer, I'll show you to your room and classroom space, and then Jonny's going to run us across to the studios."

Without waiting for an answer, Britt took Charlie's bag from Jonny and headed through the most opulent doorway Charlie had ever seen, turning left past a magnificent staircase before heading down a plushly carpeted hallway. "So, the production company have taken over the whole hotel for the next three months, so you'll quickly get used to both it and what will become very familiar faces. Not all production companies do this, but this one likes to, something about creating a community-feeling amongst the cast crew." She paused briefly and threw a slightly sardonic smile Charlie's way. "It doesn't always work, but I suppose it's better than the cast being put up in luxury and the crew being in the local hostel as some other companies like to do! Even though there is clearly a hierarchy, with those at the top getting the suites, it's still nice to be treated to your own bathroom," she laughed, and Charlie glanced at her in horror, the thought of having to share such an intimate space never having crossed her mind.

"Thank god for small mercies," she muttered, pulling another laugh from Britt. Charlie decided there and then that she liked the production assistant, something she considered rather more humongous than a small mercy. If she had to be cooped up in this crazy scheme for the next ninety days, she was going to need at least one friendly face to survive it.

"So, whilst you're not at the top of the pecking order, Charlie, I think you're still going to be pretty pleased with your room. You've got one of the garden ones," she said, holding a card to a door which clicked open loudly. She pushed it open and ushered Charlie inside.

Britt was right. Although the room wasn't overly large, it more than suited Charlie and she was aware of the small gasp that escaped as she noticed the bi-fold doors leading out onto her own private terrace.

"Wow," she uttered in awe. "This is stunning."

The room was warmly furnished in browns and pinks, a sofa located at the end of the king size bed, a small table with a beautiful vase of flowers, a functional desk, and a wall-mounted TV about twice the size of Charlie's at home. She peeked her head in the bathroom, relieved to see that not only was it private, but that it had a bath and separate walk-in shower. One of Charlie's pet hates was clambering over the side of the bath to take a shower and she was relieved she wouldn't have to do that here. The grey and white marble was a bit over the top for her tastes, but she supposed she'd manage to cope with it.

"I hate to rush you," interrupted Britt, "but we really do need to get going."

"Of course," Charlie apologised. "I'm going to have plenty time to get used to these surroundings over the next few weeks. You said something about a classroom space?"

"Yep. We'll look at that next, on our way to meet Jonny," Britt replied as she headed out of Charlie's room and back down the hallway. "It's just one of the meeting rooms, so if there is any equipment that you're going to need, please just let me know and I'll arrange to get it for you. Anything at all."

"Thank you," Charlie replied as she followed, trying to take in the directions so that she'd be able to find her way around later.

"If you'd like to meet again in the morning, I can show you what else the hotel has to offer," Britt said as she wound her way through the corridors like she had an in-built GPS. "The company make it so that you can use any of the facilities: fitness room, indoor pool, outdoor pool, spa. All of it." She grinned at Charlie, who returned the expression. Maybe her work/life balance would benefit from this jaunt. "Here we go," Britt said, pushing open a heavy oak door that opened into a high-ceilinged, oak-panelled square room, just big enough to comfortably fit a round conference table with six leather chairs. "There's also a space for you to use on set," Britt added.

"This is great, thank you. It should be perfect for what I need."

As they rode in the back of the Merc, Charlie listened to Britt make small talk, filling her in on some of the more mundane aspects of the next three months. The way things worked on a film set, what things like 'call time' meant, and how often she could expect to see Lucinda.

"Lucy," Charlie couldn't help but correct. "She hates Lucinda."

"Noted," Britt grinned. "Anything else you think we should know about her?"

"Is her mother here?" The words escaped before Charlie could pull them back in, but her momentary chagrin dissipated immediately as Britt giggled.

"No, she's not. And she has limited visitation rights," Britt added with a wink, to which Charlie mimed wiping the sweat from her brow.

"Then I can't imagine there's anything else. Lucy's a great kid, she just doesn't always get to be herself. The Armstrong-Miller's have high expectations. To be honest, I was pretty surprised that they were supporting Lucy with this adventure." A look crossed Britt's face, and Charlie understood immediately that all had not been plain sailing. "What?" she asked.

"Well," Britt began. "It seems that Lucy didn't tell them she was auditioning. Not for the first, second or third rounds. In fact, she didn't mention it until she had the part secured. By that point, she'd secured herself an agent and signed contracts. Pretty clever really. Her parents had no choice but to go along with it; the names attached to this project are too big to piss off," she added with a wink.

"Let's just hope that Lucy is able to put as much effort into her studies over the next three months as she has this elaborate ruse."

"I wouldn't bet on it," replied Britt. "She's likely to be exhausted, especially over the first few weeks while she adjusts to the pace and pressures of a film set. It's ah, a unique experience," she finished softly.

"Sorry to interrupt, ladies," came Jonny's voice from the front. "We're here."

Charlie looked out the window as the gatehouse came into view, the words 'Pinewood Studios', spelled out in capitals across the top. Jonny slowed and said something Charlie couldn't hear to the guard, who laughed and immediately raised the bar for their car. The Mercedes continued through, and Charlie tried not to let her astonishment show as they drove past the iconic 007, Roger Moore and Richard Attenborough stages, building after building that had housed some of the greatest films ever made. She glanced across at Britt, lost for words, but hoping her emotions showed on her face.

"It never gets old," Britt said.

The car pulled to a stop outside one of the buildings. Such was her awe at her surroundings, that Charlie made no move to let herself get out of the car, happy to wait for Jonny this time. He smiled at her as she slowly climbed out. "Have fun," he said.

Charlie didn't think that would be at all possible. She couldn't imagine allowing herself to relax enough to enjoy it here. It had been a very long time since she'd felt so far out of her depth. Having gone straight from university to Harewood Grammar to undertake her training year, then securing a position there as a newly qualified teacher, it struck Charlie that for the last thirteen years, she had been going to work in exactly the same place every morning. She was more than a little out of her depth and the constant fluttering in her stomach suggested it was going to take more than good wishes from Jonny to put her at ease.

"Come on then, let's go and meet some people and check in with Lucy," said Britt, the gentle smile on her face suggesting she could see exactly what Charlie was thinking. "Trust me," she said as they headed inside the building, "the novelty wears off pretty quickly and it becomes just another job." Somehow, Charlie couldn't imagine that would ever be the case. Wandering next to Britt, it occurred to her that she hadn't asked what was possibly the most important question.

"So, now that I'm here, am I allowed to know anything about the film?" she asked.

"What do you mean?"

"Well, what it's called. What it's about? Who's in it?"

Britt stopped dead and it took Charlie a second to notice. Turning back to look at her, she almost laughed at the look of incredulity on her face. "You don't know any of those things?" she asked, her voice rising a pitch beyond its normal level. "None of them? What do you know?"

Charlie laughed. "Well, I know it's Thursday afternoon. I know that I found out on Monday morning that I was coming here to tutor Lucy," she paused, a thoughtful look on her face. "Yep. That's it. That's what I know."

"Oh my god," breathed Britt. "I knew this had been last minute, but this is ridiculous." A hint of annoyance coloured her tone. "I can't believe they would tell you so little." She looked at Charlie, with something that was either confusion or respect or something that flitted between the two. "I can't believe you came knowing so little."

Charlie shrugged. "My headteacher told me it was a done deal. And besides, I couldn't leave Lucy. Her mother wouldn't have asked for me if it wasn't what Lucy wanted."

"Come on," Britt said as she grabbed Charlie's arm and pulled her towards an on-site coffee shop. "Let me fill in some blanks before we wander any further into this crazy day."

Of all the things that Britt told her, only one reverberated around Charlie's mind as they left the coffee shop and headed further into the studios. Not that this was an adaptation of one of her favourite modern novels. Not that it was being directed by a previous Academy Award winner. Not that the budget for the production was larger than the economy of a small country. Only one thing stuck, pounding in time with her heartbeat as they made their way across a courtyard and onto a sound stage. Robyn White. This was Robyn White's new film.

Charlie knew immediately that the girls were going to shit a brick when she messaged them later that night. Having discovered within hours of moving in together that they all preferred women, their in-depth discussion of likes and dislikes revealed absolutely no similarities, except for Robyn White. She was only a couple of years older than them and had become an overnight sensation as the lead role in *Branded*, what was to be the first in a series of dystopian action films. Charlie, much happier with her nose in a book rather than eyes on a film, had absolutely no idea who they were talking about, but she had been more than happy to listen, and she could still hear the heated discussions that had taken place every time a new Robyn White film came out.

For Jen, it was Robyn's physique that was her major selling point, that athletic body that just seemed to get better and better with each film. Jen was convinced it was all the hours the committed actor spent in the gym, something she too enjoyed. Whilst Charlie didn't doubt Robyn White's workout regimes were followed religiously, she felt the ever-decreasing costumes also helped to draw Jen's attention. Over the intervening years, Jen had had more than her fair share of up-close-and-personal experiences of women's bodies. In fact, Charlie thought, Jen probably remembered more bodies than she did names. As much as she loved her friend, the way Jen went through women was not at all akin to Charlie's style, such as it was.

For Lauren, it was what she described as Robyn's aura. The confident way she came across in interviews, the poise she held herself with on talk-shows and red-carpet events. Her style and attention to detail. Laur argued that even when Robyn was acting, there was something quintessentially 'her' about the character's style. Whilst it all sounded rather fanciful to Charlie at first, she understood exactly what Lauren had been describing on a day ten years ago when she introduced them to her new girlfriend. Teresa had had that same quality and Charlie knew that was what had drawn Lauren to the older architect.

For Nay, it was something different still. Something incredibly simple. According to her, Robyn White had an orgasm-inducing voice. Nothing more, nothing less. And to Nay, that was all it took.

And so, Charlie's education began. The other three had sat her down to watch the *Branded* films that very day and it had become a ritual that the four of them would go to the cinema together to see each new Robyn White release. Whilst Charlie could see what each of friends saw in the actor, for her there was something else, something she had never quite managed to put her finger on which stopped her from being as effusive as the others during their post-screening dissections. They always teased Charlie about it, just like they teased her about her inability to be passionate about anything apart from her job. Charlie didn't think that was exactly fair. She was passionate about things, she just didn't show it like the others, especially not Jen or Nay, who quite literally wore their hearts on their sleeves, the epitome of loud and proud.

Lauren had been more like them when they'd all first met, but she had mellowed as she settled into life with Teresa, become the complete opposite during Teresa's short-lived battle with cancer, and had only recently shown signs that she was coming back out of the darkness that had enveloped her after her wife's far too early death. Charlie knew her friend still had a long way to go, but she was proud of the progress she was making. Charlie had never even been in the same hemisphere of feeling a love like Laur and Teresa had, and if she was being honest, she wasn't sure she was capable of it.

"You okay, Charlie?" asked Britt, breaking into Charlie's memories.

"Yes, sorry. Just taking it all in."

"I imagine it all feels very different, but once you've been around us all for a few days, I'll bet you feel right at home. We're all just people," Britt grinned.

"Famous people," Charlie qualified.

"Not all of us. Some of us are just everyday people, who don't have millions of fans around the world. We turn up, we do our job, and we go home."

And some of you are Robyn White, thought Charlie, hoping it would be possible for her to avoid making an idiot of herself in front of the star should she have the misfortune to meet her.

Chapter Three

Robyn

A frisson of excitement ran through Robyn's body as she stepped onto a Pinewood Studio sound stage for the first time. She'd been creating blockbuster films for a decade-and-a-half but had yet to set foot on such hallowed film-making ground. When she thought about the history, those that had gone before her in this prestigious English location, she had to pinch herself to make sure she wasn't dreaming. And as if that weren't enough, she was finally getting the opportunity to work with Academy Award winning director Peter Fletcher, who she had auditioned for on a number of occasions but never managed to land a role. Finally, it was as if the stars had aligned: an adaptation of one of her favourite novels, a director she had dreamed of working with, and it was all to be filmed here. Pinewood.

She had asked her driver to bring her early this morning, wanting some time to wander and look round, to get the excitement out of her system a little bit before she met the cast and crew. It was important to her that no one realised just how thrilled she was to be part of this project. Experience had taught her that letting her emotions be known was a weakness in this cut-throat business. Someone somewhere would pounce on it and exploit her. It made for a lonely existence at times, but she had accepted that a long time ago.

Robyn sipped on the green tea she had ordered from the on-site coffee shop and checked her watch again. Right on time, a young woman entered the shop, a smile already on her face as she spotted Robyn in the back corner.

"Jeanie," Robyn said, rising to shake hands. "It's lovely to see you again."

"And you," replied the production assistant who had been assigned to Robyn as soon as she'd been cast. They had met a number of times before leaving the States, the young woman keen to make certain that she knew all of Robyn's requirements. "Everything okay at the hotel?"

"Perfect, thank you, Jeanie. It's a lovely place and great that we have it to ourselves. No crazy fan dodging needed!"

"And your room is okay?" The look of concern on her face made Robyn wonder which other actors she had worked with previously and what exactly they had demanded of her.

"Jeanie," Robyn began, placing a reassuring hand on her shoulder. "My room is perfect. The hotel is perfect. Every single thing that you have done for me has been perfect." She grinned, trying to let the younger woman know she was completely genuine. "I honestly couldn't have asked for anything more from an assistant," she added. The look of wonderment on Jeanie's face made Robyn grin. "Come on, then," she encouraged. "I imagine we have somewhere to be."

"Absolutely," Jeanie nodded. "I'll take you to the conference room so you can join the others for the first meet and greet, then I'll wait and take you to your trailer."

"Sounds great."

"Have you worked with anyone here before?"

"No," Robyn admitted, hoping the nerves she felt were disguised behind a false sense of bravado. "I've wanted to work with Mr Fletcher for years now, but this is the first time I've been successful in landing a part in his films. It's not like I haven't tried before either, believe me," she laughed. "I guess I finally must have done something right." A tight smile crossed Jeanie's face, but was gone almost as quickly as it had arrived, long before Robyn could even say with certainty that she'd seen it.

"So, it's just down this corridor," Jeanie said as she turned a corner. Robyn sent up a silent thanks that she hadn't had to find this room on her own – she'd have needed Siri's help to avoid being lost.

Next to her, Jeanie slowed her step, finally stopping outside a heavy oak door marked simply with 'Sharif'. Hallowed grounds indeed. Jeanie knocked once before opening the door, standing to one side, and motioning with her head for Robyn to enter. "I'll be right here," she said softly, not quite meeting Robyn's eye as she spoke.

Before any of the people in the room registered on her radar, Robyn felt herself get swallowed by the space. She was aware the oval table in the centre of the room had seating for about twenty, but her eyes bypassed it immediately as she took in the interior. Walnut panelling, with intricate gold filigree, lined the whole space. Some walls featured bookshelves, the leather spines slightly distorted by the wire mesh that made up the doors in front of them. Others were concave and held busts of famous faces from the studio's history: Olivier, Monroe, Connery. At one end hung a sumptuous pair of red velvet curtains, pulled slightly open to reveal the large television hidden behind, the technology seeming out of place in the traditional room.

"Ms White," a voice dripping with Southern charm broke through her reverie, shocking Robyn slightly as she remembered she was in a room full of people. "I'm so delighted you could join us." The woman stood from her seat at the head of the table and approached Robyn, a welcoming look stretched across her face.

"Mrs Covington," Robyn replied warmly, moving to greet her. "It's an absolute pleasure to see you again."

"Likewise, darling," she drawled, leaning in to kiss Robyn's cheeks. "And I'm sure I've told you this before, young lady, but you must call me Addie. Mrs Covington was my mother-in-law and an absolute beast of a woman." Her eyes went wide and she shuddered for dramatic effect. "I have never been to a party I enjoyed as much as that woman's wake." Robyn couldn't help but laugh, even as part of her was shocked at the genuineness of Addie's vitriol. The older woman had a reputation for speaking her mind and refusing to pull any punches. Robyn assumed that when you were rich like Adelaide Covington rich, you could say whatever the hell you wanted. Despite her own millions in the bank, Robyn knew her fortune was probably just loose change to someone like Addie, who financed films because she damn well wanted to, and not because she was out to make even more money. "Let me introduce you around."

Adelaide gestured towards the table, steering Robyn to one of the remaining empty chairs before settling herself back in her seat.

"This here fine-looking gentleman is our esteemed director, Peter Fletcher, but you know that already, I'm sure," Addie said with a grin.

"I do, absolutely," Robyn replied. "It's a real pleasure to meet you and I'm so excited to be part of this project." She'd told herself over and over not to gush, but now she was faced with the director she idolised, she found it hard to hold to her plans. She was more than a little disappointed when a curt nod was his only reply. She had only ever heard positive things from actors who had worked under Fletcher, so his distance took her by surprise. His reputation was stellar; a hard-working director who knew just how to coax the best from his talent. Robyn hadn't expected him to be effusive in his welcome, but nor had she expected what felt like dismissal.

Adelaide didn't seem to miss a beat before moving on and Robyn forced herself to keep her smile in place.

"Kevin Grealish," she continued, gesturing to the balding man to Fletcher's left. "Our scriptwriter who has just done amazing things with the original manuscript," Addie gushed.

"Hi," Robyn said with a nod. "I love what I've read so far," she smiled, trying desperately to hold it in place when all she received again was a nod and tight smile. Something wasn't right here. She had absolutely no idea what it was, but she always trusted her gut and it was telling her that something was off.

"Steve Cantwell and Rhona Long, two of our producers."

Slightly warmer greetings, with both actually saying hello and sporting genuine smiles.

"Elizabeth Reina, our Director of Photography."

Back to what was beginning to feel like icy, barely concealed contempt.

"Lucy Hampton, Production Designer."

A slight lift of the chin.

"Thierry Saint-Maximin, our wonderful Art Director."

The smile he sent towards Adelaide belonged in a different stratosphere to the one directed at Robyn. What had started as tendrils of unease had now fully taken root in the pit of Robyn's stomach. It had been a long time since she'd experienced the anxiety that had been a familiar accomplice throughout her late teens and early twenties. Born from her lack of self-worth and a severely underdeveloped sense of self-esteem, it had at times been crippling, but her success over the years had allowed her confidence to blossom. Never tipping into arrogance, it had at least been enough to quiet the fear that she was completely out of her depth and about to be revealed as a fraud at any second. The glacial atmosphere in this room, a room dripping in history, pitched her headlong into a regression.

Below the table, she curled her right hand into a fist, welcoming the press of fingernails against palm. She counted her breaths, in and out, refusing to let anyone in the room see how their politely masked hostility affected her. Strategies she hadn't needed for years, rushed back like welcome friends, enabling the fixed smile to stay in place, the nods to come when they were needed, even the words of greeting to tumble out at the right time. But the names and jobs of everyone else swept past her, as did the small talk that filled the room once the introductions were over. From experience, she knew that not a single person in the room would be aware of the ridiculous increase to her heartrate, or the steely control she needed to get her through to the end of the meeting. No one would notice the wobble in her legs when she was finally able to rise from her seat, the tremor in her left hand as she reached for her bag, the nausea she fought down as she said her goodbyes and left the room.

Only when she was outside the room did Robyn slowly uncurl the fingers of her right hand, knowing without looking that there would be crescent-shaped indentations across her palm. She was conscious of Jeanie falling into step next to her, but she made no effort to acknowledge her, too busy allowing her mantra to repeat over and over in her head. She wondered for a moment what the world would think if they knew that she, Robyn White, star of Hollywood blockbuster after Hollywood blockbuster, relied on a litany of superhero names to keep her panic at bay. The alphabetical list was the only thing she'd found that occupied enough of her brain to make her appear as fully functioning to any on-looker.

Antman, Batwoman, Catwoman, she silently began again, retracing her steps from earlier through the winding corridors. *Daredevil, Electra, Flash, Green Lantern, Hit-Girl, Ironman, Jessica Jones, KickAss.* The more distance she put between herself and that room, the calmer she felt. Moving always helped.

"Is there anywhere you want to go before your trailer?" Jeanie's gentle voice broke through her thoughts.

"No," she replied. "Thank you," she added as an afterthought. None of this was Jeanie's fault after all. *Luke Cage, Ms Marvel, Nick Fury, (technically not a superhero, but good enough for her), Ozymandias.*

"I know you've already found one of the cafés, but there are a couple of others just down here," Jeanie continued. "And there are also some restaurants on site. I mean, I know we'll have all the catering teams on set with us, but if you ever wanted a restaurant for some reason, they do have them."

Jeanie was rambling. Robyn wasn't sure if it was because she could sense there was something not quite right with her charge or something else. Her mind replayed for her the tight smile that had crossed her assistant's face ahead of the meeting. Did she know something?

Phantom, Quicksilver, Rogue, Storm.

"So, we're going to be filming mostly on The Roger Moore Stage and a couple of the backlots nearby, so our trailers are located over that side too," Jeanie explained as she pushed through the front doors and walked towards the waiting car, Robyn following in silence behind her. What the hell was going on? She had never felt like this on set before, not even all those years ago on her very first one.

Thor, Ultragirl, Venom, Wonder Woman.

"Oh, hey, Brittany!" Robyn heard Jeanie say as she stopped to greet someone else. Slowing her own pace to match, Robyn allowed her thoughts to percolate, playing difference scenarios over in head as she tried to work out what she had just experienced.

"Jeanie," a warm voice said. "So good to see you again." A hug took place, but it barely registered for Robyn. "You have to meet Charlie," she enthused, introducing the woman beside her. More chatting that Robyn just tuned out.

X-Man, Yellowjacket, Zatanna.

Distantly, Robyn registered a pause in the conversation beside her, but as the last name in her litany ticked through her mind, the pieces clicked into place, and she knew exactly what had happened in that meeting room. It was so obvious now she couldn't quite believe it had taken this long to sink in.

They didn't want her here.

"My trailer. Now," she ground out, barely keeping a lid on the anxiety and tension roiling through her entire being. She saw the look of shock on the faces of the three women before, but she was too far gone to do anything about it. And anyway, she'd rather they thought her a rude, demanding diva than figure out the truth. That she was just moments away from a full-blown panic attack. Her right hand had clenched tightly again, and the litany began, racing its way through her fractured mind: *Antman, Batwoman, Catwoman, Daredevil, Elektra, Flash, Green Lantern, Hit-Girl, Ironman, Jessica Jones, KickAss.* Move, she had to move. Turning her back on the small group before her, she walked briskly to the car, sliding in through the open door, all the time keeping the mantra going. *Luke Cage, Ms Marvel, Nick Fury, Ozymandias, Phantom, Quicksilver, Rogue, Storm.*

"My trailer," she said sternly to her driver, not giving Jeanie a chance to catch up before closing the door and having him drive her away. She had to be on her own. Needed it more than anything.

Thor, Ultragirl, Venom, Wonder Woman, X-Man, Yellowjacket, Zatanna.

The car pulled up at the end of a row of trailers and Robyn pushed open the door, not giving the driver a chance to get out, never mind get around to open it for her. She slammed it shut behind her and started down the aisle, her eye running over the names on the doors. She didn't care what any of them said, she just needed to find her own. She found it on the sixth door down and gratefully pushed open the door, stumbling inside and locking it behind her.

Once you'd been in one trailer, you'd pretty much been in them all and so it didn't take her a moment to locate the bedroom and slide down onto the floor between the bed and the wall. Pulling her knees in, Robyn pressed her forehead to them, wrapped her arms around her legs and allowed the worst to wash over her. Over the years, she'd found a number of affirmations that worked for her once she was calm enough to let them in. *I have survived this before, and I'll survive it this time. I am strong enough to get through this. This doesn't define me.* Robyn ignored the part of her mind that was telling her, yes, she'd survived these moments of panic before, but she hadn't ever experienced not being wanted on a film set. That was new. And that meant she couldn't know for certain that she would survive it.

Instead, she focused on the part that shouted more loudly. The part that reminded her she had lived through not being wanted before. So what if it hadn't been on a film set? So what if she almost hadn't come through it? All that mattered was that she had. She wouldn't say she'd become stronger because of it, but she had endured. And that meant she could do it again. She had to. She was Robyn White, and whether she was wanted on this film set or not, she was going to act the shit out of her role.

Drawing in a deep, steadying breath, she allowed her body to relax. She lifted her head, flexed her hands, stretched her legs. She was utterly exhausted, but she wasn't beaten. She pushed to her feet, limbs shaking, and walked slowly back to the kitchen area. Opening cupboards, she smiled as she saw that Jeanie had indeed done her job perfectly. Her favourite chocolate bars waited patiently. Robyn didn't waste any time ripping one open and taking a large, satisfying bite. The taste of the comfort food would do as much for her mind as the sugar hit would her body. She moaned as she took a second bite, chewing slowly as she turned to fill the kettle, switching it on so she could make her favourite tea.

Not only did she owe Jeanie another thank you, she also owed her a massive apology. She'd left her standing on the sidewalk outside the studio, having just ignored someone she was trying to introduce to Robyn. A groan escaped as she realised just how rude she'd been. Robyn knew she could just leave things as they were and have the other women think her a diva, but that wasn't her style. She'd find a way to make it up to Jeanie. Maybe not quite a full explanation, but enough to make things right between them.

Tea and chocolate in hand, she curled up in a corner of the large, grey sofa that filled the living space. Before she could work out what she was going to say to Jeanie, she needed to make a call. Pulling out her phone, Robyn pressed on David's name.

"Robyn!" The deep, baritone voice boomed down the line. "How's London treating you?"

"They don't want me here, David."

Silence. And that only meant one thing.

"You knew, didn't you?" she accused. "How could you just let me walk in here without any kind of warning?"

"Slow down, Robyn," he appeased.

"Slow down?" she asked, incredulous. "Do you have any idea what it was like, David? To be introduced to a room full of people who could barely keep their disdain hidden? How could you do that to me?"

"It's not what you think," he began.

"It's exactly what I think, David." Robyn could feel her heartbeat rise again, this time with anger rather than anxiety. "They can barely even look me in the eye. What the hell is going on?" she demanded.

"Now just hold on a moment," he retorted, an edge creeping into his voice that Robyn was very familiar with. He was infamous for his short temper and Robyn had seen it unleashed on a number of occasions over the years he had been her manager. It was unusual to have it be directed at her though. "You were the one that insisted on doing something different, Robyn. That doesn't just happen easily, you know. If you'd just stuck to what you're good at, we wouldn't be in this situation."

Robyn felt as though her rapidly beating heart had just come to a complete standstill. What was he talking about?

"You need to explain this to me, David," she said, forcing her voice to remain calm, even as she heard his heavy sigh down the line.

"Look, I'll be blunt, Robyn." When was he not?, she mused. "You're pretty much typecast." She drew in a breath, surprised by the jolt of pain his words brought. "You are Hester Wilde," he said, referring to the character she had played in *Branded*. "Sure, you've done other films, but when anyone thinks of Robyn White, they see Hester. And let's face it," he continued, seemingly on a roll. "Those other roles you've had? All of them are pretty much a version of Hester."

As much as she wanted to argue vehemently against what David was saying, Robyn knew it was true. It was why she had turned down the last few parts he'd brought to her. She wanted to do something different. And that's what *Strikes Twice* was meant to be. Her chance to show not only the world, but herself, that she could play the part she'd longed to play ever since she'd first read the book as a teenager.

"What did you do, David?" she asked, unsure if she really wanted to know the answer.

"I went straight to Adelaide Covington," he replied. "That's where the power is in this film, no matter what Peter Fletcher might think." He paused for a moment and Robyn steeled herself, knowing this was where the whole truth would come out. "He turned you down," David continued, his voice gentling just a touch. "After your audition, his office contacted me to say thanks, but no thanks. So, I did the last thing you are supposed to do in Hollywood; I went straight to the source of the money. I've known Adelaide for years, worked with her a number of times, always successfully. I reminded her of that, and we made a deal."

"What kind of deal?"

"You're tied into Peaches Productions for three films," he stated, referring to Covington's company. "But you only get paid for this one."

His words hung between them, Robyn shocked into silence. Was he really saying what she thought he was?

"Are you telling me that in order to get this role, I have to do another two movies for nothing?" She knew that was what he'd said, but it didn't make any sense.

"Yes," he confirmed, no elaboration forthcoming.

No wonder Addie Covington had been so friendly earlier. And no wonder everyone else in the room was so pissed.

Chapter Four

Robyn

It had taken her a couple of days, but Robyn had finally found something resembling peace with David's revelation. She absolutely hated what he'd done, but she had managed to calm herself enough to realise there was nothing she could do about it. She had silenced the part of her that demanded she walk off set and leave them all in the lurch, because what would that actually achieve? Nothing good, she'd convinced herself.

The tentative knock at her door signalled the first item on her to do list. Apologise to Jeanie.

"Hi," Robyn said in her best version of contrite. "I know we need to head off, but do you have a quick moment before we leave please?"

"Of course," Jeanie replied. Robyn knew she was to blame for the worried look on her assistant's face and resolved to make her apology sincere.

"I need to apologise for the other day." No use in beating around the bush. "After the initial meeting, I was incredibly rude to you, which you absolutely didn't deserve." She had thought about possible reasons she could offer to Jeanie, but she didn't want to lie to her and there was no way she was going to tell the truth, so that meant a heartful apology, with no excuses. "I shouldn't have been in such a rush to get to my trailer," she continued. "It was wrong to leave you and I can assure you it won't happen again."

"It's okay, Ms White," Jeanie said, her tone and facial expression both belying the fact that the people she worked for didn't usually apologise to her.

"No, it's absolutely not alright," she countered. "I was out of line."

For a moment, Robyn thought Jeanie was going to argue, to continue to displace the blame, to try and let her off the hook. And then a different look settled across her face.

"Thank you," she said. "I really appreciate you saying all that, Ms White."

Robyn grinned at her. "So, we're good?"

Jeanie nodded.

"Then can you please remember to call me Robyn?" she teased, pulling a matching grin from Jeanie.

"Absolutely, Robyn."

Somehow Robyn guessed it wouldn't go quite as smoothly with everyone else on set.

By the time their lunch break rolled around, Robyn knew with complete certainty that she was fighting an uphill battle. Peter Fletcher hadn't met with her at all, despite doing so with every other main member of the cast; she had been delegated to the Assistant Director instead. The clipped tone told Robyn even that had been done begrudgingly. Despite spending almost an hour in the meeting, she still felt none the wiser about what they wanted from her. Her questions had been met with the kind of vague non-answer she associated with a politician and she'd had to bite her tongue to refrain from suggesting a career change.

Her time with Marge Cresswell, Academy Award winning Costume Designer, had been equally as brutal. The initial small talk Robyn had attempted was met with a stony wall of silence, and in the end, she just gave up and endured the fittings.

All-in-all, it had not gone to plan. She had hoped to start winning people over, building a few bridges, finding some olive branches and any other similar metaphors she could think of. Surely once they got to know her, they'd see something more. But that had been the biggest problem – it seemed that no-one wanted to give her a chance.

She sighed as she leaned back into the sofa in her trailer, propping her feet up on the coffee table. She gazed at the ceiling, trying to find the strength to get through the rest of the day. There was only one thing that was going to make that happen. She pulled her phone from her back pocket, did a quick calculation and dialled. Her phone rang only twice before the one person in the world who could really calm her answered.

"Hey, little sis," a warm voice cooed down the line.

"Little by two minutes," Robyn laughed, the greeting so familiar. "It's so good to hear your voice, Kate."

"Yours too, Robbie. How's England?"

"Well, it hasn't rained yet, so I guess it's not too bad," Robyn grinned.

"So, now that the pleasantries are out of the way, what's up?"

"That obvious, huh?"

"I know you, Robbie. Well, that and it's not long past 7:30am here and I know you never call me without working out the time difference, so to ring this early..." Kate let her words hang down the line between them and Robyn smiled softly to herself. This was why she needed to talk to Kate. No one else had ever come close to understanding Robyn like her twin sister, and Robyn doubted anyone could. Growing up they'd been inseparable, right up until the end of high school when they'd chosen colleges thousands of miles apart, Robyn to study economics and Kate to pursue her dream of becoming a school teacher. Even then, they'd never gone more than a couple of days without talking to each other. When Kate had met Gray, the man she'd eventually settle down with and marry, Robyn had been her first phone call. Despite the fame Robyn had found, she had been maid of honour at the wedding and was godmother to both her nieces.

"Rob?" Kate prompted.

And that was all it took to get Robyn to pour out the whole miserable tale.

"So, let me get this right," Kate said slowly, and Robyn could imagine the look on her face: eyebrows drawn together in a slightly quizzical nature, lips pursed, eyes bright with indignant fury. "David pimped you out?"

Robyn barked out a laugh. Of all the ways her sister could have summarised what she'd just told her, that one had never crossed her mind. "It's hardly pimping, Kate, if we're not making any money from it. Not that that's what bothers me. We both know I don't do this for the money."

"Hmm," Kate mused. "While you might not be making any money from the deal, I guarantee that David Neville will have weaselled himself something. I swear, Robbie, that man is trouble. I've been telling you since I first met him that you need to get a new agent." Robyn smiled sadly and shook her head. It was true. Kate had taken an instant dislike to David, and although he'd never said anything, Robyn was pretty sure the feeling was mutual. "But, that aside, we need a plan to fix this," Kate stated confidently.

"Thank you, Katie," Robyn whispered. They always knew what the other one needed to hear and right now, Robyn needed someone to tell her there was a way through the mess she found herself in. "Any ideas? I've tried being nice, but I think I've pretty much failed on all fronts with that strategy."

"Let me think on it, Rob. We're going to need something special and I can't manage to come up with that while I'm also trying to convince your youngest niece not to try out her new crayons on the den wall, am failing in my attempts to get my husband to obey the telepathic messages I'm sending him about said crayons, and your eldest niece has just arrived looking rather sheepish, clutching what I suspect is the homework she assured me she didn't have last night."

"Wow, it sounds like your mess is even bigger than mine," Robyn teased, trying to hide the sudden pang of loneliness that washed over her. Most days, she loved her job and the lifestyle that came with it. Others, particularly when she was with her sister and her family, she found herself wishing she'd made different choices.

"I'll call you when I can tonight," Kate said quickly. "I might even remember to work out the time difference this time," she added with a laugh before hanging up. Robyn had lost count of just how often she'd been woken by the buzz of her telephone at the most inhospitable hours of day when Kate called without thinking. Right now, she didn't care what time her sister called, as long as she did. No plan in the world would get her through the next few months of purgatory if she didn't have that regular check in time with Kate.

She pushed herself up out of the sofa, feeling more fortified than she had before their call, glanced in the mirror, and left her trailer to go to the read through that was scheduled to start in 20 minutes. At least this would give her the chance to be in the same room as everyone else, she hoped. Surely they couldn't side-line her for the this?

Robyn's nerves settled slightly as she pushed into the Sharif room, immediately noticing that the key cast and crew were indeed inside and this wasn't some elaborate ruse to make her go to the wrong room or turn up an hour late. There were name cards out around the table, and she felt further relief that she wasn't going to have to awkwardly try to find a seat by herself. Dropping her copy of the script and the well-loved *Branded* pencil case Kate had bought her one Christmas onto the table, she crossed the room to the refreshment table and snagged a bottle of water. She kept her eyes down, not ready to see the resentment she felt for sure would be on some of the faces around her. She hoped it wasn't obvious to anyone just how intensely she was concentrating on her breathing as she eased into her seat. *Inhale, pause, exhale; inhale, pause, exhale;* the mantra repeated in her head as she opened the bottle and took a small sip.

"Right, let's make a start," Peter said loudly into the room, which immediately quieted as everyone took their seats. "We've done most of the introductions at some point over the last couple of days, and anyone you don't know yet, you soon will, so let's not waste any time on meaningless pleasantries."

He didn't look at her once, but Robyn couldn't help but feel some of that was aimed at her. If he'd had the cast he wanted, would he have started today differently?

Clearing his throat, David continued. "A basic read through today, please. No theatrics, no egos, just read the lines from the page. We can get to the rest later. For now, we all just need to hear it." This time he had looked at her, and Robyn swallowed to keep her emotions in check. "I'll read the stage directions." And with that, he was off.

When she didn't have lines of her own to read, Robyn tried to surreptitiously take in the other cast members, not having worked with any of them before, and not actually even having heard of some of them. Experience allowed her to get a feel for them from the way the read, fidgeted, day-dreamed, or looked at her. From the few glances thrown at her by Stephen Carlisle, one of her co-stars, she knew that she would have to act the shit out of their scenes for anything resembling chemistry to appear on the screen. His character was supposed to be the best friend of hers; he didn't need to say a word for her to know he was aware of the circumstances in which she had landed the role. His disdain dripped from every pore and she caught more than one knowing look shared between him and Peter. She could only just imagine how they were going to try and make things difficult for her once they were on set.

The girl playing her younger sister, Lucinda, Robyn thought she was called, looked far more positive, however, and Robyn got the strange impression that if she did know the circumstances surrounding her hiring, she couldn't care less. There was a visible streak of steel in the young woman and she met Robyn's eyes with confidence more than once, sometimes shooting a cheeky grin or rolling her eyes at something. It was reckless behaviour from someone so young, and ordinarily, Robyn would have labelled it as arrogance, a trait she couldn't abide. With Lucinda, it was different though and she looked forward to the scenes they would film together.

Mackenzie Brewster, a stalwart of British film, barely looked up from his script and Robyn couldn't tell yet whether that was from concentration or a general contempt for the others in the room. Mary Kane and Paxton Jones were firmly in Stephen Carlisle's camp, their dislike palpable whenever they looked her way.

As soon as they were finished and Peter dismissed them for the evening, Robyn left the room, restraining herself from sprinting out, and trying to maintain a composed exit. She caught sight of the worst offenders gathering together, their stares firmly pinned on her as she made her way across the room. She refused to let them see how much it bothered them and sent a friendly smile their way.

"See you all tomorrow," she practically purred as she passed them, pushing open the door and taking a deep, calming breath. She needed a moment to herself, so rather than trying to hold it all together until she made it back to her trailer, she glanced at the schedule pinned outside the room at the end of their corridor and, seeing it was empty, pushed inside.

Closing her eyes, she sank to the floor and allowed herself a moment of weakness, covering her face with her hands and letting a ragged sob escape. Her dream job, the role she had wanted since being an awkward teenager, was all going to shit. She let out a silent scream, screwing her fists as tightly as her eyes and letting her head fall back against the door with a small thump.

A throat cleared softly, and Robyn's heart almost leapt out through her chest.

"Jesus Christ!" she exclaimed, opening her eyes widely and looking about the room as she pushed to her feet. To her left, sat a woman with the most startling blue eyes Robyn had ever seen, a fact that registered somewhere deep in her mind, a mind that was overcome with embarrassment at having been caught in a moment of weakness.

"Are you okay?" a soft English voice asked, pity coating the tone, just as it laced the woman's eyes.

"What the hell are you doing in here?" Robyn demanded, ignoring the question and attacking the sympathy she absolutely did not want to hear or see at that moment. "This room is supposed to be empty. You can't just go around sitting in any room you choose," she railed, knowing she was taking out her frustrations on this beautiful stranger, but wholly unable to stop herself. "If you want to occupy one, you book it using the correct procedures and a sign goes up outside. That way everyone knows it's been booked, and they don't mistakenly think it's empty."

At the very least, Robyn's outburst achieved one thing: the look of pity disappeared immediately, a flash of hurt there before quickly being masked by an emptiness that Robyn felt ashamed to have caused.

"My apologies," the woman uttered quietly, maintaining her even temperament, much to Robyn's dismay. The fire she felt inside needed an outlet. She took a step away from the door, moving further into the room.

"If you so much as mention this to anyone else," Robyn began in a menacing tone she wasn't aware she was capable of, before being cut off as the woman raised a hand and spoke in that gentle voice.

"You don't need to worry," she assured. "I'll leave you to it," she added quietly, pushing to her feet and going the long way around the table to the door so she wouldn't have to walk anywhere near Robyn. "I won't say a word to anyone, Ms White," she added with a sad smile, before pulling open the door and leaving.

Robyn's heart beat wildly in her chest and she sank down into a chair, shame overwhelming her. What had she just done? She didn't even recognise her own behaviour. It was so out of character. That poor woman had done absolutely nothing wrong, and Robyn had just gone all diva on her, purely to hide her embarrassment at having been caught with her guard down, even if it had been momentary.

Elbows resting on the table, she pressed her forehead into her hands and wished desperately that she could rewind the last five minutes. She could have just laughed off being caught, responded to the woman's initial question with a witty riposte. But the kindness in those too-blue eyes had caught her off guard, so different had they been from the gazes that her driven her into this room in the first place. The gentle voice had seemed genuine, the English accent merely emphasising the caring tone.

God, those eyes. Even though she didn't want it to, a stubborn part of Robyn's brain refused to move beyond processing those beautiful eyes. Perfectly at home in an equally beautiful face, framed with a stylish brown bob that accentuated her jawline. She wasn't an actress that Robyn had ever met before, but that was surely what she did. Someone that striking had to be in the movie business.

"Ms Evans," an excited voice called behind her as the door to the room burst open. "You'll never guess... Oh. Hi, Ms White," said the young woman as she stood slightly uncertainly in the doorway. The girl playing her younger sister smiled and the look of steel from earlier quickly took up residence in her eyes.

"Lucinda," Robyn greeted, rising up and stretching out her hand, which the girl reached out slowly to take.

"It's actually just Lucy," she said with a grin. "Unless my mother is in earshot and then you should probably stick with the whole Sunday name."

"Noted," Robyn laughed.

"I, um, I'm really sorry to disturb you, Miss White, I was looking for my teacher. I thought this was the room I was supposed to meet her in."

Robyn's heart sank. It hadn't been some other diva actress she had chased away; it had been Lucy's teacher.

"Dark hair, about this long?" she asked, motioning to her jawline with her hand. Lucy nodded. "She was here, but she, er, she left when I came in." It wasn't exactly the whole truth, but Robyn felt crappy enough already without confessing her horrendous behaviour to her young co-star.

"I guess I'll just try to catch her at the hotel instead. Thank you for the info." She turned to leave but stopped when Robyn called her name.

"I just wanted to say that you don't have to call me 'Ms White'," Robyn smiled. "Robyn is just fine."

To her credit, Lucy almost managed to keep the look of awe from her face as she nodded.

"Thank you." She paused before adding, "Robyn," a shy grin lighting her eyes.

"We should catch up later tonight when we're back at the hotel," Robyn found herself saying, though only god knew why. The only thing she wanted to do later was collapse into her bed and bring today to a swift end. Apparently her mouth wasn't on the same wavelength as her brain. "It would be nice to get to know each other a bit," she added with a smile.

"Wow! I mean, um, yeah, that would be great." Lucy's attempt at nonchalance missed the mark by about three miles and Robyn couldn't help but grin. "I guess I'll see you later then."

"I should be in the hotel bar by 7:30pm."

"I'll be there!" said Lucy, her grin matching Robyn's.

As the door closed fully, Robyn allowed her head to sink completely to the table.

"Great job, Robbie," she muttered to herself. Now not only did she have to socialise tonight, but she also needed to add seeking out the teacher and apologising to the top of her to do list.

Chapter Five

Charlie

"I honestly can't tell you how much of a bitch Robyn White is," Charlie said by way of greeting as she logged in to the weekly Skype group conversation she had with her friends.

"Oh, my god," Naomi screeched. "You've met her? I can't believe you've met Robyn White. I am literally beyond jealous right now."

"Yes, I've met her, Nay. And she's a bitch."

"Who cares about her personality? Is she even more stunning in real life?" Jenna asked, a dreamy look on her face.

"Is anyone actually listening to me?" Charlie asked. "She. Is. A. Bitch."

"But hot!"

"Jenna! Seriously. The woman's been an absolute monster both times I've met her."

"Twice? She said twice, Jen! Charlie's met her twice!" Naomi yelled, fanning herself in excitement.

"I give up," Charlie said, a grin lifting the corners of her mouth for the first time since Robyn had so unceremoniously chucked her out of the room she was supposed to use for Lucy's tutoring. "Help me out here, Lauren," she pleaded with the most sensible member of their group.

"I hear what you're saying," she replied, her chocolatey eyes full of what looked suspiciously like mirth to Charlie. "But I'm kind of with Jen on this one."

"Lauren Hughes, you are not that shallow," Charlie reprimanded.

"But I am?" Jenna asked, arching an eyebrow in feigned insult. She would be the first to admit that when it came to women, she had all the depth of a puddle in the Sahara. "It's not my fault no one holds my attention for longer than ten minutes," she grinned.

"Anyway...," Naomi began.

"Yes," Charlie interrupted in annoyance. "She's an incredibly attractive woman. Are you happy now?"

"Actually, I was going to ask what she'd done to annoy you so much," Nay said quietly.

"Oh." Charlie closed her eyes for a moment and took a breath. "I'm sorry, Nay."

Her friend smiled. "No harm done. So, come on, tell us all about it."

Charlie relayed everything that happened, starting with her excitement at being at Pinewood Studios that first day, at least until Ms White had completely ignored her, dismissing her presence when Brittany's friend Jeanie had wanted to introduce them. She'd tried not to let her bother her, tried to give the benefit of the doubt and assume that the actress had been tired from an exhausting rehearsal, or dashing off for an important phone call with Hollywood. Still, Charlie couldn't quite see how taking thirty seconds to say 'hi' could be such a difficulty.

Today though, today had been on a totally different level. She had felt demeaned and dismissed, like she was somehow less worthy of being on the same planet as Robyn White, never mind the same room.

"I guess more than anything," she admitted, "I'm just really disappointed in her, which I know is ridiculous."

"It's hardly ridiculous to think one human being might treat another with a modicum of respect," Jenna countered, defending Charlie, just as Charlie had known her friend would.

"We could invent a thousand possible reasons to excuse Robin's behaviour, but that's all they'd ever be: excuses," Naomi added.

"I don't know what I expected though. I mean, it's not like we were destined to become best friends or anything," Charlie said, the earlier anger gone completely now that she had shared with her friends. "I guess I just hoped that I'd be able to tell you all that she's as amazing as you want her to be. All those hours we've spent watching her films together. I wanted her to be worthy of that."

"Maybe this is why you've always held back on her, Charlie," Lauren said, using what Charlie liked to call her 'wise' tone. "Maybe there was something there that you somehow managed to sense. You never did get as giddy as the three of us," she laughed.

"Maybe," Charlie agreed because that was easier than trying to explain how she knew with absolute certainty that hadn't been what had held her back. Try as she might, she'd never been able to put words to it, but she knew it wasn't anything to do with her suspecting Robin White to be a class-A bitch. Far from it.

"You know that this doesn't spoil any of those memories of us watching the films together, though, right?" Jenna asked in one of her rare moments of showing just how capable of empathy she was. Charlie suspected that was the real reason her relationships never lasted. Not because she was unable to feel with any depth, but because she was protecting herself from falling all in.

"It doesn't?" Charlie asked in a quiet voice. "You aren't all a little bit disappointed in me for bringing out the worst in your favourite actress?"

Naomi's loud laugh rang out, before she realised Charlie was being serious. "Of course it doesn't. And why would we ever be disappointed in you, Char? You're like the best of the best and if you don't know that we are super-proud of you, then that's on us for not saying it loudly enough. You, Charlie Evans, are one of the good guys and if some Hollywood Diva can't see that, that's her loss."

"Nay's right," Lauren agreed. "Watching those movies with the three of you are some of the happiest memories I have, and nothing could change that."

"Sometimes you're such an idiot, Evans," Jenna quipped, reverting to her usual sardonic tone. "And as I said before, who gives a shit about personality?"

Charlie was still chuckling as she shut down her laptop. She honestly had no idea how she would have managed to navigate life if it weren't for her three best friends. Tucking the laptop back in her bag for tomorrow's session with Lucy, she stood and stretched out the kinks in her back. She shook her head as she took in her surroundings, still unable to get to grips with the grandeur of her room. Glancing at her watch, she knew she had about an hour before she needed to turn in for the night. Whilst most people in her situation would have headed to the hotel bar, that wasn't Charlie. Grabbing the book from her nightstand and her favourite washed out hoody that was a souvenir from a trip the four of them had taken to New York the year they all turned 30, she headed to the doors that opened onto her small patio area. She snuggled into a loveseat, opened her book, and lost herself immediately.

When Charlie woke the next morning, she found a message waiting from Lauren.

Laur: Hey, you. No matter the time, I'm here if you need me.

She wasn't surprised. There was always a little something extra in the understanding that passed between the two of them. She loved Jenna and Nay and knew they'd always be there if she needed them, but Lauren somehow got her on a slightly deeper level. They'd always been that way, and even Lauren's marriage to Teresa hadn't prevented them from being able to read each other better than they could read themselves. This whole Robin White thing had Charlie doubting herself in a way she hadn't for years. Knowing Lauren got that helped.

Charlie: Thank you. Goes both ways.

It had been just over two-and-a-half years since Lauren had lost Teresa, and for much of the intervening period, Charlie had been seriously worried that Lauren might not pull through herself. Things had been so bleak eight months ago that Charlie had taken drastic action and turned up on Lauren's doorstep, suitcase in hand, refusing to leave. Six weeks later, she had finally gone back home, secure in the knowledge that Lauren would be okay.

It had taken a few days for Lauren to say anything to her at all, and when she did it had been a tirade of anger, most of it aimed at Charlie, who hadn't once flinched or responded in any way but calmly. She had instinctively known none of it was personal and that Lauren needed to get out the ire she felt at losing her beloved wife. After the anger had come the tears, and Charlie had joined in on that one. Lauren was right; it wasn't fair. Teresa had been the life and soul of the party, one of those larger than life but utterly genuine personalities. Charlie had loved her like a sister and was devastated when she died.

A knock at the door signalled a welcome interruption to her sad train of thoughts.

"Good morning!" greeted Britt, slightly too perkily for Charlie's liking, whose raised eyebrow clearly signalled that to her new friend. "Sorry," she gushed. "James surprised me last night by arriving a couple of days early," she said, referring to her husband. "He somehow managed to convince my mother to take on babysitting duties earlier than planned!"

"Major brownie points for him, I presume?"

"Major!" Britt laughed. "I know we're ridiculous, but I don't care."

"Ridiculous, how?" Charlie asked, her curiosity piqued.

"Because we've been together for ever."

"And that means you can't get excited to see each other?" Charlie was genuinely puzzled by Britt's answer.

"Well, most people just think it's ludicrous," Britt explained. "James' parents lived two doors down from mine, and they were friends before either of us came along. Apparently, I announced when I was three that we would be getting married and everyone was invited. I can honestly say no-one else ever got a look in! It was always just him for me and vice-versa. Now I'm in my mid-forties, have three gorgeous kids and still feel like a teenager when he knocks on my hotel room door 48 hours before he's meant to, clasping a bunch of flowers and wearing a sheepish grin."

"Britt," Charlie began, reaching out to put a hand on her new friend's arm. "That is anything but ludicrous, and anyone who tells you otherwise is just plain old jealous."

"What about you?" Britt asked, her caramel eyes sparkling with mischief.

"Me? I'm pretty much the exact opposite of you," Charlie replied, keeping her tone light and upbeat. "Aside from the odd date here and there, I am Miss Perpetually Single."

"All that means is that you haven't met the right guy or gal yet," Britt replied with an authority Charlie found refreshing.

"Gal," she confirmed with a smile. "And if she could stop doing whatever it is that's been keeping me from finding her, that would be great," she quipped. "Anyhow, I'm pretty certain you didn't leave that husband of yours alone so early this morning just to come along here and talk about my non-existent love life," Charlie prompted.

"You are correct," Britt replied. "I did not. There's been a change to the schedule, so Lucy isn't needed on set until this afternoon. I took the liberty of letting her know she should meet you in the conference room here at 9:30am instead of the one on set."

Charlie hadn't told Britt about her run in with Robin White yesterday afternoon and she hoped the instant relief she felt at not having to go back to that room today wasn't completely obvious on her face. Of course, she knew she'd have to go back in it at some point but having 24 hours grace felt like a blessing.

"Thank you for letting me know. I've not seen Lucy since I got here, so it'll be good to catch up."

"Of course, I'll check in with you tonight and let you know the plan for tomorrow. See you later, Charlie." The grin on Britt's face told Charlie all she needed to know about the assistant's plans for the rest of her morning.

An hour later, she was flicking through her tattered copy of *Tess of the D'Urbervilles*, waiting for Lucy to arrive. As if on cue, the door burst open and a slightly out of breath Lucinda Armstrong-Miller rushed inside.

"I'm so sorry I'm late, Ms Evans," she blurted. "I lost track of time when I was trying to learn my lines for this afternoon." She collapsed into a chair at the table. "I have my first scene with Robin White," she grinned. "Can you believe it, Ms Evans? Me. I'm going to be acting opposite the most amazing actress on the planet!"

Charlie only just managed to stifle a groan. Could she not get a break from the damn woman?

"I'm sure that you'll be just fine, Lucy."

"Fine? I can't just be 'fine', Ms Evans. I have to be amazing otherwise I won't do her justice. God, I can't let her down." She paused before continuing. "I met her yesterday and she was so lovely, just so down to earth and really made me feel like she was looking forward to working with me too."

So, it seemed the great Robin White could be personable when it mattered to her. Just not when she was talking to a woman below whatever passed for human in her world.

"I'm glad she was nice to you, Lucy." Not a total lie. "It's important that the people who've been doing this job for years help you settle in."

"She was definitely nice. We had quite a long chat and not just about the film either, which I was pretty surprised at. I mean, who would have thought some Hollywood A-lister would want to get to know me?" she rambled on, clearly more starstruck than Charlie would have imagined. She'd expected Lucy to play it cool, to seem like nothing affected her. She was glad to be wrong as it was nice to see her usually reserved student come to life.

"I suppose getting to know your co-stars is quite an important part of the job."

"I mean, I guess so, but I really didn't expect her to spend any time with me away from the studio," Lucy gushed.

"She did?" Charlie asked, hoping the disbelief she felt came across as mild surprise.

"Yeah. I met her in the room where you're going to be teaching me, and she was just really friendly, you know?" Lucy got a dreamy look on her face and Charlie bit down on the inside of her cheek to stop the 'are you fucking kidding me?' question that so desperately wanted to be heard. "And then she asked me if I wanted to meet up here in the bar last night," she gushed.

"In the bar?" Charlie asked, unable to stop the teacher in her from coming out.

"Don't worry, Ms Evans," Lucy laughed. "Robyn made sure to tell me I had to stay on the soft stuff. She did too. She said all good actresses do."

Charlie gave a begrudging point to Robyn White, but it didn't make her climb any higher in her estimation.

"That's very sensible advice."

"She gave me loads of tips about how to deal with the intensity of a film shoot, but she wasn't patronising at all. It was all kind of 'I've learned this so I'm passing it on', stuff. You know?"

Charlie nodded despite the fact that she didn't know. Didn't have even the beginnings of a clue. How could she and Lucy have experienced two such different women? Could it really just be because Lucy was an actress and Charlie was the help?

"That was nice of her."

41

"It was, it really was. And, it wasn't all about her or work either. She asked about me, my hobbies, my experience, everything. She even asked about my lessons with you," Lucy smiled.

"She did?" Charlie knew that wasn't the first time she'd asked that exact same question, but to be honest, she was at a complete loss. Her brain couldn't seem to get over the opposing experiences that Robyn White had offered up so far. Total bitch to supportive mentor.

"Yep. I told her we were doing *Tess* in Lit," Lucy scrunched her nose up and Charlie didn't blame her; it was an interminable novel that exam boards insisted on foisting upon teenage readers. A cruel and unusual punishment in Charlie's opinion; not that she'd ever share that with her students. "She said that it had always been on her list to read and that she might try to find a copy so we could chat about it between scenes. Can you imagine, Ms Evans? Me talking to Robyn White about Thomas Hardy?"

No, Charlie thought to herself. She couldn't imagine it for one second based on her Robyn White experience to date. Too stunned to formulate a response, she just smiled and let Lucy ramble for another few minutes before grasping hold of the conversation and turning their attention to the Victorian tragedy.

Chapter Six

Charlie

"Thank you, Jonny," Charlie said as she climbed out the back of the car the next morning. She'd woken early, calmed herself with her usual morning yoga routine and taken advantage of room service for breakfast. She promised herself it wouldn't become a habit and that she'd brave the hotel restaurant at some point, but she wasn't quite at that point yet. For now, she was happy to be a hermit while she found her feet.

"Morning, Charlie!" Britt called as she pushed through the rotating door at the front of the studio, beckoning Charlie to head her way. Charlie couldn't help but smile to herself; Britt's extra perkiness caused by her husband's arrival was still very much in evidence. The assistant somehow just seemed lighter, as if she was suddenly freed from carrying a weight Charlie wouldn't have known was there if she hadn't seen the transformation. She doubted many people would even notice, but Charlie had always been attuned to the slightest shifts in other people's moods.

"Hi, Britt," she answered as she drew closer. "Everything okay so far?"

"Yeah, it's all been good, though we are running a little behind schedule, but," Britt paused dramatically, a huge grin lighting up her face. "I've checked with Mr Fletcher, and he's more than happy for you to come onto set and watch the filming." She looked expectantly at Charlie, who summoned up her best fake positivity.

"Oh wow! What an honour," she gushed, hoping she hadn't gone overboard. Whilst it would be exciting to see a major film in production, Charlie knew that dramatically narrowed the possibility of having to be in the same space as Robin White, and she was in no rush to do that.

"Come on," Britt said, seemingly unaware of Charlie's reticence. "I'll take you there via your room so you can drop your stuff off." Charlie couldn't help the involuntary bristle when Britt called it 'her' room. Tell that to Ms White, she thought snarkily. And yes, as an English teacher, 'snarkily' wasn't a word that crept into her vocabulary all that often, but she felt the situation warranted it.

"Do you know who Lucy's filming with today?" Charlie asked, keeping everything crossed that it wasn't you-know-who.

"Today's one of her scenes with Robyn," Britt replied, because of course it was. Charlie wondered why she'd even bothered asking the question. No way could she have been lucky enough to get any other response. "You're in for a treat," Britt added. "I have been on a lot of film sets over the years, but I've never seen anyone quite like her."

Charlie resisted the temptation to roll her eyes, and simply nodded for Britt to continue.

"I mean, I know that's not the popular thing to say, especially on this set," Britt lowered her voice as she spoke, looking at Charlie like Charlie was supposed to know what on earth she was talking about. She didn't, but she wasn't about to admit that. "Anyway, you'll see for yourself soon enough."

Britt pushed open the door to the cursed room, as Charlie thought of it, and Charlie dropped her bags inside, before following Britt back down the corridor and then on towards what she assumed was the set.

They stopped outside a set of double doors, the lightbox above them informing Charlie that filming was in action. She correctly assumed that meant they wouldn't be able to enter immediately, but she was a bit relieved when that gave Britt enough time to give a quick rundown of film-set etiquette.

"So, there'll likely be a lot more people inside than you're expecting and most of them will be running about the place whenever filming's not taking place. I usually find it best to stand with my back against a wall. That way I'm less likely to be in anyone's way," Britt said, shooting a grin at Charlie.

"Back against the wall," Charlie repeated, showing she was listening, and also determined to get it right. The last thing she wanted was to make an arse of herself in any space inhabited by Robyn White.

"It's usually best to stay quiet the whole time, even in between takes. There'll be a lot of important conversations taking place and we don't want to interrupt anything or disturb something vital." The seriousness of Britt's tone made Charlie want to laugh out loud; it was a film set not an operating theatre.

"Don't speak unless spoken to," Charlie uttered, earning a grin from Britt.

A buzzer sounded and the lightbox above the doors went out.

"That's our signal," Britt said excitedly, pulling open the door and tucking inside. Charlie followed and immediately forgot rule number two as an unruly "oh my god," managed to sneak out without her permission.

She was glad the look Britt shot her was one of understanding and not reprimand.

Whilst she'd seen her fair share of film sets on the 'behind-the-scenes' special features she loved to watch on DVDs, nothing could have prepared her for the real thing. To say the space was enormous was an understatement. It was cavernous, and Britt had been right, it was full of people. Everywhere she looked, groups of people seemed to congregate. By their tools, she could tell that some were obviously set designers, others worked on lighting rigs or bits of camera equipment. Some stood holding make-up accoutrement, obviously there in case an actor needed their face touching up or their hair putting back into place. There was a group clustered around a screen watching what Charlie imagined was the scene they'd just filmed, but she couldn't see the screen well enough from this distance to be certain. Still others stood with bits of paper whilst holding harried discussions, their faces animated and their hands gesturing.

Taking a steadying breath, Charlie turned back to Britt, who gestured for her to follow. Charlie was glad she wouldn't have to make conversation as her mind couldn't have formed a sentence if her life depended on it. The energy in the room was palpable and Charlie could actually feel goose bumps creep their way down her arms. She knew that when she tried to describe this to her friends on their next group call, she wouldn't be able to do it justice.

Taking a hesitant step, Charlie was relieved to find her legs seemed to still work and she felt herself relax a little at the knowledge. Staying close behind Britt, they made their way around the room until Britt seemed happy. She nodded across the room, motioning for Charlie to look in that direction.

If Charlie's breath had been stolen when they first stepped into the studio, that was nothing compared to what happened when she caught her first sight of the set. Knowing the film was based on one of her favourite novels, *Strikes Twice,* and actually seeing that brought to life in front of her, were two completely different things. It was stunning.

Charlie gazed at the kitchen set, consciously trying to stop her jaw from dropping at the minute attention to detail: the child's drawings on the Shaker cabinet fronts; the daisies in an earthenware jug situated exactly in the middle of a traditional farmhouse table; even the wooden clock on the wall with the V missing from the Roman numeral for the four. Charlie knew that was only mentioned in one sentence in the entire novel and she imagined most readers would have forgotten it after they'd read the next couple of pages. In a word, it was perfect.

Movement from the group around the screen drew Charlie's attention and she looked across in time to see Peter Fletcher clap his hands loudly.

"Let's go again, people," he bellowed across the soundstage. As he strode towards his chair, Charlie's breath hitched again. Behind him and now directly opposite her, were Lucy and Robyn White. Lucy was animatedly describing something, her hands working fifty to the dozen. Robyn nodded along encouragingly and then threw her head back and laughed at whatever Lucy said next. For just a moment, Charlie's heart stopped at the sound and the carefree look on Robyn's face.

And then her traitorous heart started to double-time, and she was aware of a strange sensation in her stomach. What the hell was happening?

"Charlie," Britt's voice whispered close to her ear and Charlie was grateful for the interruption. She turned to see the assistant gesturing her towards a couple of seats against the wall. It took all her persistence to look away from the scene in front of her, even though she knew it would only be momentary. She used the four steps she needed to take to regain control, trying to convince herself it was just a reaction to seeing her favourite characters brought to life.

She sank into the chair, her eyes immediately drawn back across the space to the set, where she could now see Robyn and Lucy receiving some last-minute touch-ups to their makeup. Charlie felt a swell of pride as she took in Lucy, who looked completely at home in her surroundings and not at all like the student Charlie had taught for the past five years. Part of it was obviously the physical changes: her hair, her costume, her make-up, but a larger part was how she held herself, how she interacted so professionally with everyone around her. Despite being a fair distance away, Charlie could see how she seemed to exude a sense of calm that Charlie had never once associated with Lucinda Armstrong-Miller, a vivacious student who always seemed to have too much energy to be completely still. It was like a switch had been flicked within the teenager and Charlie knew without a doubt that film sets were where Lucy was supposed to be.

Another shout from Peter Fletcher and the non-actors scuttled off-set, leaving just Lucy and Robyn White in the kitchen. Lucy's character, Aster, was lounging in a chair at the kitchen table, while Robyn's, Freya, was standing just off set, ready to walk through the door when given her signal. Much as she tried not to, Charlie couldn't help but allow her gaze to fall back on Robyn. Eyes closed as she waited for whatever the signal was, Charlie drank in the sight before her. She really was beautiful.

Her blonde hair, which Charlie guessed would fall below her shoulders when down, was pinned up in a messy bun, exactly as the character Freya wore hers on most days. Although dressed simply in jeans and a t-shirt, they looked tailored to her frame. The washed-out, faded blue denim was practically painted on, moulded to her slight curves. Her legs, which really did seem to go on for miles, were cocooned in the material, which looked as worn and loved as Charlie knew them to be in the novel. And the t-shirt, good god, had anyone ever looked so good in a simple white t-shirt? The contrast made her slightly tanned skin look more bronzed and as far as Charlie was concerned, the woman was an absolute goddess.

She must have missed whatever caused the action to begin, because all of a sudden, Robyn's eyes opened, and she walked confidently into the kitchen.

"Hey, kiddo," Robyn's character Freya said in the direction of Lucy's. Her voice was like honey and the feeling in Charlie's stomach sank slightly lower. "How are you feeling about tomorrow?"

"Terrified," Lucy replied, completely channelling Aster. "Excited. Nervous. Impatient." Lucy's character sank into the chair next to Lucy.

"Whatever happens, I'm unbelievably proud of you, Aster," she said softly, covering one of Lucy's hands as she spoke.

"I couldn't have done any of it without you, Frey," Lucy's character said, turning to look at Robyn.

"Nonsense. You're the one who's done the work. All that revision and preparation. God, Aster, you were an absolute machine for months ahead of those final exams. That was all you." Charlie couldn't see from her place against the wall, but she'd bet all of last year's salary that Robyn had somehow managed to make her eyes tear up as she spoke that line. It was an emotional scene between the sisters and Charlie had to remind herself to breathe.

"Yeah, I know. I did work hard, but you taught me that, Freya. How could you not have? You gave up so much for me and never once have I felt that you resent me for that."

"Because I don't, Aster," Robyn's character countered.

"Trust me, sis. Not every 22-year-old would give up on their degree five months away from graduating to return to the middle of nowhere to spend the next twelve years bringing up their half-sister."

"What have I told you about that 'half' word?" Robyn asked, a mock sternness on her face, causing a grin to spread across Lucy's.

"That it's a stupid word because you can't just half love someone."

"And?"

"And Markham sisters don't do anything by halves," Lucy finished.

"Correct," replied Robyn, giving Lucy's hand a gentle squeeze.

"And, cut!" came a loud voice, making Charlie jump. She had been so into the scene she'd forgotten she wasn't eavesdropping on a real conversation.

Both of the women in front of her were excellent, but my, did Robyn White have something else. She turned to look at Britt, who was grinning knowingly in her direction.

"Told you," was all she said.

Forty minutes later, Charlie was sitting in one of the on-site cafeterias with Lucy, grabbing a quick bite to eat before their afternoon lesson began.

"You were really good out there, Lucy," Charlie said softly between mouthfuls of her halloumi salad.

"Thanks, Ms Evans," Lucy grinned. "It's hard work, but I absolutely love it," she gushed. "And I'm learning so much all the time from the people around me. Robyn's been incredible, just sharing all these little tips that she's picked up over the years. From what some of the others had said, I hadn't expected her to be like that at all, but she really is generous."

"That's great," Charlie replied, hoping she sounded sincere. It seemed that Robyn had taken a bit of a shine to Lucy, and Charlie hoped it was genuine and not just a front put on to impress the young actress. Before she could add anything more, Lucy's face lit up as her eyes met someone behind Charlie. It didn't take a genius to work out who it was, and Charlie felt her muscles steel themselves involuntarily, as if she were about to buffeted by an incoming storm.

"Would either of you mind if I joined you?" asked a soft American voice that did that annoying thing to Charlie's insides again. How could she politely say no?

"Of course we don't, Robyn," Lucy beamed. "Do we?" she asked of Charlie, giving her the perfect opportunity to express her opinion on the matter and send the award-winning actress on her way.

"Not at all," her traitorous voice said without her permission. At least her eyes were doing as instructed and staying firmly fixed on her halloumi. It was, after all, the most interesting thing in the room.

"Thank you," Robyn's honey voice dripped as she put her food on the table and pulled out the chair to Charlie's left.

"This is my teacher, Ms Evans," Lucy said. "The one I was telling you about earlier."

"It's a pleasure to meet you, Ms Evans," said Robyn, reaching out a hand across the round table.

It wasn't in Charlie's nature to be rude, so she reluctantly took the hand with a muttered, "Likewise." She released the hand as quickly as she could, steadfastly refusing to acknowledge any of the sensations that accompanied Robyn's touch. She could feel Lucy's eyes on her and flicked her gaze away from the halloumi for a moment to meet them, taking in the quizzical look. Lucy might only be seventeen, but she could clearly read people, especially when that someone taught her for several hours every day. Charlie swallowed and sent a small smile to Lucy, chastising herself for her immature behaviour at the same time.

Lucy's eyes narrowed for a moment as if trying to work out what exactly was going on, before switching her attention back to Robyn.

"So, they all seemed pretty happy with how things went this morning," she said, her statement sounding more like a question, as if she wanted to make sure the older actress agreed with her before expressing an opinion.

"Definitely," Robyn assured her. "There'll be tougher scenes at some point but getting a really solid start under our belts is important." She paused for a moment, and even though Charlie wasn't looking at her, she felt Robyn's attention switch to her and she braced for whatever might come her way next. "Lucy mentioned you're studying *Tess of the D'Urbervilles* with her." Charlie nodded. "Not exactly the happiest of novels," Robyn said lightly.

"No," replied Charlie, slightly annoyed at herself for the one-word answer. She wanted to be the bigger person and pretend the previous slights hadn't happened, especially when she was in front of Lucy. What kind of impression was she setting for her student? But she just couldn't seem to muster up any further response. She raised her eyes finally and met Robyn's, which turned out to be the worst choice she could have made.

There was a vulnerability swirling in the depths of her blue orbs that Charlie absolutely would not have expected to see in the face of someone as successful as Robyn White. She immediately wanted to rewind this interaction and start again, but she wouldn't get the opportunity.

"Robyn," interrupted a slightly breathless Jeanie. "I'm so sorry to barge in on your lunch, but Peter would like you to join him in the conference room."

If Charlie hadn't been looking, she would have missed the look that flew across Robyn's face, before she hid it back behind her friendly smile.

"Of course, Jeanie," she answered. "Thank you so much for coming to find me." Gracefully, she rose to her feet and turned to Lucy. "Another time?" she asked, with a smile, before looking at Charlie. "It was nice to meet you, Ms Evans. I hope we get the opportunity to finish our conversation." And with that, she picked up her remaining food and followed Jeanie across the room.

Charlie knew she was in trouble. Since when had 'finish our conversation' sounded like a pick-up line? And why was her brain even going there? Not only did she have a strong dislike of Robyn White, if the male co-stars she'd been linked with in the past were any indication, she was as straight as a dye.

"So," came the voice from across the table, interrupting her thoughts and reminding Robyn that she wasn't on her own. "You were kind of frosty to Robyn." A statement. She met Lucy's eyes.

"I was. I'm sorry."

A pause while Lucy studied her. Charlie didn't look away, knowing her student was right to call her out on her rudeness.

"Well, I guess it's not every day that you get to meet a bona fide Hollywood superstar. I get that could be a little overwhelming. Hopefully next time, the cat won't get your tongue quite as badly."

Bless her, Charlie thought, realising she'd been given an out she didn't necessarily deserve.

"I'm sure next time will be much better," she agreed, knowing she needed to get over herself and move on. She'd also need to have a good conversation with herself when she was back in the safety of her hotel room and work out exactly what the feeling was that shot through her stomach whenever she was in the same space as Robyn White. She had a sinking feeling she already knew the answer.

Chapter Seven

Robyn

"Just in here," Jeanie said in a hushed voice as she pushed open the heavy oak door and stood aside for Robyn to enter.

"Thank you, Jeanie," Robyn managed to get out, even though she was pretty sure she was about to throw up. Manners cost nothing, as her grandmother had always been quick to tell her.

She forced her clenched hands to open, not wanting to outwardly show any of the nerves she was fighting. Her heart pounded, the blood racing so quickly she couldn't be sure if Jeanie had acknowledged her thanks. She had hoped to get further on this project than just one morning's filming. She actually thought the scenes they'd done had gone pretty well too. Just goes to show what she knew. Clearly it was Peter Fletcher's opinion that mattered, and Robyn was pretty certain this would be the last time she would get called to his presence; it wasn't like he could fire her a second time.

Glancing up, Robyn's step faltered slightly when she saw Peter Fletcher wasn't alone, Adelaide Covington sitting to his right. Robyn tried to read her expression: was that a hint of smugness she could see? There was definitely a glint in the older woman's eyes that made Robyn's breathing ease ever so slightly. Maybe this wasn't her trip to the guillotine after all...

"Robyn," Peter said, motioning her to a chair opposite him and Addie. "I'm not one for small talk," he began as she lowered herself into the seat. "I owe you an apology. I've treated you like crap since you got here, and I was wrong." His gaze never once wavered from hers and Robyn couldn't help but allow him to rise steadily upwards in her estimation. "I know Addie's told you that you weren't first choice, and I have behaved like a petulant child having a tantrum since she told me you'd been cast whether I liked it or not. If I hadn't wanted to make this film so much, I would have walked away, but I decided to stick with it and when you were as terrible as I knew you would be, I could get rid of you and start over with someone I wanted." He paused and looked at Addie, who by now really did resemble the cat with all the cream.

"I won't say I told you so," she drawled, turning to Robyn with a wink. "But I goddamn told you so!"

"You did, Addie," Peter agreed softly, and Robyn saw for the first time the bond between the two. Peter looked back at her as he continued. "You were magnificent out there today," he said softly. "The real deal and human with it. It didn't go unnoticed by anyone on the crew just how supportive you were of Lucinda. We all knew it was a risk to take an unknown and we were expecting to need to do some handholding, but you beat us to it and in a very unassuming way. Thank you for that."

"You're welcome," Robyn replied, more than a little taken aback. "And it's Lucy," she added with a smile. "Only goes by Lucinda if her mother's in earshot!"

Peter and Addie laughed.

"You see? Those are the little details no-one else has managed to get yet," he said. "But, Robyn, your acting. My god, you're good," complete sincerity coloured his tone and Robyn felt her cheeks flush.

"Thank you. It really means a lot coming from you," she said shyly.

"Even after I acted like a total jerk?" Peter asked with a laugh.

"Even after that," Robyn agreed, letting go of the hurt she'd experienced over the last few days.

"Anyway," Addie said, taking control. "Now that all that business is over," she gave Peter a mock glare, clearly letting him know what she thought of his behaviour towards Robyn. "We're actually here because after seeing you knock it out of the park today, we're thinking of shaking things up a bit."

Robyn's brow creased in confusion.

"I know what you're thinking," Peter said quickly. "How can we shake things up when we're adapting a novel?" He did indeed know exactly what was on Robyn's mind. She'd signed up because she'd loved *Strikes Twice* since her first read towards the end of her teens, curled up in her trailer on the set of *Branded*. The novel had helped her deal with a difficult time in her life. There was no way she could be part of a film that didn't treat the storyline with respect.

"Now, come on, sugar," Addie drawled, clearly reading the panic on Robyn's face. "We're not going to ruin it; we want to make it better."

Robyn's scepticism remained and she quirked an eyebrow at the pair opposite her.

"What exactly does that mean?" she asked.

"Well, you see, Rebecca McIntyre is one of my good friends," Addie said of *Strike Twice's* author. "And I remember her being in right old dilemma when she was writing that damn book. Couldn't decide whether to include a certain romance in the story or not. We used to talk about it regularly, and I was always a little disappointed when she decided not to. And as proud of that book as she is, I know she looks back now and is a little disappointed in herself too."

"A romance?" Robyn asked tentatively, not sure whether to feel glee or terror.

"A humdinger of one," Addie replied gleefully, while Peter nodded along next to her.

"With?" Robyn's hand clenched beneath the table, her fingernails digging slightly into her palm, willing Addie not to say the name she knew was coming.

"Well, I seem to remember you saying you were a big fan, so who do you think?"

Robyn's breath caught. She knew who she'd always hoped Freya would end up with, but if she said that name out loud and was wrong, how would that look? Robyn looked from Peter to Addie, the latter with that mischievous glimmer still in her eye. What the hell, she thought, uncharacteristically throwing caution to the wind. She'd find a way to recover if she were miles off course.

"I always thought there was something there between Freya and Grace, the woman she meets at the Art Club." There, she'd said it, put it out in the room.

Addie hooted and the smile on Peter's face was enormous.

"Right on the money, sugar!"

"So, what do you think?" Peter asked.

"About what?" Robyn asked back, needing to know exactly what they wanted from her.

"Fleshing out that storyline in a way that'll make Rebecca McIntyre proud? She's completely on board if that makes you feel any more comfortable about it," he added. "I think this one," he jerked his thumb towards Addie, "might have had this on the cards all along. Conveniently already had in writing from Ms McIntyre herself that she would support us wholeheartedly." He paused and leant across the table towards Robyn. "She's even sent us some sections from the manuscript that she wrote and then pulled out of the final draft before it was published. Scenes where the romance would have been wholly obvious to anyone who read it."

"We have original content from Rebecca McIntyre?" Robyn asked incredulously.

"I thought you'd like that part, sugar," Addie beamed. "A few thousand words, to be exact."

Robyn's heart that had previously been in overdrive came to a sudden stop. Rebecca McIntyre had written a lesbian storyline, decided against it, and now she was going to get to read it anyway? How many hours had she spent pouring over every interaction between Freya and Grace, desperate to try to find something that had in fact been there all along?

"Why did she pull it?" Robyn asked as a sudden wave of disappointment hit her. What difference might it have made if Rebecca McIntyre had left those scenes in the original?

"She was afraid," Addie replied matter-of-factly. "You've got to remember, sugar, that novel was published in the 1970s, a very different time from now, especially when it came to sexuality. There was no way a mainstream publisher would have picked up *Strikes Twice* if it had centred around a lesbian, no way at all."

"But the world has changed," Peter continued. "Now, there is absolutely nothing stopping us from telling the story Rebecca wanted to tell back then but felt she couldn't."

"You think it will be well received?" Robyn asked, more to buy herself time to recover, than any real interest in the answer.

"Oh, I don't doubt for one second that some blowhards will complain," answered Addie. "But I couldn't give two hoots about small-minded bigots. I don't make films for them," she said firmly. "I make films for the rest of the world, the world that doesn't care who somebody else loves."

"Agreed," Peter added. "We know there's a huge market who will embrace the additional content. Just look at how well *Carol* did. And, with Rebecca on board, it'll make things more genuine and not like we're shoehorning in a lesbian romance to jump on the gay bandwagon. That's not my style," he said firmly.

Robyn nodded slowly. It did make sense and she could see that Rebecca McIntyre's support would be essential. She drew in a shaky breath. The question was though, could she do this? Could she push herself this far out of her comfort zone?

"I'm in," she said, her voice sounding far more confident than she felt.

An hour later and the conference room had filled considerably. Kevin Grealish, their scriptwriter was there, complete with a hungry look in his eye, like he sensed this could possibly be award-winning material. Producers Steven Cantwell and Rhona Long buzzed excitedly around Adelaide Covington, and Stephen Carlisle, her on-screen best friend, talked animatedly with Peter. Robyn couldn't quite get over how different the vibe in the room was from the first meetings she had experienced with these people. No wonder Hollywood had a reputation for being fickle, she thought.

"Okay, people," Peter called, clapping his hands, and encouraging everyone into their seats. "So, I've apologised to Robyn for being such an ass," he announced, and Robyn caught sight of more than one face that expressed exactly the same sentiment. "I know you all share that feeling, especially after we witnessed Robyn in action this morning."

Nods and murmurs of agreement came from all corners of the room and Robyn wondered for a moment whether she was having an out-of-body experience but managed to summon a smile from somewhere.

"But that's not why we've called you here and it's certainly not the only reason you caught Addie and I acting like kids who've just been plonked in an ice-cream factory, never mind a shop." Laughter circulated and Robyn felt the anticipation ratchet up. "Addie, would you do the honours please?" he asked, handing over the floor to the formidable woman.

"With pleasure," she drawled. "Patrick," she motioned to her assistant, who began handing out folders. "No peeking just yet," she warned. "Now then, y'all have heard of Rebecca McIntyre, the author whose book we're taking to screen, but you might not know that she and I have been friends forever. Inside your folder are some pages that were written for *Strikes Twice* but didn't make the final version. Why don't you open them up and have a read?"

No-one needed to be told twice.

Robyn closed her eyes to steady her thoughts. The pages had been beyond her wildest hopes, the relationship between Freya and Grace perfectly crafted. She'd fallen in love with the book without this storyline, but with it, my god, she thought. This elevated it further, made her heart soar and then plummet when it struck her that she was now going to have to act out. Granted, there weren't any steamy sex scenes, but there were a couple of kisses and lots of longing looks. Could she do this? She wasn't convinced, but then, how could she not? What would it look like if she refused? She desperately needed to talk to Kate, and she should probably call David too, she supposed.

Murmurings around her signalled that the others had now finished reading too. She tried to pick up on the general tone, read the facial expressions. Mostly positive, some even bordering on excited. Perhaps a touch of reticence here and there. Robyn tried to school her face to neutral and sincerely hoped that Addie and Peter would ask other people for their opinions first; she wanted as much opportunity to read the room as she could get before adding her thoughts.

"Steve? Rhona?" Peter asked of his producers.

They shared a look Robyn couldn't quite read and then broke out in a shared smile.

"We love it," Steve replied, speaking for them both. "It's bold. It takes things in a different direction, but it's a direction we like."

"It works because it comes from the author," Rhona added. "It's not like we've taken it and added a lesbian love story just for the sake of it, like we're trying to capitalise on something. It feels genuine."

Addie and Peter nodded in agreement, then turned their attention to Kevin Grealish. As the screenwriter, Robyn figured he would have the most work to do.

"I love it," he said simply, and Robyn smiled as Addie's excitement got the better of her and she let out a little whoop. "I mean, there's work to do, yes, but these scenes," he said, gesturing to the pages he'd just read. "These are beautifully written, and I think we can probably lift quite a bit and weave it in with what we've already got." He glanced at Addie. "Do you think Ms McIntyre would be okay with us doing that?"

"Why, absolutely, sugar! Why do you think she sent me those papers? She's also happy for you to call her up any time you need to if there's anything else you need to know."

Kevin looked like a kid in a sweetshop, who'd just been told he'd won the lottery.

Robyn turned her attention to Mary Kane, sitting next to Kevin. If they did go ahead with this twist in the storyline, her part as Grace would grow considerably. Robyn tried to read her thoughts, but the other woman was keeping her proverbial cards close to her chest, and steadfastly ignoring Robyn.

Robyn tried to imagine herself playing out a love story opposite Mary. With raven black hair hanging just below her shoulders and eyes a shimmering green, there was no doubting she was an attractive woman, but she really wasn't Robyn's type. Not that any of her romantic co-stars had been, but given that up until this point, they'd all been male, it was hardly surprising.

Not for the first time, an image of Lucy's teacher sprang unbidden into her mind. Blue eyes flashing with anger and contempt, the only emotions Robyn's behaviour towards her so far deserved. She had hoped to see something different when she ran into them in the canteen, but Ms Evans, Charlotte, had closed off to her completely and Robyn was reminded that she hadn't yet apologised for her earlier behaviour. She hadn't wanted to in front of Lucy, but she needed to find a time to do it soon. She might well be an award-winning Hollywood starlet, but upsetting someone still bothered her in a way most people probably wouldn't expect.

"And your thoughts, Mary?" Peter's voice broke into Robyn's thoughts, pulling her away from her daydreams. Probably just as well. Where Mary Kane wasn't Robyn's type at all, she had an inkling that Charlotte Evans very well might be, but there was absolutely no way she would be exploring that. An apology to correct her wrongs was in order, but that was it.

Turning her attention back to the room and Mary in particular, Robyn saw what she instinctively knew to be a smile of the most fake order settle on Mary's face, and she smothered her own grin. After the gushing from those who had spoken ahead of her, it was unlikely Mary would be anything but positive, though Robyn suspected her true feelings lay in the complete opposite direction to positive. With a couple of decent films under her belt, Mary might have tried to stamp her foot down in lesser company, but Robyn had to give her some credit for recognising that in this particular room, any complaint would be enough to see her part re-cast. After all, they hadn't filmed any of Grace's scenes yet, so it would be no hardship at all.

"It would be a privilege to play the part," Mary gushed; Robyn hoped she'd tame down the acting when it came to their scenes together. Given the cold shoulder Mary had given her so far, Robyn couldn't help but wonder how much her reluctance came from knowing she'd have to lock lips with yours truly. She really couldn't help herself...

"That's great news, Mary!" Robyn gushed. "You and I should definitely grab a coffee sometime and get to know each other a little better. After all, we're going to have some really intimate scenes together and they always go more smoothly if a bit of off-screen friendship can feed the on-screen chemistry."

The look on Mary's face was fleeting but priceless and Robyn had to keep her perky grin in place to stop herself from collapsing in loud guffaws. She knew Kate wouldn't approve of her tactics, but sometimes her mischievous streak came out to play, and who was she to try and stop it? There was absolutely no way she and Mary Kane would ever be friends, but she'd enjoy making the woman squirm for half an hour over a coffee if she ever took Robyn up on her suggestion. It was highly unlikely she would, but Robyn thought the moment was worth it.

A glance across at Addie Covington told Robyn the older woman knew exactly what she was up to, but rather than the reprimand she knew she'd get later from Kate, it seemed the Southern Belle was enjoying it just as much as she was. A quick wink from Addie confirmed her suspicions, making Robyn think that if she were to befriend anyone at this table, it would in all likelihood be her. She admired her guts, her get-what-she-wants attitude, and she suspected that behind the glossy façade was a woman Robyn could trust, and that above anything else was what Robyn valued. She sent a wink back, and then turned her attention to Peter, who was rousing the troops.

"Okay people, so here's what we're going to do. We'll scrap the planned filming for this afternoon and for tomorrow. Give Kevin and his team some time to look over everything and work out which scenes he thinks will remain unchanged. I'm guessing everything up to when Freya and Grace first meet will stay as is, but I want to give you the space to make this perfect, Kev." No pressure from the director then.

"Thanks, Pete," Kevin replied. "I think you're probably right, but there might be the odd tweak here and there. Nothing revealing, but maybe a couple of lines where, once you've got the benefit of hindsight, you can look back and think a-ha!"

"So, that means the rest of you have a free day-and-a-half. Use it wisely!" Peter teased, leading to polite chuckles in response.

Robyn glanced at her watch, automatically calculating the time difference back to Kate. If she had ever needed a conversation with her sister, it was right now. By the time she got back to the hotel, Kate should be home from school. She gathered her things, gave a smile to the table, and started to make her way out of the room getting caught up with small talk on the way. Only one comment made any impact. Addie's quiet words as she passed Robyn, a gentle hand placed on the small of her back as she leant in to whisper in Robyn's ear.

"Well played, sugar. Well played, indeed."

Chapter Eight

Robyn

By the time she arrived back at the hotel, Robyn's earlier calmness had dissipated, and she was teetering on the edge of panic. She couldn't get to her room and Kate quickly enough. Her sister had better be in the mood for a conversation because Robyn wasn't certain she'd make it through the night without her.

"They're making Freya gay," she blurted as soon as Kate answered her video call.

"Who's what now?" her sister asked, face twisted with confusion.

"Addie and Peter. They're making her gay. What am I going to do? I can't play a gay character, Kate. What if I'm too good? What if people suspect? Oh my god, this is an absolute nightmare."

"Robbie," the calm voice came through the line. "Sis, I need you to stand still or better yet, sit on something. I can't focus when you're waving me around while you're pacing. Please, sit, Robyn."

Robyn perched on the edge of her bed, her left leg jiggling up and down.

"Help me, Kate. Please." She could hear the panic lessening slightly in her voice, but she was pretty sure it was now being replaced by desperation.

"Okay, hold on, hon," Kate replied, the endearment one Robyn could imagine her sister using with her students. She gazed at her screen as her sister moved from her kitchen to her back porch, lowering herself into the swing they had so often sat on together. "Slowly, Robbie. Tell it to me slowly."

"Addie Covington, the executive producer of the film is an old friend of the author," Robyn paused, looking to see if Kate was following, and at her nod continued. "Her friend confessed that when she first wrote the book, she had Freya fall in love with a woman." More nodding. "But because of the pressures back then, she removed those scenes, but now she wants them to be in the film. Bloody Carol," Robyn muttered.

"Carol? I thought the author was called Rebecca McIntyre?" Kate asked, stressing the author's first name.

"She is," Robyn affirmed.

"Then who's Carol?" Kate asked, clearly confused.

"The film, *Carol*," Robyn replied, unable to help the small smile that lifted the corners of her lips. Despite the anxiousness of the moment, Kate could always draw a smile. "You know, the one with the lovely Cate."

"What's that film got to do with yours?"

"Because it was such a hit, it seems Hollywood is keen for more lesbian-centric movies."

"Oh, right! I get you."

"So, as I was saying," Robyn continued. "The powers that be called us all together today, let us read the pages from the original manuscript, and then asked for our opinions. Everyone loved it," she paused. "Well, not quite everyone. I don't think the woman playing my new love interest was hugely impressed, but she did a pretty good job of faking her enthusiasm."

"Hold on a moment," Kate said, signalling with a finger for Robyn to pause. "I thought everyone hated you and they were all looking for a way to get rid of you? Is this how they're trying? Because if it is, that's pretty low, even for Hollywood." Kate's righteous indignation warmed Robyn from the inside out.

"No, Katie, it's not like that, I promise. We filmed the first scenes today and then I got called to Peter Fletcher's office. I honestly thought that was it and he was going to fire me, but instead he apologised for being such an ass."

"About damn time."

"I know. He was completely genuine. And actually, really lovely. Said he was impressed."

"Again, about damn time." Robyn felt another layer of tension lift at Kate's words. Yes, of course she was biased about Robyn's acting, but right now, that didn't matter at all. Knowing she had Kate's support was all that mattered.

"Then he and Addie told me about the scenes, ahead of calling everyone else in. They wanted to know if I was on board first."

"And you said?"

"I said yes," Robyn replied, wishing Kate could be there to give her a hug, rather than thousands of miles and an ocean away.

"I'm proud of you, Robyn. You know that you had to say yes, don't you? Maybe if you'd had more gay characters to watch on screen growing up, it wouldn't be so hard for you now."

And there it was. The issue in a nutshell. Kate was the only person on the planet who knew Robyn was gay. When Robyn had finally told her, not long after the first *Branded* film had been a global hit, Kate had just shrugged and said she'd known since they were in their freshman year of high school. And then she'd pulled

Robyn into the tightest of hugs and told her how proud she was and that she was thrilled Robyn had told her.

When Robyn had gone back to her a few months later to say she had decided to keep everything secret so as not to affect her career, although Kate had told her she respected her decision, Robyn knew a small part of her was disappointed. As a teacher, Kate had often told Robyn how important it was for youngsters to have positive role models in the media, and Robyn knew that her sister would have liked her to be one of them. But that wasn't a sacrifice Robyn was willing to make. She'd seen what had happened to actresses where there was even just a rumour of a same-sex preference. No more leading roles, no more starring opposite male romantic co-stars, which in Hollywood was pretty much all films, no more big-time. And Robyn loved the big-time. Making films was what fed her soul, and if she was going to do it, she wanted to do it on the biggest stage.

"I really didn't have a choice," Robyn admitted. "Addie and Peter were both so excited by the opportunity, it would have looked more suspicious if I'd said no."

"You did the right thing," Kate assured. "But now you're worrying?" she asked.

"I'm less worrying and more freaking out!"

"Maybe I just don't remember it, but I don't seem to recall any gossip surrounding Cate after *Carol*?"

"That's because she's been married forever, and everyone can see it's the real deal."

"And you're not."

"I'm not."

"And you're not dating anyone."

"You're doing well stating the facts, here, Kate," Robyn mused, sarcasm lacing her tone."

"And you've never dated anyone, although the media probably don't realise that as they like to try and make up that you're dating any man you're photographed within fifty feet of."

"My saving grace," Robyn's sarcasm ratcheted up another notch. "This could get really messy, Kate."

"Will it though?" she asked. "I mean, will it really? You're making a film where the character happens to be gay. And we both know that you'll act the role superbly, because that's just what you do, so yes, there will be speculation that you're able to pull it off so well because of your own persuasion." Kate paused and swallowed, her tell that she was about to say something Robyn wouldn't like. "But so what, Robyn? Would it really be the end of the world? You'd finally be able to live your life and experience what it's like to fall in love. The world is a different place to when you first came out to me, sis. It's moved on so much and there is acceptance

61

now. I'm not saying you should come out; I'm just saying that maybe you should think about it. Imagine, not having to be afraid of people finding out anymore."

For a moment, Robyn allowed herself that luxury. A world where she could go to the premiere of *Strikes Twice*, with a woman on her arm, someone who looked at her with love. She closed her eyes, enjoying the sensation, until the moment her imaginary date turned her head and gazed at her with Charlotte Evans' too-blue eyes.

"Oh my god," she exclaimed, and then tried to cover with an excuse. "David will kill me for agreeing to this before speaking to him about it."

"I'd much prefer it if you'd just let me kill him instead," Kate's anger evident in her tone. She'd never been a fan and this last debacle with Addie Covington had added further nails to his coffin as far as Kate was concerned. "Don't let him talk you out of it," Kate added. "Maybe get Addie to tell him seeing as he seems so desperate to be on her good side."

"That's actually not a bad idea at all, sis! Thank you." Robyn paused. "And thank you for listening and giving your usual awesome advice. Whether I act on it or not, your advice is always welcome."

"What is it about Charlotte Evans?" Robyn asked herself aloud after ending her call to Kate. She pottered about her hotel suite, making a cup of coffee to take out on her veranda area, wanting to spend some time looking over the script to see if she could figure out which bits would change, and which might remain the same. She'd been completely taken aback when Charlotte's face had appeared in her daydream while chatting to Kate, especially as it had been accompanied by a surge of arousal that coiled through her stomach, seemingly wanting to take up residence slightly lower.

Her interactions with the woman so far had been disastrous. Robyn had been too wound up during the first two to consciously register much about her, but it seemed her subconscious had been working on overdrive, storing up an image to throw back at her at a time when her defences were down.

Charlotte's eyes reminded her of Crater Lake, in Oregon, where her parents had taken her and Kate every summer. She remembered fondly the log cabin they'd always stayed in, the room she and Kate had shared with patchwork quilts on their beds. Hiking the trails through the National Park had been one of her favourite pastimes, a hobby she still undertook when she could. She hadn't been back to Crater Lake in years though, not since she got the part in *Branded*.

Robyn thought back to being in the room Lucy was using for her studies. She'd immediately assumed Charlotte was an actress, her beauty making Robyn's breath catch. The angled bob framed her face perfectly, and Robyn could practically feel her fingertips itch to tuck the hair behind her ear on one side, gently stroke her cheek and lean in to softly capture her lips.

"God," Robyn sank into a chair, curling her legs beneath her and wrapping both hands around her coffee mug. Over the years, she'd been attracted to a number of different women, but she'd never fantasised about kissing one with whom she hadn't managed to have a positive conversation.

She sighed, put her coffee on the table beside her and picked up her phone, sent a quick text to Addie suggesting she might want to contact David, and then exchanged the phone for her copy of the script. Maybe if she lost herself in the words for a while, that might help keep her mind off Charlotte. Well, it might if every page Robyn looked at didn't seem to have Charlotte's face watermarked in the background, like an ancient palimpsest.

Robyn managed to read a few pages, but it certainly wasn't with her usual level of concentration, and she welcomed the interruption of her phone ringing beside her. At least, she did until she saw it was David calling. Whilst she and her manager had only had one very brief conversation about her sexuality during the first *Branded* film, Robyn was pretty sure he had never forgotten. Over the years he'd brought up several stories of actors who'd come out and then disappeared from mainstream Hollywood, seeming to just drop them casually into conversation. Robyn might not have thought anything about it, if each time hadn't been preceded by her noticing an attractive woman, even trying to flirt with a couple of them. She knew there were plenty of closeted people in the movie business who took advantage of high-end clubs where NDAs were a standard part of the joining process, giving them the 'freedom' to pursue their sexual proclivities without fear of being outed in the press. But that kind of place didn't appeal to Robyn at all. So, she had just settled into a life without intimacy and tried to convince herself she was okay with that.

"David," she said on greeting. "Lovely to hear from you." Amazing how the lies just slid off her tongue when it came to her manager.

"You would have heard from me earlier if you'd picked the phone up yourself instead of handing it off to Addie Covington." No greeting, and a tone that would re-freeze the icecaps, let Robyn pitch his mood at extremely pissed.

"I felt that, in the circumstances, Addie was best placed to inform you of the changes being made to the script," she countered.

"What circumstances?"

"You know, the ones where you sold me out to get this movie." Robyn could play pissed too.

"Well, if I'd known where they were going to take the storyline there's no way in hell I'd have made any kind of deal at all. I can't believe you've agreed to this, Robyn. It's career suicide."

"Explain that."

"I really shouldn't have to; you should understand how these things work by now. Once you've turned gay-for-pay there's no coming back from that. You'll be typecast. No-one will consider you for any of the straight roles, not to mention the field day the press is going to have with this. Good god girl, have you listened to anything I've tried to teach you over the years?" Robyn bit down on her immediate reply, closing her eyes and drawing in a calming breath like Kate had taught her.

"David," she began slowly. "I have to disagree with you on this one. There are plenty of actresses who've recently taken on starring roles in same-sex relationships and then have gone on to take heterosexual roles afterwards. There is no typecasting."

"All of those women are married to men," David said, his tone dripping with condescension. "Everyone knows they're acting the role of the lesbian, because they've got some strapping Adonis to go home to at the end of the shoot. It won't be like that for you."

Robyn wondered how much he left unsaid. She had outright refused to date any of the men he had tried to set her up with as a means of keeping her in the media spotlight. All Robyn wanted to do was work, not get dragged into games with the press. David had never understood that, and Robyn was pretty sure his opinions about her sexuality stemmed from the vehemence with which she refused his plans. His words stung and her earlier fears, the ones Kate had so successfully quashed, began to rear their heads again. Was she making a mistake with this role? She had so much to lose if it all came tumbling down around her. However, there was no way she would be admitting any of this to David.

"Look, I made a choice, David, and I'm not changing my mind. It was the right choice to make in the moment. Addie and Peter were so excited by the changes, and I had to consider what message I would be sending them if I said no. You know how reluctant Peter was to have me on board in the first place. Any hint that I wasn't prepared to take the role would have seen me replaced. Not even Addie would have fought to have me on board with a refusal. She's desperate to make her friend happy and I honestly don't think she'd have hesitated to cut me."

"Humph," Peter replied. "I'm not surprised she's keen on the storyline." His voice was bitter and dripping with vitriol as he stressed the 'she'. Robyn decided not to dig; she could do that another day.

"It's not just them," she shared. "When the pages were shared with the team, the other producers, the head writer, the other actors, everyone was excited. It would have looked horrific if I'd flat out refused after that. If it had leaked out of the set, which you know it would have done, I would have been branded a homophobe. Imagine the shitstorm that would have followed..." Robyn said, hoping she'd manage to calm David down.

"I suppose," he grumbled in agreement. "But I still don't like it."

"I know you don't, David," Robyn placated. "But it was the right thing to do and we'll handle it. You'll handle it," she corrected, playing to his ego. "You know how to work the media; you've got most of them wrapped around your little finger." She wanted to mime gagging at her own words but resisted the temptation. "Who knows, if it goes really well, we might get as many nominations as *Carol*." It sickened Robyn that she knew how easily to manipulate him. If there was anything David loved, it was an award nomination. Robyn was pretty sure he liked the nominations more than winning. He got such a kick out of all the gossip, the parties, the backstabbing.

"Well," he said, drawing the word out for far longer than needed. "I suppose there is that," he added grudgingly. "If you're going to do it, you might as well do it fantastically."

Robyn allowed a smile to herself, appreciating that some things really didn't change.

"Of course," she said meekly, not wanting him to realise how pleased she was with herself.

"Just don't blame me when the press start calling you a dyke." He hung up, leaving Robyn staring open-mouthed at her phone, not quite able to believe what she'd heard.

Of all the terms David could have used, he had to go for the one that hurt the most. Shaking her head in disbelief, she thought back to Kate's offer to get rid of David once and for all, an offer she'd made several times over the past 20-years. It was more tempting than ever to accept. She wasn't sure what it was, but Kate had never liked David, not even for a second, and she tried to persuade Robyn to change her manager at least once every six months.

But Robyn had always felt like she owed David something, since he'd been with her since her break with *Branded*. Kate was adamant that since it was Robyn who'd landed that role for herself, she would have kept the part in the sequels no matter who her manager had been, but Robyn wasn't so sure. David knew everyone in Hollywood and told her exactly which strings he'd pulled to secure the position. And without the *Branded* franchise, where would Robyn have been? Certainly not sitting on a veranda overlooking a beautiful British landscape, that was for sure.

Chapter Nine

Charlie

Charlie smiled as she leaned back in her chair and listened to Lucy express her opinions about whether Tess's downfall was a result of fate or her own poor decision making. Although she didn't enjoy reading Hardy's classic, it never failed to engage students and get them fired up, particularly in discussions that revolved around the villain, Alec. Lucy was making incredibly valid points as she spoke, and Charlie knew she wouldn't have got this level of detail from her if they'd been back in their regular classroom. Whether Lucy was reticent in front of her peers, or just distracted more easily and therefore less certain in her opinions, Charlie wasn't sure. It seemed her fears that Lucy wouldn't keep on top of her schoolwork were unfounded. Granted, all she'd had to do so far was read, but Charlie sensed Lucy would approach her essays with this newfound maturity too. She'd soon find out as the reason for today's discussion was to provide a solid foundation of knowledge for the essay Charlie was setting at the end of their session.

Today's hour had been fruitful. Charlie had prodded and probed with her questioning, forcing Lucy to elaborate on her opinions, to support them by referring to the text, and to unpick the authorial methods Hardy had employed in his writing. Lucy had coped well for a student in her first year of A-level studies.

"Well done, Lucy," Charlie praised. "I was tough on you today with some of those questions, but you coped superbly well, drawing on your knowledge of the time period as well as the text."

"Thank you, Ms Evans," Lucy beamed.

"I'll be honest, I was a bit worried that you wouldn't be able to manage the tricky balancing act between working and studying, but you've clearly managed to keep on top of your reading and had some time to think about the novel too."

"Actually, I have to admit that I'm finding it a lot easier to focus away from my friends," Lucy grinned. "I mean, I text them a bit when I get back to the hotel, but it's not like they can convince to go out at night or distract me when I'm supposed to be studying in the library or the common room."

"How are you finding being away from home?" Charlie asked, unable to resist slipping into the pastoral side of her job.

"It's okay, yeah," replied Lucy. "A bit weird being in a strange hotel, surrounded by strangers, and doing a strange job, but I know this is what I want to do with my life, so I'm just trying to make the most of it, you know."

Charlie nodded. "It's an amazing opportunity and one you seem to be relishing."

"I'm conscious that everyone is older than me, but I suppose that has its advantages. Everyone has been super-kind and they all look out for me, make sure I understand how everything works, that kind of thing. It's like I've suddenly gained a whole load of older siblings and cousins!" Lucy paused and looked down at her copy of the novel, unable to meet Charlie's eye momentarily. "What about you, Miss? How are you finding it? I know this isn't what you want to do with your life and that you didn't really have a choice in coming." She looked back up, her face more serious than Charlie had ever seen it. "I haven't apologised to you for that, and I should have done."

Charlie felt her heart catch. Teenagers rarely thought outside the bubble of their own world, but when they did, it never failed to move her. She decided honesty was the best policy.

"I'm enjoying it a lot more than I expected to. Actually, I really wasn't sure what to expect, but you're right. The people here are lovely, and they've made me feel welcome even though I'm not really a part of the film." Well, not everyone had made her feel that way, but Charlie didn't need to get into that with Lucy. "And you absolutely do not need to apologise, Lucy. You did nothing wrong. I'm happy to be here supporting you and getting to see just how incredible you are when you're on that set." She smiled warmly at her student and was pleased to see Lucy return to her usual self.

"I'm glad," she said simply, before checking the time on her phone. "Speaking of the set, I'd better go and get ready for filming later. Thank you for today, Miss."

"You're welcome, Lucy," Charlie replied as her student packed her things and stood. "I'll email you your essay title," she added lightly, before laughing at the groan Lucy released as she left the room.

An hour later, Charlie left the tutoring room and headed to the set to meet Brittany where they were due to watch more filming. She glanced at her watch, noting she was a bit early. She wasn't sure she should go on to set without Britt, so she wandered down the corridor slightly, stopping every now and then to look at the film posters that lined the walls, presuming all of them had been filmed here at Pinewood.

"Hey, Charlie!" Britt called as she came around the corner at pace, clutching a pile of folders to her chest.

"Hi, Britt. Can I help you with anything?" Charlie asked, moving towards the production assistant, ready to take something off her.

"Bless you. Thanks, but I'm all good and balanced." She hefted the folders in her arms as she came to a stop. "I'm really sorry, though, I'm not going to be able to come and watch the filming with you. This all just landed on my plate, and I need to take care of it right away."

"Oh. That's absolutely no problem," Charlie replied. "Why don't you let me take some of those and I'll head out with you?"

"What? No! Don't be silly, Charlie. You don't need to leave. Just because you're not with me, doesn't mean you can't still go in and watch. You've got your pass," she said, pointing to the lanyard Charlie was wearing. "That grants you access to the sets whenever you want it."

"Wow. I hadn't realised."

"Sorry, I should have made that clear. Anyway, go on, head in. The light's off, so you're all good. I'll catch up with you later back at the hotel."

"Sure, that would be nice," Charlie replied, before turning and letting herself through the stage door.

Once her credentials had been checked, she took a couple of tentative steps into the vast space, remembering what Britt had said about trying to stay close to the walls to keep out of everyone's way. It didn't seem quite as frantic as it had the first time she'd visited, but Charlie wasn't sure if that was because it actually was less busy or because, having experienced it once already, her senses weren't quite as far into overdrive.

She paused for a moment and looked across to the set itself, smiling again when she recognised the same kitchen. Briefly she wondered to herself if they would film all the scenes that took place in that room first and then move to another part of the set, or whether they moved around between them depending on the day. That seemed like a question for Brittany.

From where she was standing, Charlie couldn't make out any of the actors, though she guessed from the kitchen that it would probably be Robyn and Lucy again. Charlie tried to think back through the novel to see if she could remember any other characters being in the kitchen and was pretty sure she couldn't. Freya and Aster had a lot of their most meaningful conversations in that room of the house, and it was a set they would return to again and again as the novel progressed.

"Hi, Charlie?" asked a quiet voice next to her and Charlie realised she'd been so focused on the set that she hadn't registered the approach of the friendly looking woman now standing in front of her.

"Yes," she replied.

"Great. I'm Lizzie Carter, a friend of Britt's and one of the scriptwriters," she explained. "She texted me to say she'd had to abandon you and she wanted me to make sure you're okay."

Charlie laughed softly.

"Britt's a delight," she said. "And, yes, I'm fine, thank you. I'm not in the way over here, am I?" she asked.

"Not at all, but you're so far away from the action that you won't see a thing!" Lizzie grinned. "Come on, you can sit with me." She beckoned for Charlie to follow her as she began moving towards the set.

Charlie went willingly, excited to be able to see things in a more up close and personal fashion. Even if it was Robyn White on set today, she wouldn't miss the chance to see Lucy in action. She followed Lizzie towards a small group of chairs, just slightly behind the director and writer. She swallowed hard, not quite able to believe she was going to be this close to the action.

Easing down into the chair next to Lizzie, Charlie could see Lucy huddled together with five or six other people in the kitchen area of the set.

"Just some last-minute direction from Peter to Robyn and Lucy," Lizzie explained, leaning in to speak quietly. "We'll start filming in probably about five minutes, so is there anything you want to ask?"

"Can you tell me which bit of the novel they're filming today?" Charlie asked, her voice tinged with excitement.

"Of course. It's a scene a couple of days after Lucy has received her A-level results and the sisters are discussing next steps."

"Did you write it?"

Lizzie laughed.

"No, not this scene. I've been working on some other bits recently, so I haven't had any input on this. That's one of the main reasons I'm here," she explained. "To make sure the tone of what I'm writing matches with this scene."

"I always thought film scripts were written before the filming started," Charlie replied. "I didn't realise you would still be working on it."

"There's always a little bit of tinkering that goes on with every script, but we've had some pretty major re-writes over the last couple of days, which is a bit more unusual." Lizzie turned her attention back to the set as the conversation came to an end the group broke apart, everyone going to their rightful places.

Charlie mused on what she'd just heard, wondering which parts had required major overhauling and hoping they weren't doing anything to ruin her favourite book.

"Don't worry," Lizzie said kindly, clearly reading Charlie's thoughts. "We won't spoil it. In fact," she paused and gave Charlie something akin to an insider's smile. "I think it'll probably make you like it even more."

Charlie raised a sceptical eyebrow, drawing a laugh from Lizzie.

"I love the novel too," she said. "I wouldn't do anything that didn't feel right, Charlie, I promise." Her look of sincerity convinced Charlie of several things, all in that quick second. That she was telling the truth and honestly believed whatever they were working on would improve the storyline. That she trusted Lizzie, which was weird because Charlie didn't trust easily anymore. That, despite the ping to her gaydar, there was no romantic spark between them at all, but there were clear signs of embers of friendship that Charlie intended to nurture.

"I'll hold you to that," she quipped back to Lizzie, who looked like she was about to answer when someone suddenly called for quiet on the set. She settled on a wink instead, then leaned back in her chair to enjoy the action.

Charlie was swept away by what she saw unfurl before her. No matter that they filmed the same scene over and over again, sometimes from different angles, sometimes with different intonation, it was like being transported straight into the middle of a scene she'd read a hundred times. The writing style of the author had always been rich enough for Charlie to feel like she had a thorough understanding of the characters and their settings but seeing it in front of her was something different entirely. And much as she was loathe to admit it, a large part of that was because of Robyn White.

She brought a realness to her work that Charlie felt was utterly genuine. Time and again she forgot she was watching someone act, and instead wholly believed it was the character of Freya brought to life in front of her. Everything that Charlie associated with Robyn was swept away entirely and she became the embodiment of an older sister discussing her younger sister's future. Gone was the diva attitude, the dismissive and rude persona that Charlie had met, and in its place was someone so warm, so full of pride, joy, and passion, that Charlie's brain resolutely refused to believe they were in fact the same person. No wonder the crew hung on her every word. No wonder the director was full of praise as they re-set the cameras for 'take 14', from what seemed to Charlie's untrained eye to be just two centimetres further left than 'take 13' had been.

What staggered Charlie the most though, was that in between the takes, when the crew were bustling about them, Robyn radiated a sense of calmness that permeated the space around her. Charlie could see that Lucy was definitely caught up in it, none of the teenage eagerness that wasted so much energy was evident at all. The conversation between them as they awaited instruction was light and easy, and

Charlie marvelled that Robyn had established this with Lucy in such a short space of time. It was no wonder Lucy never shut up about Robyn during their lessons.

"Final take everyone!" a loud voice called across the set, causing a sensation of disappointment to settle on Charlie. She wasn't ready for this to be over yet.

"Don't worry," Lizzie interjected, clearing reading Charlie's mind again. "It might be almost over for today, but we've got a shit ton of days left to go!"

"I like you, Lizzie Carter," Charlie grinned.

"Great. That means you won't leave me hanging when I ask you to join me for a coffee after this scene."

Half an hour later, they were tucked into a corner table in the cafeteria, chatting with the ease of two lifelong friends and not people who'd only met that day. Charlie didn't tend to make friends easily, but with Lizzie it had taken no effort at all. She was pretty sure Lizzie was gay too, she just projected that aura that Charlie was convinced all lesbians have, but it hadn't been confirmed in conversation yet. Not that it mattered; whilst Charlie really liked Lizzie, there was no spark whatsoever between them. If Charlie was being honest, that brought a feeling of relief rather than disappointment. She wasn't in the market for an 'on-set' romance. She wasn't really in the market for romance at all, really. It was just too much faff. She was perfectly content on her own, thank you very much.

"So, Britt said this is your first time on a film set," Lizzie said, interrupting Charlie's daydreaming train of thought and bringing her back to the real world.

"That's right," she confirmed.

"And? What do you think so far?"

"Well, it's certainly different from being at school," Charlie said with a smile. "The swanky hotel, the chauffeur driven cars, decent food and coffee in the cafeteria! Couldn't be more different. What about you?" she asked. "What number is this one in your list of film sets?"

Lucy laughed out loud, drawing a couple of looks from the other people around them. No one seemed to mind though.

"I couldn't possibly begin to count. I started out with short scripts for adverts, moved into television and then across to film, so I've worked on a lot of sets," she replied, stressing the phrase 'a lot'. Her eyes twinkled as she spoke and something about them put Charlie at ease.

"Do you have a favourite?"

"Even though we're only a few days in, I can say hand on heart, that this one will surpass everything I've done before it."

"Wow. You sound so certain. How come?" Charlie asked, genuinely fascinated to hear her answer.

71

"Lots of reasons, I guess," she said, and began listing them on her fingers as she spoke. "It's my first time with Peter Fletcher as director and he's someone I have a lot of respect for, so to be involved with him is awesome. I love the book; read it as a teenager so many times the front cover of my copy dropped off! I've done three scripts with Kevin before, but this is the first one where I feel it has the potential to actually matter," Lizzie paused and looked more closely at Charlie, excitement sparkling through her whole body. "The new stuff I was talking about earlier has got me all a quiver!"

"But you're still not going to tell me what that is are you?" Charlie asked, receiving an adamant shake of the head in response.

"My lips are sealed."

"Fine," Charlie huffed, exaggerating it slightly, but only slightly. She was desperate to know, and Lizzie was fully aware of that and using it as a form of torture. "Any other reasons?"

"One more," Lizzie said emphatically. "And this is the main one really. The other things are great, but not a patch on this one."

She paused as if gathering herself, and in that moment, Charlie somehow knew exactly what was going to come out of the other woman's mouth. She steeled herself against any involuntary reaction.

"It's my first film with Robin White and she's just amazing."

Yep. There it was, just as Charlie had known it would be. Seriously, what was it about Robyn bloody White that caused everyone to get their knickers in such a twist?

"I have worked with some incredibly talented actors, don't get me wrong," Lizzie continued. "But I have never seen anyone just become their character so completely and so effortlessly. She has an extraordinary ability and it's an absolute privilege to watch her."

Charlie guessed she agreed with that one, so she nodded along politely.

"She's so personable and human and humble. She keeps things light when it's appropriate but can turn on her professionalism like the flick of a switch. Seriously, you are so lucky to have the opportunity to see her in action."

Great, Charlie thought. Another superfan.

Chapter Ten

Charlie

"I think I spend more time in this cafeteria than anywhere else at the moment," Charlie quipped to Lizzie as they joined the queue for lunch.

"That's the glamorous world of movie-making for you. Set, food, sleep. That's pretty much it."

"At least the food's decent. If we were filming at my school, you would not want to be eating in the canteen every day." Charlie pulled a face that could better sum up her opinion than any words.

"That good, huh?" Lizzie laughed. "You don't talk about your life at school much. In fact, that might be the first time I've heard you mention it."

"There's not a lot to say, really. Teach, food, sleep," she said with a shrug. "At least here I have the added bonus of being able to lounge about in a director's chair and watch magic happen. Again, and again, and again. From a slightly different angle each time."

"Don't think I don't hear the sarcasm, Ms Evans. Just last week you thought it was amazing to be on set and already you're bored!"

"I'm not bored," Charlie clarified, as she picked up a salad and some fruit, adding a water and heading to what had become their regular table. "I just hadn't realised exactly how many takes there would be of each scene."

"Oh yeah, there's a whole lot of takes," said Lizzie as sat down, looking around the table to see who had been able to join them for lunch that day. "You should ask Melissa about the whole angle thing," she added, nodding towards one of the junior camera operators.

"What's this about angles?" Melissa asked, her whole body seeming to perk up at the very mention of the word.

"Charlie was just saying she hadn't expected all the angle adjustments between takes," Lizzie explained, sending a small smile Charlie's way. If there was one thing Melissa loved to talk about, it was angles.

Charlie gave Lizzie her deadpan 'I am not impressed' face, before switching her attention to Melissa and pretending to listen, hoping she was nodding along in the right places. She tried to concentrate and take it in, she really did, but her mind wandered in a nano-second, flitting from the lesson she'd had with Lucy that morning and adjustments she'd need to make tonight to tomorrow's as a result, to the filming she'd watched that day, to the group call she had planned with her friends tonight. It was only when she realised the topic had switched from angles that she zoned back in.

"So, Lizzie," began Rachel from the props department, elbow on the table and chin resting on her fist. "Is there any truth in the rumour that your script changes have finally greenlighted?"

Lizzie's face lit up with what Charlie could only describe as pure unadulterated delight.

"They did! All of them," she exclaimed.

"I honestly can't believe it," Rachel said, her grin matching Lizzie's. "No way in hell did I think Kevin would be able to convince them."

"He didn't need to," Lizzie clarified. "It was Addie Covington who brought it to us, and you know Addie. She almost certainly gets what she wants!"

"Wait, Addie brought it to Kevin and you? How did that happen," Melissa asked, enunciating her 'that' more loudly.

"Because she's a friend of the author," replied Lizzie, a twinkle in her eye that Charlie couldn't quite interpret.

"And they accepted all the changes? Like all of them?" asked Talia, a make-up artist.

"Yup."

"And Peter Fletcher's okay with it too?"

"According to Kevin, he's more than okay with it. What's that phrase you Brits use?" Lizzie asked, turning to Charlie and pulling her into the conversation. "Cock-a-hoop?"

"Oh, yes," Charlie replied, her face deadpan. "We use that phrase all the time."

Lizzie nudged her good-naturedly with her shoulder before continuing the conversation.

"And, most importantly, all of the cast are on board too. Kev said that Peter and Addie explained the original circumstances to them, and everyone agreed it was the right thing to do." Lizzie sat back proudly and, even though Charlie had absolutely no idea which changes they were discussing, she couldn't help but feel happy for her new friend. This obviously meant a lot to Lizzie and Charlie was pleased it had been a success. Her curiosity couldn't hold out much longer though.

"Anyone care to fill me in on what you're actually talking about?" she said in a teasing tone. "New girl to the group and all that. Assuming you're allowed to unseal your lips now," she added to Lizzie. remembering the phrase from the last time Lizzie had skirted around script changes.

"Oh, my goodness," cooed Talia. "We're so sorry. I completely forget that you haven't been joining us for these coffee breaks since day one. You tell her, Lizzie, It's your work after all."

Lizzie turned so that she was square on to Charlie, the chagrin she felt at having excluded Charlie doing little to taint her delighted demeanour.

"Okay, so about ten days ago, I was in a meeting with Kevin when Addie interrupted by just marching in and pulling up a seat. You've got to love that woman's attitude to life! She pulls out an old manuscript, very obviously done on a typewriter, plonks it down on the table in front of us, fixes us with that stare of hers and launches into this tale about how she and the author of *Strikes Twice* go way back and, whilst she's happy we're finally turning her friend's book into a film, she wants us to make the actual book."

"The actual book?" Charlie asked, her puzzlement written plainly on her face. "What does that mean?"

"That's what Kev and I asked. So, then we get this whole history of how Rebecca McIntyre wrote a book that no publisher would touch unless she made some pretty major changes. She didn't want to, but eventually her agent convinced her she should, so she gave in and made them. Apparently, Rebecca has regretted it ever since."

How could anyone regret anything about *Strikes Twice*?" Charlie asked, her confusion genuine. "It's one of the most amazing, if not the most amazing, book I've ever read."

"Oh, wait until you hear this," Rachel said, a mischievous twinkle in her eye. "I guarantee you're going to like it even more."

Charlie wrinkled her brow in thought.

"I mean, the only thing that could have made it any better, especially to teenage me, would have been if Freya was gay, but that's never going to happen!" Charlie laughed as she said it, and then realised none of the other women were laughing with her. In fact, they all wore exactly the same shit-eating grin.

"Holy fuck!" Charlie exclaimed softly. "Freya is gay?"

"Yep!" replied Lizzie, as Rachel, Mel and Talia joined in with exaggerated nods. "I thought you'd like that."

Charlie hadn't considered for one moment hiding her sexuality from these women, sensing in them a kindred preference.

"And the scenes that you've written..." Her question hung in the air, and Lizzie nodded again.

"Yep. We wrote in the romance. The very gay romance," she laughed, waggling her eyebrows.

"And now we get to watch Robyn White be a lesbian," Talia, sighed dreamily.

"Oh, please!" scoffed Mel. "Like that's going to be hard for her!"

Charlie took a moment to read the emotion on Mel's face, not one she'd seen there before and therefore she didn't instantly recognise it.

"What do you mean?" Charlie asked Mel, but it was Talia who jumped in to answer.

"Mel is absolutely convinced that Robyn White plays for our team. It's absolute rubbish."

"It is not rubbish," Mel said calmly, clearly having had this conversation with Talia on more than one occasion. "And, before you start, it's not just the press making something titillating up because she's single. I've told you before that I have it on good authority."

"I know, I know," sighed Talia. "A friend of a friend's aunt's niece's cousin, or some such convoluted thing."

"It's true," Mel stated emphatically.

Charlie thought back over her two run-ins with Robyn. Was there something there Charlie had missed? Some kind of aura or presence she hadn't picked up on? She didn't think so, which was unusual as she was known for her pretty stellar gaydar, but Charlie supposed there was a tiny chance she may not have seen it. Especially as Robyn White had made her so irate during their second meeting that even if she'd been wearing one of those cheesy 'this is what a lesbian looks like' t-shirts, Charlie probably still would have missed it.

"There's a difference between you wanting something to be true and it actually being true," Rachel joined in. "Just because she was in the *Branded* films and her character wasn't overly feminine, doesn't mean she's gay."

"It's got absolutely nothing to do with the characters she plays," Mel countered. "She could act any part you asked her to in an absolutely convincing manner. You know how good she is, there's no disputing that. So, you absolutely can't tell from her acting. It's the away from set time that tells you the truth. And the truth is that she's been spotted at parties looking very familiar with other female guests."

"Yes, but, looking 'familiar' and actually being gay are two totally different things. Wouldn't you agree, Lizzie?" Talia asked, clearly trying to get some support for her side of things. It wasn't until she did that Charlie realised Lizzie hadn't joined the argument at all. She studied her for the second or two it took her to reply to Talia.

Charlie could tell that this wasn't a conversation Lizzie wanted to be drawn into, but she couldn't fathom the reason for that reluctance. Whether it was because she didn't like idle gossip, or because she was trying to stay professional, Charlie couldn't divine. Lizzie's face was shuttered in a way Charlie hadn't seen before, and she was left with the unshakeable knowledge that Lizzie knew something about this topic, something she wouldn't share no matter how much Talia pressed her.

"I don't think anything," Lizzie said when her reply came. Her face momentarily serious, before regaining its usual lightness. "I'm too busy trying to write the scenes that are going to blow *Carol* out the park!"

Charlie listened as the other women fell back into rapturous conversation about how excited they were with the new direction of the film, how it made them even more happy and proud to be part of it, and so on and so on. Charlie's attention drifted and she hoped her nods were mostly in the right places.

Something about Robyn White bothered her, and she couldn't quite put her finger on it. Robyn certainly wasn't the first person to be rude to Charlie, and she doubted she'd be the last, but it was so unlike Charlie to hang on to it for this long, and even less like her to have an actual grudge. So, what was different? Usually, she was the forgive and forget type, being, as Jenna liked to say, 'so anti-confrontational you're practically Sweden'. Charlie knew her friends worried that she let people walk all over her, but she didn't see it that way. She'd grown up in a loud and busy household, the second oldest of five siblings, and had been the peacekeeper. She'd learned early on how to smooth tempers, curtail arguments, and placate opposing viewpoints.

However, none of those long-earned talents came into play with Robyn White. Rationally, Charlie knew if it had been anyone else who'd treated her the way Robyn had, Charlie would have found a way to gloss over it. She'd have been able to ascertain the reason behind Robyn's words and understand where she'd been coming from. In fact, Charlie knew the most likely outcome of that scenario with any other person would have been a heart-to-heart a few days later about what was bothering them.

With Robyn being a global superstar, Charlie knew a heart-to-heart would have been out of the question anyway, but she'd had the opportunity to be pleasant to Robyn that day in the canteen and she hadn't taken it. She had, in fact, done the opposite, which was completely out of character for her.

And that led her back to the question of what was so different about Robyn White?

Yes, she was a world-famous actress, probably worth millions of pounds, but Charlie honestly didn't think that was it. Maybe those facts were slightly intimidating, but they certainly weren't enough to prevent Charlie from being her usual polite self.

She wondered for a moment if it was because of how much her friends liked the actress and she wouldn't want Jen, Nay or Lauren to feel let down by meeting the actress in the flesh. Was that it? Did Charlie herself feel let down by Robyn? It was a ridiculous thought, but it rankled for longer than it should have, and Charlie knew there was only one reason for that: she'd stumbled onto the answer. Or at least part of the answer.

After the uncountable number of hours she and her friends had spent watching Robyn White or discussing Robyn White, Charlie had expected more from her. She knew the pedestal the other three had the actress on was unachievable, and had always held back from that herself, but she couldn't balance her friends' passion with the reality she had faced. When she thought back to the encounter in the teaching room, she felt humiliated and bitterly disappointed.

For all the time Charlie had listened to Jen rave about Robyn's amazing body, her yoga-toned arms, muscular thighs and washboard stomach, Charlie had expected to fall into a stupor when she eventually got to see that body in real life. That all it had radiated was anger and dismissiveness ruined anything else for Charlie.

Every conversation Jen had held about Robyn's body had been equally matched by Nay lusting after her voice, the one she described as 'orgasm-inducing'. When Charlie had pushed her for more, Nay had explained the tenor of it was just perfect. That there was a hint of huskiness to her tone that made Nay's knees go weak. The hint of an accent caused the hairs on Nay's arms to prickle in a good way. There had been no 'good way' about the effect Robyn's voice had on Charlie.

And the aura that Lauren loved to discuss, that certain 'je ne sais quoi' her friend had never been able to describe fully but found utterly fascinating? Where had that been as Robyn lambasted her for having the temerity to be in what she claimed was the wrong room?

How could the three women she loved and trusted more than any other human beings be so wrong? Granted, they'd never met Robyn in person and their suppositions about her were all based off films, articles, interviews, appearances, but Charlie knew that each of her friends was an excellent judge of character, and it was unlike them to be so wrong. There were plenty of other celebrities they wouldn't give the time of day to, who they could tell were utterly fake, but their faith in Robyn White had never been shaken in all the years Charlie had known them.

So, yes, she acknowledged, she did feel disillusioned on their behalf and that partly explained her reaction to Robyn in the canteen. She'd go to hell and back for her friends and she wasn't about to let Robyn off the hook so easily.

But Charlie knew she had to be completely honest; she was also disappointed for herself. She had always held something in reserve during the discussions she and her friends had about the actress, something she could sense but couldn't name. Maybe that thing she had recognised was Robyn's duplicity.

But it didn't feel like that was right. If she had somehow sensed Robyn wasn't what she seemed, why would she be disappointed to have that come true?

Her mind flashed back to the incident in the room, throwing up a clear image of Robyn, hands on her slim hips, blue eyes pinning Charlie in place. God, those eyes. Charlie had spent hours gazing into those eyes when watching Robyn's movies and now she loathed to admit how much they affected her, how much they brought on a tingling feeling right throughout her body. She definitely hadn't felt that sensation during their meeting in the infamous room, but there had been a hint of it when she'd watched Robyn on set and even when she'd encountered her in the canteen. And that pissed her right off. Her righteous indignation didn't burn quite so brightly on those other occasions, and Charlie really wanted it to. She wanted to be annoyed rather than attracted, but it seemed her traitorous body had other plans, much to her dismay.

"You okay?" Lizzie asked softly, leaning in so that only Charlie would hear.

"Yeah, sorry," Charlie replied, adding a smile. "I just drifted off for a moment there."

Lizzie looked as though she wanted to ask more, but Talia and Mel erupted into raucous laughter, breaking the quiet moment.

"To be continued," Lizzie, said with a wink before turning her attention back to her friends.

Chapter Eleven

Robyn

A burst of laughter caught Robyn's attention as she wandered into the canteen in search of something to get her through the afternoon scenes. She could see the group of women on the other side of the room who were responsible for the frivolity and was a little taken aback by the pang of loneliness that thrummed through her. She hadn't expected to feel it so acutely given it was something she experienced on every film set.

It hadn't always been this way, but the more films she did, and the more successful people judged her to be, the harder she found it to fit in. She missed the early days of her career when she could wander into a room, sit with any group, and join in with the gossip. Now people tended to clam up, or worse still, fawn all over her.

Robyn had discussed it with Kate during one of their many phone calls, and her sister's words came flooding back.

"You need to show them that you're still you, Robbie."

"What does that mean?" Robyn asked, perplexed.

"Well, what have you done since people started treating you differently?" Kate had asked. "Wait, don't tell me, let me guess. You've let it go, retreated in case you make someone feel uncomfortable by your presence, hidden away in case someone manages to dupe you in some way."

Kate's words hung between them for a moment while Robyn worked out what to say. There was no point denying it; her sister knew her too well.

"So, what do you suggest?" she asked in a quiet voice. "How do I help people to see me and not the name from the billboard?"

"Spend time with people, Robbie. You can read people well enough to know when they're trying to take advantage, so that's not something you need to worry about. And if you think someone is feeling pressured, put them at ease, it's what you're good at."

Grabbing a salad and a bottle of water, Robyn decided there was no time like the present if she was going to act on Kate's advice. Taking a fortifying breath, she headed to the table where the laughter was coming from, hoping that the good mood would make people more amenable to her presence. Her step faltered momentarily as she spotted Charlie next to Lizzie. She knew the writer by name as they'd crossed paths at a number of parties back home; she'd come close to knowing her by more than name at one of those events when they'd both had a little too much to drink and Robyn had felt like stepping out of her self-imposed cage for a few moments. They had enjoyed a conversation in a quiet corner before leaning in for what Robyn had expected to be a quick smooch. Something had stopped them both as their mouths were just inches apart and they'd looked at each other for a few seconds before laughing uncontrollably and agreeing there was no spark whatsoever. Lizzie had been quick to reassure Robyn that she wouldn't ever share their nearly kiss, but Robyn hadn't been at all worried. If Lizzie had wanted to take advantage of her, she wouldn't have stopped. They hadn't quite become friends after that, but Robyn knew that was mostly on her and that she'd held back in future interactions. Now it was time to stop being so aloof and take a gamble.

It wasn't Lizzie that had caused the falter in her step though. No, that was all down to Charlie. Charlie and those damned eyes of hers that lit up with a sparkle when she laughed. Robyn swallowed hard as she realised just how much she would like to be the one to put that sparkle there. To bring Charlie some pleasure rather than the pain she always seemed to inflict. She had some serious damage control to do.

"Hi," Robyn said breezily as she came to a stop at their table. "Do you guys mind if I join you?" she asked, motioning towards an empty seat. "It kind of seems like this is the table to be at," she added with a grin.

"Of course," Lizzie replied instantly. "Make yourself comfortable. Let me do some quick introductions," she continued as Robyn settled into her place at the table. "Mel is with the camera team, Rachel's in props, Talia's with make-up and Charlie is Lucy's teacher."

"It's nice to meet you all," Robyn said, meeting each woman's eyes for a moment, Charlie's included. Rachel and Talia's were full of warmth, Mel's were slightly more star-struck and Charlie's revealed nothing at all. At least that was an improvement on the cold dislike she'd seen earlier in the week.

"We were just discussing the script changes," Mel announced excitedly, either unaware of the look Lizzie shot her or choosing to ignore it. Robyn didn't mind. She was happy to talk about them, especially as she knew it was Lizzie who was doing the writing.

"How are they coming along?" she asked the scriptwriter. "I have to say that I love what we've had so far," she added, causing a faint pinkness to creep across Lizzie's cheeks and some good-natured elbowing from Rachel beside her.

"Thank you. I'm pleased with the progress we're making," Lizzie replied.

"Ah, the 'I'm keeping everything close to my chest until it's finished' response," Robyn teased. "Well, I for one can't wait to see them."

"And to act them out?" Mel asked, her eyebrows bouncing around on her forehead with untethered excitement.

"Mel!" scolded Talia, who shot an apologetic look at Robyn, who wasn't remotely fazed.

"I can't wait. I'm not sure Mary's quite so pleased, though," Robyn added with a laugh.

"Her loss," Mel sighed dreamily, leaning her chin on her palm as she rested her elbow on the table and gazed at Robyn with over-the-top adoration, batting her eyelashes for full effect. Robyn couldn't help but grin at her.

"Oh, good god," sighed Rachel, "We literally can't take her anywhere."

"Like anywhere," Lizzie repeated, enunciating the 'anywhere' for dramatic effect as Talia rolled her eyes and Mel let out a breathy sigh. Even Charlie almost cracked a smile. "But you're really okay with it?" Lizzie asked, her tone turning serious.

"I am, absolutely." Robyn affirmed with a nod, holding the young writer's gaze. "I'm a long-time fan of the novel and when Addie and Peter told me the story of its history, it just kind of made sense that Freya would be in love with Grace."

The others, including Charlie, Robyn noted, nodded as she spoke. Her own heart rate did a sudden flutter, and she knew it was a result of finally being on the same page as Charlie, even on something so small as this. "Plus, I mean, nobody says no to Addie Covington!" she quipped, pulling a laugh from the girls on the crew. Everyone knew Addie's reputation and that it was actual career suicide to turn her down.

"Especially when she's the only reason you got the role in the first place!" laughed Rachel, before realising what she'd said. The look of mortification on her face suggested she was praying to some invisible god to make the ground beneath her open up so she could slink away. Instead, she met Robyn's eyes and offered a quiet apology.

"It's okay," Robyn replied softly, taking in the faces around her. She had already suspected that most, if not all, of the crew knew the story behind her hiring and Lizzie, Talia and Rachel's ashen faces did nothing but confirm that. "Seriously, guys," Robyn continued. "I know what happened, but it's okay now. Peter and I have worked things out and we're all good." She smiled, trying to convey to them that she meant what she said. The awkward silence continued a moment longer and Robyn chanced a look at Charlie. For whatever reason, she didn't mind the crew girls looking at her with sympathy, but she really didn't want to see the same expression on the brunette.

She needn't have worried. Those bottomless blue eyes held nothing but confusion. It seemed not everyone on set knew her story after all.

"I found out after a couple of days here that the reason everyone seemed to hate me was because I wasn't first choice for the part. Hell, I wasn't even in the top five, but Addie did a deal with my agent, which he conveniently forgot to tell me about, and voila, the role was mine." She smiled sadly at Charlie and shrugged in a self-deprecating manner. "It's not easy being thousands of miles from home and discovering no one actually wants you here and isn't going to be particularly subtle about letting you know that."

Robyn saw exactly the moment that Charlie worked things out and realised their encounter in the infamous meeting room had come on the back of Robyn's discovery. Understanding replaced the earlier confusion, along with a little bit of chagrin that she probably hadn't helped to make Robyn feel any better.

A warm hand covered her own and Robyn glanced down to see Charlie's fingers give a slight squeeze before retracting.

"I'm sorry to hear that," Charlie said quietly. "Really sorry," she added, with a soft smile that sent Robyn's pulse into overdrive. Good god. One hand squeeze and a little smile and she was practically melting into a puddle beneath the table. She needed to get a grip.

"Me too," she added, hoping that Charlie knew she was referencing her own awful behaviour towards the teacher.

"Well," said Mel, breaking into the moment that Robyn hoped only she and Charlie knew they'd just shared. "Now that the awkward is out of the way," she glared at Rachel, who sunk a little lower in her seat, "let's get back to more interesting gossip. Lizzie, when's the first kiss scheduled for, and can we all watch?" she asked excitedly, effectively dispersing any remaining tension and pulling groans from her friends.

Robyn liked this group, she realised, and sent a silent thank you to her sister for reminding her that she needed to give people a chance. She had retreated to her trailer far too often on previous sets, not wanting to make anyone feel awkward around her, and only now was she realising how isolated she had become.

"You know," Talia began, her voice taking on a more serious tone. "You're both doing an amazing thing," her comments directed at Lizzie and Robyn. "You for writing this, Liz, and you for being willing to play the part, Robyn. It's utterly ridiculous that we're in the twenty-first century and we're still talking about the underrepresentation of anything other than hetero relationships in our film industry."

The panic that gripped Robyn was fleeting as she wondered if this was going to be the moment where her sexuality was revealed but knew that was ridiculous and Talia wasn't talking about her the person, she was talking about her character, Freya.

"I mean, I'm a bit older than all of you, Talia continued. "And I grew up with nothing other than sub-text really. Plus, the odd murderous lesbian, which obviously does wonders for the confidence of a teen struggling with her sexuality," she added dryly, pulling a sympathetic laugh from the others.

"Trust me," Charlie joined in. "As someone who works with teenagers, day in, day out, there is still a lack of decent role models for them. You're right, Talia, that there is far more queer representation, but that doesn't mean there's enough, especially not enough that is aimed at their parents' generation. Generally, the kids are all accepting of each other, it's the adults in their lives that have more of a problem with it. So, I'm hoping that everyone who loved the book as a teen themselves will want to go and see the film, maybe even take their own teenage sons and daughters with them, and they'll see a message of acceptance." Charlie paused and looked between Lizzie and Robyn. "They will see a message of acceptance, won't they?" she asked quickly, as if suddenly realising she'd made assumptions based on her own wants and desires.

Lizzie was quick to reassure her. "Of course, they will! In fact, the plan is that the relationship won't even be a 'thing'," she said, adding air quotes to emphasize her point. "The moral of the story will remain the same as always, Freya just happens to fall in love with Grace along the way."

"And fall into her bed too?" Mel asked, the hopeful look back on her face.

Robyn let out a loud laugh, drawing attention from some of the surrounding tables and noting the glances cast her way were considerably warmer than they had been a week or two ago.

"Yes, to the bed," Robyn reassured Mel, who gasped and mock fainted into Rachel's arms. "But only for some on-top-of-the-covers make out action," she added, pulling a pout from Mel. "And yes," she continued, turning to Charlie. "It will be a message of acceptance. I wouldn't have it any other way."

For once, Robyn didn't care that Charlie might be able to read more into her comment than she was ready to reveal; seeing the grin on the brunette's face was worth the risk of accidentally outing herself. And anyway, she thought, as she glanced around the group of women she was sitting with, would it really be such a bad thing? She had no doubt they would accept it and move on to the next topic of conversation.

No sooner had Kate's encouragement to come out popped into her head, than she could hear David, and his response whenever another actor had made that same announcement. Career suicide in his opinion. And whilst that didn't necessarily seem to be the case with actors who were younger than her, she could see a definite shift in the roles they were offered afterwards. Kate had argued this point, asking her if she'd ever considered reaching out to her sapphic peers to find out if the roles were what they were offered or what they chose to accept. Kate was firmly of the belief it was the latter. As she saw it, why wouldn't someone who had just announced to the world they were a lesbian actually want to play a lesbian on screen? Robyn supposed her sister's argument had merit, but it didn't stop her from being too chicken shit to find out.

Shaking off thoughts of David and the gloom they always plunged her in to, Robyn turned back to the group, an invitation suddenly on her lips that she didn't want to censor.

"Listen," she said. "I wanted to make the most of the free weekend we've got coming up, so I've booked an Airbnb on the outskirts of Oxford. Well, it's a pretty huge, secluded farmhouse in the Oxfordshire countryside, actually," she confessed. "I couldn't resist the views. Or the pool," she added sheepishly. "It's about an hour's drive," she continued quickly. "How about we have a bit of a party on Saturday to celebrate the film's new direction?"

It didn't take much predicting that Mel would be the first to react.

"Hell, yeah!" she shouted, standing to capture the attention of the room. "Party at Robyn's mansion this weekend!" she yelled, before Rachel managed to wrestle her back into her seat, chastising her as she did.

Robyn laughed at her antics before standing up herself. In for a penny, she thought slightly recklessly before adding to Mel's announcement.

"You're all invited!" she confirmed with grin. "I'll post details on the set noticeboard!" she added before being drowned out by the whooping and hollering. "Once I've worked them out," she muttered as she sat back down.

"Are you sure?" Lizzie asked. "I don't want you to feel pressured, especially not by this one," she said, jerking her thumb towards Mel.

"I am," Robyn said, nodding and feeling more sure of herself than she had in a long time. Turning, she caught Charlie's gaze and leaned into it slightly. "You'll come?" she asked, not being particularly fond of the nervousness she detected in her own tone.

"I will," Charlie replied, eyes full of sparkle. I was right, Robyn thought. It does feel pretty damn awesome to be the one responsible for that look.

Chapter Twelve

Robyn

"Well, when I got on a trans-Atlantic flight to keep you company over your free weekend, I really didn't expect to spend my Saturday morning helping you cater for a party!" Kate quipped as she diligently worked her way through the piles of vegetables Robyn had laid out for her to chop.

"I still can't believe you're here," replied Robyn. "Honestly, if I'd known you were coming, I wouldn't have organised anything."

"You're such a drama queen," Kate retorted. "Who cares if you would have preferred to spend the weekend just with me? I get to meet other famous people and the people who make them famous!"

Robyn couldn't help but laugh. She had actually wept when she returned to the hotel on Thursday night and found Kate waiting for her in the lobby. Robyn still didn't know how she'd managed to convince her principal to give her an extra two days' holiday before the start of spring break, but she would have hugged the man herself if he'd been there.

When they'd settled into Robyn's enormous suite, Kate had confessed that she'd been worried about her sister. The long-distance conversations they'd been having had left Kate in no doubt that her sister was struggling more than usual, and Kate couldn't have that. She knew that Robyn had booked the place in the Oxfordshire, so thought she'd tag along and try to do something to combat the loneliness she could feel seeping into their chats.

Robyn had immediately offered to cancel her impromptu party, but Kate wouldn't hear of it. Instead, she'd told Robyn how proud she was of her for trying to step out of her comfort zone, a conversation which had resulted in more tears as Robyn realised just how much she needed her sister's guidance and praise.

As soon as filming wrapped on Friday afternoon, the sisters headed to the farmhouse. The car journey had passed in a flash as Kate buzzed with her experience of being on set. It wasn't something she had done very often at all, and this had been by far her favourite time. She had immediately felt the camaraderie of the cast and crew, and at home amongst people she had only just met.

"I'm really excited to meet people tonight," Kate continued. "And to be able to have actual conversations and not just whisper at them in between takes! So, come on, tell me again who's coming."

"Well, not any of the bigger names that you might know," Robyn confessed. "They all had plans lined up for the free weekend already, but most of them seemed genuinely disappointed to miss this."

"Of course they're disappointed," Kate said like it was totally obvious to everyone by Robyn. "And, anyway, I'm glad they're not coming. I can't stand egos."

"They're not too bad at all," Robyn laughed. "Well, except Mary Kane, who has a stick up her ass most of the time."

Kate joined in with the laughter. "I think it's hilarious that she's the one you have to pretend to fall in love with. I guess we'll really get to see whether you have any decent acting skills after all," she teased, earning herself a swat on the butt with a tea towel.

"Ha ha," Robyn said drily.

"Oh, and speaking of falling in love, who is the one you almost kissed at that party that one time?"

"Lizzie," came Robyn's short retort. "And I've told you, there's absolutely no chemistry there with her at all."

"I know, I know. I'm just looking forward to being able to put faces to the names I've heard you mention before. It's not often I get to meet someone you've almost kissed."

"You're incorrigible, Kate. Honestly. You're 37-years-old. Surely you're beyond wanting to tease your little sister by now?"

"Little by two minutes, as you so often like to remind me, young lady. Which means that you're 37-years-old too, and by now, I should have met someone you'd actually kissed, not just be getting excited by an almost smooch."

It was a conversation they'd had many times. Many, many times, actually. And not one Robyn was in any hurry to revisit today.

"Just shut up and chop" she said instead, a mock firmness to her tone, letting Kate know that she wasn't really angry, but that this was the end of the conversation.

"Yes, ma'am," her sister retorted, adding a mock salute for full comedic value.

A few minutes passed in a silence that was punctuated only by the rhythmic knocking of knives against chopping boards. It hadn't even occurred to Robyn to organise an outside caterer for her party, particularly when Kate had turned up out of the blue. They shared so many happy memories of hours spent like this. Robyn reached for a tomato and turned to Kate, holding it up.

"Remember what Nonna told us?" she asked, a grin splitting her face.

"If it's not Italian, it's not a tomato!" Kate replied, in a heavily accented voice so reminiscent of their paternal grandmother that Robyn's breath caught for a second before she could add her part of the anecdote.

"In fact, if it's not from the soil of Vesuvius, it's not a tomato!"

The girls had spent many summers staying with their grandmother in her home on the outskirts of San Marzano in Italy, the world-famous home of the best plum tomatoes on the planet. And not just according to Nonna. Chefs the world over refused to use any other variety of the fruit when making a tomato-based sauce. It was here, under the guidance of Nonna, that they had both learned to cook, one of the few past times they enjoyed together. They were very different, she and Kate, but their bond was strong, and it didn't matter how much time they spent apart, they fell back into their routine with ease.

"So, how come you ended up throwing a party?" Kate asked, and Robyn was impressed with how long Kate had managed to wait before asking.

"Wow! I can't believe it's taken you this long to ask me," Robyn teased. "Your patience is admirable."

"Well, now I've asked, are you going to answer?"

"I guess it's your fault, if you really must know," Robyn replied, trying to keep the tone of her voice serious as she teased her sister.

"Oh, this should be good," Kate quipped. "Come on then, hit me with it. How exactly is this my fault?"

"You told me not to shut myself off from people. Not to isolate. To give them a chance." Robyn turned away from her chopping board to look at her sister. "This is me giving people a chance." Her voice dropped as she spoke the last words, and it took Kate milliseconds to cross the kitchen and wrap her sister in a hug.

"I'm so proud of you," she crooned softly into Robyn's ear as she held her, tightening her grip before stepping back so she could look her sister in the eye. Robyn held her breath as she waited for her sister's next words, no doubt some other pearls of wisdom that she would eventually see the merit in. "So, which hot women did you invite?" Kate asked, a sly grin pulling her mouth to the left.

"Oh, my god," Robyn laughed, pushing her sister away. "You have a one-track mind!"

"Judging by the blush on those cheeks of yours, so do you," Kate needled, laughing loudly as Robyn closed her eyes and tried to will away any reddening on her face. "Well, we've established that it's not Lizzie," Kate began, holding up her thumb to indicate she was going to start counting. "Now, let's see, who else have you mentioned since I arrived?" She raised her index finger. "Jeanie?"

"My production assistant?" Robyn screeched. "She's mid-twenties at best, Kate."

"You could be a cougar," Kate quipped. "Hmm," she mimed thinking, even though Robyn was pretty sure she had a list of names already lined up and this was just for dramatic effect. "Mel?"

"God, no. Lovely girl, but utterly bonkers."

"Talia?"

"Nope. A bit like Lizzy. No spark." Robyn was happy to feign playing along as she wracked her brains trying to remember who else she'd mentioned and whether she was going to need her poker face.

"Mary Kane?"

Robyn just arched an eyebrow and folded her arms at that one. Kate knew damn fine how she felt about Mary.

"Ooh," Kate went on excitedly. "I've got it. Addie Covington!"

"Jesus, that woman would eat me alive, Kate. I'm not kidding. There is no way in hell I could hold my own in any kind of relationship with her. Plus, the pedestal I've got her on is way too high for any good to come out of it."

"Huh," Kate responded, sounding like she was stumped. Robyn knew better. "I guess that just leaves Charlie the tutor then," she smirked, a knowing look in her eyes. "And don't even try the poker face with me, Robbie," she added quickly. "Some people might think you're pretty decent at acting, but you can't do it for shit in front of me."

"Some people? Pretty decent?" Robyn replied, hoping she could distract Kate from a conversation she really didn't want to have just a few hours before guests started arriving.

"Yep, definitely Charlie the tutor. I can't wait to meet her," she said, backing away from Robyn and heading back to her chopping board. She stopped part way and swung back around, fixing Robyn with what was affectionately known in the family as her death stare. "I will meet her, won't I? You did actually invite this woman that you like to your party, didn't you?"

"Of course I did," Robyn bit back before realising that her answer had just confirmed her sister's suspicions. "Shit," she muttered.

"Tell me about her," Kate said softly, picking up her knife and returning to her chopping task, knowing without a doubt that Robyn wouldn't be able to have this conversation face-to-face. Turning back to her own board, Robyn started to speak.

"Well, for starters, she's not a tutor, she's a teacher. And yes, before you ask, there is a difference. Jeanie is friendly with Brittany, who has been assigned to help Charlie. I have it on good authority that Charlie teaches at the school Lucy, the actress playing my younger sister, goes to, and that when she got the part, Charlie was sent with her."

"Is that how it usually happens?" Kate asked. "I thought there were like specific tutors who worked on film sets or something?"

"You're right, it's not something I've ever come across before and I've worked with quite a few kids now over the years. I don't know the whole story."

"You know you could find out, right?" Kate asked. "I mean, you could just ask Charlie."

"Yeah, I don't think that would go too well."

Robyn heard Kate put her knife down and chanced a glance over her shoulder in time to see her sister turn around, lean back against the granite counter, and fold her arms.

"What did you do, Robbie?" How did she always know?

"I might have gone full on Hollywood diva the first time we met," Robyn mumbled.

"You did what now?" Kate asked, her arms unfolding and coming to rest on her hips.

"I fucked up," Robyn admitted.

Sighing, Kate crossed the room towards the kettle. "We're having a coffee break," she announced in a tone that said it wasn't up for discussion. "And we're going to work out how to fix whatever it is you've done."

A few hours later, Robyn finally left the kitchen, feeling as though she'd been trapped in it all day. Nonna would have turned in her grave if Robyn had hired a caterer, but at moments like this, she did wonder if that would be such a bad thing. Nevertheless, the food was all prepped and the drinks were ready. Now Robyn just needed to work on getting herself to a state that would be considered presentable.

Standing in the shower in the master en-suite, she replayed her conversation with Kate. It had hurt to admit to her sister that she had treated someone badly and Kate hadn't held back in expressing her disappointment. As ever with Kate though, the scolding lasted minutes and then she went into fix-it mode. Her plan was simple enough really. Accost Charlie as soon as she arrived, apologise profusely, then spend the rest of the party proving that she wasn't a bitch.

Robyn had agreed to the apology bit but argued she didn't need to spend time with Charlie after that. It's not like she would ever act on her blossoming attraction, and surely any more time she spent in her company was just going to be like rubbing salt in the wound and showing Robyn what she was missing out on.

Kate's counterargument had been delivered vehemently, most of it focusing on her absolute inability to understand why Robyn had sacrificed any hope of personal happiness for her career. Surely, she'd remonstrated, if the good people of Hollywood really were so small-minded and bigoted, they weren't worth working for. Robyn had tried to point out the flaws in this line of thought– she was a

Hollywood film star; she kind of had to work for the people there – but Kate had just listed a whole host of other film industries, television industries and even the theatre if Robyn was determined to keep acting. When Robyn had pressed Kate on her use of the phrase 'if', Kate had shrugged and replied she wasn't convinced acting made Robyn happy anymore. Before Robyn could muster any kind of response, Kate had told her that was a discussion for another place and time, repeated her 'win over' Charlie plan, and announced she was going to shower and thought Robyn should do the same. Apparently those two minutes counted for a hell of a lot as Robyn didn't even consider arguing with her 'big' sister.

Pulling on skinny jeans and her favourite Dolly Parton concert t-shirt (yes, she had more than one, and wasn't ashamed to admit it), she forced her hair into something resembling a style and added a quick coat of make-up, before shoving her feet into her black suede Tony Lama boots. And voila, she was done. It was a casual party, one that she was hosting, so why the hell shouldn't she wear what she wanted to?

"I can't believe you still have that shirt," Kate moaned, leaning in the doorway to the bedroom Robyn had claimed as hers for the weekend. "You're supposed to be trying to charm a woman tonight, and that's the outfit you pick? I would have hoped all the time you spend around glitz and glamour would have rubbed off on you just a teeny bit," she said with an eye-roll.

"First off, I am not trying to charm a woman, I am merely going to apologise. Second of all, it's a small gathering of mostly film crew and a couple of cast members. It's not a premiere night at Grauman's Theater, Kate. I can wear jeans and a t-shirt."

Kate laughed. "You do realise that Dolly is a gay icon, don't you? And that you're basically going to spend the evening wandering around with a massive pair of boobs on your chest. Maybe you should make sure Melissa Etheridge, The Indigo Girls and Tegan and Sara are all lined up on your playlist. Then we can strategically place Sarah Waters novels next to your DVD of *Carol* and you'll be all set."

Robyn just glared at her sister for a moment before shaking her head and turning back to the mirror.

"When did you become such an expert in lesbian pop-culture?" she asked snarkily.

"I figured if my oh-so-gay sister was going to stay firmly ensconced in her closet at least one of us should be aware of these things, just in case she ever decides to pop her head out and see what she's missing."

Before Robyn had a chance to formulate any kind of response, Kate pushed off from the wall and walked away. She had perfected the art of throwing a verbal grenade and retreating when they were in their early teens, and Robyn still hadn't worked out how to avoid the blast.

It seemed that Kate was bringing up her sexuality more and more these days, quickly becoming exasperated with Robyn when she wouldn't discuss it. Robyn couldn't believe that Kate was being so stubborn about it all of a sudden. It's not like it was hot off the press news for her; she had been the one Robyn had gone to when she suspected this was where her feelings lay at 17. Now, twenty years later, it seemed that Kate was finally losing patience with her and managed to bring it up in almost every conversation they had.

Robyn blew out a breath, looking herself in the eye for just a moment. She smiled sadly at her reflection, a part of her wishing Kate could be right and that she could just announce she liked women and move on with her life without it becoming a massive issue. But she lived in the real world, not the small-town friendly world Kate inhabited, but a denizen of chat shows, gossip rags, paparazzi, and the worst of them all, social media. Robyn couldn't see a way to keep her career, her image, her lifestyle, and have a woman on her arm. Not even one with the eyes of a goddess, like Charlie.

Chapter Thirteen

Charlie

"Here we go, ladies," Jonny said, breaking into the conversation Charlie and Britt were having about who made the better Tomb Raider, Angelina or Alicia. Britt was firmly in the Angelina camp, but Charlie much preferred Alicia, the Swedish actress epitomising everything Charlie loved about Scandinavia.

"Gosh, that hardly seemed to take any time at all!" Britt said, looking at her watch. "Are you sure you stuck to the speed limit, young man?" she teased Jonny.

"Absolutely, ma'am," he replied, adding a mock salute for full effect.

Charlie looked out the window in time to see the wrought iron gates they were driving through and struggled to hold back a 'wow' as the house came into view down the winding driveway. The early afternoon start to the party meant she could make out every detail and not have it obscured by darkness. It looked to be in the style of a traditional farmhouse, just on a pretty enormous scale, with a few additions added over the years. The grounds were well kept and the oak trees she could see to one side of the house hinted at ancient lineage.

Jonny pulled to a stop at the end of the drive and jumped out, as was his usual style. Charlie had learned to wait for him to open her door after he'd explained it was part of the protocol of his job; it didn't sit easily with her, but he'd seemed so disappointed early on when she had done it herself that she now let him. She gathered her bits and pieces – a small clutch bag and a bottle of Prosecco for Robyn. She might not be Charlie's favourite person, but Charlie's manners had been drilled into her as a child and she knew better than to turn up anywhere empty handed. She waited for Britt to join her, and they set off up the path together, calling their thanks to Jonny and agreeing they'd see him again at midnight when he came to collect them.

"This is stunning, isn't it?" Britt whispered as they approached the wooden front door, a pot of spring bulbs to either side of it.

"Amazing," Charlie replied, unable to put anything else into words. The bay windows to either side of the door hinted at not only the size of the place, but also the luxury. She doubted the Georgian sash windows were the originals, but they were definitely wooden and tasteful. The brick work screamed old, and she bet the flagstones she was walking on could tell a tale or two of previous visitors over the generations. The house wasn't doing anything to settle her nerves, which she was trying to convince herself were just the normal butterflies she felt ahead of any social event, and nothing at all to do with knowing she was going to be in the same place as Robyn White for the next few hours.

The story Robyn had told in the canteen earlier in the week had gone some way to explaining why she'd been the way she had with Charlie. Even though her voice had remained light throughout her retelling of events, Charlie could read in her eyes and slightly defeated body language that Robyn had been hurt by the discovery that she wasn't initially wanted on set. The urge to wrap Robyn up in a hug had been almost overwhelming and Charlie had made a concerted effort not to spend anytime analysing that response; she certainly hadn't shared it with the girls when they'd Skyped late last night. Actually, she hadn't even told them about Robyn's experience, not feeling like it was her story to tell. She had though made the mistake of telling them about the party today and then had to endure a nightmarish 15-minutes where they all reverted to their student days and talked fifty to the dozen about the many, many qualities of Robyn White. It had taken Charlie threatening not to tell them a single thing about the party to shut them up, and even then, they'd all texted her separately that morning with specific instructions: Jen wanted a selfie as proof Charlie wasn't making it up; Nay wanted a word-for-word account of any and all interactions Charlie had with the actress; and Lauren, well, Laur was the worst of all. She had just insisted that Charlie relax, enjoy herself and take advantage of the opportunity, a statement that was accompanied by a lascivious winking emoji with its tongue hanging out. Honestly, she'd expected more of Lauren.

As Britt reached for the door knocker, the door swung open, and Charlie's step faltered when she saw that Robyn had opened it herself. She'd imagined a full complement of staff to be in place tonight, not a Hollywood goddess doing the menial tasks herself.

"Hey!" Robyn greeted, an enormous grin on her face as she took in the arrivals. "Welcome! Come in, come in," she gestured. "And please, make yourselves at home. I certainly have," she quipped. "It's really good to see you, Britt," she said, pulling the red head into a half hug. "We've hardly had any time on set to catch up and I'm dying to see some photos of those beautiful kids of yours."

"Well, I certainly have plenty of them that I can bore you with later," Britt laughed. "I heard a rumour that Kate was here too, is that right?" she asked. "Maybe I can compare notes and see if she's got any top tips on making them less wild."

"The rumour is correct, for once," Robyn confirmed. "And I know Katie will love to talk children with you. I swear to god the woman could discuss that topic all day long," she said with exasperation as she rolled her eyes.

Charlie wondered whether anyone would notice if she quickly pinched herself, just to check she wasn't actually dreaming. This certainly looked like Robyn White, but the way she was behaving was so far removed from Charlie's previous interactions that she couldn't quite wrap her head around what she was seeing. The woman in front of her, the drop-dead gorgeous, stunningly attractive woman, to be precise, was friendly, caring and apparently had a decent sense of humour. She also looked sexy as hell in her fitted t-shirt and Charlie had to silently tell her heart to slow down. She could do without the tingle that zipped through her as Robyn threw her head back and laughed at something Britt had said, before ushering the assistant inside and pointing her in the direction of Kate.

Before she had any chance of recovering, those too-blue eyes were on her, warm, welcoming and softening even further.

"Hi, Charlie," Robyn said in what sounded like a shy tone. "Come in, please," she added, reaching for Charlie's shoulder to encourage her over the threshold."

"Hi," Charlie managed to say, holding out the gift bag with the Prosecco. "Thank you for having me." Oh god, was she 8-years-old?

A soft smile appeared on Robyn's face as she accepted the bag. "It's my pleasure," she added, a flush creeping up her neck as she reached for Charlie's now empty hand, taking it in her own. "I need to steal you for five minutes," she explained in a gentle voice, tugging Charlie behind her down a hallway in the opposite direction to where Britt had gone. There were a million things that Charlie wanted to ask right then, but it seemed she had completely lost the ability to form words, so she just followed, trying not to focus too much on how good it felt to hold Robyn's hand.

They entered a cosy room, with a sofa, easy chair and bookcase, and Robyn closed the door behind them, took in a visible deep breath and turned to face Charlie.

"I owe you an apology," she said, her voice small and filled with a pain that was mirrored in her eyes. "In fact, I probably owe you more than one."

"Robyn, no, it's okay," Charlie began.

"It isn't," Robyn interrupted. "It isn't at all." She moved across the room and sank down into the armchair, her eyes on the floor.

Charlie took a seat on the sofa and tried again.

"You don't have to say anything."

"Yeah, I do," Robyn replied, lifting her eyes to look straight into Charlie's. "It doesn't matter how much of a shitty day I was having, there is absolutely no excuse for the way I spoke to you in that room. I know that you have no reason to believe this, but that kind of behaviour is completely out of character for me and all I can do is apologise. I treated you despicably and I am so sorry for that."

Charlie had been on the receiving end of more than one apology in her time, usually from students who had lost their temper and taken it out on her, their teacher, who they knew would forgive them and move on. Some of those apologies had been more heartfelt than others, but none had ever been as genuine as Robyn's. Charlie held her gaze, easily reading the shame Robyn felt, the courage it had taken to deliver her speech, and the desperate need for Charlie to accept it. It was the latter that touched Charlie the most. As a teacher on set for one film, it really didn't matter in the grand scheme of things whether Charlie thought well of Robyn or not. Their paths were unlikely to ever cross again, and Charlie would have absolutely no bearing on Robyn's future career. And yet, Charlie could sense that it mattered to Robyn that she make this effort to apologise.

Without thinking, Charlie scooted along the sofa, so she was closer to Robyn's chair, and then she reached out and took Robyn's hand. If she had been thinking, she never would have been brave enough to touch Hollywood royalty without express written permission, but the sensible part of her brain seemed to have deserted her.

"I appreciate your apology, thank you." She rubbed her thumb over the back of Robyn's hand. Yep, sensible brain was definitely elsewhere. "I'm guessing from what you said the other day that you ended up in that room immediately after learning that you weren't wanted on set." Charlie spoke softly, her eyes never leaving Robyn's. "I can't begin to imagine how that must have felt and I'm sorry you had to experience it."

"It wasn't the best," Robyn laughed sadly, blinking away the tears that had sprung up.

"I think what you did is perfectly natural," Charlie continued. "You walked out of a situation you had absolutely no control over, and you took control of the next situation you found. It's what humans do. I understand it now and I'm really grateful that you took the time today to explain it to me." She paused, before grinning and adding, "I guess I should probably remove all the pins from my Voodoo doll when I get back to the hotel tonight!"

Her humour worked and Robyn laughed with her, breaking the tension that had been on them. Charlie gave Robyn's hand one last squeeze before letting it go and pushing to her feet. "Now, don't you have a party to host?" she asked, smiling, and trying desperately to look completely at ease and not like her heart was about to hammer its way out of her chest. If she had to spend one more minute in this tiny room with Robyn White looking at her with those beautiful eyes, she wouldn't be held responsible for her actions. She couldn't help but glance at Robyn's lips and then berated herself for her idiocy. Of course they were perfect, and of course they looked as though they would be incredible to kiss, but that wasn't going to happen, no matter how much she wanted it to.

"Everything okay?" Britt asked as Charlie joined her on the back patio, overlooking the pool and the countryside behind it.

"Yeah, actually," she replied. "Everything's good." Britt gave her a quizzical look, so Charlie elaborated. "Let's just say that my first couple of meetings with Robyn didn't paint her in the best light and she wanted to apologise and clear the air." Charlie didn't offer any more than that, and she was grateful when Britt accepted her response.

"Well, I'm glad she did that. She's not like many of the other actors I've worked with over the years, and I would hate you to have a negative opinion of her."

"We're all good," Charlie confirmed. "I'm pretty blown away by the fact she would go out of her way to do that today, so lots of brownie points for that. I wouldn't have expected the opinion of a lowly teacher to matter that much to someone of her stature."

"That's what I mean about her," Britt went on. "She wouldn't consider herself to be of any higher or lower stature than you, regardless of what job you had. To Robyn, everyone really is just another person, and she certainly doesn't use her fame and status for anything negative."

"You really like her," Charlie said, a statement, not a question.

"Yep. Not like you do though!" Britt said, tossing a wink at Charlie before striding across the patio to intercept someone else, leaving Charlie to almost choke on her beer and wanting to ask Britt what the hell she meant.

"You okay there?" asked a soft voice, the American drawl easily perceptible, and Charlie turned to find herself looking at a woman who resembled Robyn. "I'm Kate," she said quickly, "Robbie's sister. You sounded like that last swallow went down the wrong way."

"I'm okay, thank you. Charlie," she added, holding out her hand in introduction, which Kate squeezed quickly.

"Charlie, it's lovely to meet you. You're Lucy's teacher, right?"

"I am," Charlie replied, somewhat taken aback that Kate would know who she was.

"Robyn's mentioned you a few times," she added cryptically. "I teach too," she beamed. "I just love it!"

"I know the feeling," Charlie replied. "It's the only thing I've ever wanted to do, and even though it's a long, long way from glamorous, I can't imagine doing anything else."

"Exactly. And people who've never done it, can't understand that we feel that way about. They just look at us and commiserate that we have to spend all day surrounded by kids."

"Or they look with a kind of jealous disdain that we get so much holiday."

"As if we actually get all that time off though," Kate scoffed. "When was the last time you didn't spend at least half a vacation either trying to catch up with marking or planning lessons?"

"And every Sunday," Charlie added. "And if one more person tells me it must be great to just work from 9:00am to 3:30pm, I think I might have to bop them on the nose!"

"Oh my god," laughed Kate. "You get that one here too? It's just ridiculous." She paused for a moment to sip from her glass before continuing. "So, I'm curious. If you love teaching so much, how did you end up on a film set with just one student?"

"One student who happens to have very rich parents who like to make regular contributions to the school fund, you mean?"

"Ah," Kate replied, understanding dawning in her eyes. Eyes that were a couple shades lighter than her sister's, Charlie noted.

"Yep. One minute I'm planning to teach six different classes, ranging from 11-18, and the next, I'm in a swanky hotel with one A-level student."

"A-level is for your oldest students, right?"

"It is. Lucy is in her first year of A-levels, which are a two-year course. She just turned 17 earlier in the year. And as much as I found it gut-wrenching to leave all my other students behind, I have to say that I'm enjoying the experience so far. It's been amazing to see Lucy on the set, slipping into someone else's skin so easily. I had absolutely no idea she was so talented - she's never once even auditioned for a role in a school production, so I have to admit to being blown away by her talent. And your sister's too," Charlie added hastily lest it appear she had forgotten who she was talking to.

"It's kind of freaky though, isn't it?" Kate asked. "Seeing someone you know so well transforms to someone else right before your eyes?"

"I think freaky sums it up pretty well!" she laughed.

"Sums what up pretty well?" asked a voice that was beginning to send shivers down Charlie's spine; not the bad kind either. The American twang was less obvious than Kate's and Charlie wondered whether that was a conscious decision or the result of playing characters with different accents. When she listened to Robyn as Freya, Charlie would have sworn Robyn was more English than she was.

"We were just talking about how weird it is when you do your thing on a film set," Kate answered, giving Robyn's shoulder a gentle bump with her own.

"Weird?" Robyn asked. "I'm pretty sure that word wasn't used in my Academy Award nomination speech last year." Although her face looked deadly serious, Charlie could see just a hint of mischief in the actor's eyes as she teased her sister. This was clearly how the sisters operated as Kate gave as good as she got, turning to look at Charlie as she spoke.

"You'll note she referred to the nomination speech and not the acceptance speech," a smirk playing at the corners of her mouth. "That's because she was too weird to actually win the damn thing."

An hour ago, Charlie would have expected a comment like that to result in another diva tantrum, but now she knew better, and it came as no surprise that Robyn threw her head back and laughed.

"Ouch, you wound me sister of mine," she exclaimed, miming a stab to her chest, before rolling her eyes in Charlie's direction and flitting away from their conversation to join Lizzie, Tali and Rachel across the patio.

"She loves to ham it up," Kate said drily, looking at Charlie carefully when she didn't reply with anything but a small smile. "She spoke to you earlier, I hope?" Kate asked softly, switching the topic of conversation so quickly it took Charlie a beat to catch up. Clearly Robyn had told her sister about their less than friendly interactions. Charlie felt her heart pick up, not certain where Kate was going with this.

"She did," Charlie confirmed, not giving away anything more in case her suspicions were wrong, and Kate didn't know the focus of their conversation. It most definitely wasn't Charlie's place to tattle on Robyn to her sister.

The smile Kate gave her told Charlie this was the right instinct. She did know what had gone on and she appreciated Charlie keeping it to herself and not rushing off to sell her story.

"She might be one of the most successful actors in the world, but that doesn't make her any less human than you or I. She's flawed," Kate said, looking wistfully at her sister, who had easily integrated herself into another conversation.

"Aren't we all?" Charlie muttered, the irony of having just discovered another of her own flaws not lost on her: not being able to easily forgive someone when they fell off the pedestal on which she'd put them.

"I'm not going to try and make excuses by saying she's had a difficult life, because she hasn't," Kate continued. "We had an amazing childhood and have such supportive parents, who've always loved us unconditionally. She gets to travel the world and meet all sorts of people, has made more money than one person could spend in a lifetime..."

"Sounds pretty lonely to me," Charlie interrupted, not realising she'd spoken aloud until she glanced at Kate to see why she'd stopped speaking.

"Very lonely," Kate confirmed with a nod, her eyes radiating sadness. "And that's not what someone like Robbie deserves," she added, the admiration for her sister a palpable pulse that radiated around her. She fell quiet for a moment, looking at Robyn, before slowly turning to Charlie and holding her gaze. "But maybe it won't be that way for much longer," she mused before taking a healthy swig of her wine and grinning at Charlie like she held the key to some ancient mystery. "Not much longer at all," she added, clinking her glass against Charlie's beer bottle and sauntering back inside the house.

Chapter Fourteen

Charlie

First Britt, and now Kate, thought Charlie as she took a moment to let the meaning of Kate's words sink in. Was her attraction to Robyn so obvious that someone she'd only just met could sense it, an attraction she'd only just acknowledged herself? It was more than a little embarrassing really and all just so clichéd; lonely teacher falls for Hollywood goddess. Honestly, couldn't she do any better than put herself through this? Some unrequited crush to see her through the nights when she was back at school and her life fell into the predictable pattern she'd been in for years. And since when was she lonely? That was new too. She'd always told herself she was happy on her own, that she enjoyed her independence and had a good life that satisfied her. Now, as she stole another glance across the patio at Robyn, those walls she had created and hidden behind crumbled away and left her feeling raw and exposed.

She wished that such a crushing realisation could have struck her when she was at home alone, where she could have grabbed her yoga mat and worked through her feelings, not when she was standing in the middle of the biggest social gathering she'd attended in years. The nagging voice in her head chose that moment to point out that yes, there were a lot of people here, but yet again, she was on her own. Looking around the enormous garden, she recognised a lot of faces, mostly the film's crew, with a couple of the actors. Lucy had been devastated not to be able to come, the weekend shopping in London with her mother, which she had been looking forward to, now just an annoyance preventing her from being here. She'd told Charlie she expected her to tell her all about in their next lesson, but Charlie didn't think the youngster would be particularly impressed with "I stood on my own on the patio and watched everyone else get on with living their lives, pretty much the same thing I've been doing every day for the last decade come to think of it." No, she certainly wouldn't be sharing that with anyone any time soon. Though a conversation with Lauren might not go amiss.

"Charlie!" a voice called to her and she turned to see Mel beckoning her to their group. The group Robyn was still standing with. Fixing what she hoped was a smile to her face, she crossed the space between them.

"I hope my sister didn't bore you too much?" Robyn asked lightly.

"Not at all," Charlie assured her. "We were talking teaching," she said with a smile.

"Oh god, so she was in full-on bore mode," Robyn said, rolling her eyes and earning a laugh from the group.

Charlie took the barb good-naturedly.

"We can't all have the skills, personality and patience required to teach," she countered, grinning as she took a long swallow from her beer bottle.

"Oooh," Talia crowed. "I think she just sassed you," she said, nudging Robyn gently with her shoulder. Robyn's eyes danced with delight, and it looked as though she was about to continue their banter, when Kate's voice cut across from the house.

"Robbie! Your timer's going off!"

"To be continued," Robyn said playfully as she extricated herself from the group and headed inside.

As soon as her back was turned, Mel fanned herself and swooned dramatically into Rachel.

"Oh. My. God," she breathed dramatically. "That woman should not be allowed out in public dressed like that. I mean, come on! It's hardly fair to us mere mortals that she can just wander around poured into an outfit that screams lesbian goddess."

"Lesbian goddess?" Rachel asked. "I get that she's hot, but where did you get that from?"

"Umm, did you see her top?" Mel asked, pinning Rachel with a 'I can't believe you're asking that question' look.

"Yeah. It's a concert shirt. So what?"

"For Dolly Parton," Mel said, speaking slowly and enunciating each syllable as though trying to explain an incredibly difficult aspect of rocket science to a young child.

"Yeah. And?" Rachel asked, completely unoffended by her friend's tone.

Mel looked exasperatedly at the others. Lizzie shrugged at her and Talia looked as clueless as Rachel.

"Help me out a little?" Mel asked Charlie.

"I'm not sure I can," she confessed.

"Really? None of you know this?"

A shake of heads.

"Dolly's like the biggest gay icon on the planet. Bigger than Barbra and Bette for sure, especially with the lesbians."

"Right," said Rachel. "But plenty of straight women like her too. You can't say someone is gay just because they like Dolly."

"Well, of course not," Mel said, as if this was the most ridiculous thing she had ever heard. "I'm not trying to say that either."

"It kind of sounds like you are," said Talia dryly.

"No, what I'm trying to say is that only a lesbian would wear that t-shirt to a party she was hosting. You have all seen the massive boobs on it, right?" she asked, hands on hips as if challenging someone to argue with her. The other four women looked at her, looked at each other, and then fell about laughing.

"What?" Mel asked. "You know I'm right."

They were saved from having to answer by a yell from Robyn to let them know the food was ready. Charlie fell in step beside Lizzie as they trooped across the garden and back in through the bi-fold doors. The space across the back of the farmhouse was incredible; kitchen nestled at one end, comfortable seating in the middle and a huge dining space at the other, the table laden with incredible looking food, the smell of which made her stomach rumble and reminding her she'd skipped lunch through nerves.

Charlie couldn't believe the spread in front of her, the dishes presented in a stylish way, with little handwritten cards in front of them to let the guests know what was what. Rather than a formal sit-down meal, Robyn was encouraging people to load their plates and head back out into the garden or to the seating area beside them. From the faces of those closer to the table than her, Charlie could tell it wasn't just her who was impressed with the feast.

Grabbing a plate and napkin, with the cutlery folded inside of it, Charlie could barely hold back of gasp of wonder as she came to the front of the queue. Ahead of her, Mel and Talia were making all the right 'ooh' and 'ahh' sounds, while Lizzie and Rachel chatted excitedly about what they were adding to their plates.

Charlie glanced around, taking in the labels: 'griddled chicken with quinoa Greek salad', read one, 'herbed lamb cutlets with roasted vegetables' announced another, 'pancetta wrapped fish with lemony potatoes', 'fried haloumi with Greek peperonata'. She reached for a roast pepper, stuffed with goat's cheese and olives, added a slice of broccoli and red pepper frittata, and piled on some of the freshest looking salad she'd seen in a long time. Charlie didn't think she'd ever been more grateful she'd skipped a meal. She could live off the food here, but then she supposed she shouldn't really be surprised. Robyn probably had a nutritionist who had liaised with the catering company to ensure everyone had delicious but healthy food to eat.

She eased herself into a seat around one of the large outdoor tables, sitting between Lizzie and Talia. For the first minute or two, there was absolute silence around their table as they sampled from their plates.

Finally, Rachel spoke.

"This is beyond good," she moaned. "I don't even have the words for it. It should be criminal to serve food that tastes like this!"

"I can honestly say that I've never seen a spread like it," added Talia. "That table is enormous and there wasn't a spare inch left on it! It's like the God of Food arrived and emptied that horn thingy out all over it."

"Cornucopia," Lizzie supplied. "And yes, whilst I wouldn't usually buy into your hyperbole, I think you might be right on this occasion. I honestly can't get over the flavours in this chicken; it's divine."

Mel nodded animatedly across from her, mouth too full to add any actual words.

"It's great to have so much vegetarian choice, too," Charlie added. "Too often, you turn up to buffets to find the only offering is a shop-bought, too warm cheese and onion quiche and a bit of wilted lettuce."

A laugh sounded behind her as Kate came out to join them.

"Well, you definitely don't need to worry about that at anything Robyn's hosting," she smiled. "Nothing shop bought and a range of options for those going meat-free."

"I have to get the name of the caterer," Britt said in a slightly breathy voice as she swallowed something that had clearly had a positive impact on her palette. "This is just incredible. James' parents have a big wedding anniversary coming up and I might actually be able to survive it if I know I've got food this good to look forward to."

Kate's grin grew and she signalled Robyn as she was passing with her own plate of food. Rather than continuing to whichever table she'd been heading to, she slid in next to her sister, a patient look on her face as she waited to hear what Kate was up to.

"Britt was just explaining that she'd like the name of your caterer for an upcoming event."

Charlie watched Robyn's face closely, wondering what was going on between the twins, as Robyn nodded sagely and turned to Britt.

"When is it? Do you have a date yet?" When Britt replied with a date in mid-July, Robyn rested her chin on her arm and turned back to Kate. "What do you think, sis?" she asked. "You wanna come back over here in your school holiday and help me out again?" The slightly cheeky grin did all kinds of things to Charlie's insides. There was a moment of silence.

"You two made this?" Britt asked, her voice rising with obvious astonishment.

"I mean, don't sound so surprised, Britt!" Robyn laughed. "You think just because I act, I don't know how to cook?" she teased.

"God, no, not at all," Britt fumbled, turning a lovely shade of pink as she spoke. "I just meant that, well, all of this is amazing, and there's so much of it that I couldn't believe just two people could make it."

"Nice save, Britt," Mel whispered loudly enough for everyone to hear, the ensuing chuckles enough to break any residual tension.

Charlie found it hard to take her eyes off Robyn, the way her face lit up as she looked and laughed with Kate. She could see the bond between them and found herself being strangely relieved and grateful to find that Robyn had that in her life. She hadn't been lying earlier when she'd told Kate that Robyn's lifestyle sounded lonely. She couldn't imagine not being able to put down roots and make something comfortable to exist in day in, day out. She allowed a slightly sad smile as she realised that whilst she had done the latter, she'd probably become too comfortable. If she was going to be completely honest with herself, she wasn't any less lonely than Robyn.

"We had the most amazing teacher growing up," Kate announced, launching into the story of their childhood and the summers spent with their grandmother in Italy.

"She was your typical Italian matriarch," Robyn joined in. "A big family, eight children, too many grandchildren to count. Our grandfather died before we were born, but according to stories from our dad, aunts and uncles, she ruled their household, and he just did as he was told!"

"Her passion was cooking," Kate continued. "And god help anyone in the family who didn't want to learn! As soon as you were old enough to hold a wooden spoon, you were taught the basics. With us living in the States, we obviously didn't get as much input from her, but she had drilled it into Dad so much that he did the same with us at home and she topped us up when we would visit."

"I don't think he dared not teach us," Robyn laughed. "Do you remember those weekly phone calls when we were kids?" she asked Kate. "Dad had to begin each one by telling her what he'd had us do that week."

"And then we had to go on the phone and confirm it," Kate laughed. "She'd ask us questions to make sure he hadn't just made it up!"

As questions broke out around the table, guests keen to find out more about their cooking lessons, their childhood memories, or just steal a recipe or two, Charlie was content to just sit back and watch. She may well have had several opportunities to sit and watch Robyn on film or on set, but none of those experiences were like this. Being able to see Robyn, the woman herself and not playing another character, was quite simply breath-taking.

This Robyn was a million miles away from the woman who had torn her to pieces when they'd first met. Charlie didn't know how she'd missed it back then, but the tension radiating from Robyn had been immense. Now, that had all slipped away and the relaxed woman in front of her looked so at home in her simple clothes in the middle of the countryside, that Charlie found it hard to equate her with the actress responsible for some of the world's most successful blockbusters. It was obvious that Robyn drew strength from being with her sister, but Charlie felt pretty certain Robyn would have been almost this relaxed if Kate hadn't been there. She seemed so at ease with herself, easily sliding from one memory to another, keeping her guests thoroughly entertained with stories of Nonna and her kitchen.

It took Charlie a few minutes of just sitting and taking Robyn in before she realised just how much trouble she was in. She liked this woman. Like, really liked this woman. Of course, she'd always found her attractive, she'd known that, but the more she got to know her, the more she got to see of her, especially in situations like this, the more she realised that this wasn't just her lusting after a famous actress. This was her wanting to spend time with her, preferably just the two of them, to be able to go on dates with her, to hold her hand... Charlie's eyes dropped to Robyn's lips, watching as she talked, smiled, laughed. Yep. She wanted to kiss her. Pretty badly.

Forcing herself to look away, Charlie focused on her bottle, took a healthy swallow of the now slightly warm beer and then made herself look back up, anywhere but at Robyn. The other guests at the table were all focused on the sisters, drinking them in and enjoying their tales. Charlie saw Mel's eyes growing wider and wider with whatever Kate was talking about, Talia beside her with her trademark smirk, Lizzie and Rachel talking animatedly together, seemingly caught up in their own conversation. Britt was nodding along to Kate, who was now gesticulating wildly to add to the scene she was describing.

Charlie felt safe watching the others, felt as though she was giving her heart time to calm itself down, giving her mind time to process her new realisation, but she couldn't help it. Her eyes drifted from Kate back to Robyn and she was pretty sure her heart stopped beating altogether for a few seconds as she turned to find Robyn looking right at her. Robyn's eyes immediately flicked away, and Charlie could see a slight stiffening in her body language, as if she'd been caught doing something she shouldn't. Had Robyn really been gazing at her, or was Charlie's imagination running riot?

The moment those blue eyes looked back at her, Charlie had her answer. Robyn White was looking at her, and not just in the friendly way she'd looked at the others that night. Her eyes had darkened, pupils slightly dilated, and Charlie saw something akin to hunger before Robyn looked away again, seemingly engrossed in whatever it was Kate was now saying.

This time it was Charlie who looked away, unable to trust that she wouldn't do something crazy like walk over and kiss Robyn if she kept looking at her like that. She turned her attention to some of the groups sitting around in the garden, anything to try and settle her focus elsewhere. She could see a group clustered together under an old oak tree, some on patio furniture, others just lounging on the ground as they chatted together. If she looked over Lizzie's shoulder, she could make out the group who were sitting around the pool who she thought might now be playing a game of charades. Moving her gaze further, she could make out a couple on their own, totally oblivious to everything else around them, as they talked quietly, heads leaning together. She watched them for a moment, partly because she found their intimacy warming, but mainly because she knew the next turn of her head would bring her to Robyn again. Charlie was fast realising she couldn't stop herself from looking, but she could try to force herself to put it off as long as possible. A challenge, she thought. You can't look at her until you've counted down from 10…

At 7 she gave up and allowed her eyes to drift back, roaming over the blonde hair, taking in the way it gently curled around Robyn's shoulders, and when she tucked an errant strand behind her ear, Charlie became mesmerised by her hand, her fingers. She followed them as they made a looping motion and then reached for a glass of wine, carefully wrapping her fingers around the stem before lifting. As the glass reached its destination, it was only natural for Charlie's attention to slowly track up the height of the glass, to take a couple of moments savouring the lips which drank from it, and then to begin the slow crawl back to eyes she knew would be looking her way.

Charlie wasn't disappointed, and this time, Robyn's gaze held, the nervousness that had initially caused her to look embarrassed at being caught staring now completely gone. And the hunger Charlie thought she'd seen last time paled in comparison to what she saw now. If one of her friends had described a moment like this, Charlie would have laughed at them. Would have accused them of being overly dramatic and blowing everything out of proportion, of reporting on fiction, not reality. For the first time in her life, Charlie experienced that moment when everything but the person you're looking at disappears, melts into the background, ceases to exist. The sounds fade away until all you can hear is the beating of your heart and your blood as it pumps its way around your body, again and again and again. When the attraction and lust pool together just below your stomach and all rational thought ebbs away, leaving you with a single solitary phrase reverberating around your mind: I want her.

Chapter Fifteen

Robyn

I want her.

It was the loudest thought in Robyn's mind as she locked gazes with Charlie, pulsing in her mind like a garish neon sign. Hot pink she thought it would be, maybe with a hint of purple creeping in around the edges. She drew in a steadying breath, and sent a small smile in Charlie's direction, which was returned immediately. Good god, those eyes. She'd known they were going to get her into trouble from the moment she'd first looked into them when they'd been flashing with anger. Now, now it definitely wasn't anger she could see. It also wasn't the same of look of desire that Robyn was used to seeing directed her way. As someone who could potentially open doors for other people, Robyn had lost count of the number of times she'd seen want in a person's eyes. This time though, Robyn knew without doubt that Charlie wasn't looking at her because Robyn held the key to getting something she wanted. Charlie was looking because she wanted her, wanted Robyn, not the actress, not the millionaire. Just Robyn.

She broke the gaze, needing a moment to herself, a chance to calm down, to step back and garner some perspective. She needed to remember where she was, who she was with. As much as it might have felt like it was just her and Charlie for a few seconds, that wasn't the case. Robyn was surrounded by people, any one of whom might catch on and cash in on what they thought they were seeing. Robyn couldn't afford that kind of press. Another breath, and she felt like some control was seeping back in, like she was back in the garden with everyone else and not in some weird version of reality where there was only her and Charlie.

"Do you remember, Robbie?" came Kate's voice from across the table.

"Sorry," she began. "I didn't quite catch that," she added, trying to sound as normal as possible and not let on to her sister that she was being anything but the attentive host she should have been. A slight crinkling of Kate's brow told her she hadn't been successful, but she knew Kate would let it go for now.

"The first time Nonna took us into Naples to visit the fish market?"

"Of course," Robyn replied, grateful for a memory that was so easily accessible. She joined Kate in telling the others about their experience, Kate's rendition of Robyn's reaction to a stall selling squid and octopus drawing laughs from the others. Had Charlie joined in with the laughter? Robyn didn't want to look, but she couldn't help herself, her gaze easily flitting back to the other woman. Charlie hadn't laughed, rather a wistful smile played at the edges of her mouth as she stared intently at her beer bottle, one thumb picking gently at the edge of the label. She looked sad and Robyn was surprised at the force of the urge that shot through her, the one demanding she wrap Charlie in her arms and tell her everything would be okay. God, that was worse than the lust that had coiled in her belly moments earlier.

Charlie chose that moment to look up from her bottle, and Robyn met her eyes head on.

I want her. The thought was back, had never really gone anywhere. But this time, Charlie's eyes didn't mimic her own. No, Charlie's were sad, resigned, and that affected Robyn to her core. She wanted to go to her and find out the cause. A moment ago, she'd have sworn that Charlie was just as lost in a lust-filled haze as she was. What had happened to cause the change? She needed to know.

Charlie turned to Lizzie next to her and muttered something, motioning towards the house, then rose, turned her back on the group and headed across the patio. Without giving herself a moment to think, Robyn was on her feet and following, throwing an excuse about dessert when she caught Kate's quizzical look. Her heart pounded in her chest, and she wouldn't have been at all surprised if her legs had given way beneath her. She had absolutely no idea what she was going to say to Charlie when she caught up to her, she just knew she needed to follow.

As she stepped inside the kitchen, she saw Charlie heading through it, just about to step out into the hallway.

"Charlie," she called, wincing at how breathless she sounded.

Charlie stopped walking and turned slowly, surprise etched on her face. She clearly hadn't expected Robyn to follow her.

"Robyn. Is everything okay?" Charlie asked, from where she stood in the doorway.

Robyn didn't reply; she couldn't. She reduced her pace, walking slowly until she was standing in front of Charlie. Their eyes were locked to each other and this close, Robyn could see a ring of silver around Charlie's pupils before the blue took over. Robyn had no idea how long they stood like that, chests heaving, eyes never wavering. It could have been seconds, minutes, hours. Slowly, Robyn took another step closer and then another. There could be absolutely no doubting what was happening between them now. This was much too close to be considered purely platonic. Another moment of indeterminate length passed; a moment in which they both seemed to be trying to read the other and choose a course of action.

And then Robyn had absolutely no idea who moved first, but all of a sudden she had her arms wrapped around Charlie, Charlie's arms around her as they desperately tried to pull each other closer. Their lips met, slightly frantically, as a frenzied kiss took over them both. The moment their lips touched, Robyn knew she had lost control of her body as it pressed Charlie's up against the nearest wall, her hands pinning Charlie's hips in place. A small part of her brain was screaming at her to slow the kiss down, to savour it, to enjoy the languorous movement, but that part was drowned out by the primal part of her that wanted to get as much as she could as quickly as she could.

She felt Charlie's hands grip her ass, pulling her even closer, which Robyn hadn't actually believed possible. She could feel the wonderful sensation of Charlie's breasts, pressing into her own. She traced one hand up Charlie's side, letting her fingers follow the outline of her curves, caress her shoulder, and slip to the nape of Charlie's neck, urging their mouths further together. Robyn had no idea who released the soft moan, but it thrummed through her, and all she knew was that she wanted to hear it again.

Another moan, this time definitely her own; Charlie's hands had slipped beneath her t-shirt and were sliding up the length of Robyn's back, applying the perfect pressure. Before it had time to register fully, Charlie had flipped their positions and Robyn, not usually one to relinquish control, enjoyed the feeling of Charlie dictating. She ran her hands over Charlie's shoulders and down her back, until they came to settle on her hips. Looping her fingers through the belt hoops on Charlie's jeans, she tugged her closer, desperate to feel more. She continued to explore with her tongue, completely overwhelmed by the sensation of Charlie's duelling with her own.

Gods, she was magnificent, this woman in her arms. Robyn didn't have to search her memory banks for the last time she had felt like this; she hadn't. Not ever. Not once in her thirty-seven years had she experienced something so all consuming, so exhilarating, so reckless. If she was being completely honest with herself, Robyn had never understood what all the fuss was about. And yet, here she was, feeling more turned on from one kiss than the handful of times she had actually let her guard down enough to have had the few kisses she'd experienced before this one. At first, she had thought it was because she had kissed a couple of guys before she'd fully accepted she was gay, then, after the fireworks still hadn't erupted when she'd finally kissed a woman, she'd blamed herself for being uptight. Another two women down the line and Robyn had finally accepted she just wasn't a sexual being. Sure, it had been fairly enjoyable kissing those other women, but nothing like the way the people around her discussed their experiences, and certainly nothing at all like what she'd read in her secret guilty pleasure: lesbian romance books. In those, writers described women losing their minds and practically having out-of-body experience. Robyn wouldn't have used an adjective any more gushing than 'nice' to describe her own trysts, and that was a word she tried to avoid at all costs given how banal it was.

This right now, this was a million miles away from nice. It had her all hot and bothered and wondering whether it was at all possible to climb inside Charlie's skin and never leave. No matter how hard she tugged at her hips, Robyn just couldn't get close enough, couldn't cleave to Charlie in the way her body demanded. As she slid her hands under Charlie's top and splayed them possessively across her back, she felt a tingle in her fingertips and palms, wherever her skin came into contact with Charlie's. She whimpered, actually whimpered, when Charlie's mouth pulled away from her own and then groaned as Charlie's lips peppered light kisses down her jaw, down her neck and then across her collar bone which Charlie had revealed by tugging down the neck of her t-shirt. She couldn't do anything more than lean her head back and try to make her neck as long as possible in the hope those kisses never ended. Each time Charlie's lips touched her skin, she felt it in her core, a small zap of lightning coursing through her. If this was how she responded when Charlie's lips touched her neck, what was going to happen when they came into contact with other more sensitive parts of her anatomy. The thought brought a new rush of desire, leaving her wet and wanting. She shifted her stance slightly, manoeuvring Charlie's thigh between her own legs. She needed the release, craved what she knew was within touching distance.

Charlie's mouth captured Robyn's possessively and Robyn knew without doubt that she wasn't the only one turned on by their tryst. Every time Charlie's tongue tangled with her own, Robyn needed more. Her hands slid up Charlie's back, curling around her shoulder blades and pulling her in further. Without conscious thought, she moved one in between them and ran it across Charlie's breast. Needing to feel it and not the satin of Charlie's bra, Robyn lifted the bottom of the cup and ran her fingers across the pebbled nipple, cupping her breast and allowing her thumb to circle Charlie's nipple. She felt rather than heard Charlie's moan, and used her other hand to try and pull their bodies even closer. One of Charlie's hands was now in Robyn's hair, and Robyn felt the gentle pressure as Charlie too tried to close the non-existent gap between them, pulling Robyn's head forward.

And then, a raucous laugh from outside on the patio invaded Robyn's senses and all thoughts of where she wanted this kiss to go disappeared.

What on earth was she thinking, kissing this woman senseless in her hallway when just metres away was a large group of people, any one of whom who could stumble upon them and have photos posted on social media in seconds? Her body reacted.

Where moments ago, her arms had been pulling Charlie closer, now they were pushing her away, forcing as much distance between their bodies as they could. As soon as the gap was big enough, she strode through it, away from the wall, away from Charlie.

"This was a mistake," she said coldly, her eyes unable to meet Charlie's as she moved down the hallway and further into the house. She couldn't look back, knowing what she would see if she did. Knowing the glimpse of confusion she'd seen register on Charlie's face as she had first pushed her away would by now have transformed into hurt, maybe even anger. Robyn didn't want to see either of those emotions and know that she was the cause. Distance, that was what she needed.

She took the stairs two at a time and leant heavily against the bedroom door as soon as she managed to close it behind her. Bent double, hands resting on her knees, she tried to drag in a breath, tried to push down the panic.

Antman, Batwoman, Catwoman, Daredevil, Elektra, Flash, Green Lantern, Hit-Girl, Ironman, Jessica Jones, KickAss.

She slid the rest of the way to the floor, pulled in her knees and wrapped her arms around them, leaning her forehead against them.

Luke Cage, Ms Marvel, Nick Fury, Ozymandias, Phantom, Quicksilver, Rogue, Storm.

How could she have been so stupid? She knew better than to give in to lust. She'd seen her share of pretty faces over the years and had always been able to resist them, especially when she came across them in public. The few women she had kissed had all been met in private and vetted prior to that. What made Charlie Evans different? God, she'd practically thrown herself at the woman, had been moments away from a fully clothed orgasm. That didn't happen to Robyn White. She needed to get a grip.

Thor, Ultragirl, Venom, Wonder Woman, X-Man, Yellowjacket, Zatanna.

Her breathing began to slow as some of the control returned. She was almost certain no-one had seen them, and if she could pull herself together and get back downstairs quickly, it might be that her absence wouldn't start to be noticed yet. Well, Kate would have noticed, but she wouldn't call Robyn on it until all their guests had gone.

Pushing gingerly to her feet, Robyn took a moment to steady her legs, draw in one last deep breath and then headed back downstairs.

"Dessert is served!" she announced in her cheeriest voice as she stepped out onto the patio, fixed grin in place. Nothing to see here, folks, she thought. Her eyes slid to Charlie's seat: empty, and then to Kate's, knowing eyes looking directly at her. With a swallow, Robyn upped the ante on her fake delight at having provided sweet treats for her guests. "Tiramisu, profiteroles, panna cotta. Take your pick," she said, with a flourish, directing people back inside to sample what was on offer.

Even as she moved across the patio, chatting with people as she went, Robyn knew that Kate's attention never left her. It was like being caught in the crosshairs, something she had experienced innumerable times before. Kate could read her even more easily than a book. Damn twin thing, she cursed, as she finally made it back to their table and slipped into her seat, allowing a long drink from her glass before lifting her eyes to meet Kate's.

"Later," her sister mouthed across the table, her eyes inscrutable. It hardly seemed fair to Robyn that Kate could read her so easily, but she always struggled to do the same. Robyn might be the actress, but she couldn't get anything past Kate, whereas her twin seemed to have been blessed with the world's best poker face.

She nodded, knowing it was inevitable and that trying to avoid it was absolutely pointless. Only the slight tightening around Kate's lips as she stood to leave their table confirmed for Robyn that she really wasn't going to enjoy later at all.

Chapter Sixteen

Robyn

Robyn knew exactly what she was doing, and that it wasn't going to work. She'd tried her hardest to keep the conversation going with the last remaining partygoers, anything to prevent her from being alone with Kate. She knew she wouldn't get a moment's respite once they were on their own, and that Kate would needle at her until Robyn confessed to everything that had happened with Charlie. However, knowing what was coming and being ready to face it were two entirely different things, and if she had to keep up the façade of being fascinated by Mel's detailed analysis of which camera angle was best for building tension, then keep it up she would. Talia's eyes had almost rolled back into her head with boredom, and Robyn was certain that if Rachel and Lizzie hadn't been so engrossed in their own conversation, they too would be utterly fed up with the topic of choice.

"Enough," snapped Talia, clearly reaching her breaking point. "I love you to bits Mel, but you could bore the tits off a nun when you start talking about angles."

Mel looked chagrined, and from the snorts of laughter which erupted from Rachel and Lizzie, Robyn got the impression this wasn't the first time Mel had gone off on one. She felt a twinge of guilt for encouraging her as much as she had, especially given her selfish motivation.

"As a lowly actress," she began, determined to try to make it up to Mel a little bit, "I'm relieved to know as much thought goes into each shot as it clearly does. I've always known your department was thorough, but I'm afraid I've been doing you an injustice by not appreciating the level of detail you consider." It was true actually. Robyn knew the camera operators had storyboards of all the shots they wanted to take, and that the Director of Photography worked closely with the Director, but Robyn really hadn't understood the amount of work that happened away from the set. It made her see the crew in a different light and she resolved to make sure she showed her gratitude more often whilst on set.

Mel blushed and stammered out a thank you, making Talia's eyes begin their latest round of rolling.

"I think that's our cue to leave," Lizzie said, smiling at her friends.

"Absolutely," replied Rachel, pushing to her feet immediately. Robyn hid a smirk; it didn't take a genius to work out why she was so keen to leave, and from the glance Lizzie threw her way, Robyn figured they were in for a good night.

A pain hit her in the solar plexus as she realised she probably could have enjoyed a similar night too.

"Come on, then," Mel said, fishing her keys from her pocket. "Your designated driver is ready to roll."

"Rachel gets shotgun," Talia announced loudly. "That way we know she and Lizzie aren't getting up to any mischief in the back seat." She grinned widely, laughing at the twin blushes that accompanied her words. "So obvious, ladies," she drawled as she swaggered her way around the table to Robyn. "Thank you so much for today, I had a blast," she said sincerely, leaning in for a one-armed hug. The move surprised Robyn momentarily, but not nearly as much as discovering she liked this show of affection from Talia and each of the other three who all repeated the gesture.

Robyn followed them through the kitchen, past the point where she'd made out with Charlie; there really wasn't any other phrase for it. They had properly made out. An uncomfortable sensation roiled through her stomach, and she swallowed hard against it. Not yet, she cautioned herself.

She leaned against the frame of the front door, smiling slightly at the women's antics on their way to the car, and then waved as they drove away. She closed the front door slowly and pressed her forehead to it, drawing in a fortifying breath. She'd been on an emotional rollercoaster that day and knew it wasn't over yet. A clearing throat behind her signalled the end of her peace and quiet.

Slowly, Robyn turned to face her sister, who was leaning against the wall further down the hallway, arms crossed and a stony expression on her face.

"So?" Kate asked. No small talk first then, Robyn surmised. Just like Kate.

"Yes?" she asked, too cowardly to jump straight in.

"Don't give me that. One moment you're stalking Charlie into the house, like a hunter after its prey, and the next she's making up some bullshit story about a migraine and asking Britt if she minds heading back to the hotel with another group as she needs their driver to take her straight away. Then you show back up all transformed from the casual you into the fake, over-the-top you." Kate stopped and fixed Robyn with a stare. "Now either you join the dots up for me, or I'm going to start making assumptions."

Robyn sighed, accepting defeat.

"Fine, but I'm going to need wine."

They sat together across the kitchen table, Kate's wineglass still full and Robyn's missing the large gulp she'd taken as soon as it was poured. She looked at Kate, into those eyes that were so familiar to her, currently eyes that were radiating a steely determination. This was a topic they had danced around so many times and Robyn recognised immediately that this was where her avoidance ran out. They weren't just going to discuss the event with Charlie tonight; they were going to talk about it all. She grabbed her glass and took another long swallow.

"I kissed her," she said softly, not looking up from where her fingers twirled the glass stem nervously.

"Mmm, hmm." Okay, so Kate wasn't going to help her out with this at all.

"We kissed," she began again, immediately faltering.

"And it was so terrible you gave Charlie a migraine?" Kate asked, clearly annoyed at her sister.

"No," said Robyn honestly. "It was anything but terrible. It was the best damn kiss of my life," she confessed, finally lifting her eyes to meet Kate's, which seemed to warm slightly, before hardening again.

"And again, I'll remind you, she left, Robyn."

A silence hung between them, one that was desperate for Robyn for fill it, but which she was equally as desperate to avoid. She needed a tighter grip on her emotions before they had this conversation. She wasn't in control, and she couldn't talk about stuff like this if she wasn't dictating things. She looked desperately at Kate, trying to convey everything she was feeling, trying to make Kate see that she needed to let her off the hook right now, that she would fall apart if they kept going.

The slight shake of her head was the only signal Kate gave. She knew exactly what Robyn needed and was refusing to give it. Something broke inside Robyn. Kate had always backed down when she saw how close Robyn was to the edge, but this time it felt like she had pushed her over. Despite wanting to rail against her, part of Robyn was grateful. She'd known this tsunami was building inside her for a long time now, cresting ever higher, ever closer to the surface. She also knew there was absolutely no way she would ever have allowed it to reach its crescendo if left to her own devices. But Kate had taken over and that was enough for Robyn to finally let go.

The sobs were all-encompassing, great wracking heaves that made Robyn feel like her lungs were trying their damnedest to rip themselves out of her body. She couldn't stop them or the shaking that accompanied them. Tears ran down her face as she fought for breath, and she couldn't have pinned down a single thought if her life had depended on it. Her insides burned, a physical pain to match her emotional turmoil.

Distantly, she registered that Kate had rounded the table and pulled Robyn from her chair into her arms. She tried to focus on the comforting feeling of her sister's hand lovingly rubbing a soft pattern on her back. Burying her head into Kate's shoulder, she clenched at fistfuls of her t-shirt in an attempt to ground herself, to know that Kate was really there, holding her.

Robyn didn't know how much time had passed before she felt able to pull herself together enough to talk to Kate. She sat back, wiping the tears from her face, and offered a sad smile to her sister.

"I fucked up again, Katie."

"Tell me."

"We kissed. It was awesome."

"I got that part already."

"And then," Robyn faltered, her eyes welling up as she looked at Kate. "I pushed her away. Literally pushed her away from me and told her it was mistake."

A silence hung between the sisters for a while, each passing second only serving to make Robyn feel worse. The moment played on a loop in her head, over and over and over again. The look in Charlie's eyes. The feel of her mouth on her. The feeling of their bodies against each other.

"Why?" Kate asked, finally breaking the silence.

Robyn thought about her answer. The easy response was to say the noise from outside had made her realise what they were doing and where they were doing it, and that she'd worried about being caught. It wasn't a lie, but it also wasn't the whole truth.

"Because I felt something that I've never felt before and it scared the hell out of me."

"Thank you for being honest, Robbie." Kate sighed before pushing herself from her knees back to a chair. "We have to talk about this."

"I know."

"I'll go first. I can't decide whether you genuinely believe your career will suffer if you come out or if you just use that as an excuse. And if it's an excuse, I don't really get what the problem is," Kate finished, taking hold of Robyn's hand and squeezing to let her know that she didn't mean what she'd said to be malicious in any way.

Robyn laughed sadly.

"I guess if we're being all upfront and open tonight, then I don't really know either," she confessed. "I mean, I came out to you, and Mom and Dad so long ago that I know that has nothing to do with it. You've all only ever been wholly supportive of me, so it isn't anything to do with family," she reassured.

"But your experience with David was very different," Kate added for her.

"You know, when I first told him, I didn't think his response was negative at all. He just seemed to accept it and then moved the conversation on. It wasn't until a few months later that I realised he had been setting me up to be seen in public with eligible men far more often than he had beforehand. When I asked him about it, he told me horror stories about other actresses who had come out, or tried to come out, and basically been shunted out of Hollywood."

"And at the time, I can understand why that would have had an impact on you. You were still fairly new on the scene and tied into the *Branded* franchise. You couldn't afford to take the risk." Kate paused and leaned forward in her seat slightly to catch Robyn's gaze. "But I don't think you can use that as a reason now, Robbie."

"You're right, I can't. I'm far more established within the industry, but I've also managed to break out of the mould with this current role, so I don't need to worry so much about maintaining a certain image."

"While we're in the middle of a heavy topic of conversation, let's add another layer to it," Kate said. "Let's say you came out and David was right, no one in Hollywood ever hires you again. How would you feel?"

"I think you know how I would feel, Katie," Robyn replied, not quite ready to bring herself to admit the truth out loud.

"I wouldn't want to presume."

"Wow, you really are laying it on me tonight, aren't you?" Robyn laughed.

"Well, seeing as we're in England, I'm channelling the British sentiment of 'in for a penny, in for a pound.' I figured we might as well cover everything in one conversation rather than me having to wait a few months to be in the same room with you again."

"Lucky me," Robyn muttered.

"You still haven't answered, Robbie," Kate chided gently.

Robyn sighed and ran a hand through her hair.

"I wouldn't be the slightest bit upset," she admitted. "In fact, I'd probably be relieved. There, I've said it. Happy now?"

"Almost," Kate said with a wink, trying to keep the tone as light as possible, which wasn't an easy feat. "So, to surmise, you kissed Charlie and liked it so much that you stopped it and pushed her away because you're afraid kissing her again could negatively impact on a career you don't really want to have any more anyway." Kate sat back in her chair and looked at Robyn, allowing her words to hang in the space between them.

Robyn looked at her sister, letting what she had said filter through, playing around with it in her mind, before finally nodding and collapsing in a fit of giggles, which quickly infected Kate too.

"Oh my god," Robyn said, gasping for breath and trying to regain some control. "I'm such a dick!"

"You really are!" Kate laughed, before sobering and taking hold of Robyn's hand again. "For the first time in your entire life, you've met someone who transforms you and you're just going to throw it away. I can't stand by and watch you do that, Robbie. We need to work a way out of this that means you get the girl and the happy ending."

"Wouldn't that be something?"

"We both know that this has been a long time coming, Robbie. And the first step you need to take is finding a way to make peace with your sexuality." She held up a hand when Robyn would have interrupted to protest. "I know you're going to say that you don't have a problem with it, but I know you, and I've watched you struggle with this for decades now. You feel guilty about it."

"What?" Robyn asked incredulously.

"I thought once you'd come out to us and saw that it didn't matter in the slightest to me or to Mom or Dad, that you'd feel better about it, and maybe you did a little bit, but not enough. You carry it like a millstone around your neck. Like you need to work harder to make up for something you've done wrong. You've thrown yourself into acting, being the best you can possibly be, despite not enjoying it. You work hard for charities and other initiatives that benefit people who are disadvantaged in some way. You earn millions of dollars and give a lot of it away."

Kate moved from her seat to kneel in front of her sister, one hand still gripping Robyn's while the other tucked an errant strand of Robyn's hair behind her ear. Robyn felt the tears well up and willed them not to spill over. When Kate had said she wanted to lay it all out tonight, Robyn had not envisaged the conversation ever being this deep. She struggled to find a response, and Kate took pity on her.

"You haven't done anything wrong, Robyn. You can love whoever you want to love without feeling like you need to apologise to the world."

As the tears spilled over yet again, Kate gathered her sister in her arms and held her tightly, allowing Robyn to let out the pent-up emotion. If it had been anyone else who had tried to have this conversation with her, she would have vehemently denied the truth in what they were saying. But this was Katie, and she had always been able to get past Robyn's defences with astonishing ease.

In the comfort of her sister's arms, Robyn took a moment to acknowledge just how right Kate was. She had always felt as though she was letting people down by being gay, as though she wasn't living up to the norm demanded by society and it weighed heavily on her conscience. She hadn't consciously set out to work hard to try and make up for it, but in her core, she knew that Kate was absolutely on the money. She'd buried her desire for happiness deep inside herself and instead used her energy to make other people happy.

Robyn eased back out of Kate's arms, wiped her tears and took a slow, deep, steadying breath.

"You're right," she said her voice tentative at first, but growing in strength as she spoke. "I have used the industry as an excuse. I already felt as though I'd let my family down by being who I am, and I wasn't brave enough to come out publicly and let all my fans and colleagues down too. It was more than I could bear feeling as though I'd disappointed the three of you." She paused and wiped away one of Kate's tears. "That's not on you, Katie. You've always been fully supportive of me and deep down I know that you love me for who I am, and you really don't care who I kiss."

Kate's face cringed and she let out a hollow laugh.

"I care who you kiss, Robyn; I don't care who you love. You've made some god-awful choices in the first category over the years!" she teased, drawing a laugh from her sister.

"Touché," Robyn replied. "I'm the first to admit my judgement hasn't always been sound, but I guess that's what comes of only being able to kiss women in secret. You don't always get the best choice." She shook her head at herself. "Thank god I never let it get any further than that," she quipped and then looked wide-eyed at Kate, realising what she had just confessed.

"I already knew that Robbie," Kate said gently. "You don't have to look as though you've just confessed to the worst crime in history! So, you've never had sex with a woman? So what? I'd rather hear you say that than a litany of conquests you regret."

"I'm thirty-seven years old, Katie. It's more than a little embarrassing," Robyn mumbled.

"I bet Charlie would disagree with that," Kate teased, causing the mild blush on Robyn's face to explode into something resembling a tomato. Kate threw her head back and laughed.

"I hate you right now," Robyn said, shaking her head at her sister.

"Yeah, right, whatever," Kate sassed. "So, you and I need to spend some time working out a plan. We need to get you this girl and come out to the public so that you can actually be with said girl." She paused, looking deep in thought for a moment. "I'm thinking Operation Deflowering," she said managing to maintain a serious tone while her eyes danced with mirth. Robyn gave her a withering look. "Or Operation Cherry Pop!"

"Fuck you, Kate," Robyn said, unable to stop the grin that came with her sister's teasing.

"Nah, been there done that lots of times," Kate said with a wink. "This time it's about getting you well and truly fu-." Her words were swallowed behind Robyn's hand, which clamped down firmly across her sister's mouth.

"Enough!" Robyn laughed, removing her hand and pulling Kate in for a tight hug. "I love you, Katie," she said quietly as she held her twin. "I don't know what I'd do without you."

"Probably die a virgin," Kate quipped sarcastically, earning a groan of despair in response.

Chapter Seventeen

Charlie

"THIS WAS A MISTAKE."

The words had reverberated inside Charlie's head all night, as they drove back to the hotel, as she drank a cuppa before bed, as she lay in bed, staring at the ceiling.

"This was a mistake."

She couldn't get them out of her mind, couldn't shake lose the coldness in Robyn's eyes as she'd pushed her away. Charlie had tried to rationalise them: Robyn was a Hollywood superstar; she wouldn't want to get caught kissing a teacher at a party. In every article Charlie had ever read, Robyn was presumed to be straight, which meant that she either was and therefore kissing a woman was a mistake, or she was in the closet and therefore kissing someone where they could get caught was a mistake. Either way Charlie looked at it, she couldn't come to any conclusion other than that Robyn had been right. It *was* a mistake.

So, why didn't it feel like one to Charlie?

She turned on her side, looking at the clock on the bedside table. 3:17am. Twelve minutes later than the last time she had looked, and twenty-three minutes since the time before that. With a sigh, Charlie sat up, pushed the covers off and swung her legs out of the bed, grabbing the plush white robe from the hook by the wardrobe and padding over to the kitchenette. There was no point in trying to sleep any longer. She flicked on the kettle and waited for it to boil.

"This was a mistake."

Argh! She wanted to reach inside her brain and turn off Robyn's voice. She sighed, made her tea, and took it to the armchair by the French doors, curling her legs beneath her and sinking in.

None of it had felt like a mistake to Charlie. Not the feeling of Robyn's body pressed against hers or hers pressed against Robyn's as they traded positions. Not the sensation of Robyn's lips against her own, Robyn's tongue gently seeking entrance, or when it battled with her own. Robyn's hands as they'd slid beneath her t-shirt, the ever-so-soft skin Charlie had discovered when her own hands had made the same journey. None of had a been a mistake to her; it had felt more right than any other kiss she had ever had. That moment just before they'd grabbed each other had been the sweetest moment of anticipation Charlie had ever experienced, and she'd give anything to have it again.

"This was a mistake."

It wasn't going to happen again though, and Charlie had to find a way to move on from it. She shook her head at herself, musing on the idea that if she hadn't been so understanding and forgiving when Robyn delivered her apology, none of this would be happening right now. Her friends had chastised her more than once for being what Jen liked to call 'a right softy', and it seemed perhaps they were right. Surely Robyn wouldn't have followed her inside, wouldn't have shoved her up against the wall with such abandon, if Charlie had told her where to shove her apology?

But then, if she'd done that, she wouldn't know how utterly amazing it felt to be kissed by Robyn White, and by all the gods, it had been amazing. More than anything, Charlie wanted to be able to press pause on her memories and stop the night before Robyn uttered that final statement, just like she did whenever she watched *Kissing Jessica Stein*, which she always stopped right after Jessica dismissed Josh at the wedding and finally committed to Helen. She hated the rest of the movie, just like she hated the rest of last night.

"This was a mistake."

It had taken a few moments for her lust-addled brain to catch up with what had happened, but not long enough for her to miss the complete detachment in Robyn's eyes or to notice that she didn't once look back at Charlie after she'd walked away. Charlie's heart, already thudding loudly with passion, had slumped into despair and she'd struggled to catch her breath. She'd debated going after Robyn, trying to talk to her, to understand where she was coming from, but she knew it would be pointless.

Charlie's body moved mechanically through the next few hours; she knew she'd done her yoga practice, drunk more tea, eaten breakfast, showered, and dressed, but her mind hadn't been present for any of it. Now, she was sitting at the small desk in her hotel room, waiting for the clock to move so she could log in to her weekly Skype call, which the girls had insisted take place earlier this Sunday, so they didn't have to wait to hear all the gossip from the party. She had resolved to be upbeat about it and not to tell them about the kiss; she wasn't ready to dissect it with them yet.

Wrapping her hands around her mug, she listened to the familiar tone as her call connected and couldn't stop the tug of a smile as she saw all three friends ready and waiting for her. This never happened. Charlie was always the first one there and often had to wait for her friends whose hectic lives stopped them from always managing to be on time. It seemed however, that with the right motivation, they could actually be present.

"About time," Jen said sharply. "We've been waiting for you to get here for ages," she scolded.

"It's 8:30am," Charlie replied. "The call is supposed to start now, and you lot are never early." She narrowed her eyes at them all. "What gives?"

"We're never early because we're never waiting on tenterhooks to find out how Robyn White's party went," Nay outlined, using her hands to express her point as was her want.

"Exactly," Jen agreed. "Come on, spill. Was it amazing? Did you have canapes and caviar? Champagne poured by waiters wearing perfect uniforms?" Her eyes drifted off dreamily as she let her imagination wander.

"Good morning, Charlie," Lauren said softly. "Apologies for these two," she added, rolling her eyes as she gestured at her friends. She shook her head affectionately at their antics, then fixed Charlie with a mischievous stare. "Right, pleasantries over. Tell us everything!"

"I kissed her," Charlie blurted out. So much for not sharing that with them yet, she chastised herself.

Excitement bubbled amongst her three friends, and she heard much whooping and hollering. She even caught Jen and Nay trying to do a virtual high-five.

"Wait," Lauren said, capturing everyone's attention. "By 'her' you do mean Robyn White, yes?"

Charlie nodded, wishing to all the things you could wish to that her traitorous mouth had kept itself shut.

Her confirmation signalled the start of more celebration and the conversation between her friends moved at a hundred miles an hour. Nay congratulated them all on having always known Robyn was gay. Jen was doing some kind of dance whilst proclaiming she'd always known Charlie had a massive crush on the actress, and was trying to convince everyone (and herself, probably), that she wasn't jealous of Charlie at all. Even Lauren, usually the quietest and most restrained after Charlie, was joining in with their antics.

A pang of sadness shot through Charlie. This was how the aftermath of kissing Robyn White should have been, not the ache in her soul she'd been left with. And yes, she knew that was an extreme response to just one kiss, but she couldn't help it. That was how she felt. Like she'd been offered something more amazing than she could ever imagine with one hand, and then had it ripped away with the other.

"Charlie?" Lauren's gentle voice prompted, and it took Charlie a moment to realise that Skype had gone quiet and the partying had stopped. She turned her gaze back to her screen and met the concerned faces of her three best friends. Her eyes immediately filled with tears and she looked away again, needing a second to try and rein her emotions back in.

"Oh no," she heard Nay console softly.

"Charlie?" Lauren asked again.

"I'm going to kill that bitch," Jen muttered, typical in her instant leap to defend Charlie. At least her threat drew something of a smile from Charlie, the first she'd managed all day.

"What happened, babe?" Lauren's use of the endearment was enough to make Charlie close her eyes, a tear escaping from each as she did so. Wiping them away, she took a deep breath, turned back to her friends, and allowed the whole story to tumble from her lips.

The arrival and the heartfelt apology. The amazing house and even better food. The ease of conversation. The longing glances. And finally, Robyn calling her name and kissing the hell out of her, right up until the moment she pushed Charlie away. And even though she didn't want to, had planned to keep them locked up for herself, she shared those words that had haunted her ever since.

"This was a mistake."

Nay's sharp intake of breath and Jen's colourful curse let Charlie know their thoughts immediately, and even though she knew they would always be utterly biased in her favour, it still felt good to hear. Only Lauren remained silent, and Charlie wasn't the only one to notice.

"Lauren," Jen challenged. "You haven't said anything. What's going on inside that head of yours."

Lauren looked slightly chagrined and before Charlie could say anything, Nay beat her to it.

"No, Lauren. Whatever you're thinking now, don't you dare say it. That woman has fucked up and there is absolutely no defending what she did."

"I know," Lauren replied, her voice quiet, but strong.

"But?" Charlie asked, knowing there was one.

"But I think we need to pause for just a moment."

"The hell we do!" Jen stated emphatically, flipping her hair back in a trademark move of frustration. "Did you listen to anything Charlie just said? How can that be seen as anything but shocking?

"It's okay, Jen," Charlie said, wanting to know what Lauren was thinking. "Go on, Laur. Please."

"I just think that in the emotion of the whole thing, we've lost sight of the context."

Nay snorted and Charlie fixed her with a look that told her not to interrupt, to which the other woman held up her hands in surrender and motioned for Lauren to continue. "We don't actually know what Robyn meant by what she said. Was it a mistake to kiss Charlie, or what it a mistake to kiss Charlie at the party?"

"What the hell is the difference?" Nay asked loudly, no longer able to hold her tongue.

"Well, we don't actually know which of those two things Robyn was upset about. Maybe she kissed Charlie in a moment of reckless abandon and immediately regretted it because Charlie wasn't the person she wanted to be kissing, hence it's a mistake. Sorry, Charlie," she added softly as she caught her friend's wince.

"Nice going," Jen said sarcastically with a roll of her eyes.

"Or," Lauren continued, "perhaps Robyn did want to kiss Charlie, but as a closeted actress, because we're guessing that's what she is, she realised that doing so in a hallway where they could get caught at any second, wasn't the best plan and she panicked." Lauren sat back from her screen and smiled sadly at Charlie.

"Both options kind of suck," Charlie replied, her voice small and still full of hurt.

"I know, babe," Lauren said softly.

"They do," Jen said thoughtfully, "but both have very different potential outcomes. In scenario A, there is no more kissing between Charlie and Robyn, but that's not true of scenario B." She warmed to the discussion, and Charlie could see her journalist's brain kicking into gear as she pondered the points. "With B, we need to establish safe parameters, to find a way to make more kissing a viable option, away from party-goers and other potential social media users. The last thing we want is for this to be trending on Twitter if it's not being properly managed." She trailed off, lost in her thoughts.

"So, let me get this right," Naomi said firmly. "In the case of scenario B, you're both suggesting that Charlie should just forgive Robyn for what she did? For making her feel small and worthless?"

"That's maybe a slight exaggeration, Nay," Charlie intervened. "I'm hurt by her words and actions, but I wouldn't go as far as to say I feel worthless."

"Semantics," Naomi said, waving her hand in dismissal. "All I'm saying is that we need to take a moment to stop and think." She looked towards Lauren and Jen. "Do we really want to be suggesting that Charlie get involved with this woman? I mean, if it was B that made her react like that, who's to say she won't do the same again? If she isn't out to the world, our Charlie is going to have to sneak around, constantly worrying that they're going to get caught. Is that the kind of relationship we want for her?"

Charlie sat back and crossed her arms, shaking her head slightly. This wasn't the first time the other three had seemingly forgotten she was part of the

126

conversation and held a deep and meaningful discussion about her. Whilst on the one hand it could be pretty irritating, on the other, being able to listen in to their conversations had always made Charlie feel reassured that her friends really did care about her.

"That's what we need to talk about," Jen declared. "I mean, this is Robyn White, right? I imagine if this had been any other woman, we wouldn't need to think like this, but Lauren has a point. We know what Hollywood is like. We've all read the stories and I've heard a whole load of other rumours about people coming out and having their careers end or thinking that's what might happen and so avoiding it."

"So, we want to sentence Charlie to a lifetime in the closet?" Nay asked, the indignation evident in her voice.

"Absolutely not," Lauren declared at the same time as Jen also gave a firm negative. "We need to find out what Robyn's motivation is. Is she gay or just curious? Does she want to come out or stay as she is? Does she see a future with Charlie?"

This time it was Charlie who snorted.

"Did you hear anything I said? She doesn't see a future, she sees a mistake!"

"No," corrected Jen. "In the heat of the moment last night she saw a mistake, and let's remember, we're not sure what that mistake was. Today, tomorrow? Who knows what she sees?"

"Well, if you think I'm going to ask her, you've got another thing coming," Charlie replied, her voice rising. "I will steadfastly be avoiding any situation that involves me being in the same room as Robyn White until this damn filming is over. In fact," she announced, her irritation becoming more obvious, "if I could work out how to get out of the whole ridiculous situation, I'd be on the first train home tomorrow."

Silence.

Charlie could count on one hand the number of times she'd lost her temper in front of her friends. She was known for her infinite patience and her ability to find a logical and reasonable way through any issue. With this though, Charlie couldn't find the usual well of reason that sat in her gut; it was as if it had evaporated the second she'd felt Robyn's hands push her away.

She tipped her head back and looked at the ceiling for a few seconds, closing her eyes and trying to centre herself.

"Look, you guys, I appreciate everything you're saying, I really do, but it's just too raw right now. It wasn't my intention to tell you about this this morning because I guess I just need some time to wallow in it. I'm sorry that it burst out when it did, and I know you've got my best intentions at heart, but could we please just leave it for today? Please?"

"Of course, we can, Charlie," Lauren said quickly, beating her friends to the answer. "We can leave it and come back to it whenever you're ready to, or never if that's what you need to do." She smiled softly into her camera and Charlie thought the tears she'd only just managed to keep at bay might now tip over. "Now, where I had I got up to in telling you about Mrs Neoclassical and her ridiculous Pantheon?" And with that, the conversation was moved away from Charlie and her disastrous night as Lauren wove a comedy of errors with her eclectic client.

Never in her life had Charlie wanted so much to be in the same room as Lauren and to be wrapped up in one of the rare hugs she gave.

For the rest of the day, Charlie threw herself into work, marking an essay that Lucy had submitted mid-week, planning their next few lessons, re-reading *The Handmaid's Tale*, the text she had to start with Lucy in the next couple of weeks. Anything to keep her mind busy and away from thoughts of Robyn and their kiss the day before, or seeing Robyn on set in the days to come.

Over yet another cup of tea, she plotted out the changes she would need to make to the patterns she'd fallen into. Over the last few weeks, she'd enjoyed being able to be on set watching the filming during any time she wasn't teaching Lucy. She sighed, acknowledging that would probably need to stop. Not only would she find it incredibly difficult to be in the same space as Robyn, she also needed to consider the other woman's feelings; Charlie couldn't imagine Robyn would want her anywhere near when she was trying to work.

Despite her best efforts to remain hurt and angry by Robyn's words and actions, Lauren's comments kept invading Charlie's thoughts. Could it be that Robyn had panicked and acted out of self-preservation? Even if that was the case, did it make any difference to Charlie? She wouldn't deny that kissing Robyn had been beyond incredible, and she couldn't say, hand on heart, that she wouldn't do it again if the opportunity arose. She wanted to say categorically that she wouldn't put herself in a position where Robyn could hurt her again, but a nagging voice told her not to be so ridiculous; did she really think she'd be able to resist those lips if they were offered? Not a chance. She'd just have to hope that Robyn thought differently on the matter and kept her distance until the damn film was finished.

Chapter Eighteen

Charlie

"TYPICAL," CHARLIE THOUGHT AS SHE pushed open the door to her teaching room to discover her luck had already run out. Seriously, the universe couldn't let her get through more than 10 minutes before it presented her with Robyn White? And not just any version of Robyn White either. Oh no, it had to be this exquisitely put together model, perfect hair, little make-up to emphasise her natural beauty, and yet another Dolly Parton concert t-shirt. As if the one from Saturday night wasn't already indelibly embedded in her mind, now she had a second one to add to it.

Thinking it best to get out of there as quickly as possible, Charlie reached for the handle on the door, which was just about to close behind her. "Sorry," she muttered as she turned to leave.

"No, Charlie, wait," Robyn called behind her. "Please."

Charlie sighed and slowly forced herself to face Rachel. "You don't need to worry," she said quickly. "I'm not going to go to the press or post something on social media. It was one kiss," she shrugged dismissively, determined to play it down.

A clouded look took up residence on Robyn's face and she sagged back down into the seat as if no longer able to bear her own weight. Charlie might have thought it was with relief if she hadn't been able to see the hurt so clearly in her eyes.

"That's not why I'm here, although I can completely understand why you would think so. It's not like I've done anything to build a particularly positive image of myself in your eyes."

Charlie folded her arms and channelled her inner Jen, knowing her friend wouldn't give an inch until she had the answers she wanted. Charlie's first instinct was to soothe Robyn, but she buried it down deep, pushed her shoulders back a little more and tried to fix her face in the resting bitch pose Jen had perfected. She was pretty sure it didn't work on her own face, but she might as well give it a go.

"Then why are you here?" Blunt, forceful, to the point, and from the way Robyn swallowed, it hit its mark.

"To apologise."

"Been there, done that," Charlie snarked. "It begins to lose its impact after a little while." If her friends could see her now, she had no doubt they'd be cheering her on. Well, to be fair, Lauren probably wouldn't. Lauren would tell her to give Robyn the benefit of the doubt, to hear her out before she dismissed her.

The barb hit and Robyn visibly winced; Charlie wondered if she was supposed to feel as bad as she did for being the cause of that pain. She sighed again, knowing she couldn't keep up the front of being blasé about this conversation. Holding her hands up in surrender, she shook her head at her own behaviour.

"I'm sorry, that was out of line." She looked at Robyn, letting her know she meant what she was saying. "Is it okay if I sit?" she asked, gesturing to the chair opposite the one Robyn occupied.

"Of course it is," Robyn motioned and Charlie sank down, sliding her satchel from her shoulder to the floor and slipping her hands beneath the table so Robyn wouldn't be able to see how tightly she had balled them into fists to try and get her through this conversation; she really didn't want to participate. Her left knee bounced up and down, and her heart rate picked up. Having to replay any part of Saturday night hadn't been on her agenda for today, especially not with the woman she hadn't been able to get out of her head right there in front of her.

Across from her, Robyn cleared her throat and looked at Charlie for a moment before looking back down at the table to where her hands rested. As Charlie looked closer, she could see them trembling, and that was the moment it really hit her. She wasn't sitting across the table from a global superstar who was untouchable by everything; she was sitting opposite another human being, a woman who probably experienced many of the same emotions as Charlie herself. Just because Robyn was known the world over, didn't mean she was impervious to doubt, to fear, to any of the emotions a non-famous person would feel.

Pushing back her chair, Charlie stood up and when Robyn's eyes grew wide at the suddenness of her movement, Charlie smiled at her, walked around the table, took a seat next to Robyn, and covered her hands with her own. "Talk to me," she said softly, looking Robyn in the eye so she could see she was being genuine. "Talk to me, Robyn." Tears immediately welled up in the blue eyes she was gazing into and as they spilled over, Charlie used one hand to gently wipe them away. "It's okay," she reassured Robyn. "I promise."

"Is it?"

"It can be."

"God, Charlie, I'm so sorry," Robyn breathed out quickly as she turned her hand over and interlaced her fingers with Charlie's. "I have to admit that I was more prepared to deal with the angry you that first arrived than I am with this sweet, understanding you. I deserved the anger; I don't think I deserve your kindness."

"Well, as you said, it's my kindness, so I get to decide where it goes, and if I want to direct some of it at you, I'm afraid there's nothing you can do to stop me."

As more tears fell, Robyn used her free hand to swipe at them. "I swore to myself I wasn't going to cry this morning. Thirty seconds in a room with you and I'm weeping like a baby." She shook her head, blew out a breath and fixed her eyes on Charlie. "I owe you more than an apology. I owe you an explanation. A full, detailed, warts and all explanation, but I can't do that here." She gestured to the room and grinned slightly as she motioned her head towards the door. "Especially when my precocious young co-star could come bounding through there at any moment."

Charlie felt Robyn's grip on her hand tighten and sensed she was about to say something that didn't come easily to her. Not that any of this did, of course. Charlie could sense the courage it had taken for Robyn to be here this morning and to say what she had so far. It seemed a far more mature response than Charlie's determination to avoid Robyn at all costs. Funny, if you'd asked her last week, Charlie would have said she thought she was pretty good at the whole adulting thing. Now she wasn't quite so certain.

"If you need to talk, I'll be available."

The relief on Robyn's face was obvious. "I'd like to do it away from here altogether, if that's okay with you? Not because I don't want to be seen with you," Robyn rushed to reassure. "I'd just really like to have the time and space to talk to you properly without having to worry about being interrupted. I think you deserve that at the very least."

Charlie smiled and nodded. "I'd like that."

"Maybe at the hotel this evening? I should be back by 4pm today. There are some scenes scheduled that I'm not in, so I get an early finish."

"Perfect. I'll be back by then too," Charlie confirmed.

"Great," Robyn smiled. "Why don't you come along to my suite for 4:30pm? I'm in The Cedar Room."

Charlie couldn't help herself. "The Cedar Room? You're in a room that has an actual name rather than a number? Wow, the perks of being you," she winked, causing Robyn to laugh as an adorable blush tinted her cheeks.

"Hollywood Diva," she said, laughing at herself.

"I'll be there," Charlie said, her voice completely sincere. "And thank you for believing in me enough to share the details of your room."

"Of course," Robyn replied as she reached out to tuck Charlie's errant strand of hair back behind her ear. "I trust you."

Charlie closed her hotel room door behind her and lent against it, glancing at her watch: 3:55pm. Time had done its usual trick of slowing right down the moment Robyn left her teaching room that morning. It seemed to always do this when Charlie wanted the day to rush by and left her feeling like she was wading through molasses, believing she was checking her watch once an hour only to find out it was more like twenty minutes. Her lesson with Lucy had been a slog; all Charlie could think about was the sensation of Robyn's fingers as they'd grazed her cheek after Robyn had tucked her hair back. Trying to focus on the intricacies of Hardy's language choices in *Tess of the D'Urbervilles* had been nigh on impossible. But she'd toughed it out and made sure that Lucy's learning wasn't affected by her wandering mind.

When Lucy had left, it took all of Charlie's willpower to stay in her teaching room rather than rushing to the set. Just because Robyn had seemed gentler that morning and wanted to talk didn't mean she needed to just up and forget how hurtful Saturday had been. She wanted to keep an open mind and really listen to Robyn, to try to understand what had happened. Watching Robyn act wasn't going to help at all with that; the only thing it helped with was increasing Charlie's libido.

She glanced again at her watch, dismayed this time to discover time was doing its opposite and careening out of control. Surely she hadn't wasted five minutes just leaning against the door? Pushing herself upright, she crossed to her wardrobe and pulled open the doors. Charlie had a feeling she might need to be comfortable for this upcoming conversation and her work suit wasn't going to cut it. Slipping out of the tailored pants and jacket, she hung them back up, tossing her shirt in the laundry. She flipped through the casual clothes she'd brought with her, eventually settling on her grey skinny jeans and a long-sleeved black Henley top, leaving the top couple of buttons open. She might want to be comfortable, but she wasn't above showing a bit of cleavage.

Charlie checked her reflection in the mirror, ran a hand through her hair and shrugged at herself. She had no idea what this conversation held and for all she knew Robyn could just dismiss her again. There'd been a look in Robyn's eyes this morning though that hinted at something else, and it was that something else that had kept Charlie on edge all day. Even if this encounter ended as painfully as their last one, Charlie knew she wouldn't miss out on the possibility of kissing Robyn again if she had the opportunity. If she focused on that part of Saturday, ignoring the words that had cut her to the quick, she would have to admit that she'd never experienced anything like it before. It wasn't like Charlie had kissed a huge number of women, not that many at all if she were being honest, maybe just more than she could count on one hand, but none of them had made her feel anything like Robyn had, not even the ones she'd ended up dating for a few months.

"Don't get ahead of yourself," she muttered quietly to her reflection before turning away and lacing up her burgundy Converse. Another look at her watch revealed she had 10 minutes, just long enough to navigate her way from the numbered rooms for the masses to the named rooms for the privileged. The Cedar Room sounded so grand and for a second, Charlie's resolve faltered. What was she doing heading off to the room of a global superstar and fantasising about kissing her? No, she wasn't going to let her doubts hold her back today. Robyn had asked to see her, had said she wanted to talk to Charlie, so Charlie had to accept she was good enough for this.

Charlie ran her fingers over the oak plaque announcing she was outside The Cedar Room. She took a moment, trying to calm her nerves. Come on, she urged, and before she could second guess herself, knocked lightly and took a step back from the door.

As the door opened, she realised all the efforts she had taken to release her tension had been in vain. Robyn White was stunning. Her blonde hair was pulled back in messy bun, blue eyes looking at her shyly. "Hi," Robyn said.

"Hey."

"Come in," Robyn said, pulling open the door fully to her suite and moving aside so Charlie could enter. As she passed her, Charlie couldn't help but reach out and tug on the hem of Robyn's hoodie.

"I'm noticing a theme," she said playfully, laughing at the 'Dolly for President' logo stamped on the front.

A cute blush crept across Robyn's face. "I'm kind of a superfan."

"You don't say!" The grin fell from Charlie's face as her gaze left the hoodie and swept around the suite. "Holy shit," she muttered. "Look at this place."

"Yeah, it's something, isn't it?" Robyn closed the door and crossed to the kitchenette. "Coffee?"

"Please. Just milk."

"Of course," Robyn replied.

As Robyn busied herself with their drinks, Charlie removed her shoes and then stood rooted to the spot, her eyes sweeping the room. The décor wasn't the over-the-top garishness that hotels sometimes went for. Instead, it was Nordic chic, all whites and greys, with splashes of colour from the plants and flowers that rested on most surfaces. Three of the most comfortable looking sofas had been placed in a u-shape around the fireplace, a sumptuous deep purple rug on the floor between them. To their left, bi-fold doors led out to a large patio area, with privacy fencing around all three sides. Planters of colour dotted the area, which was dominated by a hot tub nestled in one corner. Charlie was fairly convinced The Cedar Room came with more outdoor space than her own house. She swallowed against the nerves that rose up in her stomach as she took in all the visual reminders that she was standing in the hotel suite of an honest-to-goodness celebrity. She'd thought her room in this hotel was extravagant, but it paled in comparison to this.

"Here you go," Robyn said gently, her voice breaking into Charlie's thoughts, which had been in danger of spiralling out of control. "Shall we sit?" Robyn motioned to the sofas and Charlie followed, watching as Robyn placed one of the mugs on a coaster on an end table before crossing to the opposite sofa and repeating the motion. Charlie sank into the comfort of the couch, one leg curled beneath her and picked up her cup, wrapping her hands around it and taking a sip.

"Mmm," she moaned. "This is really good, thank you."

Robyn drank from her own mug before answering. "You're welcome."

A silence fell between them and Charlie was grateful for the coffee, needing to have something in her hands to distract her from the stillness hanging between them. She couldn't help but sneak a look at Robyn across from her. The hoodie was cute, but what really had Charlie's pulse racing was her bare feet. It seemed so ordinary and not at all what she'd expected. Even from this distance, she could see the tremble in Robyn's hands again, reminding her she wasn't the only one feeling nervous about being in the same space.

"So," she said, smiling softly at Robyn.

"So," Robyn replied, nodding. She paused, and Charlie saw her chest rise as she took what Charlie guessed was a steadying breath. She leant forward, elbows on her knees and hands tightly clasped together. "I'm gay," she announced, keeping her eyes on the floor. "But I'm not out. Well, I am to my family, but not to, you know, the world."

"Thank you for telling me." Charlie's heart pounded as she took in the enormity of what Robyn was trusting her with.

"I've known since I was in high school and I pretty much told my family right away. They've never been anything but supportive," Robyn smiled sadly, finally lifting her eyes to meet Charlie's. "I kept it quiet when I first got the *Branded* contract, but after a couple of movies, I wanted to change that. I was tired of hiding and not being able to be myself. But my agent had other ideas." Robyn closed her eyes and let out a self-deprecating laugh. "I was naïve and stupid and believed him."

"It's never easy to come out," Charlie soothed. "And having to do so globally? I can't even imagine."

"Kate and I spent a lot of time talking after the party on Saturday." She paused and looked intently at Charlie. "I can't tell you how sorry I am that I pushed you away, Charlie. I really didn't mean to hurt you."

"I know," Charlie said sincerely. "I won't pretend that you didn't, but I know it wasn't intentional."

Robyn dropped her head into her hands for a moment before running a hand through her hair and fixing Charlie with eyes filled with guilt. "I panicked and I wish to god I hadn't because that kiss..." She paused, as if searching for the words.

"I know that too," Charlie said with a smile. "It was pretty good."

"Pretty good? It was better than that, Charlie. Better than anything I've ever experienced." Charlie scoffed, laughing out loud. "I mean it," Robyn said earnestly, pushing to her feet and crossing the rug between them. She knelt in front of Charlie, took her mug from her hands, and placed it back on the end table before taking Charlie's hand in her own. "That kiss, Charlie, it was everything to me. It's made me see what I've let my life become. What I've let myself become." Without letting go of Charlie's hand, Robyn stood for moment before sitting next to her on the sofa and interlacing their fingers. "I'm 37-years-old, Charlie, and I've never had a proper relationship," she confessed. "I've hidden away, buried myself in work and tried to pretend like that's all I need. As if somehow making movie after movie could fill the aching hole in my heart."

"And now?"

"Now I know that's not enough."

Charlie searched Robyn's face, trying to get a read on what, if anything, Robyn was trying to hint at. "What does that mean?" she asked, unable to trust the feelings of hope that were building inside her.

"It means I need to make some changes. Kate and I talked about it and came up with a plan." Robyn looked across the room, searching for the words she wanted. "I want to be able to be myself, Charlie, you know? Eventually, I want a relationship, a real one. But it's going to take time. I can't change everything overnight."

When Robyn would have let go of her hand, Charlie tightened her grip. "I'm grateful that you trust me enough to tell me all of this, Robyn, but I have to ask why? You hardly know me."

"Honestly? I don't know. I just know that I can." Robyn shrugged as if it wasn't something that concerned her.

"So, asking me here this afternoon?" Charlie asked, needing to know the answer.

Robyn shrugged again. "I couldn't help myself. I hate what I did to you on Saturday and needed to put that right." She turned, and stroked Charlie's cheek with her free hand. "I am so sorry I pushed you away," she whispered. "And I never should have told you it was a mistake because it wasn't. Kissing you could never be a mistake, Charlie." She closed the gap between them and gently pressed her lips to Charlie's.

This was nothing like the lust-filled kiss from Saturday. It was soft and tender and meaningful. Charlie leaned into it, pressing closer to Robyn, feeling the warmth of her body as they leant together.

"I promise this wasn't in my plans for tonight," Robyn laughed. "I wanted to apologise, to talk to you."

"I'm not complaining," Charlie teased, pulling a laugh from Robyn.

"Me either," Robyn whispered as she leaned in again for another gentle kiss, which made Charlie feel warm to her core. "We do need to talk about this though. Things could get really messy when I come out, so I completely understand if you want to distance yourself from me."

Even though she knew Robyn was trying to look out for her, the words cut Charlie and she couldn't help but flinch from them.

"Is that what you want?" she asked, not completely certain she wanted to hear the answer.

"Not at all," Robyn said in a quiet voice. "I just know that my world is very different to yours and it's likely to become even more crazy for a while. I'm not sure any sane person would want to sign up for that."

"Do you have a plan for coming out?"

"I do."

"And does that involve you parading me in front of the press?"

Robyn shook her head vehemently. "Absolutely not."

Charlie smiled. "Good." She stole another quick kiss, needing to close the distance between them just for a few seconds. "So, we would need to be careful and take things slowly?"

"If you're okay with that?"

Charlie nodded her agreement. "I am. I actually think that would work out best for both of us. You're right when you say your world is very different to mine, so this would be a way for me to learn about how it all works without just being thrust into the limelight."

"And I would be able to work out the things I need to work out and put into action the process of announcing that I'm gay to the world." The last part came out sarcastically and Charlie made a mental note to re-visit that sometime with Robyn. If she didn't know better, she might think Robyn resented her fame.

"Well, I guess that just leaves one thing to do," Charlie said as she rose to her feet and tugged Robyn with her to the suite door. "I'm going to leave you my mobile number," she said as she wrote it down on the handy notepad the hotel had left out for guests. She'd often wondered what people used them for and now she had an answer. "When you're ready, you're going to text me so we can go on our first date." She winked at Robyn while her mind reeled at this brazen attitude that had come out of nowhere. She had never been this forward with a woman before, but she had to admit to quite liking it.

Robyn grinned and nodded, tracing a finger over the mobile number Charlie had left. "I will."

Charlie reached for the door handle and then turned, took a step into Robyn's space, cupped her cheek, and brought their mouths together. Their kiss started out as another of the gentle ones they'd already shared, but then somebody's tongue requested entrance and the other one leapt to join in; Charlie absolutely couldn't say whose had moved first, but she really didn't care. She was aware of Robyn's hands pulling their bodies together and her own hand had somehow slipped from Robyn's cheek to the back of her head and was urging them closer.

With every ounce of willpower, Charlie wrenched her mouth away, gasping, as she leaned her forehead against Robyn's. "Slow," she managed to get out between breaths. "We need to take this slow." Chest heaving, she took a step away, back towards the door. "See you tomorrow, Robyn," she said, her voice husky and laced with a passion she was desperately trying to keep a lid on. Reaching behind her, she opened the door and stepped out into the hallway.

"See you tomorrow, Charlie," Robyn echoed.

Chapter Nineteen

Robyn

It had been a week since she'd last BEEN in a room with just Charlie and now that the wait was almost over, Robyn felt nervous, and more than a smidge excited. She had agonised over the planning of their date, wanting something completely private that wouldn't be interrupted by a fan or, worse, the press, but at the same time, she didn't want Charlie to feel like she was being closeted away. In the end, she need not have worried as Charlie had expressed the same sentiment when Robyn had called her to discuss their plans. It had calmed Robyn's nerves to hear Charlie say she was looking forward to some time for just the two of them.

Not wanting to just make do with her hotel suite, Robyn had made use of the company she had booked the Oxfordshire farmhouse through, knowing they catered to exclusive clients and could be trusted not to leak anything. They had found her a small apartment in a quiet area just half an hour away from the studio, and she'd headed there as soon as they wrapped for the day.

A knock at the door signalled a fresh burst of nerves, which zinged through her body like a pinball, accompanied by a healthy side of excitement. Growing up, she'd never for one moment imagined that her first date would come at the ripe old age of 37, but, as Kate had pointed out to her in a text earlier that day, 37 was better than 47!

"Breathe," she reminded herself softly as she checked her appearance one last time in the hallway mirror before pulling open the door.

The advice was not unwarranted as Robyn was pretty sure her body had completely forgotten how to do that simple action as she drank in the vision before her. The rich plum colour of Charlie's tailored shirt made her fingers itch to touch it. Her eyes followed the buttons down the front to where they disappeared, tucked into the soft, grey dress pants Charlie wore. The strappy sandals were a similar colour to the shirt, as were Charlie's toenails. Dragging her eyes back up, over the hint of cleavage visible where the buttons had been left unfastened, Robyn's breath suddenly came rushing back as her eyes drank in the sight before her.

"Hi," Charlie said softly, a hint of amusement colouring her tone.

"Hey," Robyn managed to utter, swallowing hard around the lump in her throat, and feeling immensely proud that she had managed to form an actual word. "You look... Wow," she said, shaking her head slightly in disbelief. It had never failed to register that Charlie was an incredibly attractive woman, but tonight was on a different scale entirely, especially when she caught sight of the faint flush that crept up Charlie's exposed neck as Robyn's compliment landed.

"You look pretty wow yourself," Charlie replied with what Robyn was pretty sure was an equal amount of wonder.

They stood, looking at each other for a few more moments before Robyn remembered herself.

"Oh, god," she said hurriedly, "please, come in." She stepped back and gestured into the apartment. "Sorry, that shouldn't have taken me so long to say," she laughed, and Charlie chuckled with her.

"Don't worry about it." Charlie stepped inside, almost tentatively, and Robyn felt her nerves ease slightly as she realised she wasn't alone in being a bit off balance at the thought of their date.

Without giving herself time to think it through, Robyn closed the door and leaned into Charlie's space, running a hand down the other woman's arm, and placing a gentle kiss on her lips. It was intended as nothing more than a chaste hello, but Robyn felt the tingle all the way down to her toes.

"Hi," she whispered softly as she pulled back. "I'm so happy you're here."

"I'm happy to be here, too" Charlie replied, leaning in for a second soft kiss. "These are for you," she said, holding out a bunch of tulips that Robyn hadn't even noticed, such was her focus on drinking in Charlie. A shy blush crept across Charlie's cheeks as she waited for Robyn to take the flowers.

"They're beautiful, thank you." She took them in her right hand and slid the fingers of her left through Charlie's, entwining them, and gave a slight pull to indicate Charlie should follow her down the short hallway and into the open plan space at the end. She kept hold of Charlie's hand until she reached the sink in the kitchen and recognised the pang of disappointment she felt as she let go to take care of the flowers. The tulips were simple, pastel shades of pink and purple with some white ones dotted in between, but they immediately made the lavish bouquets she had received in the past pale into comparison. Those had been sent to impress, to cajole, to persuade, and they'd been as impersonal as they were unwanted. As she filled a jug with water and carefully placed them into it, the warmth of Charlie's gesture eased her remaining nerves.

"This room is gorgeous," Charlie said, bringing Robyn back to the moment. "I wasn't really sure what to expect when you said you were renting an apartment for the night," she added, her voice light and teasing making Robyn grin.

"Were you expecting more of a boudoir?" she asked, matching the light flirtation, and quirking an eyebrow in Charlie's direction.

"Complete with four-poster bed, velvet curtains and a cupboard full of whips and chains," Charlie deadpanned.

"Dammit, I forgot the chains," Robyn muttered, hamming it up with an overly dramatic hand to her forehead. They shared a laugh together, and Robyn thought she detected an undercurrent of a sizzle in the gaze they shared.

"It's actually a beautiful space," Charlie continued, breaking their eye contact and taking in the open-plan room. "Modern, light and airy. It's perfect," she said, returning to look at Robyn. "Thank you."

"You're welcome," Robyn smiled. "I know it's a bit weird having a first date in an apartment and I really hope you know that I have no ulterior motives at all. It's just part of the curse of who I am."

As if sensing Robyn's unease, Charlie closed the gap between them and took both of Robyn's hands in her own.

"I don't feel uncomfortable at all," she assured, squeezing Robyn's fingers to express her sincerity. "We're both miles away from our homes, so it's not like either of us could invite the other one round for the night. I don't think we would have fully relaxed using one of our rooms at the hotel, and I am certainly not ready for night out on the town with all that entails for someone with your level of fame. This is perfect, Robyn." She punctuated her words with another of the soft kisses Robyn was coming to adore, this one lingering slightly longer than those they'd shared by the front door.

Robyn freed one of her hands from Charlie's and used it to run her thumb softly along Charlie's cheek bone. "It is perfect," she agreed, her voice unexpectedly husky as she fell into that too-blue gaze. "So," she said, pulling herself together and letting her hands drop from Charlie's. "Can I get you something to drink?"

They agreed on sparkling water and carried their glasses to the table Robyn had set earlier. She had wondered whether the freesia in the stem vase and the single candle were too much for a first date, but she'd gone with it anyway, and if the look on Charlie's face was anything to go by, she'd made the right decision.

"This is beautiful, Robyn, thank you."

"It's just simple," Robyn said, dismissing the compliment, feeling slightly uncomfortable. "Nothing special."

Charlie reached across the table and covered one of Robyn's hands with her own and Robyn felt the tingle everywhere their skin touched. "It's beautiful," Charlie repeated firmly, making sure Robyn held her gaze as she said it. Robyn nodded and swallowed down the involuntary urge to disagree again. "Really beautiful," Charlie added, a soft smile lifting the corners of her mouth. She squeezed Robyn's hand and then let go, sitting back in her seat. Robyn missed her touch immediately. "So," Charlie said, a glimmer in her eye as she pinched a bit of the fresh bread Robyn had put out on their table. "Tell me how you got into this acting malarkey then."

Robyn let out a laugh, instantly feeling her discomfort dissipate.

"Malarkey is a good word for it! Some days more than others." Robyn shook her head. "I shouldn't complain, it's been very good to me."

"They don't just pay you for nothing, Robyn. I've seen you on set. I've seen how hard you work. You've earned every penny. Or every cent, I guess I should say." Charlie took another bite of the bread. "This is amazing, by the way," she said, motioning to the bread. "It's focaccia, right?"

"Yep. With rosemary and garlic."

"And I'm guessing it's not shop bought?"

"You guess correctly."

"Damn. Those are some skills you've got, Ms White. Anyway, enough distraction. Come on, tell me. How did you get into acting?"

"You really want to know?"

"I do."

"Okay, then," Robyn agreed, sipping from her glass. "It was never my plan," she began. "I had never even considered acting. Didn't audition for any parts when I was in high school. My plan was to go to college, what you call university over here," she clarified with a grin.

"I've seen enough American TV to know what college is," Charlie laughed.

"I did well in my SATs, very well actually, with a 1580, and I had a 4.0 GPA. I had applied to and been accepted to study English at Brown University. It's a pretty exclusive place and tough to get into. Kate had a place at the University of Virginia to do Elementary Education. The two schools are 500 miles apart and up until then, we'd always been together. As part of our last hurrah that summer before we started school, our parents paid for us to go to New York. When we were there, we saw some posters advertising open auditions for *Branded* and thought it would be a laugh." Robyn shrugged as she looked at Charlie. "And the rest, as they say, is history."

"Are you kidding me? You landed the main role in one of the most successful franchises of all time because you went 'for a laugh'?"

"I know. I struggled with that for a long time, actually. As you wait in line for these things, you naturally get talking to other people around you, and some of those girls had been auditioning for years, slogging their guts out to try and make the big time. And I waltz in and take something without having put in any of that graft. I spent a lot of time looking over my shoulder, waiting for someone to realise I was a complete fraud."

"I guess, at the end of the day though, the people who cast you knew what they were looking for and they saw that in you."

"Sometimes you sound just like Kate," Robyn grinned. "She told me that over and over until it eventually sunk in."

"I'm glad you have Kate. I don't mean to be rude, but your lifestyle strikes me as one that could be quite lonely. Like you're surrounded by people pretty much all the time, but those people change regularly. You don't get to be part of a long-standing team I guess is what I'm trying to say." Charlie paused and Robyn took a moment to let her words sink in, somewhat taken aback that this woman she barely knew could be so insightful. "So, if I compare it to my situation, it just couldn't be any more different. I've been going to the same building for nearly a decade-and-a-half. Some of the people I work with were there when I arrived, and yes, others have come and gone, but I can't think of anyone who was there for less than a year. You arrive on set and meet a whole bunch of new people who you're surrounded by day after day, but only for about three months and then that's it, you all head off back to where you came from and never see each other again." The look on Charlie's face was one of utter bewilderment, and Robyn couldn't stop the chuckle that escape.

"It's not quite that extreme," she countered. "When I made the *Branded* films, it was a lot of the same cast and crew each time, so that did feel like being part of a team. *Strikes Twice* is different because it's a standalone film and, yes, you're right, a lot of these people I haven't worked with before, but there are some that I kind of know. Not any friends, I guess, but at least faces that I know because our paths have crossed before."

"I don't know," Charlie said. "It just sounds so different. Don't get me wrong, I don't actually work with any of my three closest friends, but I am good friends with some of my colleagues. Not all of them though," she quipped, twisting her face into a grimace and making Robyn laugh again.

A timer sounded from the kitchen area, pulling Robyn's attention back to the moment.

"Let me just grab us some food and then I'd love to hear about those three friends, if you're happy to share?"

Charlie laughed. "I'd love to. Can I help with anything?" she asked, motioning towards the kitchen.

"Nope. You just sit there and let me wait on you," Robyn replied, leaning in for a quick kiss as she stood from her seat. As she crossed the room, she called back over her shoulder, "I made a lasagne. A vegetarian one," she qualified as she opened the oven. "I noticed at the party that you just ate the veggie dishes. I guess I should have checked, rather than just assuming." Her voice tailed off as the thought struck her for the first time.

"You are very observant," Charlie confirmed, and Robyn felt a flush of heat creep up her chest. That hadn't been the only thing she'd noticed at that party.

Giving herself a mental shake, she focused her attention back on the food, carrying their plates of lasagne and salad back across the room.

As she put in her last mouthful of lasagne, Robyn took a moment to acknowledge that all the nerves she had felt before Charlie's arrival had been a waste of energy. She didn't have to think hard at all to know she'd never felt so comfortable eating a meal with anyone outside of her family. The conversation had flowed naturally, and she'd loved hearing about Charlie's best friends, watching the way her face lit up as she talked about them. The momentary pang of envy she'd felt melted away as they laughed at their university antics. It wasn't all one-sided though. Charlie had deftly encouraged Robyn to open up about her childhood visits to Italy, what it was like being a twin, and some of her more amusing experiences on set. At no point did Robyn feel as though Charlie was trying to dig for information she would later be able to profit from, a tactic Robyn had borne witness to time and again. No, Charlie's interest seemed entirely genuine.

"That was absolutely amazing, Robyn," Charlie said gently, leaning back and patting her tummy. "If you ever decide you've had enough of Hollywood, you could easily open a restaurant. You're so talented," she smiled.

"Wait until you've had dessert!" Robyn quipped, brushing away the compliment and standing to collect their plates. "I thought we could be really naughty and eat it in front of the TV while we watch a movie."

"A Robyn White movie?" Charlie teased. At least Robyn hoped she was teasing; she absolutely did not enjoy watching her own films at all. Clearly whatever expression was on her face communicated that exact sentiment to Charlie, who laughed. "Good to know an effective torture method; I'll make sure to store that one up for another day!" As the words left her mouth, Robyn saw the dawning realisation on Charlie's face. "Not that I'm saying there will be other days, you know," she faltered and then carried on, her pace picking up even further in an attempt to climb out of the hole she was digging. "I mean, I'd like there to be other days, of course I would, I just meant that I'm not presuming and it's up to you too. Jesus," she muttered as she hung her head slightly.

Robyn honestly didn't think her own grin could be any wider. Flustered Charlie was hella hot. She moved around the table and crooked her finger under Charlie's chin, lifting her face so she could lean in, stopping just centimetres from her lips.

"There will most definitely be other days," she confirmed, her voice low and husky, and then she sank into the kind of kiss she'd been dreaming of ever since that moment in her hotel suite. Not the soft gentle type they'd shared so far this evening, but one that made her brain short circuit and then stop working altogether as she felt the gentle pressure of Charlie's tongue playing across her lips before taking advantage of Robyn's slight gasp and slipping inside. The gentleness of Charlie's fingers as they crept up her arm, across her shoulder and into her hair, the other hand a gentle force at her hip.

"Jesus, indeed," Robyn muttered as she drew her lips back, leaning her forehead against Charlie's, trying to quell her hammering heart.

As if sensing she need a moment, Charlie didn't respond immediately. Her hand slid out of Robyn's hair, and she gently trailed it up and down her arm instead, the sensation gentle and calming rather than arousing. When Robyn finally opened her eyes, the smile on Charlie's face and the sparkle in her blue eyes told Robyn she wasn't the only one enjoying their moment. If she was honest, it was all a little overwhelming and she had to take a steadying breath. This was like nothing she'd ever experienced, and if she let it, her anxiety would sweep in and take control.

As if she could sense it, Charlie softly squeezed Robyn's bicep and spoke, breaking the intensity of their stare.

"I'm pretty sure you said something about dessert and a movie," her words the balm Robyn desperately needed.

Chapter Twenty

Robyn

Warmth. Glorious, all-encompassing, warmth. That was the first thing that registered for Robyn. A warmth that wrapped around her, permeated her skin, and settled itself inside, its tendrils softly licking the length and breadth of her entire body. It emanated from Robyn's right-hand side, and blossomed outward, sending with it the sense of calm that had frustrated her in the mindfulness meditation classes she'd once attended with Kate, who had convinced her to try them as a means of combatting her anxiety. It hadn't worked, but at this moment in time, she struggled to even remember what that state of anxiousness felt like. Blinking open her eyes, she dimly registered the TV playing quietly in the background, as most of her attention was focused on the brunette curled into her side, head tucked against Robyn's shoulder. It was exquisite, this feeling of absolute contentment, and she allowed her eyelids to drift closed and took in the deepest breath she'd taken in years. This was right.

The second thing to register was longing, a deep longing that went beyond her body and into her soul. A dull throb ached between her legs and as she acknowledged it, she felt her nipples harden. So, this would be the infamous lust she'd heard so much about. She wanted Charlie with an intensity that took her breath away. Swallowing hard, she leaned down and placed a gentle kiss on Charlie's forehead, part of her hoping she'd awaken and the more timid part wanting her to remain asleep.

Blue eyes blinked slowly, slightly unfocused at first and then rapidly clearing as they registered Robyn's proximity. The usual too-blue darkened, the pupils dilating, and what had been a dull throb between Robyn's legs stood up and demanded attention. Her chest heaved, heart thrummed, and breath quickened. She couldn't have even tried to guess at how long they stayed like that, neither of them moving, barely even blinking, and then suddenly, stillness was the last thing they had.

Their mouths came together, crashed together really, and it was wet and messy and so damn perfect. Robyn couldn't touch enough of Charlie, but suddenly that didn't matter because Charlie was in her lap, straddling her, a knee either side of Robyn's hips and there was absolutely nothing for Robyn to do but wrap her arms around Charlie's, hands on her ass, and pull her even closer. The frantic kissing broke momentarily as Charlie leaned back and pulled off her shirt, not bothering to unbutton it and treating it like a t-shirt. Robyn could have pressed pause then, to take in the vision before her, but she didn't get the opportunity because Charlie pressed back in and captured her mouth with an intensity that left Robyn in little doubt as to who was in charge. Charlie's hands seemed to be everywhere: in Robyn's hair, trailing lightly across her collar bone, scraping against her abs through her top, skimming over her breasts, cupping her face. God, it was too much, and then it wasn't enough.

Robyn's own hands suddenly seemed to realise there was now naked flesh in front of them and they moved from Charlie's ass to her back with lightning speed. As she touched Charlie's skin for the first time, someone moaned, maybe Charlie, maybe Robyn herself. It really didn't matter. One hand splayed across Charlie's lower back and the other trailed up to Charlie's shoulder, desperately trying to urge their bodies closer, as if that were even possible right now. The hand at Charlie's back slipped to her hip and tugged with urgency, wanting something to satisfy the raging ache at her centre. Robyn's hips took on a life of their own, bucking and thrashing, frantically seeking contact.

And then Charlie's lips were gone, and she was pushing back, away from Robyn.

"God, I'm so sorry," she said. "I didn't even ask if you were okay with this," she managed to get out in between ragged breaths.

"Do I seem like I'm not okay?" Robyn asked, her hands holding Charlie firmly in place on her lap. "Do I seem like I'm not right here in the moment with you?" she asked, her eyes searching Charlie's. "Do I seem like I don't want this, don't want you, just as much as you want me?"

"But I promised you we would go slowly," Charlie said quietly, tracing her thumb across Robyn's cheekbone. "And going from being asleep against your shoulder to writhing around on your lap in a matter of seconds is hardly going slow."

"Fuck slow," Robyn husked, leaning in to try to re-capture Charlie's lips, giving a growl of frustration when the brunette leaned back, just out of reach.

"I'm being serious, Robyn," Charlie countered, brushing a strand of her hair behind her ear. "I made a promise and that matters to me."

"It matters to me too," Robyn promised. "And it matters to me more than you'll ever know that you had the heart to try and stop this, but you have to believe me when I tell you that I don't need you to stop. I don't want you to stop, Charlie."

"And what if that's just you being swept up in the moment, being dragged along by lust? I know that this is important to you, Robyn, and I want to get it right, to make it perfect."

"This is perfect, Charlie. You are perfect. This whole night has been perfect. For the first time in my life, I'm ready for this, Charlie. That's how perfect it is. I have never been on this precipice before, not once. I've always held a part of myself back, known exactly where my boundaries are and never come close to crossing them." She paused for a moment, gathering herself. "I don't know what it is about you, Charlie Evans, but those boundaries have melted away."

She leaned in again, and this time Charlie didn't move away. The kiss they shared had none of the frenzy from a few moments ago, though Robyn knew that simmered just below the surface. This kiss was full of unspoken promises, and Robyn knew that this time there'd be no stopping.

"As far as I can see, there's just one problem," Charlie murmured between kisses, her tone warm and teasing.

"Tell me and we can find a solution."

"I seem to be the only missing some clothing."

"Then maybe you should do something about that," Robyn whispered, loving the sense of confidence that flooded her system. It didn't matter anymore that she was the novice in the room. Charlie made her feel powerful, like for once she got to direct the scene rather than just participate.

"God, you're so sexy like this," Charlie ground out, her fingers reaching for the hem of Robyn's top and tugging upwards impatiently, drawing a chuckle from Robyn. "I take that back," Charlie moaned as her eyes greedily drank in the sight before her. "You're so sexy like this," she said, emphasising the last word as she sank back down against Robyn, skin-to-skin for the first time.

"This needs to come off," Robyn said, fumbling with the clasp of Charlie's bra. She was pretty sure she'd have worked out how to open it eventually, but without breaking their kiss, Charlie slid her own hands around her back and popped the clasp.

"They're fiddly little buggers," she said before sucking Robyn's bottom lip, running her tongue along it, and then sinking back into their kisses.

Being able to roam her hands from shoulder to lower back without any material interruptions, poured oil on Robyn's already burning core. Without any conscious thought, she pushed to her feet, hands beneath Charlie's ass, holding her in place, and, without breaking their kiss, turned so she could lie Charlie back on the couch, her turn to be on top. She'd probably have been pretty impressed with her manoeuvre if she weren't just utterly desperate to see Charlie before her. She broke their kiss and sat back for a moment. Her desire kicked up another notch as she drank in Charlie's perfectly formed breasts and wasted no time in acquainting herself with them. Her touch was far from tentative as she stroked her thumb across the already puckered nipple, her lips kissing gently beneath Charlie's jaw. As they made their way down her neck and across her collar bone, she felt the hitch in Charlie's breath and increased the stroke of her thumb, adding her forefinger and rolling Charlie's nipple between them. Charlie's back arched and something mostly unintelligible fell from her lips. Robyn felt Charlie's hands on her back, encouraging her. She sucked and licked her way down from Charlie's collarbone, wanting to take her time to explore, but not having the willpower to do so, not when the destination was so close.

"Good god," Charlie moaned as Robyn's tongue circled her nipple, and she let out a throaty moan as Robyn closed her lips around the sensitive bud and sucked, lightly at first and then as Charlie's hands moved into her hair, pulling Robyn's head closer, she sucked more firmly. She loved the immediate response of Charlie's hips, bucking into her own and worried for a moment that she might set a new record for the fastest orgasm ever as she ground back into the woman beneath her.

Although, suddenly, Charlie wasn't underneath her anymore, she was on top, and somehow, as she'd reversed their positions, she'd also managed to divest Robyn of her bra, a fact that seared itself into Robyn's brain as they came breast to breast for the first time and Charlie claimed her mouth. The power she'd revelled in moments ago had been ripped away from her and nothing could have made her happier.

Despite their bodies being practically melded together, Charlie had somehow managed to get her hand between them and was returning the exquisite torture Robyn has bestowed on her. Robyn had no idea how the direct connection between her nipple and her core had so suddenly been established but established it had been. Warmth and wetness flooded her jeans, and she knew no matter how much she wanted to draw this out, she wasn't going to last much longer.

Wrenching her mouth from Charlie's, she drew in a ragged breath and resorted to begging.

"Please, Charlie. God, I need you."

"Patience, darling," Charlie whispered in her ear, licking the shell of it before sliding her lips lower and settling to feast on Robyn's nipple.

It was too much. It was not enough.

"Charlie," she moaned, not able to recognise herself in the throaty sound. "Please," she tried again, resulting only in a hearty chuckle from her lover.

"Patience," Charlie repeated, as she moved her lips away from Robyn's nipple and swirled her tongue in an intricately infuriatingly slow pattern down the sensitive skin of Robyn's side, nipping gently here and there, before moving to her stomach. The hand that had continued to play with Robyn's nipple now moved and Robyn felt its absence keenly, only to rejoice in its movement a second later when it landed on the button of her jeans. As if she could somehow influence its intent, Robyn surged her hips against it, but it remained still.

Opening eyes she didn't even know she'd closed, Robyn gazed down the length of her body into blue eyes that were waiting for her to meet them. She watched as Charlie took a steadying breath and relished in knowing she wasn't the only one struggling to hold on.

"Are you absolutely certain?" Charlie asked gently, the look in her eyes making Robyn temporarily unable to respond. This wonderful woman, who wanted her so badly, would stop now if Robyn asked her to. And she knew without doubt that Charlie would do so without making her feel even the slightest bit guilty.

"I am beyond certain," she replied, proud of the fact her voice came out without a waver. She hadn't even known if she'd be able to form words, never mind string a coherent sentence together, she was so far gone. "I want this. I want you. I want you to take me."

The hunger in Charlie's eyes was enough to steal Robyn's breath. And then Charlie's lips were back on her stomach and her hand was finally popping open the button. A sigh of relief escaped Robyn, quickly followed by a sharp inhale of breath as Charlie's tongue followed the route that Robyn's jeans took, down over her hips, torturously slowly down her thighs to her knees, on down past her calves, ankles, and feet. It wasn't until Charlie's tongue had languorously made its journey back up over the expanse of her skin that Robyn realised it wasn't just her jeans that had been removed; her panties had gone too, and Charlie's warm breath was coming tantalisingly close to her centre.

And then it was gone.

And somehow Charlie's lips were back on hers.

And Robyn thought she might come undone completely as she felt Charlie's fingers glide up the inside of her thigh, come so, so close to where she desperately wanted them, ghost over her centre.

And then they were gone too, and Charlie's lips left hers, her body moved away.

Robyn's eyes flew open, panic creeping in that she'd done something wrong, and then immediately fleeing as she took in Charlie removing her own trousers, pushing them down frantically, before sliding her gloriously naked body back up over Robyn's and sinking into a deep kiss.

Then Charlie was off again, taking her time as she moved her mouth lower, and somehow, this time, Robyn just knew, she wouldn't alter her course, wouldn't stop until Robyn had burst into a million pieces.

When Charlie's tongue finally reached her centre, the storm that had been raging inside Robyn suddenly stopped; tranquillity spread through every nerve ending and she knew without doubt that it had all been worth waiting for. Charlie had been worth waiting for.

And then, a tiny flick of Charlie's tongue against her most sensitive nerves triggered a tsunami and waves of pleasure flooded against a backdrop of the most guttural noise Robyn had ever heard, a noise she realised was coming from her own throat. As she crested and her pleasure peaked, her hands reached for Charlie's head, simultaneously wanting to hold her in place forever and wrench her away. The feeling from before was back: it was too much; it wasn't enough. And it was perfect.

Chapter Twenty-One

Charlie

Excitement buzzed through Charlie's veins, her pulse pounding in her ears. It had been four days since she'd seen Robyn. Four horrifically long and lonely days since they'd woken up, limbs and bed sheets tangled together. Four days since they had spent the morning making love, still not satiated despite their marathon from the night before. If it had felt like Robyn was trying to make up for lost time with her sex life, Charlie certainly wasn't going to be the one doing any complaining.

If she'd known when she kissed Robyn goodbye that afternoon that she'd have to wait four whole days to see her again, she would have taken her time. Not that their kiss hadn't lingered, morphed from singular into god-knew how many, but it still wasn't enough.

They'd had plans to meet again earlier in the week, but there'd been some kind of issue on set that meant Robyn couldn't get away when she wanted to and had been stuck there into the wee hours. Charlie had an early lesson the next morning, so they'd had to postpone, agreeing to wait until Friday night.

But today, Thursday, Charlie had a lunchtime lesson planned with Lucy, squeezing it in between morning and afternoon filming, and Brittany had asked if she minded coming to the studio earlier than planned to save Jonny an extra shuttle between Pinewood and the hotel. Charlie had tried her best not to appear too excited at the thought of being able to see Robyn in her element. The slightly quizzical look Brit had flashed her way suggested Charlie hadn't been as nonchalant as she'd hoped.

Now, as Brit pushed through the doors and onto the set, Charlie gave up any pretence of calmness. Granted, she wouldn't be able to greet Robyn with a kiss, to let her hand rest against her lower back, brush an errant strand of hair off her face, but she would be able to drink her in, to let her eyes roam over every millimetre of her skin, to gaze into those eyes that held such bottomless emotion.

The soundstage was a hive of activity, people toing and froing with evident determination and focus. As Britt crossed the room and fell into discussion with Jeanie, Charlie sought out a quiet space a good distance behind the cameras. Lizzie caught her eye and Charlie returned her wave and mouthed "hello" before the writer turned back to a discussion she'd been having with Kevin and Peter, the latter's hands clearly demonstrating what he was hoping to get from the scene.

Charlie turned her attention to the set itself, wondering which part of the novel they were filming today. It was pretty obvious from the backdrop and props that this was the Art Club, the one hobby Freya had for herself, and the place she met Grace. A surge of something that she thought might be pride, settled in Charlie's stomach. She knew the risks Robyn was taking by agreeing to the new storyline, but the actress seemed to have taken it all in her stride and Charlie knew she would never give anything other than 100% to the role.

Turning her head to the door to the soundstage, Charlie immediately located the source of the energy surge she'd just felt pulsate through the room. Robyn had arrived, and with that, everyone seemed to lift their game a little, as if they felt they needed to raise their standards a little more now that the main star was here.

And good god, was she a star. She exuded confidence as she walked through the space, greeting everyone by name, making people laugh, smiling and relaxed. It was a sight to behold, and Charlie couldn't help but stand a little taller, a little straighter, improve her posture, as if she too were caught in the wave. Of course, all of this would have been slightly easier to accomplish if her heart weren't hammering its way out of her chest and her core hadn't suddenly morphed into molten lava. Gods, what she wouldn't give to be able to stride across the room and throw herself into Robyn's arms. Instead, she turned her gaze away, drew in a steadying breath and pulled her phone out of her pocket, checking for the forty-seventh time that it was on silent.

"Okay, people," a loud voice boomed around the set. "Let's get this scene rolling." Peter Fletcher grinned as he spoke, and an almost reverent hush fell over the room. "So, as a quick reminder, Freya has been coming to Art Club for a few months now, and that's where she met Grace. Today we're filming one of the new scenes, written for us by our amazing team of scriptwriters," he added with a flourish, pointing towards Lizzie and Kevin. Charlie loved the mix of excitement and embarrassment that flushed Lizzie's face. "Let's see what they've got for us!"

Charlie couldn't help it. Her gaze was drawn back to Robyn, following her as she settled herself onto the set, absently running her fingers over some of the art equipment. Even though her costume was decidedly Freya, there was still something quintessentially Robyn about her, which Charlie knew was a ridiculous thing to think, because of course she was still Robyn. But the longer she watched her, the more those pieces of Robyn fell away until Charlie felt she was truly looking at Freya.

Freya, whose eyes tracked Grace's movements around the Art Club as she pottered about, tidying up after the members who had just left. Freya, who now left

152

the easel she'd been working at and slowly made her way across to where Grace was sorting through paintbrushes. Freya who leant back against the bench next to Grace, too close to Grace in Charlie's opinion. Freya who dropped her gaze and spoke quietly.

"It's not just me, is it?" she asked, her voice timid, her eyes raking over Grace's profile. Grace's eyes didn't leave the brushes. "Grace?" Freya prompted, turning so her hand could cover Grace's, stopping her from continuing her nervous sorting. "If it is, tell me, and I can die of embarrassment and then we can pretend this conversation never happened," Freya laughed, and finally Grace put the brushes down and turned to face Freya.

"It's not just you," Grace whispered softly, her fingers coming to cup Freya's cheek.

"Cut!" Peter yelled, and Charlie jumped, so sucked in by the scene that she'd forgotten that's what it was: a scene. "Let's run that again."

And they did, a few more times, until seemingly Peter was happy with what he'd seen.

"Okay," Peter called. "Let's roll further through this time. Ladies, we'll just start from the same place, but this time I won't interrupt. Well, I might not," he chuckled.

This time, when Grace made her announcement, Freya's face spilt into a radiant smile and she reached up, covering Grace's hand with her own, pulling it down and intertwining their fingers.

"Well, that's a relief," she chuckled. "For a moment there, I thought you were going to tell me I was imagining things." Freya paused, and a look passed between them. "So, would you maybe like to go out to dinner sometime?" she asked, a slight tremor in her voice giving away her nerves. "You know, like on a date?"

"I would," Grace replied, her own smile slightly tighter and not quite reaching her eyes. And Charlie marvelled again at just how good an actress Robyn was, certainly in a different league to Mary Kane, whose portrayal of Grace was growing stiffer by the second.

"Cut!" Peter yelled again, and Charlie thought it was probably a timely intervention.

As Peter huddled in to talk to Mary, no doubt trying to warm her up a bit, Robyn wandered away from them and turned to look out into the space beyond the cameras. Charlie knew the exact moment Robyn spotted her there in the darkness, a wash of arousal coating over her as a warmth settled low in her stomach and her mouth involuntarily lifted into a small smile.

It faltered though when the look wasn't mirrored on Robyn's face. In fact, the way Robyn's brows drew in and her mouth pursed, Charlie got the distinct impression she was unimpressed to see Charlie there. Before Charlie could begin to interpret things any further, Robyn turned on her heel and strode towards Jeanie, her assistant. Charlie's heart picked up as she watched Robyn pull a page from Jeanie's notebook, scribble something on it, fold the paper over and then pass it to Jeanie with a curt instruction. Robyn's eyes never once glanced back in Charlie's direction. Instead, she turned her back and strode onto the set, looking intently at Peter and Mary who seemed to be finishing up their conversation.

Charlie's heart sank as Jeanie moved towards her, lips pressed in a firm line.

"Ms Evans," she said, her tone absolutely professional. "A moment please." She signalled with her hand towards the exit and waited for Charlie's leaden feet to make their way across the room. This was not going to be good.

As soon as they were on the other side of the doors, Jeanie held out the note, her eyes not quite able to meet Charlie's. The moment Charlie's fingers took hold of it, Jeanie was gone, heading straight back onto set and leaving Charlie alone in the corridor.

There was no name on either side of the note, not that there needed to be for Charlie to know she was the intended recipient. She just stood there, looking at it, as if by not opening it, she could somehow delay the inevitable. But, a rational part of her argued, the contents weren't going to change, no matter how long she stood there, no matter how hard she willed them to. Might as well bite the bullet and move on.

Fingers shaking, she slowly opened the piece of paper, pressing a hand over her mouth to stifle the gasp the words drew from her.

You can't be here.
You need to leave.

No greeting, no use of her name, no use of Robyn's name. Just a cold, clear directive.

A sob escaped and Charlie pressed her lips tightly together, blinking ferociously to hold back the tears threatening to escape. How could she have been so stupid? How could she possibly have thought for one moment that a global superstar would have the slightest interest in her? Of course, Robyn wouldn't want her on set, wouldn't want her anywhere near. Everything about Charlie threatened the stability of the life Robyn had built. Everyone knew Charlie was gay, so obviously Robyn would be worried about any associations between the two of them. God, she was such an idiot. She should have known it was nothing more than curiosity on Robyn's behalf, and now that it was out of her system, she was done with Charlie. Dismissed. Pushed aside. Discarded.

At some point, Charlie's feet had started to move, and she found herself pushing through the main doors and heading to where Jonny usually parked. She fumbled her phone out of her pocket and sent Brittany a text.

Charlie: Could you let Lucy know I need to cancel please? Migraine. Heading back to the hotel now.

Reaching Jonny's car, she uttered the same excuse and settled back against the cool leather interior, using the box breathing she'd learned at yoga to keep her emotions in check for the journey. Her phone buzzed in her hand.

Brittany: Of course. Hope you're okay. Will check on you later.

Charlie shut off her phone, closed her eyes and leaned back. Brittany probably knew she was lying. Jeanie would no doubt have told her that Robyn had instructed her to leave. Great, just what she needed. Her humiliation being made public. All she wanted was to curl up somewhere and disappear. She put her phone back on and pulled up The Velociraptor's number. Her finger hovered over the call button, desperately wanting to press it and make it clear that she wanted to return to school. But what would she say? I slept with Hollywood Royalty and now she doesn't want me? I may have gone and fallen for the star of the film, but it turns out an English teacher isn't quite what she's looking for? Shaking her head, she put her phone away. There was nothing she could do, no way out of the situation. Sighing, she turned and gazed out the window at the passing countryside.

Just because she needed to stay, didn't mean she had to see Robyn again. She could try to organise as many of Lucy's lessons as possible to take place at the hotel, and on the odd occasion she did need to go to Pinewood, she wouldn't venture any further than her classroom. There was no need for her to be on set. No need to use the canteen. No need to be anywhere that might lead her to cross Robyn's path.

"We're here, Charlie," Jonny said quietly, his voice breaking into Charlie's thought.

"Thank you," she replied, and tried to muster something that might pass for a smile.

Charlie lay on her bed, exactly where she'd been for the past four hours, ever since she'd arrived back. Multiple times she'd tried to convince herself to move, to do some yoga, lose herself in lesson planning, take a bath, go for a run. And yet, here she lay, utterly exhausted from the mental gymnastics she'd been doing. Blaming herself, blaming Robyn, being angry, being sad, frustrated. Now she just lay, wondering quite how she'd managed to get herself into such a mess. She'd had one night with Robyn, and yes, it had been spectacular, but it was still only one night. Before that, they'd kissed twice, so why did she feel like her heart had been ripped out and put through a blender, leaving her with an aching hole where it used to be?

Charlie never fell this quickly. She was always stoic about relationships, especially in the early days of getting to know each other and figure out their compatibility. She had always led with her head, never her heart, despite Lauren's pleas for her to do so. And now that she had, look at her. She was practically comatose in a hotel room, a billion miles away from home and all on her own. What was it about Robyn that had her acting so differently? Feeling so differently?

With a sigh, she reached for her phone.

Charlie: This is all your fault. I hope you're happy.

The dots told her a reply was imminent.

Laur: Any chance at all I could get a clue as to what you're talking about?

Charlie: This. This absolute misery. This bone-deep, all-encompassing, utter misery.

There might have been some slight exaggeration in that, but Charlie was feeling melodramatic.

A sudden sharp knock at her door broke into her pathos and she groaned. Another knock, even sharper this time. Probably Brittany coming to check on her. She sighed and forced herself to move, muscles complaining that they had to do something other than sink into the mattress. Another knock and she pulled the door open more forcefully than she'd intended to, ready to explain to Brittany that banging on the door of a migraine sufferer wasn't best practice.

She never got the chance.

No sooner was the door open, than a whirlwind of blonde was surging inside, pushing Charlie backwards, flinging the door shut, and pressing Charlie against the wall. Lips crashed against hers and Charlie had to fight to get her hands against the body writhing against her own, to push that body away, to look into Robyn's lust-filled eyes and take in her heaving chest.

"What the fuck are you doing?" she demanded, holding out her hands to ward Robyn off when it seemed she would try to step back in.

"Isn't it obvious?" Robyn moaned, trying to press past Charlie's hands and sink back into their previous position.

"I'm serious, Robyn. What the fuck is going on?"

Whether it was the tone of her voice, the expression on her face, or her defensive body language, Charlie didn't know, but something seemed to get through to Robyn and she faltered, stepped back, a quizzical look on her face.

"Charlie?" she asked, as if not understanding what was happening.

"Don't Charlie me, Robyn," Charlie replied tersely, pushing away from the wall, and walking further into her room to give herself some space.

"Did something happen?" Robyn asked, concern evident on her face. "Are you okay?" She seemed to take Charlie in for the first time. "Have you been crying?"

"Of course, I've been crying," Charlie replied in exasperation, throwing her hands in the air. "What exactly did you expect me to do? Brush it off and just move on or worse still, pretend it never happened? Well, we're not all like that, Robyn, you know." Her arms crossed defensively against her body and her jaw clamped shut.

Robyn's gaze swung wildly about the room, as if looking for some sort of hint as to what was going on. How she could be so clueless was beyond Charlie. Was she for real?

"Charlie," Robyn said softly, taking a tentative step towards her and immediately stopping when Charlie held up a hand. "I don't understand, babe. You're scaring me right now. It's obvious that you're not okay, but I don't know what's going on." Her use of the endearment only fuelled Charlie's rage.

"This, Robyn," she spat, pulling the note from her back pocket, and flinging it at Robyn. "You made your feelings abundantly clear in that," she said, pointing a finger at the piece of paper Robyn was bending down to retrieve from where it had fallen. "Your dismissal was received loud and clear. I did exactly what you asked and then you turn up here, barge into my room and try to molest me? What. The. Fuck. Robyn?" Charlie raged, every emotion she'd felt since first reading that note combining into a maelstrom of pure anger that burned through her. Charlie, the level-headed one amongst her friends, the one who never showed any emotion too extreme.

The cloud of confusion cleared from Robyn's face as she opened the note, and then understanding dawned before being replaced with something Charlie was pretty sure was devastation, with a healthy dose of shame.

"It's not... I didn't..." Her voice trailed off as tears filled her eyes. Robyn shook her head and slowly crossed the room to sink onto the sofa, leaning her head back and closing her eyes. Charlie tightened her arms around herself, determined to hold onto her anger and not be tempted by the utter defeat etched onto Robyn's face. "Mary is the worst actress I have ever worked with," Robyn announced, the non sequitur catching Charlie off guard. "I'd get more from working with a cardboard cut-out."

"Interesting," Charlie said sarcastically. "But I'm not sure that's entirely relevant right now," she added, her impatience getting the better of her.

"It is entirely relevant," Robyn whispered, the tears finally spilling over to course down her cheeks.

She made no move to wipe them away and a small voice in the back of Charlie's mind reminded her she was standing opposite one of the world's best actresses and this could all be for show. She almost winced as soon as the thought fully formed, knowing she was doing Robyn a disservice, but she needed her anger to stay in place. She was not a plaything to the rich and famous, thank you very much.

"You're going to have to explain."

Robyn nodded. "I know." She smiled softly at Charlie, glanced down at the note, shook her head, and looked back at Charlie. "Mary's terrible and she very clearly does not want the film to go in the direction it's being taken. I don't know whether it's the lesbian storyline in general that's the problem, or whether it's the lesbian being me." She shrugged. "But whichever it is, she doesn't like it, and she can't pretend she does. At least, she can't to me. And for Freya to fall in love with Grace, she has to feel it. I have to feel it," she added on a whisper. Robyn paused, swallowed hard and looked Charlie right in the eye. "So, I pretend she's you. Every scene we're in together, every longing gaze, flirtatious comment, or lingering touch I have to do, I don't see Mary. In my mind, I see you."

"Me?" Charlie asked, her voice coming out as more of a squeak than she'd have liked, pulling a gentle smile from Robyn.

"Yes, you. And today," she faltered. "Today was their first kiss, which I was absolutely dreading for a whole multitude of reasons we don't need to get into right now, but I'd convinced myself it would be okay if I just made it about you. If I got to kiss you. And it was going okay, pretty well actually, until I saw you, standing there watching me, with that adorable look on your face. And I knew that I couldn't do it. I couldn't pretend you were Grace if the real you were watching. I couldn't forget it was Mary Bloody Kane I was having to kiss and not you if you were inhabiting the same space as her."

She paused again, as if looking to see if her words were reaching their intended mark. Whatever she saw on Charlie's face must have convinced her one way or the other as she continued.

"Charlie, I couldn't kiss Mary with you there, because I wanted to be kissing you so badly I almost strode across that room and planted one on you. I couldn't kiss another woman with you standing there and not worry about how that made you feel." She motioned between them. "This is all so new, and I didn't want to jeopardise it by making you watch me kiss someone else. I didn't know how that would make you feel, and I couldn't have risked coming across to check with you because I was so turned on, I wouldn't have been able to resist kissing you, and I don't think either of us is ready for that kind of announcement yet."

The smile reached her eyes this time and she pushed onto shaky legs, taking a step towards Charlie but still respecting her space. "When I wrote this, I wasn't thinking clearly, and I forget, I forget that even though at times it feels like you can, you can't actually read my mind, or read between the lines in this case." She looked down at the letter in her hand again. "I thought you'd understand, Charlie, that you'd know exactly what I meant and why I was asking. It was a rushed scribble, and I should have known better. I'm so sorry."

Charlie stood for a moment, letting Robyn's words sink in, letting them wash over her.

"There's a strong chance my own insecurities didn't help," she admitted quietly, taking a step towards Robyn. "I think a part of me was waiting for you to change your mind, to say you'd explored your curiosities and were moving on." At the look of hurt on Robyn's face, Charlie quickly continued. "Nothing you said or did ever made me think that Robyn. It's all up here," she said, tapping the side of her head. "Why would a beautiful, rich, successful, sexy as all hell superstar, be interested in a boring English teacher?" She tried to laugh it off, but it sounded hollow even to her.

Robyn took the final step to close the distance between them, a gentle thumb wiping away the tear Charlie hadn't realised had escaped.

"Maybe because that woman is the kindest, most passionate person the superstar has ever met? Maybe because that woman makes the superstar feel things she hadn't even dreamed were possible? Makes her want to be braver than ever before? Makes her feel things with an intensity that almost causes her to forget how to breathe?"

Somehow, as Robyn had spoken, their bodies had inched closer and closer together, their faces so close Charlie could feel Robyn's breath tickle across her skin.

"Well, I suppose when you put it like that," Charlie muttered, the rest of her sentence lost as their lips came together again. The animalistic passion Robyn had launched at her on arrival was gone, and Charlie couldn't help but smile at what was left in its wake. Something deeper, something she wasn't quite ready to name just yet.

Chapter Twenty-Two

Charlie

Charlie groaned loudly as the incessant knocking on her hotel door finally broke through into her consciousness.

"Make it stop," Robyn muttered beside her, and Charlie chuckled despite the rude awakening. Pressing a gentle kiss to Robyn's temple, she clambered out of bed and pulled on a hotel robe.

"The place better be on fire," she grumbled as she pulled open the door, squinting into the light of the hallway.

"Oh, so you're alive then?" Lauren asked testily, arching an eyebrow and bringing a hand to her hip. "Alive but incapable of texting for what reason exactly?" she demanded.

"Lauren?" Charlie asked, the sight of her best friend far too much for her sleep-addled brain to wrap itself around. "Lauren?"

"We've established that already," her friend replied testily, as she shoved her way past Robyn into the room. "You leave me with some bullshit message about misery and then don't reply, don't pick-up. What did you expect? That I wouldn't get into my car and drive god-knows how many miles into the wee hours of the morning to check that you weren't dead?"

"Oh, god, Lauren, I'm so sorry," Charlie replied, finally remembering the text conversation she'd been having with Lauren before Robyn had arrived. "I got distracted," she mumbled, trying to figure out a way to get Lauren out of her hotel room without appearing to be the rudest person on the planet.

"Distracted?" Lauren practically screeched, making Charlie wince. "What the hell distracted you so completely that you didn't check your phone and managed to forget that you'd pretty much announced you were feeling suicidal?" Her chest heaved with the anger Charlie knew her friend was right to feel.

"I think that might have been me," said a small voice, as Robyn sheepishly made her way around the corner from the sleeping area, looking utterly adorable with her blonde hair a ravished mess and wearing nothing but the bed sheet.

Lauren whirled in the direction of the voice and Charlie might have laughed at the look of astonishment on her friend's face if she wasn't already in enough trouble. Lauren's mouth hung comically open and her head swung between Charlie and Robyn, obviously trying to put together the pieces of a puzzle she hadn't been expecting to need to solve.

"Lauren, this is Robyn. Robyn, this is my best friend, Lauren," Charlie said, hoping her voice sounded more confident than she felt.

"Lovely to meet you," Robyn said sincerely, crossing the room and holding out her hand for Lauren to shake, which her friend did, albeit with a sense of disbelief etched on her face. "Charlie's told me so much about you."

"It's really lovely to meet you, too," Lauren managed to get out, her voice only shaking slightly, which Charlie thought was admirable given the situation. "Charlie clearly hasn't told me nearly enough about you," she said, arching that damn eyebrow again and fixing Charlie with a look that told her she was in all sorts of trouble.

Robyn blushed and clutched the sheet more tightly to her chest.

"I'm guessing you've probably had a long drive, so if you give me a second to get into something more," she paused, looking down at the sheet before adding, "more clothes-like, I'll get out of your hair. Give you a chance to catch up," she added before turning on her heel and disappearing around the corner.

Lauren immediately swung to Charlie, who held up a finger.

"I need one minute with her, Laur. One minute and then I promise, I'm all yours." Charlie thought for a moment that Lauren might argue with her, but in the end she nodded softly.

"Take all the time you need. I'm going to get my bag out of the car," she added, before turning to leave.

Charlie sucked in a deep breath and ran a hand through her hair, steeling herself for Robyn's response as she made her way back towards the bed that had been their haven for the past few hours.

What she didn't expect when she rounded the corner, was to find Robyn sitting on the edge of the bed, trying to hold back what to Charlie's mind looked like a fit of giggles. She'd expected outrage, maybe tears, definitely something resembling concern at being outed. She did not expect laughter.

"Oh my god," Robyn managed to gasp out between breaths. "I'm guessing this is what teenagers feel like when they get caught by their parents?" She dissolved again into a peal of laughter, clutching her sides. "I thought she was going to tear me a new one and ground me," she laughed.

"I think she's saving that for me," Charlie replied. "Seriously though, Robyn. Are you okay? I'm so sorry about this."

"Of course, I'm okay," she said with a grin. "Kate is going to lose her shit when I tell her about this." Robyn's giggles took over again, and Charlie watched, slightly unsure how to handle this. Clearly Robyn was hysterical. Surely, she couldn't actually find the situation funny?

"Robyn," she began, using her serious teacher voice for good measure. "I'm serious. This is a big deal and I need to know that you're okay."

That seemed to sober Robyn and she looked at Charlie as if it were only just occurring to her that she was being serious.

"Charlie, I'm absolutely fine, I promise you. Why wouldn't I be?" she asked, her eyes searching Charlie's, her confusion genuine.

"Maybe because you were just outed to someone?"

"To someone who is your best friend," Robyn clarified. "Who has been your best friend for nearly twenty years. Someone I'm guessing that means you trust implicitly?" Her voice was so steady, so sure, it took Charlie by surprise.

"Well, yes, but..."

"It's okay, Charlie," Robyn assured her. "It hadn't even crossed my mind that Lauren might run off to the press until you went all weird on me. She's not going to do that, babe. Not after she's driven through the night to check on you." She paused, taking Charlie's hand and giving it a gentle squeeze. "And that was my fault, remember, so it should be me checking on you. I'm so sorry I hurt you yesterday."

"It's okay," Charlie said, and it really, really was. She leaned in and gently kissed, Robyn. "I wasn't concerned about Lauren going to the press, she absolutely wouldn't do that. I just wasn't sure how comfortable you were with this," she motioned between them. "I didn't know if you'd told anyone and I thought you might freak out that Lauren knew."

Robyn's brows drew together.

"You mean she didn't know already? You hadn't told her? Hadn't told your other best friends either?"

Charlie shook her head. "You and I hadn't talked about it and I didn't want to just assume that something like that would be okay." Charlie shrugged and looked down at her lap. She'd been trying to protect Robyn.

"Charlie," Robyn husked, her voice more than enough to make Charlie lift her head and meet her gaze, a gaze that darkened with a desire Charlie was beginning to recognise. Robyn's lips captured her own with a deep kiss that spoke of things Charlie wasn't ready to name. "Thank you."

Charlie swallowed and nodded, taking a moment to steady her breath. "So, so it would be okay with you if I told them about this?" she asked quietly. "About you? About us?"

"Absolutely," Robyn assured her, adding another promise for good measure. "I phoned Kate the second you left the apartment on Sunday," she teased, her eyes dancing with mischief.

"Oh yeah?"

"Yeah."

A gentle knock at the door broke the moment, which was probably just as well because if Robyn kept looking at her like that, she wouldn't be putting her clothes on for a few more hours.

"That's probably Lauren, back with her bag."

"I should probably actually get dressed then," Robyn quipped, leaning in to place a peck on Charlie's cheek, before standing to gather her clothes, allowing the sheet to drop as she did so. Charlie swallowed.

"Not fair," she griped to Robyn's chuckles.

*

"So," Lauren began, and Charlie marvelled that she'd managed to wait until room service delivered their breakfast before starting this line of questioning, the interrogation she'd been preparing for since the moment she opened her hotel room door and saw Lauren there with her bag.

"Ask whatever you want," Charlie said wearily. "Let's just get it over with."

Lauren laughed delightedly. "You make it sound like I'm lining you up in front of the firing squad!"

"Aren't you?"

Lauren's smile faded and Charlie immediately regretted her tone and apologised.

"I've known you for nearly twenty years, Charlie, and I've never seen you like this over a woman." Lauren lent forward and took hold of her friend's hand. "You scared me yesterday, Char. You've gone through break-ups before and never once sounded as utterly miserable as you did in those messages."

"I'm sorry, Lauren." Charlie hung her head and blew out a breath before tentatively lifting her head and looking her friend in the eye. "It's never hurt like that before, which I know is utterly ridiculous because I've only known Robyn for five-minutes."

"It isn't ridiculous at all," Lauren countered. "That's what it feels like when you think you've lost the person you love."

"Love?" Charlie laughed. "Which part of having only known her five-minutes did you miss, Lauren?"

"I knew in less than two-minutes when I met Teresa," Lauren confessed, the familiar sadness that always came when she talked about her late-wife settling on her features.

"How?" Charlie asked. "How did you know?"

"The same way you do," replied Lauren, holding Charlie's gaze, as if daring her to disagree, but Charlie couldn't. As much as she had avoided going down this path in her own mind, now that Lauren had led her there, there was nothing left to do but accept it.

"I love her", she muttered sadly. "I'm in love with her."

"And that's supposed to be a wondrous thing, that fills your life with light and happiness, not gloom and despair," Lauren said, her eyebrows drawn together in concern. "Talk to me, Charlie."

"It isn't one thing," Charlie began, taking her hand back from Lauren to fold her arms in what she knew was a defensive position, but she needed the comfort it brought. "It's everything," she added, blowing out a breath. Lauren's quirked eyebrow told her immediately that she wasn't going to get away with being so vague. "We don't just live in different countries, Lauren, we live in completely different worlds. She's a global superstar who jets around the world making blockbuster movies. I teach in the same school I used to attend as a student. She spends her evenings at film premieres, awards nights, and glitzy galas. I like nothing better than a night in with a cuppa and Netflix. I'm kidding myself if I think this is going to last beyond the little microcosm we currently find ourselves in. I am not going to give up teaching to go and be a housewife in Hollywood, and she's not going to come here and satisfy herself with an annual performance in the village panto."

Charlie stood abruptly and began to pace, ticking off everything that was against them.

"She's hidden so far in back of the closest she's past Narnia and I've been out since I was 17-years-old. I can't go back to hiding who I am, and I don't want to have to. It'll take a journalist all of 60-seconds to find out that I'm gay and then that'll be it."

"Have you talked to Robyn about this? I thought you said she was going to come out?"

"Well, she says she is, but I guess we won't know that for certain until she does, will we? We haven't talked about the specifics of it at all. We haven't talked about the specifics of anything if I'm honest."

"If I remember rightly, there's never really a lot of talking taking place at this stage in a relationship," Lauren winked and Charlie felt her cheeks heat up, the blush giving her away immediately, much to Lauren's delight if her evil cackles of laughter were anything to go by.

"Shut up," she mumbled.

"Could you please sit back down? The whole pacing thing is wearing me out," Lauren complained. Charlie rolled her eyes before complying, crumpling into the corner of the sofa.

"It's doomed, Lauren," she moaned, holding her head in her hands. "I've fallen in love with the worst possible person on the planet and when this stupid film is finished, I'm going to get my heart ripped out." Charlie could see Lauren trying not to laugh at her melodramatics, but it really didn't appear that she was trying all that hard.

"I had absolutely no idea you could be like this," Lauren giggled. "You're always so sensible, so stoic, so strong, and now you sound like a bratty teenager. Where has level-headed Charlie gone?"

Charlie sighed. "You're right. I can hear the words coming out of my mouth and I want to slap myself and tell myself to get a grip. How do people do this, Laur? How do they fall in love every day and not lose the ability to function like a regular human-being?"

"Quite often we do. But it passes and things settle into a new normal. And the same will happen for you and Robyn, Charlie, if you let it. You do need to talk to her about this, though. All of it."

"All of it?" Charlie asked, her voice tremulous with nerves.

"All of it," Lauren affirmed. "Why would Robyn even consider going through the trauma of coming out if she doesn't know how you feel? I certainly wouldn't risk my multi-million-dollar career for a woman who just seemed content to spend a bit of time with me here and there. No, if I were going to do that, I'd need to know that when the dust settled, she would still be there, loving me even more strongly than she had before."

The tears that welled in Charlie's eyes and the lump that settled in her throat prevented her from replying. She desperately wanted to be that person for Robyn, wanted to be able to wake up with her on all the mornings, not just the ones they could sneak without being caught. She looked across the room at her best friend and lost her grip on holding back the tears.

"Do you think I'm strong enough for that?" she asked in a quiet voice.

"Oh, Charlie," Lauren said as she crossed the room and wrapped her arms around her friend. "Of course, you are."

"I'm so glad you came," Charlie said as she held onto her friend.

"Why didn't you let me in on all of this earlier?" Lauren asked gently.

Charlie shrugged. "I didn't want to bother anyone with my drama."

"God, if I didn't love you so much, I'd be so mad at you right now." Lauren pushed back so she could look Charlie in the eye. Charlie swallowed hard at the unfamiliar stern look. "You're the first one to drop everything and come running for any of us. You have to learn to let us do the same, Charlie. It's not a weakness, and it's most certainly not any bother, damn it. After everything you did when I lost Teresa, how could you possibly think I wouldn't want to be here for you over this?" Charlie supposed she should be relieved that Lauren sounded more exasperated than annoyed, but it didn't do much to ease the guilt that settled on her chest. Time and time again her friends had encouraged her to open up to them, to let them support her, but she honestly didn't know how one was supposed to ask for that kind of help. It just wasn't in her nature.

"You've got that oculus thingy going on. I know you're busy Lauren, and this just seemed smaller than that."

"My best friend falling in love for the first time is smaller than me trying to satisfy an old woman's craziness?"

"Well, I guess when you put it like that..." Charlie's voice trailed off. "I think I avoided talking to you about it because then it was real, you know? Like if I didn't say it out loud to anyone then I would have been able to protect myself from it. I know that doesn't make any sense." She laughed. "It seems like you've traded one crazy woman for another!"

"Of course it makes, sense," Lauren countered. "You've loved women before, but you've never been in love with anyone. I watched you hold a piece of yourself back every time, and I always knew when the right one came along, you would fall hard. And, of course, you couldn't pick anyone easy, could you?" Lauren teased. "The women of Britain were never going to be good enough for you. No, you had to hold out for a Hollywood starlet," she waggled her eyebrows and grinned, and Charlie felt the weight of their conversation lift and couldn't help but laugh.

"It's so me, isn't it?"

"Absolutely! Easy path," Lauren said motioning to her left. "Hard path." She motioned to her right. "And damn near impossible path," she said as she motioned straight up towards the ceiling. "That would always be the route you'd pick."

"Ugh. I hate that you're right! Why do I do this to myself?"

"In this instance, I don't think we can really blame you. It's not like you can pick and choose who you fall in love with," Lauren shrugged. "But you can choose what you do about it, and you, my friend, are going to do everything in your power to make this work. That's what you do."

"I know," Charlie sighed.

"So, what's your first step, lover girl?"

"Don't ever call me that again," Charlie shuddered as Lauren grinned at her. "I guess there's only one thing I can do. Tell her how I feel."

"Atta girl."

Chapter Twenty-Three

Robyn

"I love you, so much. And I know that it's going to be complicated, but I really want to try and make this work. For us to try to be together. It's all I want."

To say the irony of Freya delivering these words to Grace wasn't lost on Robyn would be an understatement. If it hadn't been the twelfth time she'd had to deliver the line, she might have allowed an out-of-character grin, but she was sick of the scene and really just wanted it to be over and done with.

"Cut!" Peter yelled again, just as Robyn knew he would. She couldn't understand what Mary was finding so hard about his direction, but time and time again, she failed to deliver on his requests. "Let's take 20," he added, and Robyn felt her heart sink a little further. An unexpected break here would just push their schedule off, meaning it would be even longer before she could get away from set later that day. She'd hoped to drop in on Charlie's lesson with Lucy, under the pretence of wanting to spend some time with her younger co-star. Robyn winced to herself, realising what that sounded like when she played it back in her head. She wanted to use a teenager to spend some time with her girlfriend. *That's low, White,* she thought as she tried to get her head back in the moment.

"You okay?" she asked Mary quietly, not really expecting much of a response from the other actress. All of Robyn's attempts to make nice had so far had been rebuffed, and the stiffening of Mary's spine and tightening of her face suggested this one was going the same way.

"Of course," she bristled.

"It might be a little easier to play the scene if we took some time away from the set together. You know, grab a coffee or something?" Robyn wanted her mouth to stop talking, wondering why she kept putting herself out there, only to be shot down.

"I don't think so," Mary replied curtly, visibly turning herself away from Robyn to face Peter who was approaching.

"Robyn," he began. "Why don't you go and take a load off in your trailer? I'll send someone to get you when we're ready to get going again."

Robyn nodded, sensing that her dismissal wasn't because of anything she'd done wrong. On the contrary, she thought it might be his way of getting her out of the way while he spoke to Mary. Her suspicions were confirmed when, as she'd turned to follow Robyn, Mary was stopped by Peter's gentle hand on her forearm.

"Let's grab a coffee somewhere quiet, Mary," he said, turning her in the opposite direction from the one Robyn was heading. The smile he threw over his shoulder at Robyn made any last concerns disappear. She'd known it was Mary who was throwing off the scene, but there was always that undercurrent of anxiety that it might be her in the director's crosshairs again.

With a deep sigh, of both relief and frustration, Robyn turned and left the set, heading straight to her trailer, pulling out her phone and texting Charlie as she went.

Robyn: So, I have an unexpectedly free 20-minutes... I don't suppose you happen to be at the studio? □

There were no dots to signal an immediate response, and Robyn felt her heart sink a little, even though she'd known it was a longshot. Twenty-minutes wasn't anywhere near long enough for what Robyn wanted to have with Charlie, but she'd take anything she could get. Since leaving her room early yesterday morning when Lauren had arrived, they hadn't managed to find a way back to each other. They'd texted and had spoken on the phone last night, but Robyn wanted more. So much more.

As she neared her trailer, her phone buzzed with an incoming call. Hoping it was Charlie, she hustled up the steps and pushed through the door, closing it behind her. Looking at the screen, she groaned aloud.

"David. Hi," she said in greeting, realising she hadn't spoken to her agent since the conversation where she'd learned the truth about her employment on the film.

"Robyn! I hear things are going well. Peter and Adelaide are raving about you!"

"I didn't know you were in touch with them."

"Of course, I am. I'm always completely up to date on everything involving my number one star." Though his tone was light, Robyn frowned, feeling slightly uncomfortable at his words.

"That sounds kind of stalker-esque, David," she said, trying to match the lightness of his tone. His slightly forced laugh did nothing to relieve the tension she'd felt creep across her skin.

"I'm looking forward to seeing it for myself," he added.

"The first screening's a little while off yet. I'd be happy to talk you through anything you were particularly interested in or concerned by," Robyn replied, doing her best to be the accommodating client she always managed to be, despite David's tendency to run her up the wrong way. Another laugh, this was less forced and more... She faltered. More triumphant maybe?

"Robyn, you know I won't have to wait that long," he chided, and the tension settled deeper within Robyn, seeping into her very bones. "I'll see you on set this afternoon." The air left her body in a sudden rush and she closed her eyes in dismay, grateful this was a voice call only and not David's preferred video call.

"This afternoon?" she managed to ask, her voice notably more feeble than it had been at the start of the conversation. "Have I missed something?"

"My plane landed an hour ago and I've just got into the car that's bringing me straight to the studio. My assistant was supposed to email you the details days ago. Do I need to have words with her?"

"No, David. I've not checked my mail in a while," she lied. "You know how busy it can get when we're in the middle of filming. I'm sure Bernice sent all the information you asked her to." Which would have been absolutely nothing at all. Robyn knew Bernice well, had always found her to be competent and thorough, not to mention friendly and caring. If she'd been asked to email Robyn, the email would have come. Bernice didn't make mistakes, which meant David had purposefully kept his arrival from her, and not for the first time.

Kate called him a sneaky bastard any time Robyn let on what he'd done, and Robyn was beginning to think her sister was probably right. Kate was convinced it was all part of the massive power trip David was on and that he did it to try and remind Robyn that he was in control.

Robyn pinched the bridge of her nose, desperate to try to stem the headache she felt building. This was going to be an absolute nightmare. For the first time in all of his unannounced arrivals, she actually had something to hide. No, she chastised herself. Charlie wasn't something to hide, not at all. Hadn't Robyn herself just told her that she wanted them to have a future together? One that involved doing the exact opposite of hiding?

So David's arrival was unexpected, that didn't have to mean it wasn't well-timed. She just needed to take advantage of it. To have the conversation she'd been putting off for years. To make him see that this time, what she wanted couldn't just be swept under the carpet. She thought she'd have more time to prepare for it, but now that it was here, she was just going to have to grasp the nettle and tell him.

"Well," David mused, bringing Robyn out of her thoughts and back into their conversation. "You must be doing something right to have two of the biggest names in Hollywood raving about you. I'm glad we were able to prove them wrong," he said smugly. "And I hope this means that I'm forgiven for the sacrifices I had to make to get you this gig?" Sacrifices he'd made? Robyn fumed, but there was no way she was getting into this with him on the phone, especially not when she needed to head back onto set shortly.

"Oh, someone just came to get me, David," she lied. "I'll see you when we wrap." She hung up quickly, let out a loud groan and flopped onto her couch. "This has got disaster written all over it," she muttered to herself as she gazed at the ceiling. She should have listened to Kate and changed agents years ago, but she'd always felt this strange sense of loyalty to David, as if she somehow owed him for helping her get established in such a fickle business. This latest stunt he'd pulled with Addie though, that might just be the last straw. She didn't know of anyone who worked for free in Hollywood, not that she imagined anyone would be shouting about it if they were, but to be tied into three films for the price of one? Well, it just kind of stung a bit. Robyn would be the first to admit that she absolutely did not need the money, it wasn't greed fuelling her annoyance, more the idea that David had made that kind of deal without telling her, without discussing it with her.

If she was honest, he didn't really discuss much with her at all. She had no say in the press junkets she participated in or the talk shows she went on. The same with radio interviews and the other events he had her doing. Robyn knew all the promotion around a film was organised by the production company, and neither of them had any control in that, but it was what David had her doing outside of those commitments that irked her. She'd asked to do more charity events, but apparently there weren't any that were interested in having her as their spokesperson. Robyn wondered now whether that was true or whether it was another case of David dismissing her wishes, just like he'd done all those years ago when she'd wanted to come out.

Her phone buzzed, signalling the arrival of a message. Good timing, she thought, as it would hopefully save her from falling into that pit of misery she was well on her way towards.

Charlie: Hey you! Sorry, I missed your message when it arrived – Lucy and I were caught up in *Tess...* Gutted on two fronts: 1) I'm not at the studio so can't crash your trailer for a quickie (I know that's what you were hinting at □) and 2) Fifteen of your twenty minutes have already gone, so I've probably missed you entirely.

Robyn: Not entirely, I still have three-and-a-half before I have to head back...

Charlie: Do you think we're the only people on the planet who type numbers out as words when texting? It's like I've died and gone to heaven every time I get a grammatically correct message from you...

Robyn: I bet we're the only two people who use the time we could be flirting to discuss grammar.

Charlie: Are you trying to suggest to me, Ms White, that grammar discussion does not constitute flirting? I guess that's where I've been going wrong all these years ☐ Anyway, how come you got an unexpected break?

Robyn: Because Mary can't act.

Charlie: Ouch! That bad??

Charlie: And yes, before you point it out, I know double question marks are a no-no!

Robyn: We only have limited time so I'm not wasting it by trying to be nice to her! Honestly, I don't know why she took this role, and I definitely don't know why she stayed on when they added the romance. Sometimes it's like trying to get a response from a cardboard cut-out. Today is one of those days, I guess.

Charlie: Well, stick with it babe, you'll get there.

Charlie: We still on for dinner later? I totally understand if you want to take a rain check after a crappy day.

Robyn: I absolutely do not want to take a rain check at all, but I'm going to have to. My agent called just before to announce his plane arrived earlier this afternoon and he'll see me on set later. I know he'll want to get together later...

Charlie: Is it unusual for him to arrive without letting you know? Is everything okay?

Robyn: Completely like him. Macho bullshit is his preferred method for everything.

Charlie: Gotcha. It's okay though, I completely understand. Your work is important and it's likely to have to take priority at times in the future.

Robyn: In the future? Well, I like the sound of that, Ms Evans!

Charlie: Crap. Sorry for assuming.

Charlie: Actually, no, I'm not sorry. I would like us to have a future.

Robyn: Oh, we absolutely do. I can assure you of that.

Robyn: On that note, though, I have to dash, sorry. I'll text you later xx

Charlie: Hope it all goes well with David. And with Mary! xx

Robyn turned her phone back off, grinning widely. She loved that Charlie had talked about them having a future, had been brave enough to put it out there and not retract it. Robyn couldn't think of anything she wanted more, and whilst she wasn't naïve enough to think it would all be plain sailing, she was willing to do whatever it took to make their future together a reality. Even if those things included acting opposite Mary Kane and having difficult conversations with David Neville.

Pushing to her feet, Robyn felt lighter than she had all day. And happy. She felt happy, something she hadn't felt in a really long time. Probably since those first few days on the *Branded* set if she was going to be completely honest with herself. The novelty had quickly worn off and been replaced by the almost crushing weight of the responsibility she'd felt to make the movie a success, particularly when she'd felt so out of her depth in the acting world, like an imposter who could be uncovered at any moment. There hadn't been much opportunity for her to really fall in love with acting, not when all she was conscious of, thanks to David, was the amount of money being gambled on her. And it was a gamble, he'd told her, time and time again. One that he was responsible for making pay and that she was responsible for not fucking up.

Robyn laughed as she opened her trailer door. She really should have seen the warning signs right back then and realised that David only had his best interests at heart, not hers. But that was the benefit of hindsight, she supposed. It had been years before she had finally garnered an understanding for an industry that had been completely foreign to her and her parents, who'd also been taken in by David's charm.

Not this time though. If he didn't support what she wanted to do, wasn't completely behind her coming out, then she'd be asking her lawyers to find her a way out of her contract with him, no matter the cost. She wasn't going to let him ruin what she was building with Charlie. Wasn't going to let him do anything to mar what she felt, to spoil in anyway this experience of falling in love. Because that's what this was to her, and she knew it deep in her bones. She was falling hard for Charlie Evans.

As she pushed back onto set, Robyn scoffed. She wasn't falling; she'd already done that. She was head-over-heels in love with the grammar-loving English teacher.

Chapter Twenty-Four

Robyn

Two weeks later and Robyn knew the time had come. She was done putting off the conversation with David, done having to sneak around trying to find time to actually see Charlie face-to-face and not just have a few rushed text messages and phone calls here and there. She'd talked it through with Kate the previous night and her twin agreed she needed to act now. Actually, Kate had said she was several years too late, but Robyn had chosen to ignore that.

A knock on her hotel room door signalled David's arrival. Taking a deep breath and smoothing non-existent creases out of her jeans, she crossed the room and didn't hesitate as she pulled open the door and ushered David inside.

"I'm meeting with Addie in twenty-minutes, so this will have to be quick," he said tersely. David wasn't a fan of being summoned.

"We'll be done in five," she countered, closing the door behind him, and crossing to the chair closest to the fireplace, motioning for him to take the one on the opposite side of the coffee table.

"Well, what is it that couldn't wait?" David demanded.

"I've met someone, and I don't want to have to hide her." She delivered the words even more confidently than she had when she'd practised with Kate last night. They'd run through several different ways of telling him and in the end had both agreed that Robyn should be straight to the point and use as few words as possible. Kate had argued it was better than Robyn trying to remember a long speech, to which Robyn had pointed out that was kind of her job, but she knew what Kate meant. Fewer words meant less time to get nervous.

A brief look on David's face told her he hadn't expected her to say what she had, but his poker face was back in place so quickly Robyn wondered whether she'd imagined his initial response.

"Well, that's just great, Robyn. I'm happy for you." Not the response she was expecting. Not at all. Although he was smiling and looked relaxed, Robyn wasn't sure he was being genuine. Or maybe she was doing him a disservice and his thinking had in fact actually moved on since the last time she'd broached this subject. She decided to proceed with caution. And honesty.

"Thank you, David. I have to say, that wasn't the response I was expecting from you. Not after how this conversation went the last time I tried to tell you that I wanted to come out."

"That was a long time ago, Robyn. Right around *Branded* if I remember rightly. You've grown up a lot since then."

"I have," she agreed. "And this is what I want to do, David, and I'd prefer to do it with your support than without." That had been Kate's line. A way to make sure he knew she was serious and was going to make the announcement whether he agreed with her or not.

"Absolutely," he nodded. "Have you thought about how you want to do it? We could arrange for an exclusive interview on *Ellen* if you like. Or you could do it live on social media. There seems to be a trend for that kind of thing."

"There does, but I had something different in mind, actually. Next weekend is the UK premiere of *Lethal Shadows*, the indie film from last summer where I got my first taste of being a producer. I thought that would make the perfect venue. You know I'm not one for making speeches, so I figured if Charlie came with me as my date, that could be how I do it. I know there'll probably need to be follow up interviews afterwards, but I'd really like to do it this way."

"Well, it sounds like you've put a lot of thought into it and have a plan that you're comfortable with. To me, that's got to be the most important factor. I'm guessing you don't want me to put feelers out about interviews until after the premiere?"

"No, I don't want there to be any rumblings beforehand."

"No problem at all, Robyn. I'm pretty sure the TV shows will be coming to us actually," he smiled. "They'll all want the exclusive," he added with a slight roll of his eyes. "I'll make sure we go with the ones we know will do a respectful job." David glanced at his watch and then pushed to his feet. "I need to get going if I'm going to keep that meeting with Addie – she's not a woman you want to keep waiting!" He crossed the room and as Robyn stood, he squeezed her arm and leaned in to kiss her cheek. "Congratulations," he smiled before turning and letting himself out of her room.

Robyn sank back into her chair, her eyes narrowed at the closing door. This was not at all what she had expected. In fact, when she and Kate had run through multiple scenarios last night, not one of them had contained a positive response. Had the passage of time really made all that much difference to his way of thinking? Granted, there were now more openly gay actresses in film and television, but she found it hard to believe his prejudice had morphed so much. He'd barely even batted an eyelid at her. Hell, she'd faced more ire and irritation when she'd spoken to him about her initial reception on set.

Maybe the conversations he'd been having with Peter and Addie had changed his mind. Robyn was starring in a film as a lesbian after all, and if someone as powerful as Addie Covington could support that, then maybe David saw this as an opportunity, the best time for her to come out while associated with such high-profile names in the industry.

She felt kind of deflated, like the whole conversation had been something of an anti-climax. It had nestled at the back of her mind for years, knowing that one day she'd probably have to bring it up with him again, and in recent weeks and days, it had been front and centre, keeping her awake long into the night. She'd been absolutely convinced he would be dead against it and that she'd need to involve her legal team to somehow get her out of contract with him. Then she'd need to find a new agent, a less homophobic one, who would support her with her career in the way she wanted them to.

The following evening, Robyn wandered around the kitchen of the apartment she had rented for that first night with Charlie. It had brought them a happy ending that time and she was hoping for more of the same magic. Spooning the warmed blackberries onto the top of her freshly baked cheesecake, she couldn't hold back a grin as she thought about the conversation she wanted to have with Charlie. The one where she asked her to come to the premiere. As her date.

With Taylor Swift playing quietly in the background, she swayed her hips gently as she moved between the kitchen area and the table, laying out the cutlery, twisting the small vase of flowers one way and then the other, trying to find the perfect angle from the chair that would be Charlie's.

When the doorbell rang, the flutter of excitement in her stomach no longer came as a surprise; it was there every time Robyn was about to see Charlie, a welcome reminder of how deeply she had fallen. This time when she opened the door, the bouquet of tulips was the first thing she saw, and she couldn't keep the chuckle from escaping. It seemed she wasn't the only one who remembered every detail from the first time they'd been in this apartment.

"They're beautiful," Robyn murmured, pulling Charlie towards her, and leaning in for a gentle kiss.

"Mmm, they really are," Charlie replied, her eyes never leaving Robyn's lips.

"Smooth," Robyn quipped, taking hold of Charlie's empty hand and pulling her through the apartment, repeating the actions of putting the flowers into water while Charlie took off her jacket. A gentle laugh had Robyn looking over her shoulder and then following Charlie's gaze to the tulips already on the table.

"Great minds," she murmured, coming to stand behind Charlie, pressing her body up against Charlie's back and gently moving her hair to one side so she could lean in and kiss her neck, moving her lips to suck on the sensitive pressure point. She snaked an arm around to Charlie's front, splaying her hand across her stomach and forcing their bodies even closer, as if that was actually possible. At Charlie's throaty moan, she used her other hand to cup her chin and turn Charlie's lips to meet her own. They sank immediately into a deep kiss, tongues battling. The hand on Charlie's stomach fisted in the material of her top, wrenching it up and over her head, forcing their mouths to part for seconds before hungrily finding their way back together.

Robyn dropped Charlie's top without thought and ran her left hand possessively upwards from her navel, over the soft skin until finding her bra and yanking the cup upwards. She'd never been like this before, an animalistic need taking over as she palmed Charlie's breast before rolling her nipple between thumb and forefinger, gently squeezing. Charlie wrenched her mouth away, gasping, head lolling back onto Robyn's shoulder. Robyn took advantage, kissing and licking her way down Charlie's exposed throat.

"Fuck," Charlie moaned.

"I intend to," Robyn replied hoarsely as the hand not caressing Charlie's nipple tugged open the buttons on her jeans and was immediately inside, fingers sliding through wetness to circle Charlie's clit again and again, before plunging inside. The guttural groan that escaped from Charlie as she withdrew her fingers, returned them to her clit and then pressed them back inside, was a sound Robyn didn't think she would ever forget. She could feel Charlie's walls already beginning to tighten, and she bit down gently at the point where neck met shoulder to add yet another source of pleasure. As Charlie began to sag her body further into Robyn's, Robyn's left hand gave a final squeeze to Charlie's nipple before sliding down to take over drawing increasingly frantic circles to Charlie's clit, the fingers of her other hand driving deeply inside and curling.

"Oh my god, Robyn," Charlie moaned as she collapsed back under the onslaught.

Robyn could feel the shudders of the orgasm as it ripped its way through Charlie's body, her walls tightening deliciously around her fingers. No sooner had the shudders stopped than Charlie was pulling away from Robyn, turning and dropping to her knees, eyes fixed on Robyn's as she yanked open Robyn's jeans, hands on the waistband tugging them down over Robyn's waist to pool at her ankles. It wasn't until she felt Charlie's hand taking hold of her ass that she realised her panties had gone the journey with her jeans. Before she had the presence of mind to consider what might happen next, Charlie's tongue laved the length of her before doing something indescribable to her clit and now she was the one moaning in absolute pleasure, a small part of her mind marvelling at the fact she was somehow still managing to stand. As Charlie replaced her tongue with her mouth, sucking on Robyn's clit, she knew she wouldn't last much longer. Something deep below the pit of her stomach tightened and she stood on the precipice; the moment Charlie's fingers slid inside her, she tumbled over the edge, crying out as her entire body shook.

Panting, she rested a hand on Charlie's shoulder, knees beginning to buckle.

"Hi," Robyn managed to say, her voice deeper and throatier than she'd ever heard it.

"Hey, yourself," Charlie replied, a lazy grin on her face as she traced a gentle pattern on the back of Robyn's knee. "I could get used to that kind of welcome," she added, a teasing tone to her voice that made a flush sweep across Robyn's body.

"Get up here and kiss me."

"Shall I bring your pants with me?" Charlie asked with a wink, earning herself a playful swat as she stood.

"As long as that's not the only time they come off tonight," Robyn said as she re-buttoned them, watching as Charlie pulled her bra back into place and scooped up her top from where it had been dropped.

"Oh, that is not even in question," Charlie murmured as she leaned in to capture Robyn's lips. The ferocity from their earlier kisses had gone, replaced by something much, much deeper.

"This looks even more amazing that I was expecting, and after my last few experiences of your cooking, those expectations were pretty high. Thank you for this," Charlie said sincerely as she raised her glass to meet Robyn's.

"Well, I wanted tonight to be special," Robyn replied.

"I think you managed that without the food," Charlie grinned with a wink.

"I'll have you know that part of the evening wasn't planned at all. I just couldn't help myself," Robyn admitted with a slight wince.

"Do I look like I'm complaining?" Charlie teased. "So, any particular reason for wanting something special tonight."

"Yes."

"Are you going to tell me or make me guess?"

"Last summer I took on my first role as producer, for a film called *Lethal Shadows*. It's making its premiere in London next weekend and I would love it if you came with me. As my date," Robyn added in case it wasn't clear what she was asking. A myriad of emotions flashed across Charlie's face: shock, concern, pride, excitement.

"As your 'date' date?" she asked quietly, clearly needing some clarification.

Robyn covered her hand with her own before replying equally as softly.

"As my 'date' date." She smoothed her thumb over the back of Charlie's knuckles. "I want to ride in the back of the limo with you, hold your hand on the red carpet, sit next to you in the cinema, and dance with you at the after party."

A silence hung in the air between them. If anyone had asked her what she thought Charlie's answer might be, Robyn couldn't have answered them. The face she could usually read so well was now emotionless. In that moment she realised she hadn't actually considered that Charlie might say no. She'd been so caught up in wanting to do this, to take her girlfriend to a premiere, that she hadn't once thought about what it would mean for someone who had no experience of the limelight whatsoever. And not just that, the press and fans who already went crazy at these things were likely to go absolutely wild when they saw Hollywood's darling hand-in-hand with another woman. What was she thinking by even suggesting Charlie subject herself to that? God, she was a selfish tit at times.

"I would love to."

Those four simple words immediately silenced the panic in Robyn's mind and a stillness descended over her.

"Really?" she asked, needing to be certain she'd heard correctly.

"It would be an absolute honour."

"I mean, I probably should have thought it through from your point of view before asking, because it could get pretty intense, you know? The press. The fans. It's always like some crazy humdrum cyclone you have to get through, and if I'm there with you then it's likely to be even more wild, and I didn't even think that it might all be too-"

"Robyn," Charlie interrupted, a smile playing at her lips. "I would love to be there, at your side." She flipped their hands over so that she could interlace their fingers, stood, and pulled Robyn up to meet her. Taking a step closer, and then another, Charlie ran gentle fingers down Robyn's cheek before tucking a strand of hair behind her ear. Their bodies pressed against each other as she leaned in and placed a gentle kiss to Robyn's lips. "I understand exactly what you're asking of me. I understand exactly what this moment will be for you. I understand exactly what the press and the fans will see when we walk down that carpet, and I am more than alright with that, Robyn. I love you, and I don't want to be anywhere than at your side."

The words rang in Robyn's ears and her heart, which had been beating at double-time throughout this whole conversation, suddenly shot up into triple time.

She searched Charlie's eyes, needing to see the confirmation of what she'd just said, and it was there alright. In bucket loads. Charlie loved her.

"I love you, too," she whispered gently before capturing Charlie's lips in a kiss she hoped would signal the truth behind her words.

Chapter Twenty-Five

Charlie

"I know it's not our usual night to chat, so thank you for fitting me into your hectic schedules," Charlie said as she looked at her three friends on the screen. After sending out an SOS message to them that morning, they'd all shown up for her tonight.

"Are you kidding?" Jenna asked in an incredulous tone. "In all the time we've been friends, you've never been the one to send the SOS message. Not once, Charlie. Of course we were going to show up for you."

"Plus, you know, there was always the slim possibility that you might bring Robyn on screen with you, and there was no way we could have missed that," Naomi quipped, never one to get too sappy.

"Well, I hate to disappoint you, but I won't be doing that tonight."

Naomi pouted and sighed dramatically before grinning as Jenna rolled her eyes and Lauren shook her head.

"A girl can try!" she said, shrugging her shoulders.

"However, you will get to see me on TV next weekend with her when we walk the red carpet at the premiere of the first film she's produced."

Charlie's words were greeted with a silence so loud you could have heard a pin drop. Well, she might have been able to hear it if her blood hadn't been racing around her body at such a pace it was like an orchestra had taken up residence in her ears. She hadn't felt a moment of nervousness last night when Robyn had asked her to go, but she'd woken in the early hours crippled by doubt. If Robyn was going to come out to the world, surely she couldn't really want to do it with Charlie on her arm? Charlie the teacher from a small town in England, a million miles away from being a global superstar. And, as she'd worked herself into more of a frenzy, it suddenly occurred to her that she and Robyn were yet to have a conversation about their future. What was going to happen when Robyn finished filming? She would head back to the States and Charlie would return to school. Their lives and worlds couldn't be more different.

Her friends' faces registered a myriad of emotions, most of which Charlie had experienced herself in the early hours. Jenna mostly looked shocked, Naomi was excited, Lauren was worried. What had Charlie been thinking by accepting Robyn's invitation? She didn't even know if Robyn had thought it through properly or whether it was just a reaction to the ridiculously hot sex they'd had when Charlie arrived at the apartment.

"The *Lethal Shadows* premiere?" Jenna asked, her journalistic knowledge giving her an advantage over the other two. At Charlie's nod of confirmation, she continued. "That's getting the full Leicester Square treatment. It's a really big deal. There'll be hundreds of fans and a lot of press there." She left the question about whether Charlie was aware of that unasked.

"Did she say exactly in what capacity you'll be there?" Lauren asked, pragmatic as ever.

"As her date."

Naomi's excited face fell as the reality of the situation sank in.

"Holy shit," she muttered.

"Yep," said Charlie, her right leg beginning to bounce uncontrollably.

"And how did all of this come about?" Lauren again, ever the one for details.

"She rented that apartment again last night and invited me for dinner. When I got there, there was a whole romantic table set. Flowers, candles, the whole shebang." Charlie deliberately skipped over the hottest sex she'd ever experienced. "She cooked, we ate, and then she asked me to go with her, as her 'date' date."

"And you said?"

"Yes," Charlie replied quietly. "I said it would be an honour."

Jenna let out a low whistle.

"Is she giving a coming out speech beforehand?"

"No."

"So, she's hoping that the two of you walking the red carpet together will be enough of an announcement?"

"She's planning to hold my hand," Charlie said, her voice still low. "And then there's also going to be some dancing at the after party."

"And how do you feel about it today?" Lauren asked, cutting straight to the crux of the matter.

"All over the place, if I'm being honest," Charlie sighed. "I wasn't lying when I said it would be an honour. I know how much this means to her and the fact she's asked me to be the one she does it with is amazing." She paused as she gathered her thoughts, wanting to find the right words. "But I guess the full weight of it hit last night."

"Ah, the infamous 'wee hours' got you," said Jenna. "They're an absolute bitch sometimes."

"I'm just a teacher," Charlie said helplessly. "I've never been to an event like this, and I've certainly never been the target of the press. How am I supposed to support Robyn through that? What are the media going to say about me? I don't look like a celebrity for god's sake, I'm just me." She knew her voice was getting more and more frantic, but she couldn't rein it in. "We haven't even talked about what happens when she finishes filming *Strikes Twice*. Does she expect me to give up my job and just follow her around the globe, because that's not going to happen. And what the hell am I going to wear?" She dropped her head into her hands. "This is an absolute disaster," she groaned. "And to top it all I went and told her that I bloody love her!"

"Enough," Lauren said in a voice that sounded surprisingly like Charlie's teacher voice, the one that could silence a class of excited girls in an instant. "You're spiralling, Charlie, and you really don't need to. Take a breath," she instructed. "Right, let's work through this logically."

Jenna jumped in, taking over from Lauren's lead.

"Firstly, you don't need to worry about what you're going to wear, Charlie. No one goes to these events without input from a team of stylists. At the very least, you'll have someone pick out an outfit for you. You might even get make-up and hair done. Robyn will definitely have people who do that for her, and she'll likely extend to you.

"Secondly, you absolutely do not need to be worrying about how you look, babe. You're an absolute knock-out in your slobbing around clothes. The only thing you need to worry about in that department is whether Robyn will still be able to stand upright when she sees you in whatever designer outfit they put you in."

"Thirdly," Naomi went on, picking up with barely a pause. "If Robyn has asked you to do this with her, it's because she wants you there. And if that's the case, there's no way she won't make sure you're prepared for it. And as terrifying as it will be for her, knowing the statement that she's making, she will absolutely be looking after you, Charlie. She's been dealing with the paparazzi for nearly two-decades. She will know exactly how to protect you. And before you try to tell me you don't need protecting, you need to let her do it, Charlie. Apart from anything, it'll give her something else to think about when she's on that red carpet, rather than just being focused on knowing she's coming out."

As her friends' words sunk in, Charlie couldn't help the tears that escaped. She was usually the logical one, laying out options, decisions, pathways with absolute clarity for them. To have the tables turned made her feel more supported than she had expected, and she was finally able to take that breath Lauren had instructed her to.

"As for what happens after the premiere," Lauren began. "You already know the solution to that, Charlie."

"I need to talk to Robyn," she replied quietly.

"You do," Lauren confirmed. "You are two intelligent women who love each other. You'll work it out," she said confidently. "Don't put it off, Charlie. As soon as we hang up, you need to call her and talk this out, okay?"

"Yeah, okay."

"I mean it, Charlie. I know you and your avoidance tactics. Don't let this become bigger than it needs to be."

"I promise," Charlie smiled, both loving and hating that her friends knew her so well.

"And keep talking to us," Jenna pleaded. "You just have to pick up the phone and we'll be there."

"Thanks, you guys."

"Anytime," Naomi said, her tone of voice leaving no room for discussion.

True to her word, Charlie dialled Robyn's number once her friends had gone, tucking her phone between ear and shoulder as she pottered around her room making a much-needed cup of tea.

"Good morning, beautiful," Robyn purred as she answered, and a pang of longing shot through Charlie. This was a conversation that she could have had on the phone, but in that moment she wanted nothing more than to see Robyn.

"I don't suppose you have a free half hour?" she asked by way of greeting.

"Second thoughts?"

"No," she assured. "But about a million questions and maybe a teeny bit of freaking out." Charlie knew she needed to be completely honest with Robyn if she was going to make it through Saturday night in one piece.

"I'll be there in two minutes," came the immediate reply before Robyn hung up without another word.

Charlie blew out a breath and set out making a second cup of tea, knowing that Robyn would probably want one too. She'd barely finished when there was a knock on the door and she grinned, wondering if Robyn had run there from her room.

"Hey," she said, pulling open the door and feeling her breath catch at the woman standing on the other side. Dressed like this, in jeans and a hoodie, Robyn was absolutely stunning, even more so to Charlie than when she was dolled up to the nines.

"Hey yourself," replied Robyn with a gentle smile. Closing the door behind herself, she leaned in for a gentle kiss and laced her fingers through Charlie's. "I'm guessing you've already made the tea, so let's talk this all through, shall we?" She pulled on Charlie's hand, leading her to the couch.

"Are you sure it's okay that you're here?" Charlie asked, remembering how much Robyn had initially wanted to avoid meeting in their rooms.

"Absolutely." Robyn took hold of the mug Charlie had left on the coffee table and leaned back into the sumptuous cushions, Charlie mirroring her actions.

"I'm sorry about this."

"Don't you dare be sorry, Charlie Evans. I dropped an absolute bombshell on you last night, one that, if I know you at all, became a nuclear explosion at some time around 3am." Her voice held a teasing tone that made all of Charlie's remaining nerves and concerns disappear. In return, Charlie mimed said explosion with her hands, making Robyn chuckle.

"I may have spent a few minutes thinking about it," she confessed, and Robyn's chuckle turned into a full laugh.

"And what did the girls say about it?"

If Charlie had been able to see her own face, she knew the expression on it would be described as astonishment.

"How did you know that I've spoken to them?"

In reply, Robyn just arched an eyebrow. Charlie shook her head. Apparently she was becoming predictable even to Robyn.

"Mostly they just told me to breathe."

"Good advice," Robyn grinned. "I kind of like it when you're doing that," she teased.

"And that I didn't need to worry about what to wear because someone would probably pick it for me."

"Correct."

"And there might even be people who could do my make-up and hair."

"Correct again."

"That you've been on plenty of red carpets and know what you're doing, so you'd probably look after me and make sure I don't say or do the wrong thing."

A look of tenderness settled on Robyn's face before she answered that one.

"Not probably, definitely." She reached out for Charlie's hand, rubbing her thumb over Charlie's knuckles in what was becoming the quickest way to ease any tension Charlie was feeling. "I don't need to make sure you don't say or do anything wrong, Charlie. You wouldn't. It's not in your nature. But I will be right by your side, hand-in-hand." She looked deeply into Charlie's eyes. "I don't intend to let you go, Charlie."

"What about after?" Charlie asked quietly, afraid to have put the question out there, not sure she wanted to know the answer.

"After the premiere?"

Charlie nodded her confirmation.

"I'm not letting you go then, either. I love you, Charlie. I know there's things we need to work out, but I want a life with you, and if that means I need to make some changes, then that's what I'll do." She said it as though it was the simplest thing in the world and Charlie felt her heart swell. Robyn might not have been able to give her a detailed overview of what that life would look like, but it was enough to know she wanted one. Enough to know that she wanted Charlie.

Charlie took the mug from Robyn's hand and placed it with her own back on the coffee table.

"I love you, too," she said as she leaned in to capture's Robyn's mouth with her own.

Five days later and Charlie knew she was as ready as she could be for their big night. She'd been measured, prodded, and squeezed into a variety of different outfits before Robyn's stylist had been satisfied she looked appropriate. They'd visited the make-up and hair team to discuss their outfits and the possible styles that would go with them. Charlie had never seen her hair swept into as many different up-dos; if she was being honest, she really couldn't tell one from the other, but she would never have admitted that out loud.

Robyn had walked her through the whole evening, from beginning to end, innumerable times and Charlie felt like nothing could take her by surprise now. She knew what to say, when not to say anything, who to look at, who to avoid looking at, when to smile, when not to smile. The process had been exhausting and she marvelled that Robyn could do it and make it all seem so effortless.

They'd even begun to talk about options for after *Strikes Twice*. Robyn had confessed late one night that she was eager to explore options on the other side of the camera. She'd loved the experience of producing *Lethal Shadows* and hoped to do more of that. She even had a few screenplays that she'd written over the years while waiting in her trailer for something to happen on set. Maybe now would be the time she found the courage to pitch them. Charlie was still unsure of how it would all work, especially considering Robyn still 'owed' Addie Covington two more films, but she trusted Robyn when she said they would find a way. Charlie changing job hadn't come up once in any of their conversations and knowing that Robyn had no expectations on that front had relaxed Charlie to the point where she felt that there could be concessions that she made too. After all, there were schools all over the world.

A knock on her hotel room door broke into her thoughts and she frowned, knowing Robyn was on set and that both Brittany and Lucy were with her. Perhaps it was someone from the hotel staff.

A man she didn't recognise was on the other side of the door when she opened it. Charlie knew immediately he wasn't from the hotel; his suit was exceptionally smart, but it wasn't the right colour for the hotel.

"Can I help you?" she asked tentatively, the man's oily smile putting her slightly on edge.

"David Neville," he announced. "Robyn's manager," he added at what Charlie assumed was a confused look on her face. "I just needed to stop by and talk through some final points for tomorrow," he explained. "Am I okay to come in or would you prefer to go to the coffee area in the lobby?"

"Here's fine," Charlie said, pulling the door open fully and stepping aside to let him pass. For some reason she felt more comfortable talking to this man on what she considered to be her territory.

David made himself at home, sweeping past her into the living area and settling himself in one of the armchairs. Feeling she was on the back foot, Charlie didn't know what else to do other than join him.

"Is everything okay?" she asked, a tendril of something uncomfortable taking root in her stomach. She was a good judge of character, and she did not like David Neville one little bit.

"It will be now," he began, his tone ominous. "Robyn has come to her senses about the premiere tomorrow." He paused and Charlie swallowed hard. "She will be attending on her own," he said bluntly. "You're no longer invited." He stood, straightening his jacket. "Don't contact her again, Ms Evans. She doesn't want to hear from you. Ever."

As he strode past her, a million questions bubbled up in Charlie, but she couldn't make her mouth ask any of them. How could this have happened? How had things changed so drastically since their final hair appointment yesterday? Robyn hadn't seemed anything other than wholly confident and excited about her coming out. She'd been buzzing about it in fact. Had almost spilled the beans to the stylists more than once. It was impossible that she could have had such a change of heart, wasn't it?

Fighting back a sob, Charlie leapt off the sofa and strode to the kitchen, sweeping up her phone from where she'd left it on the counter. This couldn't be right. Pulling up Robyn's contact details, she pressed the call button. The wind went completely out of her, and she crumpled to the floor, as her brain took in the 'sorry, this number is no longer in use' message she heard. Robyn had changed her number. She had sent her manager to deliver the message; she hadn't even had the guts to do it herself.

With a shaky hand, Charlie opened her messages and typed in three simple letters before pressing send: SOS. She needed her friends now more than ever.

Chapter Twenty-Six

Robyn

Robyn's head swam. She looked up from the couch, unsure of how she had ended up sitting. She couldn't quite get a hold of her breathing; it was too fast, too shallow.

"This can't be right. There must be some kind of mistake..." She looked pleadingly at David, wiling him to change the words he'd just said, the words that had cut her to the quick.

"I'm sorry, Robyn," he said softly, a look of compassion on his face. "There's no mistake."

"But I don't understand. Everything was fine, better than fine," her voice broke off as emotion overwhelmed her. "She told me she loved me." Tears spilled down her face as the enormity of David's message sunk in. Charlie wasn't coming to the premiere with her. If that had been the entirety of it, she could have dealt with it, understood that it was too much, too soon for Charlie. But that hadn't been all he'd had to say, and it was the second part that had ripped her reality into shreds. Charlie didn't want to see her again, didn't want any contact with her at all.

"Sometimes people say the things they think we want to hear," David went on. "With some time and space, they often realise that's what they've done. It's not always malicious from the outset, Robyn. This just isn't what Charlie wants. She can see now that she got swept up in the glamour of it all. The fairy-tale romance. The nobody the princess falls in love with."

"She's not a nobody, David."

"You know what I mean," he shrugged. "And surely it's better to find this out now before Saturday? Imagine if she had gone through with the premiere, let herself be photographed by your side for all the world to see and then turned around and left you? At least this way you're not left looking foolish."

"Just heartbroken," she murmured through her tears.

"I know that this is how you wanted to do it, how you wanted to let the world know, but there are other ways you can do that."

Robyn let out a mirthless laugh.

"What's the point, David?" She wiped the tears from her face, hating herself for falling apart like this in front of him. "Look, I appreciate you coming to tell me yourself, but right now, I just need some space. Could we pick this up later, please?"

"Of course," he replied. "Whatever you need, Robyn. I've got your back."

The moment he pulled her trailer door closed behind him, Robyn stood from the couch and headed into the bedroom and sat on the edge of the bed. There had to be some kind of mistake, Charlie wouldn't do this to her, would she? Grabbing her phone from her pocket, she dialled and waited.

"*The number you have dialled has not been recognised,*" said the automated voice on the other end. She hung up and tried again. Same message.

She slumped from the bed to the floor, wrapping her arms around herself, using her well-practised litany to try to calm the rising panic. Pulling up Google, she found the number for their hotel, knowing that was where Charlie was basing herself for her lessons with Lucy today. The receptionist who answered had a ridiculously perky voice which grated on Robyn's every last nerve.

"Charlie Evans' room, please," she directed.

"One moment." A pause that felt inordinately long to Robyn, one in which she realised she was shaking from head to toe, her stomach a whirling pit of vipers. "I'm sorry," came the perky voice. "Ms Evans checked out about 20-minutes ago." If the voice said anything else, Robyn didn't hear it. Grateful that she was already on the floor, she curled into a ball and wept.

A gentle hand on her shoulder shook her awake.

"Robyn?" the soft voice probed. "Robyn? It's Jeanie. Are you okay?"

Groggily, Robyn pushed into a seating position and ran a hand over her face. She had less than a millisecond's peace before the truth rammed home hard: Charlie had left her. She didn't want to be with her.

"Is she okay?" asked another woman's voice, one that Robyn knew she should recognise.

"I don't know, Brittany, she's not saying anything," Jeanie replied, her voice laced with concern.

"I'm okay," Robyn assured them, her voice a rasp. "What time is it?"

"Late," Jeanie answered. "The set has pretty much emptied. Filming wrapped up a couple of hours ago. We thought you'd already left," she went on. "We popped in to re-stock your water for tomorrow and heard a noise from in here."

"A noise?" Robyn asked, trying to focus her gaze on the younger woman.

"A whimper," Jeanie replied softly, her eyes dipping away from Robyn's momentarily.

"I've had a pretty shitty day," Robyn replied, trying to dismiss their concerns and break the tension in the room.

Brittany scoffed.

"They must be going round," she said, a slight note of something colouring the tone of her voice.

Jeanie whipped her head around and gave Brittany a look that had the older woman raising her hands in surrender and looking shamefaced.

"Is there something we can do?" Jeanie asked.

Bring my girlfriend back? Robyn wanted to ask. Make the last few hours disappear?

"No, I'm good she said," pushing to her feet. "I just need to get back to the hotel."

"I'll arrange for a car," Jeanie said, finally looking relieved to have something to do, and bustling out the room before anyone could stop her.

Robyn met Brittany's gaze. From where she stood, one shoulder leaning against the door frame, arms folded tightly across her body, Robyn could feel the anger.

"Do you know where she's gone?" Robyn asked softly. She couldn't bring herself to say Charlie's name, but she knew that Brittany knew exactly who she was talking about.

"No," came the flat reply. "I got a message to say that Lucy could manage without a tutor on set for the few days of filming we've got left and that was all. She hasn't replied to any of my texts or picked up when I've called." The accusation was clear – Brittany thought it was Robyn's fault.

"I didn't think anyone knew about us," Robyn confessed, not needing to beat around the bush.

"I don't imagine anyone else does," Brittany agreed. "But production assistants are paid to be able to read their clients, and both Jeanie and I are good at our jobs."

A flush covered Robyn's neck and face and tears welled up again, where from she had no idea as she was convinced she had literally shed every drop of water in her body already.

"I don't know what happened," she said, her voice breaking. She saw the confusion flit over Brittany's face at her words, and then the realisation that maybe Robyn wasn't to blame for Charlie's sudden disappearance. That maybe she hadn't hurt her but was instead the one who'd been hurt.

"Oh, Robyn," Brittany said softly, immediately leaving her place in the doorway and crossing to Robyn before wrapping her up in her arms. The comfort was more than Robyn could take and she let the emotion wash over her, sobbing into Brittany's shoulder.

"The car will be here in five minutes," Jeanie said in a quiet voice as she came back into the room. Standing next to Brittany, she put a hand on Robyn's forearm. "We've got you."

It had taken a few hours before Robyn was able to convince Brittany and Jeanie that she was okay to be left alone in her hotel room. They hadn't once asked a question, patient enough to let Robyn share what she wanted, offering nothing but comfort. There had been no shock or judgement on their faces as she had confessed to being gay and it seemed they had suspected as much even before the start of this film. Their support had been overwhelming, along with their assurances they wouldn't be heading straight to the press or social media with the gossip. In fact, those promises had been so vehemently delivered that Robyn's tears had finally dried up and she'd had to laugh. Jeanie's swearing of Scout's honour had tipped her over the edge.

Finally alone, she made the one call she'd wanted to make since the moment David broke the news to her.

"What's wrong?" Kate asked in place of her usual greeting, and Robyn was eternally grateful for that weird twin thing they had going on.

"She left me."

"Oh, Robbie, I'm so sorry."

"I don't know what I did wrong, Kate. One minute it was all fine and then the next it wasn't. She didn't even have the guts to tell me herself. She sent a message with David."

"David?" Kate asked. "How would she even have got in touch with David?"

"She's resourceful." Robyn paused, swallowing down the ball of emotion in her throat. "We had the dresses picked out, hair and make-up planned, and I'd coached her through the dos and don'ts so many times she could recite them in her sleep. She seemed happy, Kate. How did this happen?"

"I don't know, babe. Sometimes these things come completely out of the blue. Have you tried to contact her?"

"About a trillion times," Robyn admitted. "I keep getting a message to say her number isn't recognised. God, she must have changed it, Kate. That's how much she doesn't want me getting in touch with her!"

"Have you got any other way of trying to get in touch?" Kate asked. "Social media? An address?"

"She isn't on social media. Some teacher thing, apparently. And, no, I don't have an address, but even if I did, I wouldn't use it. It's pretty obvious she doesn't want anything to do with me and I refuse to turn into a stalker over this."

"It's not stalking to check that someone is okay," Kate assured.

"Well, it feels like it when the person in question is your girlfriend and they've just broken up with you." Robyn blew out a frustrated breath. "I'm sorry, Kate. I didn't mean to snap at you."

"It's completely understandable, Robbie. I know she meant a lot to you."

"She told me she loved me. How can someone say that one day and then walk away without a word?"

"Wow. You didn't tell me she'd said that."

"I guess I wanted to keep it special for a little while."

"What did you say?"

Robyn laughed sadly.

"I told her that I loved her too."

Her admission was greeted with a momentary silence, which was absolutely out of character for Kate. If there was one thing her twin knew how to do it was to say the right thing at the right time, a gift that Robyn absolutely did not possess."

"And do you?"

"Do I what?"

"Love her, Robyn. Do you love her, or did you just say it back?"

"God, no, Kate. I would never do that. I love her. I'm in love with her."

"So why are you just accepting this? It feels like this is something you should be fighting for, like Charlie is someone you should be fighting for, not just taking what David said at face value."

"I can't fight for her when she won't pick up the phone," Robyn replied tartly, unable to keep the hurt from her voice. Didn't Kate think she would do everything she could to keep Charlie in her life?

"Okay, I'm sorry, I didn't mean to insinuate that you weren't going to do anything, Rob. Why don't you get tomorrow out of the way and then we can talk through some ideas?"

"Ugh. I don't want to do tomorrow. I was so looking forward to having Charlie with me, and to finally be getting an opportunity to take her out in public, to know that after tomorrow, we could go anywhere we wanted together without sneaking around."

"Now isn't the time to talk about it, but you can still come out when you're ready."

"I know. It's not the same though."

"I know."

A moment of silence stretched between them, and Robyn thought she might be wholly content to just sit like that forever, her sister's gentle comforting presence just a heartbeat away.

A day later and Robyn didn't think she'd ever missed Kate as much as she did right now. She'd had to field questions all day about Charlie. Why hadn't she accompanied Robyn for her dress fitting? Had she not liked the ideas the hair and make-up team had come up with? Was the driver just picking up one passenger now and not two? If she didn't think the make-up artist would kill her, Robyn could have wept every time someone uttered Charlie's name; it was quite literally like a knife to her heart. Had Kate been there with her, not only would she have run interference, but Robyn would have been able to draw comfort from her sister. The loneliness had hit her harder today than it had in a very long time. It seemed so cruel to have experienced what life could be like when someone loved her, even if it had only been in secret.

As much as she wished Kate were with her, it was Charlie she really wanted, but Robyn couldn't afford to let that thought take hold of her heart. Not if she was going to make it down that damnable red carpet, sit through a screening and the show her face at the after-party. After Charlie had agreed to go with her, Robyn had walked her through every moment of the event and was only now discovering the downside of that: in her mind she had already envisioned every second of the night with Charlie. To be robbed of that was the most acute pain Robyn had ever experienced. If this was how it felt to be in love, she wouldn't be in any hurry to experience it again.

"We'll be there in five minutes," came the voice of her driver through the intercom. She acknowledged him with the closest thing to a smile as she could muster, closed her eyes, and leaned her head against the headrest, willing her heart to slow down.

"Antman, Batman, Catwoman," she murmured under her breath while trying desperately to forget what it felt like to have Charlie's hand nestled within her own. To forget everything she had imagined about this evening and what it might be like to be able to take the woman she loved to a film premiere.

Chapter Twenty-Seven

Charlie

"I can't believe you're making me watch this," Charlie complained bitterly, not that anyone was listening to her because they were too busy ogling the celebrities who had turned up to the *Lethal Shadows* premiere. An event *you* were supposed to be at, said the nagging voice in her head.

"Stop complaining and drink this," Jenna said, shoving a beer bottle in Charlie's direction. "We've been over this already," she continued, exasperation evident in her voice. "It's like ripping off a plaster. You need to be able to see her."

"I really don't," Charlie countered.

"It's more than that," Lauren butted in before Jenna could continue. "You need answers and seeing as you can't call Robyn and ask for them, we're going to try and discern them from what we see of her on the carpet."

"Yeah, we're like regular Charlie's Angels or something," Naomi said, laughing at her own joke and pulling an eyeroll from the others.

"How long have you been waiting to use that line?" asked Jenna, the sarcasm more than evident in her tone.

"At least a decade," quipped Naomi.

"Well, I'm glad that my disaster of a love life finally gave you the opportunity to make your joke."

The look Lauren shot Naomi told her that was enough and to stop trying to employ her usual tactic of using humour to diffuse a situation in which she was uncomfortable. Charlie followed it with her own look of apology; her friends were the last people she should be sniping at.

She'd barely got five minutes into the second SOS call with them when Lauren announced that she was skipping the appointment she was currently driving to and was heading to the hotel to collect Charlie instead. She'd given Charlie twenty minutes to pack before arriving like a tornado, sweeping in and leaving again within a matter of minutes. She'd driven them straight to Jenna's apartment, where Naomi had already arrived. That had been sometime yesterday afternoon and they were yet to leave.

They had fussed around Charlie, alternating between sympathising with her when she cried, stoking her fire when she grew angry, and working hard to counter the well of emptiness threatening to engulf her. But this, Charlie really wasn't sure this was one of their better ideas. It had been Jenna who had suggested it initially, with Lauren and Naomi immediately jumping on her bandwagon. How on earth watching the woman who had just broken her heart was supposed to make her feel any better had eluded her; short of walking out though, there was no way she could avoid it.

Lauren's voice cut into her thoughts.

"Ah! Finally, someone I actually recognise! Does this mean we're getting to the more important people?"

"Yep," Jenna confirmed. "I'm not actually sure where Robyn will be in the line-up. Usually, as the film's star, she would be the last one through, but given that she produced this film, they might bring her on earlier."

"If she's even there," added Naomi.

"She'll be there," Charlie said, absolute certainty in her tone. "She's too professional to miss it."

As the next few celebrities made their way down the carpet, it felt to Charlie as though time had slowed. This was torture. She desperately wanted to see Robyn, just as desperately as she never wanted to have to look at her again. She hoped she looked heartbroken and dreadful, as much as she hoped she looked stunning and like she didn't have a care in the world.

Charlie took a deep swig of her beer and looked back at the television, still the supporting cast. Without her permission, her mind wandered, picturing the dress she should have been wearing tonight, the deep burgundy which had set off her blue eyes, and the plunging neckline that she knew would have drawn Robyn's gaze more than once. When they'd gone to choose their outfits, Robyn had been adamant that she didn't want to see Charlie's until today.

A gentle hand landed on her shoulder as Lauren folded a leg beneath her, sinking into the couch beside Charlie. She ran her hand down Charlie's arm before taking hold of her hand and giving it a reassuring squeeze.

"How are you doing, kiddo?" she asked quietly while Jenna and Naomi argued about the dress the current actress on screen had chosen.

"I've had better days, Laur," she admitted. "I just don't understand what I did wrong." The question had plagued her since the moment David Neville had left her hotel room. Somewhere between confessions of love, planning a coming out event, and discussing ideas for their future, it had all fallen apart. "If I knew what I'd done, I think I'd be able to handle it better, but it just doesn't make any sense to me."

"I think there's a bloody good chance that you didn't do anything, Charlie. This was Robyn's decision, not yours."

"She's up next," Jenna said suddenly, grabbing everyone's attention, causing Charlie's broken heart to beat out a rhythm that was more suited to a rock'n'roll drum solo than the inside of her chest.

A hush descended over the room, as if they were all holding their breath. Naomi turned up the volume as a black limo pulled into shot.

"And this, ladies and gentlemen, is the moment I know millions of you have been waiting for," said the reporter as she preened into the camera before it cut back to the limo as it pulled to a stop, and someone stepped forward to open the rear door. "In her first role as producer, Robyn White!"

A blonde head appeared out of the car, hair in a classy chignon that Charlie recognised from their visit to the hair stylist. Creamy skin, shoulders and back, drew her attention next and Charlie had a flash of the moment back in the rented apartment when she'd kissed and licked her way across that expanse of skin. Her hand gripped Lauren's more tightly.

And then the scene changed as it cut to a different camera, to a shot that took Charlie's breath away. Head on now, she could see Robyn's outfit, a black velvet gown that looked like it had been made for her.

"Breathe," Lauren whispered beside her, and Charlie obeyed, her mind not capable of making any of its own decisions in that moment. Apparently not even the ones designed to keep her alive.

Stunning didn't begin to cover it. The dress pinched in at the waist, emphasising the curve of Robyn's hips and breasts, before falling to her ankles. She looked absolutely incredible. Charlie's breath hitched as she pictured how the two of them would have looked side-by-side. Her burgundy gown would have complemented this one in the best way.

"That dress is fantastic," Naomi muttered, almost apologetically.

"It is," Jenna agreed, "but look at her face."

Charlie hadn't until that moment. She'd concentrated on taking in everything but Robyn's face, not ready to look at her, but there was something in Jenna's voice that made her change that decision.

"She looks sad," said Lauren from beside her.

"Devastated," Naomi added.

"Heartbroken," mused Jenna. "It's not obvious, and she's definitely trying to hide it, but it's there. I've seen Robyn White on enough red carpets to know that isn't a happy version of her.

They were all right, Charlie could tell in an instant. Pain radiated in Robyn's eyes and her body language screamed dejection. She didn't want to be there any more than Charlie wanted to be watching.

"What does it mean?" asked Naomi. "She was the one who broke things off, so why does she look like that?"

"It doesn't mean anything," Charlie replied flatly. "For all we know, there's been a falling out on set, or a project she had in the pipeline fell through. There is absolutely no way we can sit here and know that expression is because of me. And even if it is, it doesn't change anything, does it? I was supposed to be getting out of that car with her, but I'm not, and there isn't anything we can do about it."

Lauren dropped Charlie's hand and wrapped her arm around her friend's shoulder instead, pulling her in to her side.

"Let's hear what she's got to say," Lauren said quietly as, on-screen, Robyn walked towards the reporter.

"Congratulations on tonight, Robyn. How does it feel?" The huge smile on the reporter's face was not matched by the expression on Robyn's, who managed little more than to make the corners of her mouth turn up. If Charlie thought seeing Robyn had been bad though, hearing her was a trillion times worse.

"I'm really proud of everything the whole team accomplished," Robyn began, effectively shifting the attention away from herself. "I couldn't have asked for a better group of people to work with in my first production role. They deserve all the accolades tonight." With another tight smile, Robyn nodded at the interviewer and moved on, leaving the woman with a slightly dazed and disappointed look on her face, which she quickly tried to mask.

"That conversation should have lasted at least another two minutes," Jenna explained. "Robyn cut it short."

The camera tracked Robyn as she made her way along the red carpet, stopping here and there to interact with others on the carpet or the fans who lined it. When they'd talked about how this part of the evening would go, Charlie had felt herself falling a little more in love with Robyn, the way her face lit up when she talked about how important it was for her to make sure the fans felt it had been worth their time to turn up to the event. Robyn had regaled her with stories of times when she'd held up entire premieres because she'd lost track of how long she'd been in amongst the people who mattered most to her.

Robyn had explained that she still wanted to be able to sign autographs and pose for selfies, but didn't want to leave Charlie standing alone, nor did she expect her to be in those selfies with her. They'd worked out a plan to be able to do both, Robyn keeping hold of Charlie's hand as she leant into photos. She'd even gone as far to say she wanted Charlie to hold her right hand so that she didn't need to let go when she signed autographs with her left.

Tonight though, Robyn's interactions were short and cursory. Although there was more of a smile than the reporter had been given, it was a long way from the trademark grin Charlie was used to seeing from Robyn at these premiere events

– after all, she'd been forced to watch a good many over the years with her friends, so had a good idea of what to look for. Not once did Robyn lean in to pose for a selfie or to sign an autograph. Charlie knew her friends had been right with their earlier descriptions of Robyn; she cut a lonely and dejected figure out there on her own.

Her already broken heart splintered again. Perhaps there was more to Robyn's dismissal than she'd allowed herself to consider. She'd convinced herself it was because of something she had done or that Robyn had simply realised she didn't want someone like Charlie next to her on the red carpet; someone as provincial and inexperienced with her world as Charlie was. That had been the only thing that made any sense, to believe Robyn had been swept up in her first romance, mistaking lust for love, getting carried away with the fairy-tale of coming out to a world that wouldn't care, to an industry where her sexuality wouldn't matter. At the end of the day, Robyn had just decided that it wasn't worth the risk; that Charlie wasn't worth the risk.

If that had been the case though, surely Robyn wouldn't look as deflated as she did right now?

"I thought she would have looked happier, freer tonight. Knowing she'd avoided making a monumental error. I thought she would be floating down that carpet, laughing with her fans, safe in the knowledge she wasn't about to turn her world on its head," Charlie voiced her thoughts aloud. "I didn't expect her eyes to look like that," she whispered as a final close up of Robyn lingered on the screen before she headed inside the cinema, arriving well ahead of stars who had set off on the carpet before her.

"She has certainly never gone along a carpet that quickly before," Naomi added. "What's the phrase about being there in body but not soul? I feel like I've just watched an empty shell skulk along a back alley."

Her vivid description drew a chuckle from Jenna.

"There's more to this," she said with certainty, her journalistic nose almost twitching at the thought of a story.

"Is there though?" Charlie asked. "Or are we just desperately trying to find something to make sense of this?"

"We just watched a woman who is globally recognised for how fantastic she is on the red carpet. That was not a Robyn White performance, Charlie. Not at all."

"Social media agrees with you, Jen," added Naomi, glancing up from her phone. "Twitter is blowing up with it. #wheresrobyn is already trending. People in their thousands sharing their concerns that something isn't right. There's even the usual conspiracy theorists out there suggesting it's a body double!"

"It's not," Charlie said with absolute certainty, drawing another squeeze of the hand from Lauren.

"Maybe you should try getting in touch with her again?" Lauren suggested gently.

"How? Her number doesn't work anymore, and I am not going back to that hotel to bang on her room door, not when there are so many other members of the cast and crew staying there. I won't put her in a compromising situation no matter how much she's hurt me."

"You could try reaching out through her manager?" Jenna suggested.

"Absolutely not. He looked far too self-satisfied when he left my room. I get the impression he was not at all supportive of Robyn wanting to come out and was wholly relieved by her decision not to."

"He would be," snorted Lauren. "Imagine if she did find it more difficult to get cast in roles? It would be his bank balance suffering just as much as hers."

A silence settled on the room, all of them lost in thought before Jenna broke it, an excited look in her eyes.

"Then we opt for a more clandestine way."

Chapter Twenty-Eight

Robyn

Robyn groaned as she pushed herself out of the chair she felt like she'd been sitting in for days. Rolling her neck and then her shoulders, she shook out her hands and feet.

"God, I hate these press junkets," she complained to Freda, her assistant for the day. "I swear they make days feel like weeks."

"Only one more interview to go."

"Thank god."

Robyn knew this was her own fault. After her lacklustre performance on the red carpet for *Lethal Shadows* the studio had expressed its opinion loudly and organised another round of interviews with journalists for Robyn and a couple of the actors. No one seemed to care that she really had tried her best on the evening of the premiere, that what they saw was all she'd been capable of. The film screening hadn't even started before she'd received a message from David telling her to sort herself out, that she was embarrassing herself and not doing *Lethal Shadows* any favours at all. Robyn hadn't replied. Instead, she'd forced herself to sit through the screening and then had slipped out a back entrance she'd bribed an employee into showing her. She'd booked into a hotel and taken a couple of days to wallow in her own misery, speaking only to Kate and finally responding to one of the messages Jeanie had sent to assure her was okay and would be back on set for her call-time on Monday.

No matter what she did, she just couldn't get Charlie out of head, no matter how hard she tried. In the couple of weeks since David's announcement had gutted her, she'd struggled to sleep, found it hard to concentrate on the set for *Strikes Twice*, and could quite easily have curled up in a ball and sobbed at any moment.

"Two more minutes, Ms White," Freda said, breaking into Robyn's thoughts. "I'll go and check the journalist is here."

"Thank you, Freda."

Opening a bottle of water, Robyn took a long swig and cleared her mind. One more to get through, she thought as she settled back into chair, hoping that perhaps this journalist might have some slightly more interesting questions than the previous ones.

The door opened and a fiery redhead swept past Freda, a smile fixed on her face that could only be described as predatory, a steely determination flashing in her green eyes that made Robyn's breath catch for a second. This was not the obsequious attitude she was used to from journalists looking to get her on side.

"Ms White," came the curt greeting, a hand held out as she crossed the room in a few steps. "Jenna Edwards."

"Lovely to meet you. You can call me Robyn, no need for formality," Robyn said, a fake smile in place as she tried to turn on her charm offensive. Perhaps that would knock this Jenna Edwards off her stride.

"Noted," she replied with a nod before turning back to Freda. "As I said, my photographer had to run back down for something he left in the van. If you could go and meet him in the lobby, that would be great." There was no room for discussion in her tone, but to give Freda her due, she did meet Robyn's gaze to check she was okay with that. It wasn't usual protocol to leave the celebrity alone with the press. Robyn nodded her permission. There were security guards just outside the door if she needed them. Truth be told, there was something intriguing about Jenna Edwards that Robyn wanted to find out more about. Hostility was not something she had ever experienced during a press junket.

As Freda closed the door, Jenna settled into the chair opposite Robyn's. She made no move to take anything from her bag. No notepad, no Dictaphone, no pre-prepared notes. Instead, she crossed her legs and folded her arms, and fixed burning emerald green eyes on Robyn's, holding her stare without blinking. After a moment, she broke the silence between them.

"Ms White," her use of the formal moniker seeming like a purposeful ignoring of Robyn's request that she use her first name. "I just have one question." A pause as Jenna seemed to lean slightly forward in her seat. "Why?"

Why? Why what? Robyn's mind raced, frantically trying to work out what exactly was going on.

"Why produce this film?" she asked cautiously, already knowing that was not what was being asked.

Jenna scoffed.

"No. Why break Charlie's heart? Why ask her to the premiere, make promises about a future together and then rip it all away from her? Why?" she demanded.

At the mention of Charlie's name, Robyn's heart did its usual flutter and increase in rhythm. Her palms went clammy, and she felt the prickle of sweat beneath her arms. A flush crept up her chest and she thought the breath she exhaled might have been audible to people in the next room never mind to the woman sitting in front of her. A woman who had arched an eyebrow in expectation and who was radiating antagonism. It took a moment for her words to filter through Robyn's physical reaction to the topic.

"Why did I break Charlie's heart? What are you talking about?"

Shaking her head, Jenna snorted.

"I should have known you'd take the route of denial and feign ignorance."

"I'm not," Robyn cut in. "Not in the way you think anyway. I'm presuming that you're one of Charlie's best friends, the journalist?"

At Jenna's curt nod, Robyn continued.

"I'm not denying knowing Charlie. Hell, I'm not even denying being in a relationship with her. What I am denying is breaking her heart."

"So, you think you can tell someone that you love them, tell them you're going to come out so you don't have to hide them, and then ditch them without it having any repercussions?" Jenna's acidic voice had taken on a new level of vitriol as she spat the words at Robyn. "Christ, you didn't even have the decency to do it yourself," she snarled.

Robyn flinched at the words, her mind racing to try and keep up.

"Listen, Jenna, I honestly don't know what you're talking about."

"So you didn't tell Charlie you loved her? Didn't make grand statements about wanting the world to know who you really are?"

"Wait," Robyn said holding up a hand. She stood from her chair and paced towards the window, needing a second away from Jenna's ire. Turning back round, she tried to will herself to stay calm. "You're misunderstanding what I'm trying to say." She ran a hand over her face. "Please, just listen to me for a moment, Jenna."

The journalist made an impatient gesture that Robyn interpreted as permission to carry on.

"Some of what you're saying is true. Yes, I told Charlie that I love her. Yes, I promised her a future, wanted her by my side when I came out. But those things never changed for me, Jenna. I still love her, and I still want a future with her." At the look of disbelief in Jenna's eyes, she hurried on. "What I don't understand is why you think I took those things away from her? She was the one who pulled away, not me." Emotion welled up inside of her and she couldn't hold back the tears any longer. "Charlie broke my heart, not the other way around."

Stillness settled over Jenna and her gaze raked over Robyn.

"Fuck me," she uttered, her coldness disappearing as she seemed to melt at whatever it was she could read in Robyn's face. "You might be the world's best actor, but that right there isn't put on, is it? That's genuine emotion." She shook her head, bewilderment obvious in her expression. "What do you mean Charlie was the one who pulled away?" she asked slowly.

"She told me that she didn't want to go to the premiere, that she didn't want to be with me at all anymore. And then she walked away without looking back," Robyn huffed out a laugh. "She even changed her phone number so I couldn't harass her." If Robyn was honest with herself, that was what had hurt the most. Not that Charlie wouldn't given her a chance to try and fix things, but that she obviously hadn't trusted Robyn to stay away like she'd asked her to.

"And Charlie told you all of this herself?" Jenna asked, a sudden light appearing in her eyes, as if the pieces had suddenly fallen into place.

"No, she did exactly what you accused me of and sent a message."

"Via your manager, David Neville?"

"Yes," Robyn confirmed slowly.

"That fucking bastard," Jenna spat under her breath. Closing her eyes for a moment, she drew in a deep breath. "He did the same to Charlie," she confessed angrily.

"What?" Robyn asked, stunned.

"He went to her hotel room, told her you'd come to your senses and wanted nothing more to do with her. Told her not to bother trying to contact you."

An icy rage took over Robyn and her heart, which had been racing, felt like it stilled entirely. Nothing in her questioned what Jenna had just said. No part of her doubted that this was the truth. It was exactly the kind of underhanded move she'd come to expect from David. Well, no, that wasn't right. She'd never dreamt for one minute that he would do something this cruel, but now the possibility was out there, she believed it with absolute certainty.

"I am going to fucking kill him," she seethed between clenched teeth.

"You might need to get in line," muttered Jenna.

"What an absolute bastard," Robyn raged. "Killing him isn't punishment enough. I'm going to destroy his reputation. No one will want him as their agent by the time I'm finished with him."

"Woah, slow down, Robyn," Jenna said, coming to stand with her, placing a gentle hand on her shoulder. "We need to get the whole picture, to figure out exactly how he did this and then consider a response. You need to keep your own reputation untarnished." She paused for a moment then strode back across the room to her bag. "Give me your phone," she said sharply over her shoulder as she pulled her own out and began doing something with it.

Robyn didn't hesitate, pulling it from her pocket and unlocking it before giving it to Jenna, who immediately set about finding something in it. She drew in a sharp breath before turning the phones around and holding them out to Robyn, who shook her head in confusion.

"What am I looking at?"

"Charlie's contact details in both our phones. Look at the penultimate digit."

"One has a 2 and the other an 8," Robyn read out. "So?"

"So, the 2 is in my phone and given that I text and call Charlie pretty much on a daily basis, I think we can be certain it's the right number. On your phone though, that number has been changed to an 8. It's not Charlie's number anymore."

"And you think David did that?"

Jenna nodded once before turning Robyn's phone back around and tapping the screen again.

"I think he did this too." She held out the phone again, showing Robyn a page of blocked numbers, the one at the top matching exactly the number Jenna had stored for Charlie.

"So, he changed her number on my phone so that I couldn't call her, and he blocked her real number so that she couldn't call me? Is that what this is telling me?" Robyn asked, barely concealed fury lacing her voice.

"It would appear that that's what has happened to your phone, yes. Whether it was David Neville who did it, we have no way of knowing for sure."

"It was him," Robyn replied, a note of finality in her tone.

"I expect so," Jenna confirmed and then paused, seeming to wonder whether she should ask the question that was on the tip of her tongue.

"Ask," Robyn commanded.

"Why would he do this to you, Robyn? I can understand doing something to Charlie. He doesn't know her from Adam, but you... He's known you for years, represented you since the very beginning. Surely he would want you to be happy?"

Robyn laughed out loud.

"For a journalist, you're more naive than I expected," she said, warmth coating her voice to let Jenna know she wasn't insulting her with her words. "He did this because he's a greedy bastard, Jenna. A greedy bastard my sister has been telling me to get rid of since the end of the first *Branded* film. I went to him then, all those years ago, and told him I was gay and wanted to come out. He shot me down. Told me horror stories of people who had tried and whose careers had failed spectacularly as a result."

"Sadly, he was probably right back then," Jenna said quietly, and Robyn nodded her agreement.

"Probably. There certainly weren't any loud out and proud voices back then, and it just seemed too risky, too lonely to fight it on my own. Maybe if I'd met someone like Charlie back then, I would have felt differently, but I hadn't. So, I stayed quiet and listened to his advice. I did the same when I broached a change of genre to him, and he pretty much laughed in my face. Told me not to rock the boat.

That it wasn't worth being associated with a box office flop. God, I've been such an idiot all these years." Fresh tears spilled over and Jenna pulled her into a hug.

"We can't do anything about the past, Robyn. It's a waste of energy to look back and see what we could have done differently. But we can move on," she paused, pulling away from Robyn so she could look into her eyes. "Do you still love her?"

"With every fibre of my being."

Jenna pulled her back into the warm embrace.

"So, we fix what David has done first, and then we plot to bring the fucker to his knees."

Chapter Twenty-Nine

Charlie

The ringing of her phone for the third time in as many minutes caused Charlie to groan and put down her book. She'd been quite happy to ignore it, but apparently the caller wasn't going to allow that. Padding across her hardwood floors in her bare feet, Charlie picked up her phone from where she'd left it on the table. Jenna.

"I'm assuming this is an emergency since you're blowing up my phone," she said in lieu of greeting.

"Well, hello to you, too, Charlie. Yes, I'm fine, thank you for asking."

"Whatever," Charlie muttered.

"You're usually only this miserable when I interrupt a good book, but this time I'm not sorry."

"Are you ever?" Charlie asked archly.

"Nope! Anyway, do you remember the night of the premiere I mentioned that we needed to run a clandestine operation?"

"Vaguely."

"Well, it turned out to be so clandestine that I didn't tell you about it beforehand."

"Beforehand? So, that means you're telling me afterwards?" Charlie paused as she rolled her eyes and sent up a silent plea for strength. "You'd better not have done something that is going to result in me adding you to my kill list..."

"One day you and I are going to have to have a long and heartfelt conversation about the fact you have a list, but no, I don't think my op will land me on it. Especially not when I tell you all about it."

"Do I need to get comfortable?"

"Not right now, but maybe in about 10-minutes. Before that, you need to put the kettle on and tidy away any of those romance books you don't want me to be able to tease you about."

Charlie gasped.

"You're on your way here? Now?"

"About 9-minutes away now. I sincerely hope you've showered at some point in the last 72-hours." And on that note, Jenna hung up, leaving Charlie staring at her phone. It wasn't an out-of-character call from Jenna in the least, but she dreaded to think what kind of hare-brained scheme she'd rustled up this time. "I might just add her to that list regardless", Charlie muttered as she began to brew some coffee, knowing there was no way Jenna would accept a cup of instant. She was a horrific coffee snob.

Beans ground and the filtering process underway, Robyn crossed to her reading nook and began tidying away the pile she'd been working her way through. God forbid Jenna get a look at them – she'd never hear the end of it. It was only a couple of years ago that Jenna had threatened to report her to the teaching board, claiming that it had to be against teaching law for an English teacher to enjoy trashy romances as much as Charlie did, especially those of a Sapphic persuasion. Charlie had tried to point out that a) there was no such thing as 'teaching law' and b) no-one cared what she read in her own time, but Jenna had refused to believe either of these assertions.

Exactly four minutes after hanging up her phone, Charlie's doorbell rang. Clearly Jenna was as good at sticking to the speed limit today as she was every other day of the week. A last glance around the room told her it would have to do. It wasn't like Jenna hadn't seen her house in far worse states than this. A particularly ill-advised baking session came to mind, one that involved all four of them after far more gin than should be permitted before using a stand-mixer. She'd still been finding the detritus from what should have been banana and walnut muffins three weeks later.

Charlie pulled open the door, ready to launch into Jenna about invading her privacy, but she found herself unable to make a single utterance. Robyn White was standing on her doorstep, a slightly apprehensive smile on her lips. Charlie couldn't take her eyes off her. An amused throat cleared at Robyn's side.

"Right, I'm leaving Robyn here and you are going to listen, Charlie. Then, once you've listened and done whatever else you two like to get up to, come and meet us in the pub." She motioned over her shoulder with her final words and Charlie finally managed to make her eyes leave Robyn's to take in the sight of Lauren and Naomi leaning against Jenna's car, inane grins fixed on their faces. When Charlie turned her confused gaze to Jenna, her friend just laughed and mouthed "You're welcome!" as she turned around and headed down the drive to the others.

It took a moment for Charlie to realise that Jenna leaving on her own meant that Robyn was still standing on her doorstep. She wasn't entirely sure which emotion won out right then. Confusion in bucket loads, irritation that Jenna hadn't given her more warning or explained what the hell was going on, annoyance that

Robyn felt she could just waltz back into Charlie's life after unceremoniously dumping her. She finally allowed her eyes to meet Robyn's again.

"Hey," Robyn drawled softly.

"Hello," Charlie replied, unable to prevent the slight terseness to her tone, or her arms from folding protectively across her chest.

"If you're more comfortable having this conversation on your doorstep, I'm happy to accommodate," Robyn said. "Just let me know when you're ready to start. I understand that you weren't expecting to see me and probably need a minute."

Charlie wanted to point out that she needed a good deal more than a minute to get over the shock she was feeling, but she opted for the more mature response of pushing the door open more widely and ushering Robyn inside. Closing the door behind them, Charlie took in a deep breath and steeled herself before turning back.

"Come through to the kitchen," she said, leading the way. "Have a seat," she said, motioning to the table in the centre. "Coffee?" she asked, knowing that she needed both the caffeine and something to do with her hands. Robyn shook her head.

"Later." She pulled out the closest seat and looked at Charlie as she lowered herself into it. "We need to talk first."

Charlie didn't miss the flicker of hurt in Robyn's eyes as Charlie walked to the opposite side of the table rather than take the seat next to her. Charlie was doing her best to be hospitable, but there was a limit after all.

"So, you want to talk?" Blunt and brusque.

"David lied to you," Robyn blurted out. "That message wasn't from me, Charlie. He played us both."

"What?" Charlie wasn't following. Nothing Robyn had said made any sense.

Clearly deciding she didn't like the distance between them, Robyn pushed to her feet, rounded the table, and pulled out the seat next to Charlie's, angling it so she was facing her. Leaning forward, Robyn placed a tentative hand on Charlie's knee.

"He lied," Robyn repeated softly, an aching sadness in her eyes that tugged at Charlie's heart. "He came to you and told you that I had changed my mind, and he came to me and said exactly the same thing." Charlie inhaled sharply at the revelation. "He told me that you'd decided it wasn't worth it, that I wasn't worth it," she said, her voice breaking slightly. "That you realised you'd been swept up by the glamour and had no desire to be paraded around in front of the press as my coming out story." She paused, wiping away the tear that had escaped. "That you'd come to see that you didn't love me as much as you loved the idea of being with me."

"That's absolute bullshit!" Charlie replied, heat colouring her voice. "I said no such thing, Robyn. I wanted nothing more than to be on that carpet with you, to be at your side during what could have been both the best and worst moment of your life." At some point as she'd spoken, Charlie had turned fully to face Robyn and taken hold of both her hands. "I wanted to be there, Robyn."

"And I wanted you there. Jenna told me that David came to your hotel room. Told me what he'd said to you." She dropped her head, unable to hold Charlie's eyes any longer. "I'm so sorry," she whispered.

In a heartbeat, Charlie was on her knees in front of Robyn, gathering her into her arms and holding her as she cried, rubbing a soothing hand up and down her back.

"You have nothing at all to apologise for," Charlie intoned.

"He messed with my phone, too. That's why we couldn't contact each other."

"That bastard," Charlie ground out. She moved the hand from Robyn's back to gently stroke her hair instead. "I can't believe he did that to you."

"To us," Robyn said, pushing away from Charlie enough to look her in the eyes. "I love you, Charlie Evans. Please don't ever doubt that."

"I love you, too," Charlie breathed as she leaned in to capture Robyn's lips with her own. She allowed herself to sink into the kiss a moment longer, before breaking it off and re-taking her seat, keeping one of Robyn's hands in her own. "So, where do we go from here?"

Robyn laughed.

"I have some ideas, and I want to talk them all through with you. Our future isn't just about me, Charlie. We both have a say in it."

"Thank you," Charlie replied softly, appreciating the sentiment in Robyn's words.

"As you know, I have about a week left on set for *Strikes Twice*. I also have a couple more commitments for *Lethal Shadows*, but they're both here in the UK and within the next few weeks. Nothing overseas. About ten months from now, *Strikes Twice* will be hitting cinemas, so there'll be some marketing commitments before that, and I guess that will involve a global tour. After that, who knows?"

"Do you think you'll want to wait until the *Strikes Twice* premiere to make your coming out announcement?" It was important to Charlie to know what the next ten months might look like. Would it be as secretive as the last couple?

"Absolutely not," Robyn said firmly, no room for any indecision in her voice. "There is no way I'm keeping us quiet until then." She paused, a mild look of panic on her face as though something had just occurred to her. "I mean, if there is an us. I don't want to be presumptuous..." Her voice trailed off and Charlie smiled at her.

"Oh, there's definitely an us," she said, leaning in for another kiss. "I don't tend to kiss women and tell them I love them unless there's an us," she teased.

"Good to know," Robyn smirked, relief palpable on her face. "I want to make that announcement as quickly as possible," she continued. "In fact, I thought I'd talk to Jenna about it. About whether she would write the article."

Charlie screwed up her nose.

"She doesn't usually cover celebrities. She's the junior political editor at her paper, but I guess she might do this for us, and if she can't, she'll definitely know someone who will."

Robyn laughed out loud at the revelation.

"So, she turned up at my press junket today and doesn't even do the culture section? I thought she was a lot more feisty than the usual reporters I get put in front of. Now that you've said politics, I can see it. I bet they hate finding themselves on the end of one of her questions!"

"She came to your junket?" Charlie asked, her eyebrows disappearing into her hairline. "That woman is unbelievable."

"I'm glad she did," Robyn commented, tracing her thumb over Charlie's knuckles. "I wouldn't be sitting in your kitchen if she hadn't."

"True. But at least let me berate her for a little while before you forgive her publicly please."

"Cross my heart," Robyn teased. "Speaking of your friends, I promised them that I would drag you to the pub kicking and screaming. I am absolutely not allowed to let you to convince me to just stay here for the evening." She smiled at Charlie.

"Exactly how long were you in the car with them all for? No, wait. Don't tell me. I don't want to know what other promises they've forced on you, or worse, what else they've told you." Charlie sighed in exasperation. "You should probably know that all of them are pathological liars and absolutely cannot be trusted on any topic, particularly me."

Robyn laughed loudly, quirking her eyebrow in the way that did squishy things to Charlie's insides.

"You're incredibly lucky to have them," she added, her voice growing more serious.

"I know," Charlie replied softly. "Very lucky."

"Pay up!" Lauren said excitedly to Jenna and Naomi as Charlie and Robyn entered the village pub. "You both owe me a tenner!" She motioned with her hand for the money, and grumbling, both Jenna and Naomi dug in their wallets and handed it over.

"I can't believe you three," Charlie admonished, turning to Robyn with an explanation. "They bet on us."

"Hell, yeah, we did!" Lauren crowed, still obviously delighted to have won. "Naomi reckoned you wouldn't show up at all and that we'd have to come back and drag you out of bed."

"Nay!" Charlie scolded, her face a crimson flush.

"Jenna thought you'd arrive separately, staggering your entrance and both wearing a disguise to throw off the press. Although why she thought Charlie would need a disguise is beyond me, and where she thought the paparazzi were going to come from out here is a complete mystery."

Jenna shrugged her shoulders.

"It could happen. Those vultures will travel miles for a photo op." Despite being part of the press herself, Jenna had made her opinion of the paps more than clear over the years and was quick to distance herself from them at any opportunity, explaining at length the difference between a hard-hitting, political journalist and someone who chased cars to take photographs for a living.

"And what did you bet on?" Charlie asked Lauren, amusement at her friends' behaviour in her tone.

"That you'd be here within the hour, looking all loved up and ready to unleash hell on the world."

Charlie turned to look at Robyn, who grinned, shrugged, and turned back to Lauren.

"Very astute of you."

"So, you've talked?" Jenna asked as Charlie and Robyn took their seats. "And you have a plan?"

"We've talked, yes," confirmed Charlie. "But other than knowing we want to give this a go, together, we don't really have a plan. We have ideas about what we want to do, but we're not in any rush, we have plenty of time." She turned and grinned at Robyn, the knowledge that they did indeed have time ahead of them filling her with a warmth she thought had disappeared.

"Yeah, yeah," dismissed Jenna. "I'm not talking about all that settling down, fluffy crap. I'm talking about revenge. How are we going to make the slimy David Neville pay for what he did to you?"

"Remind me never to get on her bad side," Robyn whispered theatrically to Charlie, loud enough for the others to hear.

"Oh, you have no idea," Lauren drawled. "Sometimes I really worry about the things that go on inside that head of hers," she said, jerking a thumb towards Jenna, who let out a perfectly timed malevolent, bordering on maniacal laugh.

"Sweet Jesus," Charlie dead panned. "I take it you have suggestions."

"Oh, you'd better believe it!" Jenna exclaimed, opening up her satchel and pulling out a notebook. She flipped through the pages. "Okay, here we go." She cleared her throat and looked around the table in glee.

"She's made a list?" Robyn asked.

"Probably more than one," Naomi replied. "Jenna loves a list."

"Yes, Jenna does."

"I hate it when she does the third person thing," Lauren moaned. "It means something truly diabolical is about to occur."

"Okay, so, idea number one. We break into his hotel room –"

"No," Charlie interrupted. "Absolutely not."

Jenna rolled her eyes.

"Idea number two. We break into his office –"

"Jenna," Charlie admonished. "We are not breaking into any property or any object that belongs to David Neville. End of."

"God, you're no fun, Charlie," she complained, grabbing a pen and crossing off the first two items on her list. "I'll get rid of ideas 3-7 as well, then," she huffed.

"You had another five ideas of places to break into?" Robyn asked incredulously, earning a secretive wink from Jenna.

"I'll tell you about them sometime when the fun police aren't here," she quipped, motioning her head at Charlie.

"Sorry for wanting to try and keep you out of prison."

"I think we all know that if she did get sent down, she'd probably be running the place within a few hours of arriving," said Lauren with a roll of her eyes. "I told you Charlie wouldn't go for the breaking and entering ones. Skip to number eleven. That one definitely has promise."

Robyn turned to look at Charlie, mouthing "eleven?", a stunned look on her face.

"I told you she loved lists," Naomi laughed. "You should see what she comes up with when she'd had more than an hour to work on one."

"That is a terrifying prospect," Robyn replied.

"Okay, number eleven. We hire a private detective to dig up some dirt on him and then release it all over social media."

"Holy Christ, Lauren!" Charlie laughed. "You thought that was a good idea? You're supposed to be the sensible one in this group!"

"I absolutely am not," Lauren disagreed. "That label has always belonged to you, my friend."

"Most definitely," Naomi confirmed over the lip of her pint glass before taking a long swig.

"It's okay, babe," Robyn said softly, placing a hand on Charlie's knee underneath the table. "I like your sensibleness."

Charlie just scowled and pouted in mock disgust, hoping her face didn't show her delight that Robyn was yet to take back her hand.

"Fine," Jenna announced. "I had a feeling you wouldn't like anything that bordered on illegal or scandalous, so I'm just going to jump straight down to idea number twenty-six."

Charlie and Robyn shared a laugh.

"Idea twenty-six," Jenna began in an over-the-top impression of an auctioneer. "In idea twenty-six, Hollywood royalty, Robyn White, agrees to an in-depth, on-the-record chat with soon to be Pulitzer Prize winning reporter, Jenna Edwards. During the interview, White will reveal that's she a big ol' lesbian, whose heart has been captured by the down to earth on-set tutor hired for her *Strikes Twice* co-star, Lucinda Armstrong-Miller. When asked if this is her first dalliance in the Sapphic pool, White will demurely reveal that her wicked agent, David Neville has kept her locked in a gilded closet her entire career, threatening her with fire and brimstone should she reveal her heart's deepest desires. Edwards will then bravely push on, asking the question that will have readers on the edge of their seats. Why risk his wrath now then? To which White will break down in dramatic sobs, admitting that without her teacher lover, life itself would not be worth living and she'd rather never work again than miss out on the love of a good woman. After all, if the institution she's given her heart and soul to over the last two decades is so homophobic, why should she continue making millions for it? And when asked if she's ready to face the backlash from her fans, White will respond with genuine shock. Backlash? she'll enquire in amazement. There won't be backlash. My fans know that I am a human being and that I'm capable of falling in love. They won't care about my lover's gender, not when all they've ever wanted is for me to be happy. And then, White and said lover will float off on a cloud into the sunset and live happily ever after."

Jenna sat back with a look of triumph on her face.

"Holy Christ," Charlie muttered again when Naomi and Lauren burst into a round of applause. "I am so, so, sorry," she said to Robyn.

But Robyn wasn't paying attention to Charlie; instead, her gaze was fixed onto Jenna and Charlie was pretty sure Robyn was slowly nodding.

"That one," Robyn began, nodding her head more vigorously as she spoke. "That's the one. It's absolutely bloody perfect," she said with finality. "I mean, obviously we need to strip out some of your blether, and while we're on it, I would recommend sticking to journalism and not considering a career change to romance novelist, but the overall idea is perfect. We get to control the story, we have an explanation for why it took me so fucking long to see the truth, we put pressure on the industry to keep giving me roles, if I want them," she added, almost as an aside. "And we try to appeal to the better nature of my fans, too." She turned bright eyes to Charlie, a huge grin on her face. "This is how we take the next step, babe."

As far as Charlie was concerned, anything that made Robyn call her 'babe' was something she would get behind one hundred percent, so she smiled warmly back at her.

"If you're happy with it, I'm on board."

"See," Jenna said smugly. "I told you they'd pick that one." She put a hand out, palm up and looked wickedly at Lauren and Naomi, who both sighed heavily, pulled out their wallets and handed over the requisite tenner.

"I'm pretty sure you cheated by going through all the crap ideas first," Naomi complained.

"I still don't see what's wrong with the Private Investigator," Lauren muttered.

"When do you want to do it?" Jenna asked Robyn. "What kind of timeline are we on?"

"Tomorrow," Robyn replied without hesitation. "First thing tomorrow. I have a couple of calls that I need to make today. My lawyer to see how I get out of my contract with David, but I imagine that will be fairly straightforward because I don't care what I have to pay to do it. I want that man out of my life. My lawyer doesn't take any shit, so I'm pretty sure once I tell her what he's done, she'll find a way to make it him that has to pay me. And I need to call my sister, and my parents, just to give them the heads up. They've all known for years, but I don't want them seeing a headline tomorrow without being prepared for it." She paused, looking at Charlie. "They know all about you, so it won't come as a surprise," she added shyly.

"Your parents do?" Charlie asked in shock.

"Of course," Robyn replied. "I told them a few weeks ago, before you'd even agreed to go to the premiere with me." She squeezed Charlie's knee again. "Any family you need to contact?" she asked. "Sorry, I should have checked first. We can change the timing if you need more time."

"They all know already," Charlie said motioning her head to the women on the other side of the table," a smile tinged with sadness on her face. Charlie could tell that Robyn sensed there was more to the story, but she didn't push her for details, instead just giving her a look that said, 'when you're ready, I'm here'.

"Excellent," Jenna said breaking the silence, clapping her hands together. "So, although I have an important interview to conduct tomorrow, I'm pretty sure that I can handle one more drink. Charlie?" she asked expectantly. "If I'm going to be doing this favour for your girlfriend, the least you can do is get the next round in!" She laughed in delight at the look Charlie shot her way.

"Of course, milady" Charlie replied, dipping her head in a mock bow. "What can I get you all?"

As her friends all called out their orders, Charlie took a moment to once again thank the university housing gods who had seen fit to put the four of them together. She let her gaze drift to Robyn, who was laughing along with the group. Warmth flowed through her, and she ran a hand down Robyn's arm as she crossed behind her to head to the bar. She couldn't imagine being happier than she was right now.

Epilogue

Charlie and Robyn

Charlie moaned as Robyn pressed her lips gently to the nape of her neck.

"I don't think I'll ever tire of doing that," Robyn purred as she slowly pulled up the zip on Charlie's dress, smoothing her hands across Charlie's bare shoulders.

"Please don't," Charlie pleaded.

"I love you in this colour," Robyn replied, running her hands down Charlie's side to rest on her waist. Without letting her eyes leave Charlie's reflection in the mirror before them, she pressed in close, trailing kisses up Charlie's neck, then gently sucking her earlobe into her mouth.

"Robyn," Charlie gasped throatily. "We don't have time, my love."

"I know, I just don't want you to forget what's waiting for you later."

"As if I ever could," Charlie replied turning to face Robyn. "You'll need to re-do your lipstick," she warned before leaning in and capturing Robyn's mouth in a passionate kiss. Pulling back breathlessly, she winked. "I couldn't have you forgetting either." Using the pad of her thumb, she gently wiped away a smear of lipstick from the edge of Robyn's mouth. "Perfect."

"Are you ready for tonight?"

"Absolutely," Charlie replied confidently. "This isn't my first red carpet, you know," she teased.

"No, but it is your first Oscar ceremony," Robyn reminded her.

"It's your first one as a nominee," Charlie shot back. "And I am so fucking proud of you, have I told you that?"

"Maybe once or twice," Robyn grinned. "I still can't believe *Strikes Twice* has six nominations. It still astounds me how well-received it was, by both fans and critics."

"I've heard the lead actress did a pretty good job. She also timed her own coming out announcement perfectly!" Charlie teased. "I'm pretty sure more people went to see it because of that."

"Sadly, I imagine you're right," Robyn replied wryly. "It certainly didn't harm the film like it could have done."

"Or us."

"Or us," Robyn agreed, stealing one last quick kiss. "Come on then, let's do this thing."

"Ready?" Robyn asked for the forty-seventh time as the car slowed to a stop.

"As ready as I was thirteen seconds ago."

"Shut up!"

"Ms White! Is that anyway to talk to the woman who's about to hold your hand down the red carpet?"

"Good evening, ladies," a voice boomed as their door was opened. "Welcome to the Academy Awards!"

Robyn stepped out of the car, her right hand immediately slipping behind her, waiting for the familiar feeling of Charlie threading their fingers together. It had become an anchor Robyn couldn't remember managing events like this without. A double squeeze: Charlie's signal that she was out of the car and ready to go.

Around them, people buzzed in all directions as they waited in the 'holding pen' before hitting the carpet and the awaiting press. To Charlie it seemed as though she and Robyn were somehow removed from the organised chaos, perfectly content to stand together in a comfortable silence as they waited their turn. Whilst she didn't think she would ever quite get used to the craziness of Hollywood, or any of the film events she attended with Robyn, over the last year she had at least been able to relax enough to take in more each time. Their very first one was a complete blur, but Charlie intended to remember every moment of tonight.

Strikes Twice had finally been released to fans and critics who were desperate to see it. Jenna's article about Robyn had more than whetted their appetites when it had been released almost a year ago. True to her word, Robyn had given the interview the morning after she'd arrived unannounced in Charlie's kitchen and the story had gone to print for the very next issue. A slew of radio interviews, television appearances and magazine articles had followed, and social media had erupted, more of it positive than they had initially expected.

Since then, Robyn had stuck to the commitments she had to the marketing side of *Strikes Twice*, but Rhonda, her new agent had made as many of them happen in the UK and Europe as she could, with anything further afield timed to coincide with Charlie's school holidays whenever possible.

Rhonda had been an absolute godsend. In the wake of her interview with Jenna, Robyn had received a call from a fellow actress, one who had come out a couple of years earlier. She had been devastated to hear what Robyn had gone through and wanted to recommend her own agent, Rhonda, who she said had been nothing but supportive. Rhonda had flown to London to meet Robyn, bringing her wife with her. One dinner and it was a sealed deal, mainly because Rhonda completely understood Robyn's reasons for wanting to take a break and possibly shift her career in another direction.

Within a fortnight after signing on with Rhonda, Robyn had received an email detailing a range of options, from executive producer to a role on stage. Every single option was based in the UK, something that Charlie had been eternally grateful for. Robyn had stayed the night at Charlie's house after that first trip to the local pub, and she'd never left. Charlie didn't care if they were a cliché, they were happy.

"We're next," Robyn whispered in her ear.

"I love you," Charlie whispered back, earning a smile and a chaste kiss in return.

And then they were off, heading onto the famous red carpet, posing for the cameras, laughing and smiling at the comments thrown their way. The obligatory interview from the carpet went perfectly, Robyn's charm shining through in bucketloads. She brushed off compliments and talked up her fellow Best Actress nominees, effused about the team behind *Strikes Twice*, and stole momentary glances at Charlie whenever she could.

That part over, they were ushered past more cameras before being directed inside the Dolby Theatre and taken to their table. Charlie was pleased to see faces she recognised. Peter Fletcher, the film's director, greeted Robyn warmly, as did Kevin Grealish, the main scriptwriter. Charlie pulled Lizzie Carter into a hug, delighted the assistant scriptwriter had been given the nod to attend tonight. As far as Charlie was concerned, the scenes she had re-written to introduce the love story of the film, had been among some of the finest she had ever seen. They were just about to take their seats when a loud voice called out behind them, the Southern drawl dripping like honey.

"Don't you dare put your butts on those chairs without giving me a hug," Addie Covington demanded as she strode up to the table, wrapping her arms dramatically around Robyn and giving her what Charlie could only describe as a smacker on the lips. Addie turned and winked at her, "I expect the same from you too, gorgeous woman," she drawled, pulling Charlie into her arms. "You two look absolutely fucking stunning," she exclaimed loudly, causing the woman who had arrived a few steps behind her to wince in embarrassment and chide her.

"Adelaide Covington, you watch that mouth of yours."

Addie rolled her eyes good-naturedly, grabbing the woman's hand and pulling her in close.

"I'd like to introduce you all to Rebecca McIntyre," she said with a flourish, causing most of the mouths around the table to drop. Robyn was the first to recover.

"Ms McIntyre, it's an absolute pleasure to meet you. I know I can speak for all of us when I say we were honoured you allowed us to make *Strikes Twice*. On a personal note, I'll be forever grateful that you had the courage to send us your original manuscript." She looked at Charlie beside her, taking hold of her hand. "It helped me find some courage of my own.

"It's Rebecca," she said shyly. "And I'm thrilled I played a small part in your own love story. I have to say, I have thoroughly enjoyed following it in the press. I'm not usually one for gossip, but every now and then, when the real thing shows up, I like to keep an eye on it."

Robyn flushed and knew from the squeeze of her hand that Charlie felt the same.

"Yes, well, enough of that," Addie announced. "I wasn't able to get this one to come to the premiere or any of the other launch events for the film, but I promised myself I would get her here tonight, come hell or highwater." She threw an affectionate look at the author, and Robyn noticed that Addie was still clutching Rebecca's hand tightly in her own. "It's about damn time I got to show my girlfriend off," she finished with a flourish, grinning like the cat with its proverbial cream.

Rebecca flushed with embarrassment, a slightly mortified look on her face and Charlie got the distinct impression that this was not how they had agreed to make that particular announcement.

"I am far too old to be called your girlfriend, Addie," she chastised.

"Then you should have humoured me and let me arrange that stopover in Vegas. That way I could have introduced you as my wife."

"Good god, woman," Rebecca huffed, sliding into the chair Charlie had pulled out for her. "Sometimes I really do wonder what on earth I've got myself mixed up in." The tone was serious, but the look in Rebecca's eyes was one of love and amusement.

"I'll get that ring on your finger one of these days," Addie promised as she sank into the chair next to her. "I might even manage it before these two," she added, motioning between Robyn and Charlie.

"You can try," Robyn quipped as she took her own seat next to Charlie.

"Is there a reason it hasn't happened yet?" Addie demanded, brushing off Rebecca who was desperately trying to shut her off.

"We thought we'd get the baby out of the way first," Charlie said in her most serious voice, just as Addie took a sip of her drink, which was almost spurted right back out. She looked between the two of them, her eyes as round as saucers, trying to see through their poker faces. When the edges of Robyn's lips finally quirked upwards, Addie laughed.

"She's a keeper," she said to Robyn.

"Oh, I know that," replied Robyn in the sultry voice that did strange things to Charlie's insides.

Addie laughed loudly, settling back into her seat and falling into conversation with Peter, her hand still holding tightly to Rebecca's, who seemed content to sit back and watch.

Charlie turned to Robyn, a smile on her face.

"So, I'm a keeper, am I?"

Robyn put her elbow on the table and rested her chin in her hand, looking so intently at Charlie that it could well have been possible every other person in the venue disappeared.

"I'm pretty sure you know that already," she mused.

Charlie made a so-so gesture with her hand, grinning widely at Robyn's rolling eyes.

"I guess you've hinted at it once or twice."

"Maybe I should do more than just hint..."

"Maybe you should..."

"Later," Robyn promised, leaning in and capturing Charlie's lips with her own for a kiss that lingered longer than anything she usually gave her in public. In fact, Charlie was pretty damn sure there'd been a swipe of Robyn's tongue along her bottom lip thrown into it for good measure.

"Why, Ms White," she said in a low voice, fanning herself dramatically.

Robyn shifted her chair so that it was closer to Charlie's, close enough to put a possessive hand on Charlie's thigh as she leaned in to whisper in her ear.

"Please, please, please call me Ms White in that husky voice later tonight."

Charlie turned her head so that she was able to whisper back.

"Only if you do that thing with your tongue..." She couldn't hold back her grin at the sound of Robyn's quiet gasp and the reflexive tightening of the hand on her thigh.

Music suddenly struck up and the lights dimmed, signalling the start of the ceremony.

"I promise," Robyn purred before leaning back in her seat to take in the events on stage. Charlie stole one last glance at her, happiness radiating in every part of her, before she too turned her attention to the performers.

In that moment, whether Robyn won or not tonight wasn't of the slightest importance to either of them.

A note from K.E. Morrison

I hope you enjoyed reading the story of Charlie and Robyn as much as I enjoyed writing it. Theirs is the first in the Branded Hearts quadrilogy, a series of novels that will tell the tales of the four friends who met at university and became family. Charlie and Robyn will make cameo appearances in the remaining books, so you'll be able to follow them for a while longer.

Next up will be Jenna's story. The hard-headed journalist, with a reputation for being something of a player, will meet her match when she's assigned to follow the campaign trail of a rising politician vying to become the leader of her party.

If you have time, a review would be greatly appreciated – they really do help independent authors reach more readers.

Thank you for reading,

K.E.